THE CHINA PLAY

MICHAEL WINSTEAD

Cover design by Tim Barber of Dissect Designs

ISBN 978-0-9992421-4-8

Other Books by Michael Winstead

Ultimate Verdict
Ultimate Deception
Ultimate Truth
Ella's Wings

PRAISE FOR WINSTEAD'S NOVELS

By turns thrilling and moving, Ella's Wings is an ideal companion to the Ultimate Verdict series, taking readers deeply into the world of one whose life is forever altered by a terrorist attack. Riveting and emotionally complex, Ella's Wings will keep you turning the pages . . .
Joanne O'Sullivan, author Between Two Skies

For lovers of crime novels and courtroom drama, *Ultimate Verdict* by Michael Winstead delivers an exciting story that moves along without getting stuck in legal humdrum, builds up suspense and intensity, and makes us think hard and feel deeply while we turn the pages. Highly recommended! – *TheColumbiaReview.com*

Winstead excels at weaving philosophical questions of good and evil into realistic legal, professional and human conflicts . . . The plot is rich with creative twists and blind turns, leading to a satisfying (and surprising) conclusion . . .
Avrahim Azrieli, Author Deborah Rising

Ultimate Deception is an action-packed story that will be loved by people who enjoy suspense and legal thrillers. Laced with intrigue, yet thought-provoking, Michael Winstead's second novel successfully combines an excellent plot with a fascinating glimpse into courts and the criminal justice system. – *Susan Keefe, TheColumbiaReview.com*

This book is dedicated to all those who have given their lives to the land.

1

Oakley Walker Hitchcock sits at a polished table, eyeing the Judges. As a trial lawyer, this courtroom should be a place he is comfortable. He has been in dozens of courtrooms just like this one. Normally, he moves about a courtroom as if he owns it, laying a hand on the worn rail of the jury box as he delivers a closing argument, striding across the carpeted floor as if it is his domain.

But today he is terrified.

Because on this day, he is the one on trial.

Hitch, as he is known to almost everyone, remains seated. He sits in a hard chair behind a vast expanse of table. Alone. There is a noticeable tremble in his hands.

His three Judges perch on an elevated bench four strides away. Each looks down at him with varying degrees of intensity. The one in the middle—the one who is in charge—assesses him with a steely, unwavering gaze.

"Mr. Hitchcock," she begins. Alicia Vanderwelt is a senior partner at Atlanta's largest and most- prestigious law firm. Though her name is not on the door, she is one of the firm's best litigators. She also is a member of the Board of Governors of the Georgia State Bar. Her eyes bore into him over silver-framed glasses. She speaks in a voice that does not brook dissent.

"Do you admit that you were having an affair with your client while you were representing her?"

Hitch stands to respond. His eyes flick to the domed ceiling and wander over the cherubs and winged angels floating against a sky-blue backdrop, each figure adorned in gold leaf. He has rehearsed an answer with his attorney. His attorney is not with him at this proceeding because… well, because Hitch has decided he can handle the case on his own. As he freezes beneath Vanderwelt's scrutiny, he realizes this decision is a mistake. Making an argument in a courtroom is immeasurably more difficult when you are the accused. His rehearsed answer, full of solemnity and contrition, now seems woefully inadequate. After all, someone was murdered.

"Your Honor ..."

"I'm not a judge, Mr. Hitchcock." Vanderwelt's mouth curls in disdain, not even trying to hide her contempt.

Hitch works to produce the endearing smile he's used with countless juries. A smile of genuine humility, conveying that everyone here is engaged in the same, paramount task of finding the truth. They must work together on this journey. With this short delay, he has gained valuable time.

"Of course, but even though you are not wearing a robe, you are my Judges, all three of you, for purposes of this hearing. I say it with the utmost respect." He pauses to gauge reaction. He meets all six eyes. No one interrupts him. "We had started dating, that week in fact, but there were circumstances. Not excuses mind you, but circumstances. Ms. Summers and I had a romantic relationship for almost two years a while back, well before I agreed to represent her, *pro bono*, in her equitable distribution claim as part of her divorce."

"But that relationship had ended, had it not?" This question comes from the attorney on the left, a balding and pasty man from Augusta who practices real estate law. His name, for the moment, escapes Hitch.

He turns his head to the left to engage this new questioner. "Yes, sir. Our relationship was over a few months before Sonia—I mean Ms. Summers— married George Colbert."

"You keep referring to her as Ms. Summers," Vanderwelt resumes, "but in fact the final Decree of Divorce had not been entered by the Court at the time of the incidents in question. So she was, in the eyes of the law, still Mrs. Colbert."

Hitch nods. His eyes retreat to the gleaming surface of the table for a moment. He is trying to keep his concentration. Fighting not to go back to that fateful morning. Trying not to re-live it. For if he does, it will throw him with the force of a bucking horse. When he is ready to battle again, he locks eyes with Vanderwelt. "That's true, but the agreement for unconditional divorce had already been signed by both parties, and Ms. Summers had been using her maiden name since she had separated from Mr. Colbert, many months earlier."

Vanderwelt has a rebuttal ready. "But it remains true, does it not, that at the time, Mrs. Colbert or Ms. Summers, was still your client, and you were having a romantic relationship with her?"

Hitch notes Vanderwelt has switched from *affair* to *romantic relationship.*

A minor victory, perhaps. Hitch replies, "We were not sleeping together."

"Don't debate definitions with me, Mr. Hitchcock. During your representation of Mrs. Colbert in her divorce, did you kiss her? Simple question."

"Yes. The night before she signed the settlement agreement. The night before she was …"

Vanderwelt interrupts. "So you had a romantic relationship with her while she was still your client. And your professional judgment was therefore impaired."

Vanderwelt asserts this last as irrefutable fact, not in the form of a question. She already has decided how she will rule on the seminal issue in his disciplinary hearing: Did his personal relationship with a client impair his professional judgment as her attorney? If so, he has violated the Georgia Rules of Professional Conduct. One vote against, even before he finishes making his case.

Hitch has a response prepared. He hesitates so he can strip his tone of anger.

"Wait a minute, Alicia." David Holt Kight, who routinely introduces himself using all three names, is a fellow plaintiffs' attorney from Savannah. The one friend Hitch might have on this disciplinary panel. "The fact that Mr. Hitchcock was having a consensual personal relationship with her, in light of their prior relationship and the circumstances of this case, including allegations that Mr. Colbert physically and emotionally abused his wife, does not automatically lead to the conclusion that Mr. Hitchcock's professional judgment was impaired during representation. In fact, the marital property settlement they reached at mediation, in my estimation, was incredibly favorable to Ms. Summers. Mr. Hitchcock did his job, and he did it well."

"Per the Supreme Court's decision in *In re Lewis*," Vanderwelt counters, "with facts parallel to those in this case, such a romantic relationship establishes, *ipso facto*, an impaired professional judgment."

"I don't agree," Kight says. "Attorney Lewis admitted to having sexual intercourse with his client. There's no evidence of that here."

"But the romantic relationship here may have actually caused Mr. Colbert to stalk and shoot his wife out of jealousy," Vanderwelt declares. "Mr. Hitchcock— wittingly or unwittingly—put his client's safety at risk. She paid for his mistake with her life."

Silence consumes the hearing room. Vanderwelt's words sting. Hitch knows well he made a mistake. He never should have taken Sonia's case. He doesn't usually handle divorces. But he handled the case competently. Because he cared. He's not on trial because his advice was below par. He's here because Sonia was murdered. And each time he contemplates what happened in his conference room that morning, he concludes it was all his fault. Oh, he could argue the legal construct that a criminal act such as murder is not foreseeable, that he could not have known any of his actions would lead to gunfire, but the burden of establishing causation under the law is very different than the acknowledgment of cause and effect in the aftermath of tragedy. If he had not been so zealous in advocating Sonia's legal rights, if he had not been so profoundly in love with her, her enraged husband might not have barged into his law office and shot her. It is this knowledge that haunts him.

"That's unsupported speculation," Kight resumes, "and given the history of abuse by Mr. Colbert, we can't conclude, and it is in fact reckless for us to conclude, that Mr. Hitchcock's actions in any way contributed to her death. Let me remind this panel that Mr. Colbert has been convicted of murder and attempted murder. If not for Mr. Hitchcock's heroic actions that day—with a bullet in his lung, I might add—the casualties could have been much worse."

Hitch unconsciously flexes his left shoulder, where Colbert's third bullet ricocheted off his collar bone and ripped through the top of his lung. There are times, like now, when the wound pulses with the racing pace of his heart.

Kight is doing a fine job defending Hitch, reminding his co-judges that the attorney before them also is a victim. But Kight can't do it alone. Hitch needs two votes from this panel. Vanderwelt, probably a true believer in the sanctity of marriage and its inviolable oath of fidelity, is cemented against him. Her expression says she views the Rules of Professional Conduct in black and white, with nothing left in the margins for interpretation. That means the Augusta real estate lawyer—Archie Williams, he now remembers—will cast the deciding vote on whether Hitch violated his ethical duties.

"Is there anything else you'd like to add, Mr. Hitchcock?" Though Vanderwelt's words are polite, her eyes simmer.

Hitch glances down at the prepared notes on his legal pad. Nothing leaps up at him. *Make an argument, but keep emotion out of it*, he tells himself. He takes a deep breath.

"Yes. In my sixteen years as a lawyer, I have had only one other complaint lodged against me with the Georgia Bar. That complaint was made by an opposing party who claimed I was overzealous in representing my own client. That complaint was summarily dismissed. This ethics complaint has been submitted by a convicted murderer, who is bent on revenge, as he was the day he killed his estranged wife."

With this final phrase, he concedes the point that Sonia was, technically, still married. He hopes this concession will ease Vanderwelt's ire.

"And, although I admit it may be unwise to have a romantic relationship with a client, it is not expressly forbidden under our Rules. We all know that. As Mr. Kight has pointed out, the objective evidence establishes that my professional judgment was not impaired during my representation of Ms. Summers. That is the seminal question here. I worked just as hard, if not harder, for Ms. Summers as I have for any other client in recent memory. I gave her good legal advice regarding her rights and the standards that apply in equitable distribution cases. Given the abuse she suffered at the hands of Mr. Colbert, which is documented in at least two criminal complaints and arrests, and the fact he had attempted to hide some of his assets prior to the equitable distribution proceeding, Sonia deserved an aggressive, passionate representation. That's exactly what I gave her."

He scans the panel. Vanderwelt has her left elbow propped on the bench, her chin resting in her palm. Kight leans back in his chair with his hands intertwined across his belly, a loyalist to the end.

Attorney Williams, now the fulcrum juror, is unreadable. He wears a paisley bow tie (knotted by hand, probably) and a starched white shirt. He is clean-shaven, his face waxen from hours at a desk beneath fluorescent lights, a man devoted to the rigors of his craft. Williams' gaze conveys neither sympathy nor judgment, as if he is focused on the metes and bounds of a real property description, his mouth working as he tries to puzzle it out.

Hitch does not yet have Archie Williams on his side. But it is possible he has not lost his vote, either. Hitch must alter the ambiguous imbalance. He must convince Archie Williams he is guilty of nothing.

"My relationship with Sonia was not a mere dalliance. Once the case was officially over, which I estimated to be within a day or two when the Judge signed the consent divorce decree, Sonia planned to move into my house. I did not take advantage of her as a client. I loved her; and she loved me."

He says this less eloquently than he would like, for as he thinks of Sonia and the future they will never have, sadness and misery clog his throat. He tries to swallow it. He needs to maintain control. He will not break down. Maybe in the privacy of a bathroom stall or in his car, but not here. Not in front of Vanderwelt. With a practiced motion, he smooths his tie with his right hand, unbuttons the top button of his suit jacket, and settles into the wooden chair at the table with an audible sigh.

"Nevertheless," Vanderwelt says, "Sonia Colbert was killed by her soon-to-be-ex-husband. In your law office."

She turns swiftly to each of her co-panelists. "Anything else?"

They add nothing.

"This hearing is adjourned," Vanderwelt declares. "Since this is our last ethics matter of the day, we will be deliberating this afternoon. If you want to stay close Mr. Hitchcock, we'll have a decision imminently."

2

Now, he must wait. Attorneys call it babysitting the jury. For Hitch, this has always been his least-favorite aspect of a trial. The waiting. The second-guessing. The quietude, lost in your own thoughts, recalling all of the things you could have done better, recollecting a phrase you should have used more, or discarded altogether. The slow ebb of adrenaline, leaving you spent. Forced inaction while someone else debates your fate.

As he sits alone in the hearing room, he fingers the first page of the ethics complaint filed against him.

STATE BAR OF GEORGIA
V.
OAKLEY WALKER HITCHCOCK

To Hitch, the bold caption is as damning as a criminal charge. He doesn't handle criminal cases. Over the course of his career, he has spent little time contemplating what it must be like to face a jury who can take away your freedom. Until now. He won't go to jail. That's not an option for his Judges. But with Vanderwelt in charge of the deliberations, his vindication is in peril. He comprehends now, for the first time, that if Vanderwelt can convince Archie Williams, they could end his career.

It took a lot of work to get here. Long nights. Lost weekends. Missed birthdays and holidays. He relishes practicing law and helping people who otherwise have no voice in the legal system. He considers it a privilege. Standing in front of a judge or jury and making the winning argument fills him with a pride he has found in no other pursuit. Seeing the faces of clients for whom he is able to achieve justice is beyond gratifying. Practicing law is the fulfillment of a dream. He is a lawyer. It is not just his chosen profession. It is not simply what he does for a living. Being a lawyer defines him.

Alicia Vanderwelt could take all that away.

He ponders whether Vanderwelt's aggressive attitude toward him is retribution for his besting her in a big lawsuit five years back. It had not gone well for her client, a company that smelted lead on the fringes of a residential neighborhood near Savannah. The jury awarded $50 million in total damages to Hitch's clients, the dozens of families whose yards and houses had been permanently contaminated by lead.

After the jury's verdict, Vanderwelt begged the trial judge to overturn it. He denied her motion. She appealed to the Georgia Court of Appeals, which upheld the verdict. The Georgia Supreme Court refused to hear her next appeal. Defeated, Vanderwelt had finally wired the $50 million, plus interest, into Hitch's client trust account. She followed that surrender with a short phone message, left after working hours, in which she vowed to win the next one.

This disciplinary hearing is the next one. Hitch realizes that now. She is still incensed about a case she lost five years ago. A case she should have lost. He could see it in her face, in the set of her mouth, as she glared down at him from the elevated bench. She has probably convinced all 579 attorneys in her law firm that he is an enemy who must be destroyed. And here, at this trial, she holds almost unbridled power to do just that.

In deciding to represent himself, Hitch has ignored Abraham Lincoln's admonition: "He who serves as his own counsel has a fool for a lawyer, and a jackass for a client." But this is his mess. He will accept the consequences. Alone. Maybe he could not have predicted George Colbert would burst into his office with a loaded revolver, but he should have protected Sonia. It is a pervasive guilt he will never shed.

The memory of that morning is as fresh as the day after. He can see the speckles of Sonia's blood on the settlement agreement, the pages stacked neatly, the pen with which she had signed the documents wobbling on the conference table. Gun smoke clouds the room. The acrid smell stings his nose. His ears are ringing from the reports. And there stands George Colbert, dark half-moons beneath his eyes, his shirt untucked on one side, the gun dangling from his right hand. There is no smile, no smirk of satisfaction that in shooting his wife and her lawyer he has somehow won justice. His face emits only a look of sad resignation.

When Hitch tackled Colbert there was little resistance. There was no scramble for the gun that clattered beneath the conference table. Hitch pressed his knee into the small of the shooter's back and bound Colbert's hands with the phone cord. Colbert seemed surprised—perhaps at what he'd done, or perhaps that a man with a bullet in his chest could move with such swiftness. Hitch had eyed the gun under the table for a few seconds, as if one more bullet could erase this misery. But he left it for the police and crawled across the floor to where Sonia had toppled.

Her blood gurgled from two bullet holes. He knew as he pulled out his cell phone to dial 911 that she was going to die. The damage was too great. After he made the call, he had cradled her head in his lap and watched her slip away. Then Hitch had glared at Colbert, hating him more than he'd ever hated anyone in his life. Still, he left the murder weapon beneath the conference table.

And then the police and paramedics had arrived. He saw two cops haul Colbert to his feet and hustle him out of the law office. As his breath seized and sputtered from the collapsed lung, Hitch watched as a first responder knelt next to Sonia, checked for a pulse, then shook his head. He remembered nothing else until he awoke in the hospital the next day.

Now, his right knee jiggles beneath the table. He needs to distract himself from the memory. He needs to distract himself from the interminable waiting. He surveys the room. Except for the fresco ceiling, the room is about as sterile as the State Bar could make it. The hearing bench, crafted of oak, has dulled over time to a yellow hue. The Georgia flag, with its stars representing the original thirteen colonies, stands on one side of the dais; the United States flag on the other. He mouths the words on the state flag: "In God We Trust; Constitution; Justice; Wisdom; Moderation." He's never had much reason to examine the Georgia flag before, but he sincerely hopes his Judges will exhibit a great deal of those last two tenets—wisdom and moderation. Behind the bench, the State Bar of Georgia seal adorns the wall. There are no photographs in this courtroom. No artwork. The room does not look like a place where weighty matters are decided, but given the stakes, this is about as heavy as it can get for Hitch.

He pulls out his phone, presses the power button, and checks his messages. There is one. He lifts the phone to his ear. His two legal assistants—Natalie Anderson and Stacie Throckmorton—have left him a message of encouragement. They both wanted to come, but he convinced them the result was pro forma, that this hearing was a mere formality, something he would endure alone.

He scrolls through photographs stored on his phone: with friends at a Sand Gnats baseball game; posing next to a sailfish he caught on a fishing trip to the Keys; his bloodhound Jasper in full howl. And then he comes to one of Sonia, taken when they were first dating, long before he agreed to handle her divorce case. She is sitting in a blue kayak in red shorts and a sleeveless top, a paddle across her thighs. God, she was lovely. Both inside and out. She exuded radiance in her smile, in the tilt of her head, in a Southern drawl both precise and soft. She was kind to everyone, even strangers.

He and Sonia had started dating a year after his own divorce. For twenty-three months they lived an idyllic romance, or as close as anyone can come amid tangles of responsibility and ex-spouses. Then it ended, solely because he was not prepared to commit to a second marriage on the heels of a disastrous end to his first. His fault. Sonia had married George Colbert six months later. When she filed for divorce, Hitch had gotten a rare second chance with the love of his life. Then Colbert's bullets intervened.

An hour has elapsed since the judges left the hearing room. For a few minutes he listens to the ticking wall clock, its second-hand precise and consistent. There is no bailiff to shoot the bull with, or to ask about progress in the deliberations. Something continues to vibrate within him, a dirty finger plucking a cord deep inside. He knows what it is. He can no longer resist its thrum.

He approaches the door through which his judges exited the courtroom and pushes the handle down, putting him in a back hallway. Where he is not supposed to be. As he creeps along the plush carpet of the corridor, he can hear them talking, their voices quiet and contained. He appears in the open doorway to their meeting room. An interloper.

"I have one more thing to say," he starts before anyone can protest. "Hear me out. Off the record. Whatever you decide to do to me, whatever punishment you want to exact, do it for the right reasons. Don't do it because you're still angry about some case we had together years ago, or because you want to take a good plaintiff's lawyer off the docket. Make your decision in the best interests of my client, Sonia Summers. That's who you're supposed to be protecting." He pulls up the picture of Sonia sitting in the boat. He wants them to put a face to the client he allegedly took advantage of. He steps closer and angles his phone so they all can see her. "Just ask yourselves this: What would she want you to do?"

And then he leaves. He strides down the corridor, barely leaving depressions on the mauve carpet, then through the hearing room and down the elevator and out of the building. He exits the parking garage in a squeal of tires on slick concrete. As if distance alone can make all this go away.

He is weaving through thick Atlanta traffic, heading south, when he gets the call. He presses the answer button on the steering wheel of his car.

"Hitch, this is David Holt Kight. We have a 2-1 decision. Sorry to say, they're recommending you be suspended for one year. Effective immediately." The message is succinct, yet painful.

Hitch swallows hard. Hearing it pronounced is far worse than contemplating his punishment theoretically. It has just become real. He doesn't know what he is going to do if he can't practice law for an entire year. He gathers himself as the cars around him become a blur. "So my impassioned speech back there, showing them Sonia's picture, that didn't help, I take it?"

"Oh, it helped, my friend. That's what pulled Archie Williams back from the brink," Kight says. "Before that, Alicia Vanderwelt had convinced him to disbar you."

3

Hitch wants a drink. He has learned, through countless meetings, not to think *I need a drink*, because alcohol is not essential to life. Air, food, water—and maybe love—are necessary to sustain life, but alcohol is definitely not. Or at least that's what he keeps telling himself as he barrels south on the Interstate, rejecting each exit ramp as roadside bar signs beckon him.

Hitch confesses to being an over-drinker. He uses this euphemism because labeling himself an alcoholic would constitute an irreversible declaration. He's kept his drinking mostly under control over the last few years. Mostly. In the wake of the shooting and Sonia's death, he drank some, but not enough to interfere with his daily responsibility to go to work six days a week and to keep his mind clear and focused for his clients. But that responsibility—that privilege—has just been ripped away from him. The skin of his cheeks feels raw.

He can't believe Alicia Vanderwelt was pushing to disbar him for having a consensual relationship with a woman he was in love with. After structuring a property settlement that, by any objective assessment, was incredibly favorable to Sonia. The notion of disbarment is absurd. It's cruel and unusual punishment. It's off the charts. But, she didn't get her way. A year's suspension. Still, it goes down like shards of glass.

Standing in the courtroom, locking eyes with Vanderwelt up on the bench, she with a distinct advantage of height, he had not fully realized the evidence in his case didn't matter to her. She was motivated to punish him. He sees that now. She wanted cold revenge.

In the litigation in which he beat her, their dealings had been ferociously heated. Their accusations as acrimonious as those of divorcing spouses. They couldn't seem to schedule a deposition without a protracted argument. He and Vanderwelt appeared before the trial judge seven or eight times on motions to compel discovery and for sanctions. She accused him of distorting the opinions of his expert witnesses. He accused her of destroying documents. Back and forth, fighting over issues that litigation combatants could usually resolve without the intervention of a judge. The battles, most of which he'd won, prolonged his clients' day in court by a year or more. It was undoubtedly part of Vanderwelt's master plan. Delay, obfuscate, contrive—three essential stratagems for any lawyer whose client is standing at the edge of the litigation cliff.

After his vindication by the jury's verdict, she had scowled at him as she tromped down the courthouse steps, past the bank of microphones at which he was giving a press conference, explaining why he believed the jury had awarded such substantial damages. Vanderwelt's name came up in a question, and he may have implied she wasn't interested in truth or justice, only in covering for her client at all costs.

Now, barreling down I-75, having escaped the harshest penalty, he doesn't feel relief. He is … despondent. The foundations of his life are being slowly demolished by an incessant series of waves, and he feels powerless to stop any of it. Sonia was taken from him less than nine months ago by her crazed husband. The bullet that shattered his shoulder, tearing off a piece of his lung in the process, left a scar he sees every morning in the mirror. The wound is an emblem of his diminishing vitality, perpetual proof of his vulnerability. Now, his law license, the thing to which he has clung so desperately, is suspended for a year by a vengeful lawyer as reprisal for him doing the very thing he is supposed to do—achieve justice for exploited victims.

His fingers grip the steering wheel hard enough to turn his knuckles white. Aloud, he curses George Colbert. And Alicia Vanderwelt. When the red haze in his head finally clears, the speedometer registers 87. He is weaving in and out of lanes like someone being chased by sirens.

He takes the exit for downtown Macon, his breath coming in rapid gasps. He parks his silver SUV on Mulberry Street, in front of the Bibb County courthouse, an edifice in which he's tried a handful of jury cases. He lays his forehead on the steering wheel. He desperately needs sanctuary from this onslaught. He needs relief. He needs friends. Too embarrassed by his suspension, he decides not to call his assistants. He doesn't know how to tell Natalie and Stacie what has happened. The verdict. The unfathomable outcome. Given the circumstances, none of them contemplated this. A result as unforeseeable as George Colbert's bullets. He is the only lawyer in his firm, and his suspension jeopardizes their jobs. Their livelihoods also are in peril. Still, he can't tell them. Not right now.

He walks a couple of blocks to a bar where he has eaten lunch while in trial here. He weaves through the fallen pink cherry blossoms that litter the sidewalk, now a mucky paste that sticks to the bottom of his shoes. It is close to 4 p.m. He's missed lunch, but food is not what he has in mind.

He orders a Jack and Coke. To start slow, he tells himself. The bartender sets the tumbler down with a hearty thunk then ducks into the back room. The glass sits untouched on the wooden bar, droplets beading the glass. He inches the glass back and forth with his index fingers, like a cat playing with a dead bug. Then he picks up the glass and sniffs it, takes a deep whiff of intoxicating aroma. He puts the glass back down and peers into the mirror behind the bar.

Hitch notes his hair-line is receding, something he might not have noticed in the morning's foggy mirror. A gray curl in his left eyebrow. Tiny lines at the corners of his eyes that may not have been there a month ago. His face holds a pallor that makes him look, in the sad light of the bar, older than 41. He stands, slips off his suit jacket, and drapes it on the back of the barstool. He turns to the side, seeing a slight bulge in his mid-section profile. He contracts his abdominal muscles. He unbuttons his shirt cuffs and rolls them to mid-forearm. He loosens the knot in his tie. He is readying himself for something.

He wriggles into the bar seat, anchoring, as if he plans to stay for days. He counts the bottles of liquor lined up on the back shelf like contestants. Fifty-four. He has probably tried them all at some point. Well, not Cointreau. Two halves of him begin to fight, one bent on distraction, the other bent on … He picks up the tumbler and examines its rich, dark contents. He raises the glass to his nose. The fizz of the carbonated mixer tickles his upper lip. He takes a sip. Not a slug; just a sip. The bourbon slides down, warm but not burning. And then he sets the glass down and waits for something to happen. He waits a minute, then five. Nothing. It takes at least ten minutes for alcohol to take effect, he knows. He watches the digital clock behind the bar, its red numbers in countdown. At eleven minutes he remains flat. He is expecting some change in demeanor, something to click in his brain now that he has pulled the pin from the grenade. Something approaching a craving. The plan for a crazy late-night adventure. Instead—nothing. Sanity remains in charge. At least for the moment.

There is another patron at the far end of the bar, and two businessmen sitting in a booth in back. Not surprising for a Monday afternoon. He contemplates their situations, the catalysts that might have brought them in. The man at the end of the bar is woozy, a regular in all likelihood, the kind who comes during the first few minutes of happy hour and stays until closing. He is drinking something clear, on ice. His head is down, as though studying the grain of the wood. A laugh emanates from the booth in the back. Two younger guys in suits, tie knots still cinched. Their fists are wrapped around beer bottles. Hitch figures they are killing time before a meeting, or a child's ball game or recital, or before heading home. Someplace they don't want to be just yet. This is a musing, without any real evidence, but their circumstances certainly seem less dire than his. He doubts either of them had his professional license pulled today.

He takes another swallow of whiskey, more than a sip this time, and catalogues the possible outcomes if he were to order another. The top contender: he won't stop at two. Somewhere between four drinks and seven is his prediction, leading to a range of states from maudlin to moribund to comatose. Then a short stagger to a hotel nearby, if he is able to walk at all. Followed by a restless night amid tangled bed sheets that will leave him listless and exhausted in the morning. Maybe repentant. He has been there before. Seven years back. No eight. Right in the throes of his divorce from Mary Whisenhunt, a period of prolonged darkness.

He looks up from the greasy bar, thinking he might modulate his intake, just enough to maintain some charm, edging on bravado, but avoiding stupid and sloshed. In that event, he will want company. On a Monday night his odds are poor, and he can think of no one to call, no one from his past who might be even the slightest bit interested. His assistants are two and a half hours away. They both would come to the rescue, but he will not involve them in this misery. When he thinks fleetingly of calling his ex-wife, he snickers, wondering why he would want to pile torment atop agony. Anyway, if she knew it was him on the line, she wouldn't pick up. She hates him. Maybe for good reason.

He coddles the glass, still half-full, the Jack diluting from melting ice. He gazes at himself again in the bar mirror, for he can't avoid it unless he rotates the barstool. His eyes are rimmed in red, his shoulders slumped. His forehead has a sheen. Above, his hair is mussed, disheveled. His mouth holds an uncertain expression, as if it doesn't know what to do, doesn't know what words to utter in this most dire situation. He looks … defeated. That's the word.

Is this what Vanderwelt saw when she peered down at him from her higher perch? Despite his reflection, despite the absence of a ticket to practice law, he is not washed up. He cannot accept that. No.

He grips the glass and drains it. Then he sets the tumbler down. The ice clinks against the glass like an invitation.

"Another?" the bartender asks, his hand poised over the bottle of Jack.

Hitch hesitates, then shakes his head once. He watches in the mirror as a wry smile appears on his face. He doesn't normally do wry. Sonia said he had a winning smile, a smile that invites you in. And his mirrored self sputters into a laugh because it is the only thing he can do. His reflection mouth is animated now, lips parted, a desperate chortle leaving his throat. The chuckle leaves him shaking his head. At himself. He wipes his brow with his shirt sleeve. Then he slides a twenty across the bar.

On the stroll back to his car, he feels less burdened. Laughter? Could it be that simple? He accepts that he has achieved a small victory, regained a modicum of control on a day when he has been otherwise battered by powerful forces. The sun dips below the tops of the buildings, casting a wan light across the facade of the courthouse, turning the brick walls the color of dying embers. He stops to take in white azaleas in full bloom, drooping dogwoods surrounded by a shallow layer of white petals. He pulls a dogwood bough to his nose and inhales the sickly, sweet scent.

4

Hitch arrives at his law office in Savannah at mid-morning. He barely slept the night before, gyrating like an animal caught in a trap. A handful of reporters are milling on the brick sidewalk in front of his building. He pulls past them into the gravel parking lot behind. They follow his car along the drive. Before getting out, he stares through the windshield at the black wrought-iron fence separating his building from the neighbor's, steeling himself. He looks in the rearview and adjusts his hair, tightens the knot of his tie.

This can't be good.

He steps out of the car. Before he can close the door the reporters begin hurling questions at him, thrusting microphones in his face. He greets them with a contrived smile, as if he welcomes their interrogation. He does not.

"Good morning." He recognizes two reporters from local papers, and a television reporter and her cameraman from WSAV. "What can I do for you all today?"

"What is your suspension from the State Bar based on?" one of the newspaper reporters asks.

How did the decision become public so fast? he wonders.

He folds his hands in front, adopting a sincere posture. "Well, the State Bar is charged with the responsibility of keeping lawyers in line, and yesterday a disciplinary panel determined that I crossed that line." The smile is gone. He manages a somber face for the rolling camera.

"Based on what?" the same reporter asks.

"Well, what did the State Bar tell you, Myra?"

"All we got in the press release was a one-liner, that you have been suspended from the practice of law for one year, effective immediately. The Bar refuses further comment."

The handiwork of Alicia Vanderwelt, no doubt. Provide the media with the penalty, without explanation or circumstances, so the press can ambush me and make me explain my crime to the public.

He has a good relationship with the media, but that belief is about to be tested. They usually respond when he issues an occasional media release or holds a press conference about one of his cases, and he has never been crucified by a reporter. Yet. He knows they have only one loyalty—to the story. "Successful Savannah Lawyer Falls From Grace," the headline might read. He could refuse comment, which is what he would advise a client to do under similar circumstances, but then he would feel like a coward.

"As you know, matters between attorney and client are confidential, and I'm not at liberty to discuss those matters with anyone. Wish I could, but I can't…"

The tv reporter interrupts. "Sara Mitchell, Channel 3. So you can confirm that your suspension is because of some matter involving a client?"

"Thank you for the question, Sara. I can confirm that, but as I said I can't discuss details because of client confidentiality. I'm sure you understand." His response is mostly true. He is required to maintain the confidentiality of certain information about his clients, even deceased clients, but there might be facets regarding the disciplinary hearing he could divulge without breaching that duty—like his history with Alicia Vanderwelt and her heavy-handed vendetta. He chooses not to bring that up, in some part because he doesn't want to engage in a diatribe that will further inflame Vanderwelt.

The third reporter, Delia Covington, steps in. "Does your suspension have anything to do with the shooting at your office nine months ago? I covered that story."

His eyes veer to the back wall of his red-brick building, as if he can peer through the dense ivy and thick walls into the first-floor conference room where it all happened.

"I thought you did an excellent job on that story Delia, and in covering George Colbert's plea and sentencing. As you know, my client, Sonia Summers, was killed in that vicious, unprovoked attack. But I can neither confirm nor deny that my suspension is in any way related to what happened that terrible day."

"Can you confirm you were still having an affair with Ms. Summers?" TV reporter Mitchell asks.

The gotcha question. Where did she get that information? That tidbit is not in the public records. Who is her source? Maybe Colbert, the convicted murderer.

Hitch has used the technique himself dozens of times with cagey witnesses. Most lawyers employ it. Somewhat like asking the husband in an assault case: "Have you stopped beating your wife yet?" "Yes" means he used to beat her. "No," means he is still doing it.

He firms his jaw but softens his eyes, wills his feet and hands to remain still. No fidgeting. In a practiced maneuver, he focuses on the right ear of the reporter so her expression will not distract him. She is standing next to the camera, so it appears he is speaking directly to the viewers, making eye contact with each of them.

"It is no secret that Ms. Summers and I had a personal relationship a number of years ago. Once her divorce was finalized, which was imminent, we planned to explore a future together. Unfortunately, George Colbert took that away from us." He looks down for a moment, noticing weeds in the gravel. His eyes re-focus on the camera. "Now, thanks to all of you for your questions."

He walks the gravel drive to the front entrance, his chin down. The reporters follow but no longer bombard him with questions.

He closes the front door and leans against it, taking a deep breath. Natalie Anderson and Stacie Throckmorton emerge from the break room in the back, where they have no doubt been watching the interrogation through the window. They know. He should have told them. If not last night, then this morning, before they arrived to a gaggle of reporters.

"I was ambushed."

"I tried to text you," Natalie says. "Didn't you get the message?"

He pulls his cell from his coat pocket. The screen is dark. He forgot to charge it last night.

He hired Natalie three years ago. She has taken it upon herself to serve as messenger when bad news needs to be delivered. She has a way of softening the blow, with him and clients alike. She has an undergraduate degree from the University of Florida in political science and a paralegal certification from the national association. She is tall, blonde and athletic. Clients adore her. Natalie can do everything necessary in a law office, from billing, to client intake, to brief writing. Except, she can't practice law in his stead.

Natalie approaches and hands him a one-page letter, with the gold-embossed seal of the State Bar of Georgia at the top. "It came via overnight delivery this morning."

"Sorry guys. I should have told you yesterday. I didn't want you to find out this way. I wanted to do it in person. I just …" He breaks off, scans the short letter. Formal notification of his suspension, for one year, effective immediately. It is signed at the bottom by the Bar's General Counsel. He waves the letter. "It could have been worse. Vanderwelt was pushing hard for my disbarment," he says.

"Who is she to judge you?" Natalie says with blazing eyes. "She's a vengeful bitch."

"You're not wrong there, Nat, but it's done."

"Never liked her," Stacie says, "not since she hid those documents in the lead-smelter case."

Stacie was his first hire when he started his practice eleven years ago. A graduate of Emory with a degree in environmental engineering, Stacie switched careers at age 40, opting for the law because she thought it would be less boring and more glamorous than testing for pollutants and writing environmental impact statements. Sometimes it is. She had been invaluable in helping Hitch digest the complicated data from the environmental testing of his clients' lead-contaminated properties in the case against Vanderwelt. Stacie abhors confrontation and, in keeping with her engineering background, generally displays a scientist's distance and objectivity.

"You don't deserve to be suspended," Stacie adds, as if the thought has been dangling on her lips.

"Thanks for the sympathy, guys. I need a minute to check on some things. Let's meet in the conference room in ten." He glances at the oak door to his left, which conceals the room where George Colbert shot him and murdered Sonia. Other than an industrial cleaning service, no one has been in there since the police finished their investigation and took down the yellow crime tape. He might never be able to sit in that room again. Certainly not now. "The upstairs conference room," he amends.

He climbs the stairs to his office, hooks his suit coat on the rack, and settles into a high-backed leather chair molded to the contours of his body. Despite donning one of his best navy suits and a blood-red tie this morning, he is suddenly uncomfortable at his own desk. This is a lawyer's space, and he can no longer hold himself out as a lawyer. Not for a year, anyway. There will be a feeding frenzy when word gets out. He thought he had more time. But in a few hours, certainly not more than a day, some of the opposing lawyers on his cases will begin to press the advantage, scheduling depositions and key hearings because there is no longer a lawyer on this side. Not all of them will pounce, but some of them will. All in the name of zealous advocacy.

They huddle around the oval table in the war room, where they prepare for trials and major hearings. Schedules and deadlines are posted on a three-month calendar spread across the longest wall. He studies it, as he does at least twice a week. One trial, scheduled two months out. The next few days will be a trial of a different nature.

"Okay, if we work together, we'll get through this," he starts. "Natalie, get in touch with all of the clients. ASAP. Tell them what's happened and instruct them not to talk to any lawyers who may contact them."

"Lawyers can't talk to clients who are represented by" Natalie stops, recognizing her misstep.

The prohibition on opposing counsel contacting his clients has evaporated because he is no longer a licensed lawyer. His clients are, technically, unrepresented. Unscrupulous lawyers could contact them for any number of reasons: to offer a low-ball settlement; to scare them into believing they will lose their case and potentially have to pay the defendant's court costs; or to poach his clients for themselves. He wonders if Vanderwelt thought about this when she levied the immediate suspension, allowing no time for a peaceful transition, leaving his clients in jeopardy. Of course she did.

"Stacie, I want you to write up a summary of each case we have. Include the key facts, important documents, status of discovery, deposition summaries, the pleadings, any pending motions, and all deadlines. Provide enough detail so another lawyer can pick up the case and try it next week, if necessary. Once the summary is finished, prepare a binder for each case and include all of that information and documents, indexed and tabbed."

"We have forty-three cases," Stacie says.

"That many?"

It is not a huge docket, but he doesn't handle run-of-the-mill cases. He decided when he started the solo practice he wanted quality, not quantity, so he focused on commercial disputes, complex litigation, mass torts and class actions. Big cases; manageable case load.

Stacie nods, her red curls bouncing around her ears.

He scans the wall calendar again. "Okay. Prioritize the ones that have pending deadlines in the next two weeks. If you want to email me a prototype summary, I'll review it before you draft the others. But I don't think these summaries need much more detail than the reports we send to clients every quarter."

"We could email everything to whoever takes over," Stacie offers.

"We can do that, but I want the binders prepared, just like we're going to trial."

"You have a summary judgment hearing in the Casterline case next Monday," Natalie says.

"Has the response brief been filed?"

"Yesterday, while you were in Atlanta."

He presses his palms together at his chin, taps his lips with his index fingers, conjuring how to handle a significant hearing only six days out. "We'll refer it to David Holt Kight. I'll talk to him personally. As soon as we're done here."

Natalie frowns. "Ah, not to argue with you boss, but wouldn't it be better to hire another lawyer and keep the cases in-house? You've got a dozen resumes on your desk, all qualified candidates looking for an opportunity to work with you."

He has already decided to refer all his cases to other lawyers and take on no new clients until the suspension expires. He doesn't want to practice law through a surrogate and invite continued scrutiny from Alicia Vanderwelt or the State Bar. These days, it isn't entirely clear what "practice of law" means. A suspended lawyer certainly can't appear in court, and is not supposed to provide legal advice, but lots of non-lawyers, from accountants, to insurance adjusters, to companies providing incorporation services over the internet, are, consciously or not, providing legal advice to clients all the time. The State Bar has simply decided not to pursue these non-lawyers for the unauthorized practice of law. But once you are in the Bar's sights, they are unlikely to look away. He intends to stay well away from the spotlight.

"I appreciate the suggestion Nat, but it wouldn't be fair to the clients to have their cases handled by a baby lawyer, regardless of the talent level. These aren't slip and falls or rear-end collision cases. Most of these are complicated cases, with big money at stake. And for most of our clients, this is their only shot at justice."

Natalie is undeterred. "But if you refer all the cases out, what are you going to do about us?" She glances at Stacie.

He sips his coffee, which suddenly tastes bitter. "I'm going to set aside funds to cover your salaries, benefits and all operating expenses for a year. Without contingency cases, we won't have to front litigation expenses. It will be tight financially, but we'll be okay."

"Oakley Walker Hitchcock," Natalie exclaims. Crinkles mar her brow. "I wasn't referring to money. What are we going to *do* without clients?

What are we going to work on?"

"Oh, you're going to keep working. Both of you. All our cases will be moving forward, we're just switching out the lawyer-in-charge. One of the conditions of referral is that the new lawyer continues to work with you. You guys know the clients, and the cases. Me, they will do without. But you—you're an invaluable asset to every one of our clients."

This seems to mollify Natalie. He locks gazes with her, realizing somewhere along the line she has become a loyal friend.

"Thank you," he says, "for sticking by me." He clears his throat. "It's good to know I have friends— not just employees—who will help me through this." He includes Stacie in his acknowledging glances.

"I hate that word—employee," Natalie says.

"I said 'friends' Nat. I mean that."

Stacie, in her anxious way, gnaws on a yellow number two pencil, her eyes fixed on the client list.

"That has lead in it," he says. "Incredibly bad for your brain."

Stacie pulls the pencil from her mouth. Teeth marks dent the yellow trunk. "I've told you a hundred times, it's not lead but graphite. It's not toxic . . ." Her mouth curls. "Oh, you were trying to lighten the mood."

"Did it work?"

"In your year off," Natalie interjects, "I don't recommend you try stand-up comedy. You'll starve."

He feigns a wounded look. "I take back what I said about keeping you on .... No, I'm just kidding."

But Natalie and Stacie have moved on, hunched together over the client list, dividing up other responsibilities he hasn't even thought of. They will take care of the clients. Maybe this year hiatus from practicing law won't be so terrible. Yes, it will.

He slumps behind his desk, looking out the front window at Oglethorpe Avenue, two stories below. Live oaks arch across the center median. He bought the building as an investment eight years ago. It came with a hefty mortgage. On a legal pad he jots a note to look at the loan documents. He is concerned there might be a provision triggering a default if he is no longer practicing law. Not a provision he would have noticed at the time because that contingency was unfathomable. Was. Despite his assurances to Natalie and Stacie, he is not confident he can weather a year away from the practice, either financially or emotionally. This morning, he has tried to present a stoic countenance, but he knows it is a flimsy facade that could crack at any minute.

He picks up the phone. With only a short wait, the receptionist puts him through to attorney David Holt Kight.

"I've been expecting your call," Kight says. "I'm presuming you're calling about the press release."

"Actually, I was …"

"I had no idea Vanderwelt would do that, Hitch, but it appears she got authority for a press release from the general counsel's office right after the hearing. She's really got it in for you."

"That's obvious. I got ambushed by three reporters at my office this morning. Probably exactly what Vanderwelt intended." He gets up and peers down at the sidewalk, but the reporters are gone.

"Crap. You don't deserve that."

"Thanks for saying that. Anyway, what I really wanted to talk to you about is taking over some of my cases. I've got 43 cases I need to refer to other attorneys ASAP, and I wanted to start with you. All pretty good cases, most of them contingencies."

"I'd be honored, Hitch."

"One of the cases has a summary judgment hearing on Monday, but we filed the response brief yesterday. Disability insurance case. Our client is a thoracic surgeon. Defendant is the disability carrier. Can you take that on on such short notice?"

Kight clicks keys on his computer. "Yeah, I can handle it. Tell me about the issues. If there's something I can't get up to speed on, the judge will probably grant a continuance."

Hitch fills him in on the key points and promises to deliver a hearing binder and the case file first thing in the morning. He ends the call with confidence that Kight will not let the client down. The most pressing emergency handled, he spends the afternoon handing off other clients, trying to match them with the right lawyers. The clients always come first. He will take care of them even though suspended.

Natalie buzzes his extension. "Judge McCullough on line two for you."

He has a handful of civil cases pending before Judge McCullough. "Did he say why he's calling?"

"He didn't, but take a wild guess," Natalie says through the speaker.

He picks up the handset. "Your Honor."

"Hitch, I just heard the news. Suspended? What the hell is going on?"

In his former life, Terry Patrick McCullough was a trial lawyer, representing clients in civil cases on both sides of the docket. In his five years on the bench, he hasn't forgotten his roots and is often overly courteous to the lawyers who appear before him.

"They're suspending me for one year for impaired professional judgment."

"That may be the most ridiculous thing I've ever heard. You're probably the most level-headed, sanest lawyer among us."

"Thank you for saying that, Judge, but two members of the bar disciplinary panel disagree with that assessment."

"In what case did you supposedly have impaired professional judgment? Certainly not something in my court."

"No, sir. The Colbert divorce case."

Savannah is a relatively small legal community, one in which the lawyers mix with the judges socially. This is not the norm. In the nine months since Sonia's murder, Hitch has told most of the local litigators, and many of the judges, exactly what happened in his office that fateful morning. Other details he could not bring himself to utter came out during Colbert's sentencing hearing.

"George Colbert? The confessed murderer?"

"One and the same."

"And he filed a bar complaint against you?"

"Yes, sir. From prison."

"Ridiculous. Are you going to fight this?"

"The standard is abuse of discretion, and you know how the appellate courts interpret that."

"I do," the Judge says. "I've been the beneficiary of that almost impossible-to-reverse-standard when some of my rulings were upheld, even though I might have been wrong."

This presents an opening for a joke, but Hitch isn't up to it. "I'm not going to appeal."

Judge McCullough pauses, as he usually does before announcing his decision. "Probably the smart thing, but I hate it. By the time you'd get a decision from the Supreme Court, a year would have gone by anyway. The whole thing will be moot, and the Court's decision might be taken as approval of the suspension. Listen, I know you've got three or four cases before me, some with deadlines coming up. Don't worry about those cases, Hitch. Given the circumstances, I can re-set those deadlines a year out. Most of the other judges will probably do the same, though of course I can't speak for them."

Hitch had explored the possibility of postponing his cases before deciding to hand everything off. He taps a ballpoint against the desk blotter, reconsidering. "I appreciate that Judge, but I'm finding other lawyers to take over in my absence. It wouldn't be fair to the clients to make them wait an extra year because of my troubles."

"Proof positive that your judgment isn't impaired," he says. "Maybe that's the best way to handle it, if that's the way you want to go, but I wanted to let you know you have another option."

"I appreciate that, Your Honor."

"What are you going to do for the next year?"

"Honestly, I have no idea."

In this unprecedented situation, Hitch's future is blank. Since he opened his practice eleven years ago, he's spent most of his daylight hours in this office. He props his feet on the restored leather top of his oak desk, imported from England in the early 1800s by a Georgia shipping merchant, and somehow spared in Sherman's firestorm to the sea. He looks around at his office. The walls are leaf green, giving the vague impression you are out in nature even when confined by four walls and a ceiling. Sonia helped him re-decorate during the almost two years they dated after his divorce. Her touches are everywhere: the brass planter in the far corner; the watercolors of the Savannah waterfront and reedy marshes and the long strand of beach at Tybee Island; the lacquered coat rack he brushes with the back of his hand twice each day. God, he misses her. Her absence, and now his suspension, has dimmed the light. Everything is muted. The bustling traffic on Oglethorpe is a mere murmur. It hasn't been a full day yet, and the office has gone silent. How quickly the phone stops ringing. He isn't ready for a year of silence.

He hears Natalie's light footsteps coming up the wooden stairs. She pops her head into his office, stands in the doorway. "What did the Judge have to say?"

"A message of condolence, I think. He said he could bump our deadlines out a year."

"Did you tell him yes?"

"I did not. The hand-offs are almost complete. And besides, even if the court dates were postponed, I'd still have to take depositions, propound and answer discovery, all stuff I can't do on suspension."

She chews her lower lip, mulling whether to broach something else on her mind. "I'm about to head out for the day. You okay?"

"Working on it. Trying to decide if I should issue my own press release, or at least post something on our website."

"Not a bad idea. Although …"

"Spill it, employee."

She frowns in return, ambles into his office the way only long-legged athletes can, and takes up a position in the upholstered wing chair on the opposite side of his desk. With her left arm she sweeps his feet over to the side of the desktop. "If you don't mind." She steeples her hands beneath her chin. "I've been giving this some thought. How to respond. Whether to respond. I talked to a friend of mine who specializes in crisis management, and she says now that the cat's out of the bag, it's probably best to stay quiet."

"Sounds like a conversation I should have had before the hearing."

"Agreed. But spilt milk and all that. Anyway, what's the real upside if you do respond?"

"I get to tell my side."

"Which accomplishes what?"

He thinks about this for a minute, letting his eyes drift to the watercolor of River Street, hanging in a gold-painted frame on the opposite wall. Regardless of what he says, a short or lengthy explanation will probably land wrong. He can't conjure any public statement that will make his situation any better. There is nothing that will ease the pain of a year away from his practice.

"Okay. I'll accept my punishment in silence."

"Smart move," Natalie says. "Sometimes it's best for the lawyer to say nothing."

5

Home is a longing, an anchor. In the wake of his suspension, Hitch needs a safe harbor away from his own turbulent storm. Going to the office where he can't practice his profession only increases his frustration. His bungalow on the Half-Moon River, purchased only weeks before Sonia's murder, is a constant reminder of what he has lost. It takes him a few days of moping about before he realizes he must go home.

He loads his SUV and leaves Savannah before the afternoon rush hour. He has barely reached the outskirts of the city when his phone rings. Jasper, curled on a blanket in the back seat, lifts his bloodhound nose at the harsh ring tone. Attorney Kight is on the line.

"Hitch, good news. We won the summary judgment hearing on the Casterline case."

"That is good news," he says into the speaker in his steering wheel.

"All your doing. The brief carried the day. I hardly had to make an argument."

Hitch beams. Natalie wrote most of the brief. He edited it, adding some punch, bringing Dr. Casterline's plight to life.

"There's something else. The insurance company wants to settle. They're offering the past-due disability benefits, plus the present value of all of the future benefits under the policy, discounted at 6% per annum. Comes to $1.2 million."

"They're worried about punitive damages, or trebles," Hitch says.

"No doubt, but those are hard to recover. You know that. And Dr. Casterline isn't the most sympathetic client."

"I know. A bit of a God complex. And a jury might think a million dollars is enough to give to an arrogant doctor who has already made millions."

"The Doc wants to settle, Hitch. I told him I'd have to analyze all the issues and get back to him with a recommendation. I really just wanted to run it by you. Thoughts?"

Hitch rubs his forehead. He knows the issues inside and out, could make the closing argument right now if he were allowed to. "The past-due benefits are a lock. Two-fifty, maybe three hundred thousand at the time of trial. The insurance company had no justification for denying the claim. The usual insurance company BS. But to get the future stream of monthly benefits—that's more problematic. We basically have to prove the insurance company repudiated the policy, not just materially breached it. It's a tough sell."

"Yeah, I see it that way too," Kight says. "Crap shoot on the future benefits. The Doc doesn't want to have to fight with them whenever they decide to stop paying him in the future. Even if we get three times the actual damages now, that could amount to less than the offer on the table."

'Right," Hitch replies.

"So should I tell him to take it? By the way, I'm not taking a fee if the case settles. The one-third contingency all goes to you."

"David Holt, that's not right."

"Hitch, I've had the case less than a week, hardly put anything into it. Plus … I feel like I owe you."

"Owe me?"

"For not being able to convince Alicia Vanderwelt or Archie Williams that you didn't violate your ethical duties, or to impose a lesser penalty than a suspension. A year off is going to cost you a lot."

"We can talk fee-split later," Hitch says. "I'm okay if you settle it."

"Done, my friend. For my fee you can take me out for oysters and beers. Deal?"

"All right. You're a gem David Holt."

After the call, Hitch's hands relax on the steering wheel. He doesn't pay attention to the grassy shoulders or the bar ditches half-filled with water. He doesn't glance at the eighteen-wheeler that edges past him in the left lane, causing his car to shimmy in the draft. He is elated and dejected at the same time. Elated by the victory; dejected because the settlement proves he is dispensable. Another lawyer picks the case up, and in less than a week, he settles it. Hitch knows deep down that his own hard work and doggedness have contributed to this success, but he feels the quick settlement proves he is fungible. Replaceable.

Once he exits the interstate, the drive to Pineland rambles through farmland and timber tracts, ending at a sandy road off two-lane blacktop that sees as many tractors and logging trucks as automobiles. The farm owned by his parents sits within a few miles of the Okefenokee Swamp in south Georgia, nestled into a huge expanse of sand that was once covered by the sea.

He turns off the asphalt and rattles across a spur of rusted railroad track unused since he was in high school. The wooden railroad ties are decayed and split. In the golden light just before sunset, he pauses to look at the farmhouse in the distance. His childhood home. He feels better calling it that. With that modifier he can see it in a better light. Not as a place to which he is fleeing the storm, but a place to which he is returning. The farmhouse is two stories, clad in cypress planks painted white, a beacon at the end of the sentinel-like pines that give the hamlet its name. The fields are in full flourish, vibrant with jade grasses. Goat weed adds a border of rose at the fence lines. Brangus cattle graze the fields, their distinctive humps swaying as they turn to inspect the strange vehicle. He parks beneath the live oak in the side yard, Spanish moss hanging from its limbs like retired beards. The oak has been here since before the Revolutionary War.

His father, Hale Oakley Walker Hitchcock, inherited about 40 acres from his father, mostly pastureland, with borders of pine and a few hardwoods. Over the years, his father purchased additional land in small parcels. Sometimes he took out mortgages to finance the purchases, but they are all paid off now. The farm occupies 320 acres—half a square mile. His father raises beef cattle. Cotton has permanently sucked most of the nutrients from the soil. And his father wants to hang onto the remnants of a time gone by, when small cattle farms used to dominate this part of Georgia.

Hitch swings open the screen door to the kitchen and whistles for Jasper, who reluctantly abandons sniffing scents and slides past him into the house, his ears drooping. Jasper is a liver and tan saddleback bloodhound, whom Hitch rescued from the pound four years ago. With drooping ears, Jasper thoroughly investigates the kitchen floor before settling on his pallet in the corner next to the gas stove. Hitch fills a stainless bowl with water from the sink. Jasper stands, laps, then plops down again, his forehead wrinkled in constant worry.

Hitch hauls two suitcases up the center stairs to his old bedroom, making enough noise on the cypress treads to disturb the dead. And there are dead nearby—in the family cemetery on the north side of the tractor barn. He can see some of the graves from his bedroom window. Five generations of Hitchcocks are buried beneath granite headstones ringed by a white picket fence. The first Hitchcock to die on the farm, at least the first for whom there is a record, was buried in 1902. The most recent to occupy a plot is his brother Rip, his marker reflecting his death eight years and five months ago.

Hitch finds his bedroom much as it was when he left for college. His mother has replaced the bedding, opting for something more tasteful than the garish green and gold he was enamored with because they were his high school colors. Now, a vanilla spread with ocean blue sham and pillowcases adorn the bed.

Bridget Hitchcock has kept the room tidy and cleared out the chest of drawers, boxing old clothes and storing them in an attic that in summer gets hotter than the Mojave Desert. He hears her irregular footfalls starting up the stairs, a noticeable pause between strides as his mother slides her hand along the banister to pull herself up to the next step. She had her right hip replaced three years ago, and it still doesn't work quite right. She's moved her bedroom downstairs, to what had once been a parlor. Despite her doctor's admonitions, she climbs the stairs on a daily basis, cleaning and dusting the upper level. Or sometimes sitting in Rip's room, consumed by bereavement that will never leave.

He hangs his sport coat in the too-small closet and turns to her. "Mom, I was coming downstairs in a bit. I didn't stop to say hello because I didn't want to wake you."

"I wasn't sleeping. Not in the middle of the day, for sure." She rubs her puffy eyes.

"I know it's hard for you to climb the stairs."

"Oakley Walker Hitchcock, what was hard for me was being in labor with you for 27 hours, trying to push you out without even a local anesthetic. That was almost 42 years ago, and I may not have recovered yet. Maybe that's why I had to get a new hip."

He joins her charade. "So you dislocated your hip in childbirth and only recently dispensed with your stubbornness to get it replaced?"

"I could tell it like that son, but I don't really want to blame you for my troubles."

He wraps his arms around her small body, feeling the ridges of her vertebrae, her bones as frail as a sparrow's. His mother's head, with hair as white as unpicked cotton, rests against his collarbone, just an inch or two from where Colbert's bullet left its scar. She smells like gardenias. In season, she clips the white blooms from glossy bushes on the west side of the house and fills vases in the bedrooms and the living room. She likes the scent so much that for Mother's Day each year Hitch buys her a perfume that mimics the gardenia fragrance.

She unlocks from his embrace and steps back. "It's good to have you home, son."

"It's good to be home. I need a break, need some rest."

"Not sure how much rest you'll get. Your father needs you. It's almost calving season."

"I see the bulls have been busy," he says, looking out the window to the edge of the front pasture, where cows with low-slung, heavy bellies huddle in the shade. "How many cows do you have now?" He says it like this, as if the farm and its livestock belong to strangers.

"You'll have to ask your father for the exact count, but I think there's more than 120 now, with a lot more due in the next few weeks."

At dinner, between mouthfuls of veal provided by a milk-fed calf, Hitch recounts the details of the disciplinary hearing and his past travails with Alicia Vanderwelt. "They suspended me for a year. I have 51 weeks left." His parents know this already, but he feels the need to repeat it, as if saying it out loud helps purge it.

"She has it in for you," his father says, pointing his fork across the table.

"They just piled on to your suffering," his mother says. "As if losing Sonia wasn't bad enough."

His parents met Sonia once at a restaurant during one of their infrequent trips to Savannah, years ago. After Hitch dropped Sonia at her apartment that night with a sweet kiss, he asked his parents what they thought of her. His mother said "she's lovely," a high compliment. His father said he didn't deserve her. They were both right, Hitch realized at the time.

"Such a waste of human life," his father says now. "To be killed so young, and by such a sonofabitch."

"He'll never have a home other than a prison cell," Hitch replies.

"How's your shoulder, son?" His mother rarely uses his name unless trying to press a point. On those occasions, she often calls him by his full name, with an edge to her voice. "Hitch" is reserved for friends and contemporaries. The nickname seems a bit vernacular to her.

"It's fine. Still a little sore at times. Good thing I'm right-handed."

"You don't hold a grudge against the guy, shooting both of you like that?" his father asks.

His parents converse like this, tag-teaming him, his father usually uttering a pithy conclusion or an incisive question, his mother adding a dollop of sympathy.

"Of course I hold a grudge, but dwelling on it isn't going to bring Sonia back."

Hale Hitchcock's eyes roam over his son's face, analyzing him. He is a Georgia Tech-educated engineer who returned to the farm to help his father raise cattle and make improvements that increased impregnation rates, yield, weight and auction prices for his beef. But he retains a belief that not all things new can be deemed progress and that some of the old ways are actually better, more effective solutions to stubborn dilemmas. He examines people's words and deeds the way he might an engineering problem, taking apart syllables and facial expressions in an effort to get at the root meaning. He's perplexed by his son's seeming ambivalence about the man who murdered the love of his life.

"He's up at Reidsville, right?"

"Yes, dad. For the rest of his life."

"He got off easy."

"He did dad, but it wasn't my call."

"You gave a witness statement, didn't you?"

"More than that. I testified at the sentencing hearing. The jury voted for life in prison. The Judge had no choice."

Hale Hitchcock rakes his fork through a half-eaten pile of lima beans. "He should have gotten the needle," he says without looking up.

Hitch sets his silverware on the edge of his plate. "Dad, I don't disagree, but this is the way the system works. Life in prison without the possibility of parole is what the jury decided. Can we drop this, please?"

"If it was me, I would never drop it."

The rawness of this comment causes Hitch to gag, some of his dinner coming back up in his throat. He studies his father in the bright kitchen light. Hale turned 70 last year. His face is lined from farm work, but his eyes are bright, his mind sharp. He subscribes to the New York Times' Sunday edition and finishes the crossword puzzle every week.

They hold each other's eyes for a moment in standoff.

"Let's have dessert," Bridget says. "I made pecan pie."

Hitch awakens the next morning to the rooster's crow, about 20 minutes before dawn. His immediate inclination is to go out and strangle the fowl, but the Rhode Island Red has talons and cockspurs that can shred a man's skin, so that isn't a realistic option. Ear plugs might work. Or, he can just get used to rising before dawn.

Hale is up and dressed in work jeans and a denim shirt, sitting at the kitchen table, finishing a plate of fried eggs and bacon. He mops up the yolk with a buttermilk biscuit, a pan of them atop the stove. The buttery scent of fresh biscuits fills the kitchen.

"Do you still eat bacon and eggs for breakfast every morning, dad?"

"Four or five days a week. I need the protein to work the farm all day."

"What's your cholesterol level?" The boil of last night's argument is still on Hitch's mind.

"208. Had it checked last month."

"How's that possible? Are you taking a statin?"

"No. My theory is that if you keep the blood flowing, you won't have plaque sticking to your artery walls. Like running rice hulls through an oil pipeline."

Hitch shakes his head. He has been home less than 24 hours, and in that span they have argued twice. Internally, he calls a truce. "Well, you're probably in a lot better shape than I am."

"Looks like we have about a year to change that, son. Get some breakfast, get dressed and meet me at the tractor barn. We've got pasture fencing that needs mending. And tomorrow, maybe get up a little earlier."

They spend the morning in a field on the northern edge of the property, repairing fencing the cows destroyed in the winter as they roamed for green things to eat. Weighing more than half a ton, bulls and big cows simply push weak fence posts over, like a small car plowing down a mailbox. Once the other bovines witness an escape, they usually follow. The farm is bordered by timber, most of the pines ten to fifteen years old. In winter, the cows think those green needles, usually dozens of feet in the air, can be eaten, so they trample or jump over whatever barricades stand in their path. Last winter, they damaged over a quarter-mile of fencing in their quest for food.

Hitch hammers a u-nail over the end of a fifth strand of barbed wire, securing it to a corner post made from ten feet of telephone pole, four feet of it buried in the sand. Unrolling wire from the spool, Hale backs toward the next corner, a Stetson the color of fawn fur tipped low over his brow. Hitch follows, steering him away from animal burrows. At the next corner, Hale wraps the wire tight against the post. Hitch picks up the stretcher.

"Not guitar-string tight, but stretch it a little," Hale reminds him.

Hitch loads the wire in the puller and clips the excess with fence pliers. He works the stretcher, pulling the lever back, listening to the clack of the ratchet. The barbs inch around the pole, wearing thin gouges in the wood. Hale hammers in the last two u-nails to secure the top strand. There is a supply of t-posts in the bed of the pickup, six feet long, with the tops painted white. Hitch picks up the post driver, raises it as Hale holds the steel post straight, and begins planting the posts between the wooden corners, in ten feet intervals, measured with a tape. Hammering steel onto steel, the hearty clang of it a testament to the work. Using fence pliers and clips, Hale secures the barbed wire to the posts.

"There," Hale says. "That's one section done. At least you haven't forgotten everything I taught you about fencing. Let's take a break."

They fill plastic cups with water from the jug and settle on the tailgate of the pickup. Hitch takes a deep swallow, relishing the cool down his throat. The sun is in mid-sky, with no clouds to filter its heat. He slides the water-beaded cup across the back of his neck. "I've forgotten how hot it can get down here, even in the spring."

"Son, you've gotten used to working in an office, with air conditioning. Wait until August."

"I remember August. Football practice in the heat. Two-a-days."

"Not the same as when you were 18. The body changes. Heat is harder to bear as you get older."

Hitch rolls his left shoulder. It's tight and sore at the bullet scar. "Don't I know it. I'm out of shape." He pats the steel tailgate with his palm, noting all the scratches in the gray paint. "How old is this old farm truck, dad? Looks like she's still in pretty good shape."

"I bought this truck the year after you graduated from college. So, I guess that makes her 18 years old. She'll last another six or seven, if I take care of the engine."

"Schedule maintenance, or maintenance will schedule you." They say it at the same time, and both chuckle. It's a slogan Hale has repeated hundreds of times, usually as notification it's time to grease the tractor joints, or sharpen the bush-hog blades, or change the fluids in the truck.

"Well, it works, doesn't it?" Hale says.

"Apparently so." Hitch slides his hand across the tail gate, brushing stranded hay to the ground. "How's everything going with the farm, dad? I mean financially." He asks this in part to gauge how much of a burden he might be while living with his parents. His monthly income has dropped to zero, though his share of the Casterline settlement will re-build his bank account. He wants to help out.

Hale gazes off toward the horizon, the distant trees a blur of green in the waves of heat. "Sure hope beef prices improve this year. We've been low for four straight years, ever since the Chinese curtailed purchases of American beef. Trade wars and tariffs don't help the cattle farmer, that's for sure. And the environmentalists are blaming global warming on methane from cow farts. Seems like we're under attack from all sides these days." Hale takes another sip of water. "Maybe they'll get it straightened out in Washington."

"What if they don't?"

Hale pulls at his left earlobe. "Like I said, it's been tough with prices down. Feed costs are going up. Food and supplies are more expensive. Your mother needs a new car, but the money isn't there. We've been through tough times before. It will all work out. Always does."

Hitch swings his legs back and forth off the tailgate, the brass eyelets of his boots glinting in the sun. "I don't want to be a burden. Maybe I can help out."

Hale rubs a phantom stain on the thigh of his jeans. "You've got your own issues. What with the shooting, and Sonia being killed, your suspension. And besides, you're helping out now." Hale takes another swig of water, slides off the tailgate with a grunt.

They climb into the truck, Hitch at the wheel, and drive a few yards before the engine stalls.

"You're not giving it enough gas," Hale says.

"Something's probably wrong with the fuel pump," Hitch replies. He cranks the starter, but it won't catch. After several tries, he pops the hood. As they tinker with the fuel pump and inspect the gas line, Hitch hears the low whistle of a train. It is a couple of miles out, heading west, probably carrying cows or lumber to be processed. Something about the train nags at him. He can't quite catch it. He checks the watch on his left wrist. Straight up noon.

6

Hitch makes the weekly call to his office. He's carved this time from the daily grind of farm work because he needs to maintain some attachment to the law, to remind himself that in eleven months he will be allowed to practice again.

His assistant Stacie Throckmorton answers the phone.

"How's it going up there?" he asks.

"Everything is fine. Not one thing has changed since you called last week." Stacie's conversation, like her work, is neat and efficient.

"No emergencies you need to consult me about?"

"Everything is under control. No imminent deadlines. Nothing for you to do."

"Okay, then. Thanks for keeping everything moving, Stacie. Is Natalie available?"

The hold music lasts three seconds before Natalie picks up.

"Who is this?" Natalie asks in a playful tone. "You become a full-time cowboy yet?"

"Nope, but I've sure honed my fencing skills. Barbed wire, welded wire, chicken wire, the whole nine yards. If it exists, I've strung it. Maybe I should hang out my shingle as a litigation consultant, specializing in farm fencing. I bet I could get certified as an expert."

"Sounds like that may bring in even less income than your plan to go on tour as a stand-up comedian."

He chuckles. "I need something, Nat."

"Me too. I'm bored. Stacie and I spend half our day twiddling our thumbs. I spend way too much time on the internet, playing solitaire on my computer. I'm taking two-hour lunches. Next step could be watching porn at the office. Nobody wants that, Hitch."

"No new cases to review?"

"We're referring all the new clients out, remember?"

"Yeah, just um …thinking about what I'm going to work on when I do get back. At some point we'll need to start accepting new cases."

"Too soon, don't you think? You can't give clients legal advice while you're on suspension, and they will wonder why they're not hearing from you. Maybe we start considering new cases 90 days out?"

"That sounds about right. What's going on with you?"

Natalie sighs. "Now I know you're bored."

"I miss being involved. Tell me something exciting."

There is a pause on Natalie's end of the line. Then, "Mark has gotten weird."

Mark Sanchez is Natalie's boyfriend. They've been living together for the past fourteen months. Hitch has assumed a marriage proposal isn't far off.

"Weird how?"

"Something's going on with him. He's been super distant in the last month or so. I can't put my finger on it. Something's wrong."

"Do you have anything specific, or is this just a feeling?"

"Okay. He leaves the apartment late at night. Never says where he's going. Comes back at two or three in the morning. When he is home, he makes hushed phone calls in the bathroom with the shower running. I found five burner phones in a locker in his closet."

"This started a month ago?"

"That's when I first noticed it. Could have been going on longer. He doesn't really talk to me anymore. Not about anything real. Know what I mean?"

"Maybe. What does Stacie think?"

"Stacie says she needs more data before she can analyze the problem."

"That's our engineer," Hitch says.

The kitchen door to the farmhouse pops open, and Hale sticks his head in, interrupting the conversation. "You ready?" he asks his son.

"Two minutes," Hitch responds. "Look, Nat, I've got to run. We're overhauling a hay baler today. We need to get cranking before it gets too hot."

"Of course, Hitch. I didn't mean for all that personal junk to spill out."

"No, it's okay. I'm here for you, Nat. Whatever you need."

As he replaces worn parts on the hay baler, Hitch ponders Natalie's dilemma. He would be overstepping if he volunteered his opinion. She didn't specifically ask for his advice about her boyfriend. Hitch has met him a handful of times, and Mark usually seemed … wary and guarded. It's likely Mark is hiding something, Hitch thinks, but he has a poor track record in this area. He missed the signs that George Colbert was on the brink of becoming a killer. He lost Sonia as a result. His only marriage ended in divorce because he couldn't see how miserable his wife was. He had endless chances to save it. Given his history, he realizes it would be difficult to come up with pithy advice to offer Natalie about personal relationships. But if the subject of Mark comes up again, he vows to be a sympathetic ear.

It takes all day to clean, grease and replace worn out parts on the baler. His father directs the work from a tall wooden stool while Hitch crawls all over the machine, bending his body into places a man his size is not intended to go. He suffers a long cut on his right forearm from a rusty carriage bolt. He dabs away the seep of blood with an old rag. As Hitch walks to the house, he examines the wound, wondering when he last had a tetanus shot. At the laundry sink, he uses a coarse cleanser to scrub grease from his forearms and hands until his skin turns a pale rose.

Six days a week he rises before dawn, toils in the fields or works on farm equipment until noon, breaks for a 45-minute lunch, up on the tractor for the afternoon and done when the hay is baled. He doesn't know how his father can do this day after day. It's not the physical labor that exhausts him; it's the monotony. Every day he works the farm, he feels his legal skills draining away. He didn't think it would be this hard to endure a year away from the practice, but in just one month his brain is turning into swamp mush.

7

On a Friday at noon, as thunderheads build over the Okefenokee Swamp, Hitch meets Tobias Thomas at a restaurant housed in an old brick building on US 1. Hitch and Tobias played football together in high school. They are both lawyers now. They used to stay in touch better; now they catch up about once a year.

Hitch appraises his former teammate as they wait in the buffet line. Tobias' shoulders are broad and, two decades past his playing days, his stomach is still flat. Tobias' hair is turning the color of ash at the temples, and he has a bald spot just below the crown. His skin is two shades lighter than coal.

"You look good man. Still working out?"

"Three times a week," Tobias replies. "Got to keep up with the kids. On the go all the time. How about you?"

"Not spending much time in the gym." Hitch looks for an excuse. "You know I got shot? Still a little sore." Hitch rotates his left shoulder and his clavicle pops.

"Yeah, I might have read about that in the papers. Sheree has a clipping still stuck to the refrigerator. Every time I go in the kitchen, I see your ugly face. My kids keep asking me how come I couldn't be a hero like you."

"Sounds like they're my biggest fans," Hitch smiles.

"Your only fans, more like it."

They load plates with fried catfish, hush puppies, macaroni and cheese, and coleslaw, then settle into a vinyl booth.

"Sorry to hear about the suspension, man. How you holding up?"

"My dad's working my butt off. There's so much to do on the farm, and he's neglected some of the major repairs."

"Understandable," Tobias says. "Your dad is what, 70?"

Hitch nods. "I'm happy to help out, but I'm going to have to find something to keep my brain engaged."

"Maybe you should relax, Hitch. Some people come here so they can slow down and unwind a little."

Hitch swallows the last bite of a cornbread hush puppy and considers this. "I'm definitely not ready for slow."

While Hitch scoops thick yellow pudding into his mouth, Tobias leans toward him. "Reverse mortgages," he says in a voice barely above a whisper. "What do you know about them?"

"Not a fan," Hitch says. "They probably serve a purpose, but I haven't figured it out. If someone needs to tap the equity in their house, it's usually easier and cheaper to get a HELOC."

"Yeah, I'm thinking the same thing. You remember Melba Davidson, our eleventh grade English teacher?"

"Of course I remember her."

"Well, she took out a reverse mortgage on their farm about three months ago. Did it without telling her husband."

"Financial trouble, I presume?"

"Husband runs the farm. They're losing money hand over fist. She was keeping it afloat with her teacher's salary, but he got sick. They ran up a bunch of medical bills insurance won't cover."

"That's unfortunate," Hitch says, thinking of the recent conversation with his father about the dire state of the farm's finances. "So she borrowed money against the equity in their property. What's the legal issue?"

Tobias shrugs. "Don't know that there is one. But she thought the whole thing was odd. Everything was rushed. The guy who signed her up is an insurance agent, not a banker. It looks suspicious."

"She took out a reverse mortgage through an insurance agent?"

"Yep. His office is over in Valdosta. She met him at a church retreat."

"How much did she borrow?"

"Seventy-five thousand."

Hitch nods. "Who is the lender?"

"Don't know. It's not in the paperwork the guy gave her. The insurance agent came to her house and stuck the documents in front of her, but didn't give her time to read them," Tobias says. "Said he had to hurry to another appointment. The guy pushed her to sign, and he had the loan check with him."

"He dangled the money like bait."

Tobias nods and slides a manilla folder across the table. "Everything he gave her is in there."

Hitch opens the folder, flips through the pages. He finds a form promissory note. None of the blanks are filled in, and the document is unsigned. The only other document is a three-page mortgage, titled "Security Deed." It also is a form with none of the blanks filled and an empty signature block.

"These copies don't even identify the borrower, the lender, or the amount of the loan," Hitch notes.

"Or even the property address," Tobias adds. "They're just boilerplate forms. Guy told her he would send her copies of what she signed, but he never did."

"Then you'll have to check at the deeds office to see what's been filed."

"I was wondering if you could research that for me," Tobias says. "Keep track of your hours. I'll pay you."

Hitch stares outside at the pines bending in the wind. Low, dark clouds hang like clumps of purple grapes. Big drops begin to splatter the window glass next to their booth and clatter on the metal roof.

"Not sure how to take that, man," Hitch finally says.

Tobias furrows his brow. "What do you mean? I can use the help."

"I don't need charity just because I'm on suspension. I've got some money to tide me over."

"This isn't charity, Hitch. I mostly handle small-time stuff. You know that. If there's a case here, it's way out of my league. I need someone like you on it. You have the experience."

"Mrs. Davidson isn't paying you, is she?"

"Doesn't matter. I'll pay for your time. Starting right now. We're on the clock."

Hitch searches the eyes of his long-time friend, looking for sincerity. The eyes always speak, even if you can't hear what they're saying. He learned that from Riley O'Reilly, his mentor at the law firm he worked for in Savannah before starting his own law practice.

Tobias holds his gaze for a few seconds, then breaks away, pretending to be intrigued by the sheets of water cascading down the window. Tobias drops his hands beneath the table.

"Okay, I'll do some research," Hitch says. "I need some brain stimulation. And I'll do it as a favor to Mrs. Davidson. We'll figure out fees *if* this turns into something. My meter isn't running yet."

When the storm finally passes, Hitch drives to the county courthouse and parks in an angled space across the street. The wet asphalt glistens in the sunlight. He takes the long way to the corner, noting the names of lawyers stenciled in gold or white letters on glass doors, mostly solo practitioners, one or two of whom he contacted for possible job offers when he graduated law school, but without any real interest in returning to his hometown. Truth is, he wanted out. Not because Pineland was so bad, but because he needed to see what lay beyond the confines of the small world in which he had grown up. He wanted to test himself against lawyers in cities named Atlanta, or Jacksonville, Dallas, or DC.

In the summer between his second and third year of law school, he clerked for a firm in Dallas with 135 lawyers, and more than 500 employees. The firm operated as a medium-sized company, its assets defined by billable hours and not by brain power or legal ability. He wanted to be a litigator—he knew that much—but that's about all he knew. The money and perquisites that went with practicing law in a large firm were enticing. He'd stared slack-jawed at the opulence of the partners' houses where he was invited to dinner, huge structures that consumed lots in Highland Park and Turtle Creek. He marveled at the sleek cars that cost more than a first-year associate's salary. BMWs and Mercedes, the occasional Ferrari or Maserati, backed into numbered spaces in the garage beneath the firm's office building, vanity plates blaring like gaudy announcements.

But though Dallas is south, it isn't Southern. When his first clerkship was up, he immediately left Dallas and drove to Atlanta, with hopes his second clerking experience would be better. He soon learned that most of the 300 attorneys at the Atlanta law firm, the second largest in the city at the time, did not handle litigation. They advised clients outside the courtroom on matters relating to business, estates, property development, taxes, and how to deal with the myriad of state and federal government agencies. During his clerkship from early July to mid-August, the attorneys in the litigation section started but one trial, which settled after jury selection. Few of the litigators, even some who had made partner at the firm, had ever tried a jury case. When he mentioned this to the associate who was in charge of his clerkship, he was reminded the firm's letterhead and business cards said "Attorneys and Counselors" and that counseling was what most of them did. No shame in that. His first two years in law school had not prepared him for the reality that many lawyers practiced in areas other than litigation, their days consumed with writing contracts, handling tax matters, planning estates, or counseling clients how to evade the law. They spent zero time in court. Not for him.

After law school he took a job in Atlanta, working for an insurance defense firm. The firm needed young lawyers to bill hours, and the work provided Hitch a broad avenue to the courthouse. Two or three days a week he was in court arguing motions. He tried seven jury cases in three years. But he soon tired of representing insurance companies, whose primary goal was to avoid paying money. He was good at it, but the work chewed on his soul. In his third year, he realized he was a bit player in a game that had little to do with the lofty concepts he'd studied in law school, or the blindfolded lady with the scales who presided over the front entrance to the courthouse.

He left the Atlanta firm and did a two-year stint at a plaintiff's firm in Savannah, where he learned how to practice law under the tutelage of Riley O'Reilly. When he had absorbed what he thought was enough information to make it, he started his own shop. That was eleven years ago.

He enters the Dare County courthouse through double doors clad in brass. He empties his pockets into a plastic bin, then steps through the metal detector. The light atop the detector shows red, so a deputy in a khaki uniform draws the wand up and down his body. The wand emits a shriek each time it nears the steel tips of his new work boots.

"Take off your boots, please."

He has never been asked to remove his shoes when entering a courthouse, instead presenting his bar card as proof he is not a threat, passing through security with a mere nod to the guards. This is yet another unexpected consequence of his suspension: he is no longer recognized as a member of the bar. One deputy waves the wand over his socks; another watches the x-ray monitor as his boots pass through on a conveyor. Finding nothing nefarious, the deputy hands the boots back to Hitch.

At the office where deeds are recorded, he states his business through a piece of plexiglass. The clerk is a woman two years ahead of him in high school. He remembers she moved to Jacksonville to start a new life, but it looks like the churn of the city may have spit her out, depositing her back here. She has extra age chiseled into her face. She directs him to the grantor and grantee indices, big books with red and black leather bindings on shelves made of steel rollers. The books, organized by the sellers and buyers of real estate, hold old deeds and mortgages.

"The documents I'm looking for would have been filed about three months ago," he says.

"Well, then they won't be in the big books," she says. "All the recent filings are digital." She walks him over to a bank of three computers. "This will allow you to search our intranet. The public computers don't have internet access," she says before returning to the filing window.

He sits down in an uncomfortable putty-colored metal chair, scratches marring the seat. He types Melba Davidson into the search bar. A list of documents appears onscreen. The most recent is the security deed she signed. All the blanks in this filed version of the mortgage are filled in. The mortgage holder is listed as 4927 Sulfur Creek Road, LLC. The company name is the same as the address of the Davidsons' farm. On the last page, he finds Mrs. Davidson's neat signature. There is no signature block for her husband. Her signature is notarized by Garland T. Rogers, notary public for the State of Georgia. Hitch guesses Rogers is the insurance agent Tobias mentioned.

Hitch taps the butt of a pen against his lower lip. Predictably, the promissory note Mrs. Davidson signed to get the loan isn't in the public records. The filed mortgage doesn't mention the amount of her loan, containing a lot of jargon, the sum of which is the mortgage company has a lien on the Davidson farm. He thinks back to the bank documents he signed when he bought his own house, then his office building in Savannah, but he can't recall if the mortgages mentioned the amounts he borrowed. He maneuvers the mouse, clicks, and finds the original deed whereby Cordell and Melba Davidson bought their 96-acre farm in 1985. He finds the purchase-mortgage document, which identifies the lender as a local bank. Eight years ago, the Davidsons paid off the loan, evidenced by a filed satisfaction of mortgage from the same bank. He wonders why Melba Davidson didn't go back to the local bank to take out a home equity loan, a question he intends to ask when he and Tobias meet with her.

On his cell phone he searches the Georgia Secretary of State's website. He discovers 4927 Sulfur Creek Road, LLC was created the same day Mrs. Davidson signed the loan documents. From this information, and the name, he concludes the company probably has a single purpose—to hold the mortgage on the Davidson farm. Because the company is less than a year old, the only public filing is the one-page Articles of Organization, which contain scant information. The mortgage holder's principal mailing address is a PO Box in Atlanta. No physical address is listed. The documents don't reveal whether 4927 Sulfur Creek Road, LLC also loaned Mrs. Davidson the $75,000, or whether the lender is a separate company. The registered agent for the company is a well-known corporation that serves this role for thousands of companies in every state. The only other public information is the identity of the person who filed the organizing documents: A Smith. No address or phone number.

Hitch stares at the computer screen. Something's off. He's never seen loan documents with so little information. Given that Cordell Davidson owned the farm jointly with his wife, his name and signature should be on the mortgage. The mortgage is tight, one-sided in favor of the mortgage holder. Undoubtedly drafted by an attorney. Nothing in the document gives him a clue who the lender is. In this era of infinite information, he wonders how a company that makes a $75,000 loan on someone's home can remain completely anonymous.

8

Hitch reaches Tobias on Monday afternoon, after the morning session of court.

"I'll bet you miss being in the courtroom, don't you?" Tobias says over the speaker.

"Every minute. Please tell me you're working on something juicy—a murder, a bank robbery, an international money-laundering cartel." The longing in his own voice surprises Hitch.

"Sorry, I can't provide the excitement you so desperately need. I've got an arraignment in a DUI case in a couple of days. My client may or may not have been driving a delivery van while high on meth. If you want to come, I'll let you sit at counsel table with me."

Tobias primarily handles criminal cases to which he is appointed by the court, which means most of his clients are guilty. Innocent clients usually hire their own lawyers, if they can afford to. Hitch ponders whether a few minutes in criminal court might resuscitate him, but he knows the arraignment would be mundane.

"I think I'll pass, buddy, but thanks," Hitch says. "Hey, I did a little research on Mrs. Davidson's reverse mortgage. Couldn't find out much from the public records. The mortgage is on file, but the lender isn't identified anywhere. I don't know if you want me to dig further. More questions than answers at this point. We should probably meet with her to get more details about the loan."

"What an eager beaver you are," Tobias says. "Maybe I should bring you on as a full-time paralegal." Tobias laughs in a good-natured way, no edge to it.

But it still stings. Hitch cannot rid himself of the dark premonition he will never practice law again, that some new circumstance will intervene to make his suspension permanent. It is not a rational fear, but fear is rarely rational. He is pondering a scathing riposte for Tobias but comes up with nothing. Another of his skills on the wane.

"Hold on a minute," Tobias says.

Hitch hears him shuffling papers at his desk.

"Oh my God!"

"What?"

"While I was in court this morning, I got a message from her husband, Cordell Davidson. The message says Mrs. Davidson passed on Saturday, Hitch."

The county coroner's office is a small edifice on an out-of-the-way street next to a residential development on the eastern side of town. Tobias and Hitch walk through glass doors into a cool reception area, the air conditioning fluttering papers tacked to a cork bulletin board. They are greeted with the smell of decay, its scent undefinable and yet unmistakable.

"We're here to identify a body. Mrs. Melba Davidson," Tobias starts.

"And you are?"

"Tobias Thomas. I was Mrs. Davidson's attorney. Her husband called me and asked if I would come down to formally identify her. He's too upset to come in person. And this is Oakley Hitchcock." Tobias places his hand atop Hitch's right shoulder. "He's working with me."

The receptionist hands them a bottle of peppermint oil and instructs them to spray some into their palms and rub the oil beneath their noses. She then points to a cardboard container of blue surgical masks on a table by the door. They both use the peppermint oil and mask up. They don nitrile gloves before entering the morgue.

The coroner, garbed as if for surgery, grasps the handle of a large drawer in a stainless-steel refrigerated storage unit and tugs it open. Melba Davidson's pale face appears. She is encased in a thick plastic bag. The coroner bends down and checks the blue tag, as if he has so many bodies in storage he might mistake her identity.

"That's Melba Davidson," Tobias says. "She was a teacher at the high school. How did she die?"

"Technically, cardiac arrest," the coroner says. "She had a heart attack." Talking through the cloth mask, the coroner's voice is muffled. A sheen of fog covers the lenses of his black-rimmed glasses. "During the autopsy, I found substantial evidence of heart disease," he says.

Cordell Davidson meets them at a hamburger joint a couple of miles from his farm. He doesn't want to be here. He's felt upside down since a neighbor lady told him she'd found Melba lying out by the driveway, unconscious. He knows she's dead. It's just that he doesn't actually want to see her dead. Somehow, that keeps her alive in his mind.

He called Tobias Thomas yesterday morning because he'd found his business card in the drawer underneath the telephone. During that call, the lawyer told him he'd recently met with his wife, but the lawyer wouldn't disclose the reason over the phone.

Hitch and Tobias are already seated in a booth by the window with hamburgers and fries on their plates when Cordell Davidson approaches the table. He does not sit. "Did you see her?" the widower asks.

"Yes, sir," Tobias answers. "Would you like some food?"

"No. I can't eat."

"Mr. Davidson, I'm Oakley Hitchcock. Your wife was one of my teachers in eleventh grade." Hitch extends his hand.

The widower takes it and gives a weak handshake.

"Would you like to sit, Mr. Davidson?" Hitch slides down the booth toward the window.

Mr. Davidson slowly descends to the bench seat. "Did you find out what happened to her?" he asks Tobias. "All they could tell me at the hospital was she collapsed. By the time I got there, she was gone."

"She had a heart attack," Tobias says. He pauses for a moment to let Mr. Davidson absorb this information. "Did you know she had heart disease?"

Davidson shakes his head. "She had a prescription for cholesterol and one for high blood pressure. Just like everybody our age. Sometimes she'd get winded working outside. I don't know." He dabs his eyes with a napkin. When he regains control, he asks Tobias, "why did my wife have your lawyer card?"

"Your wife came to see me a few weeks ago," Tobias starts. "I was a student of hers back in high school, and we kept in touch while I was in college and law school, then when I came back to town. I gave little talks to her students for Career Day. I guess she felt comfortable coming to me for legal advice."

Davidson gives him a bleary look. "My wife didn't have legal problems."

"Well, she did, Mr. Davidson. Or at least she thought she did," Tobias continues. "I can see you're uncomfortable being here. Bear with me. I owe it to your wife to tell you this."

"I'm sick and I'm exhausted, that's all. I've got pancreatic cancer. Nine months at the outside, the doctor says."

"I'm sorry to hear that, sir. That's terrible. I can only imagine what you're going through. Your wife told me ya'll needed money to keep up with medical bills. That must be why she did what she did."

"Did what?"

"She took out a reverse mortgage on your farm." Tobias lays copies of the signed mortgage and blank promissory note in a clear spot on the table.

"She wouldn't do that without telling me," Davidson says.

Hitch interjects. "It is strange, Mr. Davidson. Your name isn't on any of the documents. Just your wife's. I did the research at the courthouse." He flips to the back page of the mortgage and slides the stapled sheaf in front of the widower. "That is Mrs. Davidson's signature, isn't it?"

Davidson dips his head so he can see the writing. "Looks like hers. You said a reverse mortgage. What's a reverse mortgage?"

Hitch answers him. "It's a mortgage you don't have to pay back until you die. She borrowed $75,000. To pay for medical expenses, sounds like. The company places a lien on your property. If you were 62 or older at the time, you can stay on your farm until you pass, then the loan has to be repaid with interest, or the lender takes your land."

"I'm 65, and I never saw any seventy-five grand."

"I suspect," Tobias says, "she kept the loan proceeds in a separate account and didn't want you to worry about it, just like she kept the mortgage a secret from you."

"My wife and I didn't keep secrets from each other," Davidson says in a tired tone. He picks up the pages and scans them. None of it makes sense to him. Not the paperwork in front of him, or his wife's secrecy. The cancer, her death, it's all too much for him to deal with.

"Where is the money at?" Davidson asks.

"I don't know," Tobias says. "Have you looked through your wife's papers at home?"

"Not yet. Been meaning to."

"That's where you might find the bank records. And her will. She told me she had a will. She was going to bring me a copy, but I guess she didn't get around to it."

"I don't know nothing about any will," Davidson says. "She never mentioned it."

"You should look for it. You might need to open an estate at some point," Tobias says

"Why? Doesn't the law give me all her possessions, even without a will?"

"It does," Tobias says. "But when you open an estate you make sure her creditors are notified. This mortgage, any credit card debt she had that wasn't joint, car loan, medical bills, that sort of thing."

Davidson turns to Hitch. "What do you think?"

"I think you should listen to Tobias. Go through your wife's records. Find her will. Make a list of her bills. Don't pay anything that isn't in your name or in both of your names."

Davidson shakes his head. "I don't want to deal with any of this. I'm dying. My wife is dead. Can't you guys handle whatever needs to be handled?"

Hitch and Tobias exchange glances. Tobias nods his approval.

"We can handle everything, Mr. Davidson," Hitch says. "Tobias will be the one who signs anything that gets filed at the courthouse."

"Okay. Just do whatever you need to do. I got to go." Davidson places his hands on the table and, with considerable effort, rises and extricates himself from the booth. He trudges from the restaurant muttering to himself.

Once they are alone, Hitch asks, "Did you know he had pancreatic cancer?"

"No. Mrs. Davidson just said he was sick and they had unpaid medical bills."

"The whole thing is awful. He's got nine months at the outside, his wife is suddenly dead, and now he finds out his farm is mortgaged. They've lived there for 37 years."

"Yeah, it sucks," Tobias agrees.

Through the window, Hitch watches Cordell Davidson climb unsteadily into his pickup. Except for the man's cancer and the weakened state, Hitch could be watching his father. "We need to help him however we can."

Tobias nods. "Yeah, I owe it to Mrs. Davidson. If she hadn't written letters of recommendation for me for law school, I probably wouldn't have gotten in."

"She did that for me, too," Hitch adds. "I can't believe she's gone."

9

Hitch is back in his conference room, the air infused with the smell of gunpowder. The thunderclap of the first gunshot has made him temporarily deaf. He watches Sonia fall, the blood blooming on the front of her white blouse, her mouth in the wide shape of an "O." The second bullet enters her torso, tears up things as it sails through, then thuds into a plaster wall. George Colbert moves into the conference room, two steps closer. He aims the pistol. The third bullet pierces Hitch's chest.

Hitch awakens in a cold sweat, the acrid odor of gunpowder and coppery blood in his nostrils. He sits up in mid-scream, blinking his eyes against the rising dawn. His breath comes in huge gasps, like a man who has stayed underwater too long. The aroma of coffee wafts to him from the kitchen. He wonders if that was the trigger—the acrid undertone of coffee on the air—if it is possible his olfactory bulb has mistaken that scent for gun smoke and plunged him down the rabbit hole. God no, not every time he smells coffee. He couldn't take it.

Then, he remembers. Sonia was killed one year ago today.

Ripping the soaked sheets from the bed, he tosses them in a corner. He will wash them and hang them on the line next to the house, where he hopes a summer breeze will purge them of his dream smells. He plods in sleeping shorts, shirtless, to the bathroom he once shared with his younger brother Rip, short for Ripley, who died in a suicide bombing in Ghanzi, Afghanistan during his second tour. Sometimes he talks to Rip in his dreams, but not this morning. He splashes cold well water on his face, then spritzes a palm-full of foam from the can. He slathers it on with the carelessness of a brick mason's apprentice on his first day. Picking up a razor, he begins cutting swaths through his three-week beard, the whiskers just now curling, blonde and dense and thick. Slicing away the foam like that first cut of the hay field with freshly sharpened blades.

Hitch no longer has an identity he can trust. He is not the prodigal son who returned to the struggling family farm, a place he thought he had escaped, where he has grown a beard hoping to adapt to the new role thrust upon him. Nor is he the disgraced lawyer barred from plying his trade by a stone-faced woman who probably never felt the irresistible tide of love, its surge making you do things that look irresponsible in the clarity of hindsight. The shave will at least give him a clean chin to contemplate who he has become. There are nine months and 28 days left on his suspension.

After donning canvas work pants and a denim shirt, he clops down the stairs in his new boots. He lifts the lid of the washer, noting rust at the hinges and scratches in the paint. He drops the armload of sweat-stained sheets in the washer basket and dumps in a capful of detergent. He is fiddling with the dial settings when his mother appears. She takes over, twisting the dials to the proper settings, and pushes the start button. Water begins to fill the tub. He recalls his father's comment about how she needs a new car.

"This washer looks pretty old," Hitch says.

"It cleans clothes just fine, son. It doesn't much matter what it looks like."

"I was thinking. I just bought a new washer and dryer a few months ago, with digital settings for everything. They're sitting idle at my house, gathering dust, so I could bring them down here if you want."

"You'll be going back soon enough. No need to go to the trouble. Your father's almost finished with breakfast. He'll be expecting you at the tractor barn in a few minutes."

In this way, she detours all concerns away from herself. She's been doing it so long he almost doesn't notice. She limps from the laundry room, favoring her right leg more than she should with a ceramic hip, even in the dampness before dawn. He follows her to the kitchen.

"Your hip bothering you again, mom?"

"Just stiff in the morning," she says, leaning back against the stolid farm sink, bringing a steaming coffee cup to her mouth to hide a grimace.

He pours himself a mug from the big percolator on the gas stove. It smells nothing like gun powder, thank goodness. He rummages in an upper cabinet for the protein bars he bought and plucks two from the box, stuffing them in his shirt pocket for later.

"I thought we'd put up that welded wire fence today, give the mamas a resting place away from those baby bulls," his father says from the kitchen doorway. "I've got ten-foot panels ready to go."

Hitch nods in assent. It is the same announcement his father made as they unloaded the pickup last evening, and he wonders if this repetition is some evidence of a creeping senility, or if his father is simply trying to spur him to action. Through the kitchen window he sees the sun's first rays reaching across the yard, glistening the dew.

"At lunch I need to head into town to get some new work shirts. These aren't thick enough to protect my arms from the thistle."

His father scans his attire. "Looks fine to me. Your mother can sew patches on the elbow's if that's what you need."

There is an undertone Hitch can't fully decipher, something different from his father's normal mantra to repair a thing a hundred times before buying new. The countless spare tractor and implement parts stashed in barn bins are a testament to his father's philosophy. Something is amiss with his dad, but he'll bring it up later, while they're putting up panels or driving fence posts, the toil and sweat lubricating the conversation. He pours the contents of his half-empty mug into a stainless-steel travel cup, then fills the insulated cup from the percolator.

They cross-fence a pasture near the barn with stout wooden posts and welded wire. Close enough to the house that the bellows of pregnant cows will be heard inside. Hitch slams the post-hole blades into the ground, forces the handles apart, deposits removed soil in a heap. The digger slices through the sandy soil with the sound of tires crunching winter slush. The back of his shirt is drenched before he sets the third post, the band of his gimme cap barely soaking up the sweat from his forehead. He pulls his sunglasses and wipes his face with a denim sleeve.

"Already hot," he announces. The heat shimmers off the crown of the field, hovering in waves above the emerald grass. He eyes the string line that stretches into the waves, then turns to his father. "That's more than three hundred feet."

"Nope. One hundred yards even. Are you questioning an old engineer's measurements?"

"Not so much that as my ability to plant these posts without having a heart attack in this heat."

"You're fit enough. Thirty-one posts is all. Why, back in the day, Rip and I could set a hundred posts in a morning."

Hitch does the calculation in his head. "Twenty-five posts an hour? No way."

"You're assuming four hours. We worked six between breakfast and lunch," Hale replies. "16.67 posts per hour, 3.6 minutes per post."

"You guys also put up the fences in winter, most likely." That's all the rejoinder he has, no additional facts to raise in rebuttal. Younger by six years, Rip was his physical superior, four inches taller and twenty pounds heavier, rippled with muscles from head to toe, a weight lifter and wrestler who joined the army right out of high school. Rip ultimately became a Ranger. He didn't live to see his twenty-eighth birthday.

"I miss him," Hitch says, glancing toward the family cemetery.

"I do too, and your mother, well …"

"Can't be easy for her."

"She wouldn't have made it if you had died from that bullet. She almost lost it in the hospital, seeing you lying there with tubes everywhere. She couldn't bear the thought of losing two sons. We had to sedate her."

"One year ago today," Hitch says.

"I know. It's marked on your mother's wall calendar. You going to do anything special to commemorate?"

There is no cemetery or crypt where he can visit Sonia, for her parents had her cremated. He suspects her funeral urn sits on a shelf somewhere in her parents' house. He could call them, but what would be the point? "It's not a day I want to remember," he finally says.

He's welling up thinking about it, remembering the ceremony and how he'd stared at her portrait throughout, as if that could bring her back. Recalling his inability to utter a single word at his beloved's funeral. He lets out an audible sigh.

He picks up the digger and fills the rest of the morning burying posts. He develops a rhythm that sounds like rough music, the slash into ground, a grunt on withdrawal, a slide of boots across bare soil. Hale keeps the truck close, confirming each hole is deep enough before they wrestle in a wooden post the diameter of a telephone pole, its bulk requiring their combined strength.

When the mournful whistle of the noon-day train reaches him, Hitch pauses in the work. He leans on the slick wooden handles of the digger, looking off into the distance of azure sky, then back at the straight line of posts already planted. More than half-way done, sixty percent maybe.

When the train whistle fades, an ominous sound replaces it.

Without shifting his feet, Hitch cranes his neck. It is behind him, certainly within striking distance. It has slithered this close to him before he detected any movement, before he heard a thing. Five feet long, he guesses. Thicker than his wrists. The rattlesnake raises its head.

He uses the post-hole digger to vault away. Keeping the blades of the digger between him and the snake, he sidles to the cab of the pickup and removes the 12-gauge Remington from the rack. He checks the chamber and confirms it is loaded with snake-shot. He hasn't fired a gun in years, really can't remember the last time, maybe hunting doves or quail on the farm, or wild hogs in the swamp. He takes a few strides toward the snake, which is escaping into a tall clump of grass.

The snake feels the vibration of his approach and coils. Its head angles back on a length of leathery neck, preparing to strike. The rattle shakes in warning.

As his father watches, Hitch pulls the butt of the shotgun to his right shoulder. He leans his right cheek on the stock. He lines up the bead sight. He counts six rings on the snake's rattle. Then he hesitates, as if thinking he doesn't have to banish the snake in this way. Or, he's thinking about something else. He fires. The snake's head separates from the body. Its body continues to writhe for a few moments, then stops.

Hitch knows why he hesitated. Just before he pulled the trigger, he conjured the face of George Colbert down the end of the barrel.

10

Tobias Thomas reviews the certified document Cordell Davidson dropped into his mailbox before office hours this morning. It is a notice from the reverse mortgage holder. They are foreclosing on the Davidson farm. Tobias notes the postmark from thirty days ago, the stamped notations in red ink that delivery notices were left on three separate occasions before Cordell Davidson finally went to the post office to pick up the envelope. He has seen this before. Small things drop through the cracks as tragedy staggers you. Forgotten mail, missed deadlines. In the eyes of the law, a certified letter ignored or refused is the same as receiving official notice. Judges have little patience for parties who fail to act. Important cases are sometimes decided because one party, usually a naive individual, simply ignores legal notice.

Tobias hands the notice across the table to Hitch.

Hitch examines the two-page document. On the last page, the notice is signed in a flourishing hand, by an attorney he knows well. "Alicia Vanderwelt is the attorney who wanted to disbar me," he says, as if his ethics hearing is somehow connected to the pending foreclosure on the Davidson farm.

"We told him he could stay in the farm until he passes," Tobias says.

"I told him that, and I'm looking at the federal regulation for reverse mortgages right now," Hitch says. He passes the tablet to Tobias. "As long as a non-borrowing spouse was 62 when the loan was made, he's protected, and loan repayment is deferred until he dies."

"So why are they foreclosing?" Tobias asks.

"Maybe Mr. Davidson wasn't 62?"

"Easy enough to confirm, but he said he's 65 now. The mortgage was signed only a few months ago. Why would he lie to us about his age?"

"I don't know. He didn't even know about the reverse mortgage until we told him last week," Hitch says.

"Maybe the company is just trying to pull a fast one on him. Maybe they figure he doesn't know his legal rights regarding reverse mortgages, which he doesn't, and won't go to a lawyer, or can't afford to hire one."

"Could be, but I doubt Alicia Vanderwelt would sign the notice if it wasn't legit," Hitch says. "She's not the type to risk a judge questioning the validity of her pleadings."

"She doesn't have to go before a judge to foreclose. Non-judicial foreclosure is the norm down here."

"Right. We must be missing something." Hitch reads the legal notice again. "The bank that loaned Mrs. Davidson the money still isn't identified."

"So what does that tell us?" Tobias asks.

"The lender is going to great lengths to remain anonymous."

"Why?"

"I have no idea. But this can't be a legitimate, mainstream lender."

"Maybe it's dirty money someone is trying to launder," Tobias says.

"Sounds like you've been down this road before."

Tobias shrugs. "The wiles of the criminal mind are beyond my imagination. I see a lot of stuff that falls in the category of unbelievable. Except it's true."

Hitch nods, switching gears. "There's one way we could get to the bottom of this."

"And that is?"

"We could file a declaratory judgment action in federal court. Ask a judge to rule the federal regulation allows Mr. Davidson to stay until he dies. We could get an injunction to stop the foreclosure. Otherwise, the sale is scheduled in four days."

"When you say 'we,' you mean me," Tobias says.

"I obviously can't sign any pleadings," Hitch says. "But I'll do all the work behind the scenes. This isn't right, and it's got me stirred up."

"I've never handled a civil case in federal court," Tobias says. "Criminal yes, but not civil. Can we even get a hearing that fast in federal court."

"I don't know. I haven't been in federal court down here, and I haven't had to get a federal injunction ever."

Tobias reads the notice again, hoping to gain some enlightenment. "Wouldn't we need to sue the lender as a defendant? If we're contending the lender's right to call the loan is limited by the federal regulation, don't they have to be a named party?"

"Probably." Hitch feels helpless not knowing the answers and not having enough time to figure this out before the Davidson farm is sold. "That makes sense, Tobias. The mortgage holder's rights are derivative of the lender's rights, so the lender probably needs to be brought in as a defendant. Which we can't do if we don't know who the lender is." He walks to the window facing the front yard of the law office. "This is intentional, Tobias. We can't sue an anonymous company. This whole scheme is designed to prevent anyone from pursuing legal action before the property is gone."

The following Tuesday, Hitch checks the list tacked to the bulletin board at the county courthouse. There are seven properties slated to be sold by foreclosure, starting at 10:00 a.m. this morning. The Davidsons' 96-acre farm is number three.

When Hitch told Mr. Davidson the depth of his legal dilemma, he had sighed and slumped his shoulders.

"Nothing you can do?"

"Not to stop the foreclosure," Hitch told him. "But with the money left from the loan, maybe we can buy your farm back at the foreclosure. It's like an auction. Highest bidder wins."

"And if you can't?"

"The mortgage company will take your farm. I'm sorry."

Davidson had just nodded, acknowledging the pending defeat. He'd sat back down in his worn recliner and closed his eyes.

Now, Hitch steps back outside the courthouse. He leans against the brick wall beneath the portico. This courthouse doesn't have a statue of Lady Justice, either inside or out. But the inscription on the marble facade at the peak of the roof reads: "Justice For All." Today, Hitch isn't sure that applies.

He has come alone. Tobias has a hearing inside on another case. Cordell Davidson declined to attend. He saw no point in it, and he doesn't like courthouses. Doesn't think much of the law and how it seems to operate to protect only the wealthy. This is not a place where Cordell Davidson wants to spend any of his final days.

At a few minutes before 10:00, a deputy sheriff sidles through the front doors and takes up his position on the marble slabs atop the courthouse steps. He has a brass name tag pinned to his uniform, "Dawson" printed on it. He scans something on a clipboard. He is armed, with a full complement of pistol, pepper spray, handcuffs, radio, and baton. Hitch has never attended a foreclosure sale and wonders if Deputy Dawson is armed because there might be trouble.

Sighting the Deputy, several men in suits and ties clamber up the steps and settle beneath the portico. Lawyers and bankers, probably. Hitch eyes them all, wondering which one is the man who represents Melba Davidson's anonymous lender. He settles on a dark-haired man with a graying moustache, attired in a charcoal-gray suit with a scarlet tie and buffed wingtips. The man stands alone, not hobnobbing with the others.

Then the double brass doors of the courthouse open, and Alicia Vanderwelt strides out. She is wearing a pink Chanel suit, the skirt hem hitting at the knee, with white heels. She actually shakes hands with Deputy Dawson, then takes a position next to him, surveying the courthouse grounds as if presiding over her fiefdom.

Hitch wanders over. "Is one of these guys your client?" he asks, scanning the array of men in suits.

"Not today," she says.

"What does that mean?"

"Why are you here, Mr. Hitchcock?" Her voice conveys more than mere annoyance. She eyes him over her silver-rimmed glasses, taking in his blue jeans, the polo shirt, the scuffed and stained work boots.

"I'm interested in the Cordell Davidson foreclosure."

"Interested in what way?" Vanderwelt asks.

"You'll see."

Vanderwelt doesn't respond, but her mouth turns down at the corners.

Deputy Dawson checks his watch, then makes a formal announcement. The foreclosures begin. For the first one, a man who might be a banker or a lawyer makes a credit bid, which means no money will change hands, but the balance of the loan will be reduced by the amount of the credit bid. Hitch knows the approximate location of the house, on the poorer side of town, a 2-1 bungalow on the standard quarter-acre of land, south of the railroad tracks. When no one else bids on the property, Deputy Dawson announces the bidding is closed and the sale complete. The whole process takes fewer than sixty seconds. In less than a minute, someone has just lost their home.

The second foreclosure follows the same procedure. The bank winds up with the property.

"Foreclosure number three," Dawson announces. "In Re: Cordell

Davidson."

Hitch gets ready.

"Does anyone want to make a bid?"

"Credit bid. One thousand dollars," Alicia Vanderwelt announces. She scans the small crowd for potential contenders. No one moves or raises their hand. Then her eyes land on Hitch.

"Two thousand dollars, cash," Hitch says, holding up his hand from the second step down. He won't allow the Davidson farm to be sold for a paltry sum.

Vanderwelt now knows why he is here. She stares at him in an amused way. "Five thousand, credit bid," she says. Her eyes never leave his.

"Fifty-five hundred, cash," he responds.

"Twenty thousand, credit bid," she counters.

"Twenty-one thousand, cash," Hitch responds. He is nearing his limit. There is approximately $26,000 from the loan proceeds still in Melba Davidson's bank account.

She turns to Deputy Dawson. "Deputy, hold on just one second, please." She strides across the fifteen feet to Hitch. She addresses him from the portico, one step above. "What are you doing? You do realize that still leaves more than sixty thousand owing on the note?"

"I'm trying to save the Davidson farm. Did you ever meet Mrs. Davidson, the borrower? Fine woman. Taught at the high school here for more than 40 years. Her husband wants to keep the farm and live there. He's dying of pancreatic cancer. This farm has been his home for 37 years."

"This is a fruitless exercise, Mr. Hitchcock. I won't be outbid. But if you want to waste everybody's time, go right ahead." She starts to step away.

"The loan is non-recourse, Alicia. You can't collect a deficiency on the note. He only has eight or nine months left to live. Hold off on the foreclosure so he can spend his final days in his home."

"No."

"The property won't drop in value in nine months. Are you that heartless, that you would kick a dying man out of the only home he's known for the past 37 years?"

"You're not representing him are you? It sounds like you're engaging in the practice of law, Mr. Hitchcock. You wouldn't be foolish enough to do that, not while you're suspended." She stares at him with cold eyes, her mouth a thin line.

"He's not my client, no. But I have a financial POA signed by him, and notarized. Want to see it?"

"It won't change anything."

"Tell me, Alicia, why he doesn't have the legal right to stay until he dies. He was 65 when his wife took out the loan."

She glares at Hitch, then turns her back to him. She returns to her place next to Deputy Dawson.

"The bid is $21,000 cash," the deputy reminds everyone.

"Twenty-five thousand. Credit bid," Vanderwelt says.

"Twenty-six thousand, cash," Hitch counters.

"Thirty thousand, credit bid," Vanderwelt announces.

Hitch hesitates. His last bid maxed out the remaining cash in the Davidsons' bank account.

The Deputy is eager to close this auction and move to the other foreclosures on his list. After a few seconds of silence, he says "Thirty thousand, going once."

Hitch fidgets. He scrapes the bottom of his boot against the edge of a step.

"Going twice," the Deputy announces.

"Thirty thousand, one hundred dollars, cash," Hitch says from the steps. He's just committed all of the savings Cordell Davidson has, plus more than $4,000 of his own money, to buy back the farm.

Vanderwelt glares across the marble floor of the portico at him, as if looking at a fool. Then she says, in a measured tone, "Eighty-one thousand four hundred thirty-five dollars and two cents, credit bid. And Mr. Hitchcock, I will go as high as it takes."

In her stony eyes, he sees the truth. Whatever he bids for the farm, she will top it. Her client probably has unlimited financial resources. Maybe her client really wants this land so badly it will add cash to the amount it already loaned to Melba Davidson.

Or maybe Alicia Vanderwelt just wants to beat him at this game, too.

"I'm out," he says. He descends the courthouse steps without looking back. "Sorry Mr. and Mrs. Davidson," he whispers to no one in particular. He stops just short of the street and stands next to the flagpole, the halyard whipping in the wind. Then he waits.

At 10:25, Tobias Thomas descends the courthouse steps. He spots Hitch by the flagpole and strides over.

"What's up?" Tobias says.

"I just left the Davidson foreclosure sale." His hands are stuffed in the back pockets of his jeans. "Alicia Vanderwelt came all the way down from Atlanta to bid for the lender." Hitch nods toward the empty steps where seven homes were sold at foreclosure in less than twenty minutes.

"Okay. What possessed you to show up for that?"

"I bid on the property."

"For yourself, or for Mr. Davidson."

"He gave me a POA. I wanted to save the farm for him. For her." Hitch shrugs his shoulders.

"I take it you lost."

Hitch nods. "The farm is gone."

11

Joe Park enters a glass skyscraper in mid-town Atlanta. Today, he is a Korean-American financier on his way to meet his lawyer. His hair, normally the color of tar, has been lightened to steel and buzzed short on the sides and top. He has infused his eyebrows with a gray gel, glued a graying moustache to his otherwise smooth face, and with stage makeup given himself a more pallid complexion. This make-over adds fifteen years to his appearance.

Joe Park is not his real name. Park is his *nom de guerre*, one of a dozen aliases he uses. He is a chameleon, shifting identities to suit the environment, with forged documents where necessary. He can pass for 35 or 55. With enough preparation, he can accurately mimic a woman, or an old man with a limp, or a homeless person living in a cardboard box.

He owns a house in Sandy Springs, Georgia and one outside Washington, DC. The furnishings of both homes have been staged by professionals and bear no personal touches. He has lived in nineteen separate cities since immigrating to America as a college student in the late 1980s. He attended an Ivy League college and obtained a degree in Geology, but he does not display the diploma because it is a clue to his past. He has been an American citizen since 1995.

He steps off the elevator on the 51st floor and is shown by a tall blonde in a form-fitting dress into a small conference room with an oval table made of black marble. The receptionist pours him a glass of water from a metal pitcher dripping with condensation. She sets the glass on a coaster made of the same marble, with the law firm's name embossed in gold. He watches her leave the conference room, then turns to admire the east-facing view. He sips slowly from the water glass and repeatedly checks the Seagull watch on his right wrist.

Park waits eleven minutes and twenty seconds for attorney Tinsley Stratton to appear. The attorney strides into the room with his hand extended. At 6-5, he is a former college basketball player and is eight inches taller than Park.

Park takes the man's massive hand with his own firm grip. He intends to remind the silver-haired attorney who really is in charge.

"You kept me waiting for more than eleven minutes, Mr. Stratton, A delay for which I will not be billed."

"My apologies, Mr. Park. I was getting an update on your legal matters. Please, let's sit so I can fill you in."

They sit at the table's end in chairs made of bleached lambskin. Park settles in the head seat; Stratton faces the floor-to-ceiling windows.

"Has the Davidson land been acquired?" Park asks impatiently.

"Yes. The auction was yesterday. The Sheriff's Deed transferring ownership of the property will be filed within the week."

"And you can assure me the new owner of the land cannot be traced back to me or any of the other entities we have created?"

"Yes, I assure you of that."

Park emits an inaudible sigh. Stratton is an expert in banking and finance law. According to Park's research, Stratton is the best lawyer in the state in his field. Using Georgia limited liability companies owned by closely held corporations in other states, Stratton has crafted an opaque veil for the reverse mortgage business Park operates. For each mortgage, the lender is separate from the lien holder, and every property foreclosed upon will be owned by a third, unrelated company. Though his name appears nowhere in the records, Park indirectly owns every company.

"How many companies do I now control?"

"Sixty-seven loans; 134 limited liability companies. There are six holding companies in Nevada, nominally owned by one of my law partners in the Vegas office. And, of course, the LLC we will create today to hold the Davidson land."

Park nods his approval. "Were there any other bidders at this auction?"

"I don't know," Stratton replies. "It doesn't matter. Your company was the successful bidder. You now control the land."

"Everything matters, Mr. Stratton. I thought you would have understood that by now." Park stares at his attorney, his eyes unblinking, his mouth a thin line. It is impossible to determine from Park's visage whether he is angry or amused.

In response, Stratton stretches his long arm to the telephone console in the middle of the table. He punches a plastic button.

"Danielle, have Alicia Vanderwelt come to the 51st floor immediately. The Peach Blossom conference room. I know she's in the office today."

While they wait, Stratton remarks on the insufferable heat of August, the stifling humidity. Park nods but contributes nothing. He has no patience and no time for idle banter. He glances at the dirt-brown ring of smog that will encircle Atlanta until the fall winds come.

Alicia Vanderwelt announces herself with a firm knock on the ash door, then steps inside at Stratton's answer. She stops at the head of the table and extends her hand: "Alicia Vanderwelt."

The client remains seated. "Joe Park," he says, shaking her hand.

Stratton waves her to the seat next to him. "Mr. Park is interested for some reason in the foreclosure auction process. He wants to know if there were any other bidders yesterday."

"One. But not a serious bidder," Vanderwelt says, then sits.

"How do you know this other bidder was not serious?" Park asks.

"Because he didn't bid high enough to acquire the property," Vanderwelt explains. "I made a credit bid, which means the buyer doesn't have to come out-of-pocket to acquire the property. The credit will be applied to the loan balance, but since these are non-recourse loans and you can't collect the money anyway, the lender will write off the loss."

"Do you have the name of this bidder?" Park asks, undeterred.

"It was an attorney—a suspended attorney. He was bidding on behalf of the former owner, Cordell Davidson."

Park ignores her explanation. "The attorney's name please?"

"Oakley Walker Hitchcock. He's from Savannah. Goes by 'Hitch'."

"Why is he suspended?"

"Because he violated his ethical duties to a client. He can't practice law again until next April. What is your concern, Mr. Park?"

Park ignores the question. "Why did this Hitchcock want the property?"

Vanderwelt glances at her law partner, who appears to be following the glint of a small plane crossing the eastern horizon. "Well, I don't know for certain why he wanted the property, but I believe he wanted Mr. Davidson to be able to live out his final days on his farm. He's dying of pancreatic cancer, according to Hitchcock. Hitchcock asked me to postpone the foreclosure for eight or nine months. He says Davidson will be dead by then."

"How did you respond?" Park asks.

"I told him 'no'. Firmly."

Park picks up the glass of water, takes a deep swallow. Vanderwelt acted appropriately. The Davidson foreclosure was the first of many, and he will not entertain negotiations to allow anyone to stay once the loan becomes due. The entire network of companies and loans was designed to acquire land in a well-defined corridor in South Georgia without anyone knowing who the real owner will be. For the moment, even his attorneys believe that Joe Park is a Korean-American financier. If only they knew the truth.

"How many more foreclosures are scheduled?" Park asks.

Tinsley Stratton interjects: "We have either noticed, or will notice in the immediate future, eight more foreclosures, Mr. Park."

"Do you anticipate legal challenges?"

"No. Only a fool would try."

This is what Park expects to hear. He hired Stratton precisely because he promised to design the labyrinth of companies in such a way that the lenders do not have to register with state or federal banking regulators. "One-off loans," the attorney called them. And Park has retained Stratton, who bills him $1,000 an hour in fifteen-minute increments, so all his questions and conversations about the business are protected by the attorney-client privilege. Secrecy is Park's, and his superiors', paramount concern. To ensure there are no leaks, the companies have no employees. Not one. A single CPA handles all the accounting and tax matters for the entire web of companies. That CPA, whose name Park doesn't know and to whom he has never spoken, is an employee of Stratton's law firm. And thus under the attorney's control.

"Is the insurance agent acquiring other mortgages?" Park asks.

"Yes, he has the list of properties you provided. He's trying to close as many as possible, as quickly as possible," Stratton says.

"And do you trust this insurance agent, Mr. Stratton?"

"Yes, he's an excellent salesman, and the reverse mortgages are enticing to any landowner who's in debt."

"That's not what I asked you. Do you trust him?"

"I do. He's my brother-in-law."

Park leaves the law office and descends 50 floors to the parking garage. There was no reason to prolong the meeting. He already knows the insurance agent—Garland T. Rogers—is married to Tinsley Stratton's youngest sister, Glenda. Park has a thick dossier on Rogers. He has been married to Glenda for eighteen years. They have two children, a girl eleven and a fourteen-year-old-boy. Park knows where the kids go to elementary and middle school. He knows Garland and Glenda own a home on two acres in Valdosta, and have a mortgage with Ameris Bank with a balance of $79,837, on which they are current. He has the license plate numbers for the black F-150 pickup Garland drives and the Subaru Outback Glenda drives. He knows Rogers plays golf three times a week at a country club in Valdosta. He knows where they take their tabby cat to the vet. Park has summary biographies on the two secretaries who work in Garland Rogers' insurance office, summaries that can be expanded if the need arises.

Most of the information Park has acquired comes from a hacker, whom Park knows only as APT/19. He does not know the hacker's name, age, or the country from where the hacker does what he does. For all Park knows, APT/19 could have an office in this same building as his lawyers.

APT/19 discovered that Garland T. Rogers frequently visits a dark website on his laptop at home. Park knows that Rogers has child pornography on that laptop—because APT/19 hacked into Rogers' computer and put it there. This is one of the hacker's many skills.

Park also has a thick dossier on Tinsley Stratton. The usual stuff about his college education and law degree, the bar association committees he's served on, the charitable-organization boards on which he sits. The Stratton dossier includes photographs of a striking redhead lounging in a white bikini on Stratton's sailboat on Lake Lanier. This woman is not Stratton's wife, or his daughter, though she looks young enough to be the latter. APT/19 discovered the old cocaine charge leveled against Stratton when he played basketball at Harvard. The drug charge was conveniently and quietly swept away, but not completely erased from the back files. Park knows the precise route through Chastain Park that Stratton jogs at 7 a.m., three to four days a week. He knows Stratton's Irish Setter, who accompanies him some mornings, is named "Crimson." He has listened to tapes of bugged conversations on Stratton's sailboat. Incriminating conversations Park can use as leverage, when necessary.

Before he starts his Range Rover, Park unlocks his cell phone using the fingerprint identifier and facial recognition software. Then he puts in the six-digit security code that changes automatically at midnight each day. He goes to the notes folder and types in the names Oakley Walker Hitchcock and Alicia Vanderwelt. Later, using an onion router, he will request that APT/19 begin compiling dossiers on these two. He is intrigued by the thought that Hitchcock's law license was suspended because of an ethics violation. In Park's experience, everyone has something in their past they want to keep hidden. Finding that information is an important part of his duties.

As he pulls up to the exit gate in the parking garage, Park turns away from the camera positioned there. Undoubtedly, the camera will capture some part of his profile, but he wants to give away as little of this fake identity as possible. Anonymity is a crucial asset in the work he does. He will have many meetings with Tinsley Stratton and Alicia Vanderwelt in this building, and he must maintain his cover as long as possible.

12

Park conducts his own surveillance because he trusts no one. He does not fully trust his attorneys. He does not trust his handler, a man with no name. Park does not trust APT/19, but he has no choice but to use the hacker, for he has computer skills Park could never acquire, and he was assigned by Park's handler to this important mission. Every morning, Park sweeps his laptop and his phone for nefarious files. He has never found anything. He does not know whether to conclude this means his devices are clean, or that APT/19 can easily thwart his security software and leave no trace. He leans toward the latter explanation, which is why he changes phones at least once a month.

The Hitchcock Law Firm's website contains information Park considers sterile and self-serving. Client testimonials lauding the traits Hitchcock wants other clients and the public to know. He reads about cases Hitchcock has won and settlements he has achieved. He lingers over the details of a lead smelter case Hitchcock tried, winning a jury verdict of more than $50 million. There is no mention on the website of Hitchcock's suspension, or the State Bar's determination he violated his ethical duties to a client. Park has found the particulars in other places. Park knows his litigation attorney, Alicia Vanderwelt, was one of Hitchcock's hearing judges. He has read the transcript from the ethics hearing. The tension between Vanderwelt and Hitchcock is palpable. He has studied Hitchcock's testimony and parsed the lawyer's explanation for his behavior. Hitchcock says he was in love with the client who was murdered in his law office. Park pulls old pictures of Sonia Summers from various social media sites. Here, he may have found Hitchcock's weakness.

The Hitchcock Law Firm employs two legal assistants, both women. Natalie Anderson, a tall blonde, is active on social media. From various sites, Park learns she lives with her boyfriend, drives a cherry-red Mustang convertible, and was once a promising middle-distance runner at the University of Florida. There are photographs of her finishing road races in Savannah; photos taken by someone else.

The other legal assistant, Stacie Throckmorton, appears to live alone in a small apartment on Wilmington Island, but not on the beach. She has a degree in environmental engineering from Emory University and worked as an engineer for a number of years before joining the Hitchcock law firm. She has a basset hound named Sam. She drives a gun-metal gray Tahoe.

Hitchcock's law office is a two-story red brick with black shutters. English ivy climbs all four walls between the windows. The building sits close to a popular thoroughfare among other professional offices, with a broad median of live oaks splitting the boulevard. There are no cameras or security lights on the building's exterior, or in the back parking lot. The first-floor windows are single pane and without protective bars. A single deadbolt secures the painted front door. Park takes photographs of the Mustang convertible and Tahoe as they turn into the gravel drive one weekday morning.

Hitchcock's Savannah house sits along the west bank of the Half-Moon River. For two days and nights Park surveils the house from a white panel van. The van sports the name of a fake delivery company painted on it sides. When he strides up the sidewalk with a counterfeit package in his hands, Park peers in the window beside the front door. No activity that he can detect.

On the third night, when the neighborhood goes quiet and dark, Park leaves the van two streets over. He slips on gloves and covers his shoes with booties. He pulls a rubber Halloween mask over his head. The mask caricatures the face of a movie star, complete with artificial hair. Black wind pants and a black long-sleeved shirt complete the outfit. Park creeps around to the side of Hitchcock's house where large shrubs conceal his activities. He uses a long-bladed knife to open a bedroom window. When he doesn't hear an alarm, he climbs through and begins his search.

Park notes the sparseness of furniture, the weight bench in a third bedroom, books on built-in shelves in the den—mainly biographies and tomes about sports. He sees no books about the law. The kitchen has standard utensils and dishes and cups, a wooden block of older butcher knives, the blades dull. In the cupboards there is only a modicum of food: a few cans of soup, a box of tea bags, a can of instant coffee, some stale crackers. There is no spice rack, just a shaker of pepper and one for salt, nestled next to the stove.

He searches each bedroom closet but finds neither weapons nor a safe, and only a normal number of shoes on the closet floor in the master. All male. He finds no framed pictures of family members or photo albums. A few CDs in a short tower on a side table tell him Hitchcock likes contemporary country music and instrumental jazz. There is one toothbrush in the holder attached to the wall, no medication in the medicine cabinet other than a generic pain reliever and a tube of antibiotic cream. The grout between the tiles in the shower has been scrubbed white.

In the detached garage, Park surveys shelves that contain a jumble of dusty boxes and empty coolers. There are two fishing tackle boxes; one for freshwater fishing, the other for saltwater. The cardboard boxes are not marked. With gloved hands he uses a wooden step ladder to take the boxes down from the storage area. He rummages through each one but finds nothing noteworthy, just odd cans of paint, old hand tools and assorted hardware. A carbon-fiber bicycle with a deflated front tire leans against a scuffed wall.

Back in the house, he checks his crystal-faced Seagull watch and notes it will be dawn soon. In the hallway he pulls a string on the attic door. The door descends with a croak. He unfolds the wooden stairs and ascends so he can survey the contents of the attic. The attic is comprised of exposed ceiling joists with fiberglass insulation tucked between and a small storage area covered in plywood. Even in the dead of night, the attic air is warm and humid. He hoped for a trove but discovers only an old empty desk, a few pieces of exercise equipment, and a couple of tables whose veneer has succumbed to the heat.

As he stands in the carpeted hallway of Hitchcock's house, Park reaches the conclusion the man lives like he does, with few mementos to the past. The furnishings are spare and sterile, as though he doesn't want his environs to display obvious clues about who he is. Maybe this is intentional. Park knows how to live such a life because he has spent years cultivating a protective paranoia. He knows what it's like to exist as one person inside and to depict someone entirely different on the outside. His mission demands nothing less. It is a necessary contortion, but not an easy one. If in fact Hitchcock has constructed a similar facade, it is imperative that Park discover what he is hiding.

13

In the stifling heat of a South Georgia summer, which can cook the careless man, Hitch and Hale work the farm until lunch, then retreat indoors for the afternoon. Hale goes over the books in his office. The income has been less than the expenses each month for the past twelve, and each year for the past four. As the ceiling fan stirs the sultry air, a returning sense of defeat descends upon Hale. It is not his fault, this failure to return the farm to profitability. Cattle prices are still down. The cost of diesel to run the tractor is up 24% from last year. Fertilizer is up 38%. Even hay to feed the cows has increased 31%. The spread between what he receives at auction and the prices for beef at the grocery store is as large as he has ever seen it. The farmer receives less for his beef, while the consumer pays more. The trade war with China and the imposition of tariffs on American beef is partially to blame. And other factors out of his control. No, this is not his fault. But it is his responsibility. In his consternation, his brow furrowed with deep creases, Hale repeatedly clicks open and closes the switchblade knife he carries with him at all times.

As his father works away at the farm finances, Hitch calls his law office. Natalie Anderson answers.

"Anything going on?" Hitch asks.

"Work-wise, the usual," Natalie says.

"And other than work-wise? How are you and Mark getting along?"

"I think he's having me followed."

"Having you followed?"

"I've seen a white van sitting across from the office a couple of times this week. I mean, it's a delivery van, but it stayed a lot longer than necessary just to deliver packages on the street. Plus, I think the van followed me to work yesterday."

"Could it be a legit delivery van?"

"I guess so. But it doesn't feel that way."

"Why do you think Mark is having you followed?" Hitch realizes he's slipped into interrogation mode, his tone verging on skepticism.

"We had a big fight last weekend. He's just grown so …taciturn. Doesn't want to talk about anything. Doesn't want to go out together. I told him I couldn't keep this up. If things didn't get better soon, I was going to leave him. He said if he couldn't have me, nobody else would. Then the van showed up."

"But you've stayed in the apartment with him?"

"I've been sleeping on the sofa for a while."

"Do you want to stay in my house until all this settles down?"

"Down there?" Natalie asks.

Hitch had been thinking of his empty house in Savannah, but the idea of Natalie coming down to Pineland for a bit doesn't put him off. He ponders the idea with a finger poised at his lips.

"You have cows down there, right? I've always wanted to learn how to ride a cow."

Given her dilemma, he appreciates her attempt at levity. "You don't ride cows, city girl. You ride bulls. And our bulls aren't for riding."

"Don't you have a horse? I've ridden horses a few times."

"We don't have a horse."

"What about a donkey? I think you mentioned a donkey once. I could ride him. Or her."

"You can come down here and hang out for a few days, but only if Stacie really has things under control at the office." Hitch is unsure if the invitation is wise, but perhaps Natalie's presence will help relieve his own ennui. He has eight months left on his suspension. The time stretches before him like a dense fog.

"I'll tell her to send you an email confirming such," Natalie says. With this, the arrangement is concluded.

Natalie arrives in Pineland the next afternoon in a whirl of dust, pulling her convertible into the sandy parking area in front of the farmhouse. Her candy-apple Mustang looks as out of place at the farm as a wedding gown at a funeral. She checks her hair and makes some minor repairs, tucking wind-blown strands back in place. From the back seat she pulls the leather briefcase Hitch gave her when she passed her paralegal exam. Her initials are embossed in gold on the top. In a dress the color of ripe corn, she puts the car's rag-top up and latches it.

Hitch observes her arrival from an upstairs window. He hustles down the stairs, the heels of his boots banging the cypress wood treads. He sweeps open the screen door and stops at her trunk just as she pops the lid.

"Hey, Nat. How was the drive?"

"It was fine. This is so country down here. I love your farm." Her attempt at a drawl spreads the last, single syllable into two, as if she has syrup in her throat.

"Don't try to talk Southern," he says.

From the trunk Hitch pulls a hard-sided suitcase and a suit bag. He holds the bag up by the nine or ten hangers that protrude through the opening. "Party dresses?"

She punches him in the left shoulder.

"Ouch, that's my sore shoulder." It is no longer sore, but he hasn't given up the bit.

"I know where to aim. Those aren't party dresses," she nods toward the garment bag, "they're my court clothes. I couldn't leave them at Mark's."

He shrugs and leads her into the house.

His mother, a clean apron covering her front, hugs Natalie in the kitchen. "Welcome. You must be famished from the drive. I've got a tomato salad for you, with fresh radishes and carrots. I also made deviled eggs. With mustard, not mayonnaise." This offer of food to a houseguest is a standard greeting from his mother.

"Sounds delicious, Mrs. Hitchcock. You're too kind. Let me put my stuff away and I'll be right back down."

"Okay. There are fresh towels on the bed. So glad you're here." Another hug and a cheek kiss.

Hitch leads Natalie up the stairs, stopping at the bedroom at the end of the hall.

"Are all the bedrooms this big? This looks like the master bedroom." Natalie says.

"Mom and dad moved their bedroom downstairs. Mom's hip. Really uncomfortable for her to climb stairs. So they're using the parlor as a bedroom."

From the doorway, Natalie surveys the master, the four-poster king bed with the paisley spread, the tufted burgundy leather chaise by the window, which catches the afternoon light. On the wall above the bed are two wall sconces for reading. The dressing table has been moved downstairs, leaving a faint outline on the wall where the sun hasn't yet yellowed the dove-gray paint. Landscapes of fields and forests and ocean surf hang on the walls, in golden gilt frames.

"This feels too weird," Natalie says.

"What?"

"I mean, this is your parents' bedroom."

"I was probably conceived in that bed," Hitch says without thinking.

"That doesn't make it any better, dude."

"I think mom thought you'd be more comfortable in here, with your own bathroom and everything."

Natalie considers this, sets her load down. "It's very thoughtful of her."

They re-assemble in the dining room. The oak table is set with the good china, a pattern of gold and turquoise flowers fit for a French restaurant or a European castle. Bridget has ten place settings her own mother accumulated when such things were important. She will never part with her china, regardless of financial circumstances. She's laid the table with silver-plated knives, forks and spoons, heavy to the touch, and completed the settings with crystal water glasses and champagne-toned linen napkins. A blueberry cobbler rests on a glass cake stand in the middle of the table. A sculpted server filled with deviled eggs sits next to it.

"Wow, mom. We should eat in here every night instead of the kitchen," Hitch says, using a silver pie server to settle a piece of cobbler on his plate.

"This is for Natalie, son."

He gives Natalie a disgruntled look across the table.

"It's perfect, Mrs. Hitchcock," Natalie says. "You shouldn't have gone to so much trouble just for me." She poises a fork above a salad plate filled with lettuce, tomatoes, carrots, cucumbers, radishes and olives, a few drizzles of balsamic vinegar on top.

"Everything except for the olives comes from our own garden," Bridget says.

"It looks wonderful, Mrs. Hitchcock. So fresh." Natalie glances around the table and notes she is the only one with salad. Mashed potatoes, corn and butterbeans adorn the other plates. "You shouldn't have gone to so much trouble."

"It's no trouble, dear. The boys don't eat much salad. I'm already thinking about meals for the next few days. No meat, right?"

Natalie looks up, crunching a wedge of radish. She finishes chewing before she speaks. "I'm a pescatarian. I eat seafood. I figured living in Savannah, so close to the ocean … Anyway, my diet is a work in progress."

"But you won't be offended if the rest of us have beef for dinner, since we raise cattle here," Hale Hitchcock says in a tone that could be taken for a challenge.

Natalie shakes her head. "No, sir. It's my choice. Not yours. I won't be offended at all. And Mrs. Hitchcock, you don't need to go out of your way to fix something just for me. I'll go into town and stock up on vegetables."

After his parents go to bed, Hitch and Natalie settle on the screen porch, listening to the throaty song of cicadas in the trees, watching moths flutter around the yellow bulb on the front stoop. He sips a beer, stealing an occasional glance at Natalie from the corner of his eye. He can't decipher her mood.

She rocks slowly, the old porch planks creaking with each press of the rocker, nursing a glass of Pinot Noir from a corked bottle she brought with her. She keeps flipping an unruly bang off her forehead. "It's nice out here," she says. "Very quiet."

"Hard to get the sound of silence in the city," he replies.

"Are we out here drinking because your parents wouldn't approve?"

He chuckles. "No. It's just more pleasant out here. The house feels claustrophobic to me."

"Must be nice, being able to work outdoors."

"It has its advantages, but it's hotter than hell right now and damned monotonous. I don't know how my dad does it day in and day out. But he's been doing it for almost 50 years."

"That's a long time to do anything," Natalie says.

"My parents have been married almost that long. Forty-six years, I think."

The comment settles into silence, the croak of the cicadas taking over. Out in the birthing corral, a cow lows. Hitch waits what he deems an appropriate time before bringing up the turmoil that drove Natalie down here.

"So, what did you tell Mark when you left?"

She clenches her eyes, trying to erase a memory. "Don't want to talk about it."

"All right," he says, palms out. Natalie was there through the worst of his tragedy with Sonia. After the shooting, she spent days sitting on the other side of his desk while he stumbled through work in a state of shock. He doesn't remember what she said to make it better, only that she did. Now it's his turn to be supportive. "I'm here when you're ready to talk."

"I just need a break. It's not like I really had anything to do at the office anyway," she says. "Stacie and I spend a lot of time twiddling our thumbs, waiting for the phone to ring. I already told you that, I guess."

He notes her deflection. Maybe she'll get around to it in due time.

"Just need to decompress. Do you have anything stronger than wine?"

"I've got a fifth of vodka upstairs," Hitch offers.

Natalie nods. "Sounds good. Do you have anything to mix it with?"

He comes back with the plastic liquor bottle, three-quarters full, an ice bucket, some orange juice and a can of grapefruit juice out-of-date. He arranges two heavy-bottomed glasses on the table between the rocking chairs. The table is made from half a steel oil drum, with a cross-cut swamp tupelo serving as top, its edges undulating and irregular. Hitch cobbled it together in high-school shop class, and his parents haven't been able to part with it. Still standing, he unscrews the cap on the vodka. "Orange juice or grapefruit?" he asks.

"Orange, please."

He pours half an inch of vodka in the bottom of each glass. He adds ice and mixer, then sits.

Natalie picks up her glass and holds it in front of her, her eyes fixed on the dark horizon. She takes a deep breath, then a long swallow of vodka.

"I left him a note," she starts.

Hitch remains silent, realizing they are crossing the threshold of something.

"He called me on the way down here," she continues. "Said he was sorry he's been so distant lately." She pauses.

Out of habit, Hitch tries to propel the conversation. "Did he say why he's been so distant?"

She shakes her head. "Said he would tell me when we can meet face-to-face. Not the kind of thing he wanted to discuss over the phone."

"It might be an excuse to see you again." The words escape his mouth before he can judge their impact.

"Maybe," she acknowledges. "But he sounded sincere."

"And yet you kept driving down here."

Natalie turns to him, her lips parted, as though just realizing she'd made the decision not to turn around and drive back to Savannah and Mark.

"Sorry, I didn't intend for it to sound so judgmental," he says.

"He doesn't know I was coming to Pineland. I lied and told him I was going to visit my parents in Orlando."

Hitch takes a sip of his screwdriver. "Think you guys might work it out?"

"I don't know."

Hitch takes a gulp, relishes the sting in his throat. The southerly breeze rattles the leaves of the live oak in the side yard, imitating a quiet snare drum. The honey-almond scent of night phlox in the cedar boxes along the front steps wafts through the screen.

"You'll figure it out," Hitch says finally.

She closes her eyes, as if the answer can be found behind her lids, then opens them again at the sound of a distant bark.

"Is that a wolf?" Natalie asks, leaning forward in the rocker.

"No. That's a coyote. There are quite a few out here." Hitch reflexively glances over at Jasper, curled on the braided rug. Jasper is aging, going soft. The bloodhound can still pick up scents, roaming the yard with his nose to the ground even in the wake of rainfall, but he might not fare well if he ran across a coyote. Or a pack of them.

"What do coyotes eat? Do they bother the cattle?"

"They would if they could. That's why we keep a donkey with the herd. Duke will stomp a coyote to death. Will kill a dog, too."

"Poor Jasper," she says, rubbing a bare foot across his flank. "Speaking of donkeys, did you find a saddle so I can ride him?"

"Bad idea."

"You're no fun."

They listen to night sounds, insects buzzing in the trees, moths ticking their wings against the screens.

Natalie coddles her glass, her eyes downcast, her brow furrowed. "That van wasn't making deliveries, Hitch. I know it."

Hitch gazes through the gauze of the porch screen, the vague outline of oak branches moving in the wind, shadows shifting and re-shaping themselves. The live oak tree he normally views as a welcome shade provider has suddenly become an ideal place for someone to hide. He gets up and flicks on the motion-activated security lights. The curtilage surrounding the house is suddenly awash in light.

14

Hitch is swallowing the last of two sausage biscuits his mother made from scratch when his phone vibrates. He picks up.

"I've got another one," Tobias Thomas announces.

"Another what?"

"Another reverse mortgage case. Client's name is Sharon Johnson. And she can pay for some research. You interested?"

Hitch glances at Natalie across the kitchen table. She's finishing a bowl of plain oatmeal and blueberries. He presses the phone to his chest. "Interested in doing a little legal research?" he asks her.

"Sure."

"Sure, Tobias. We'll be there in an hour."

"We?"

"My paralegal, Natalie Anderson, is down here for a few days. Great legal mind."

After picking up the thin file from Tobias' receptionist, Hitch and Natalie park in front of the county courthouse. Perhaps the stone walls, high ceilings, and regal columns restore in him some semblance of the lawyer he once was, as though the edifice itself can transport him back to when he carried a briefcase full of documents and a head full of cogent arguments. In Savannah, he knows the name of the clerks and assistant clerks in every department in the courthouse, and what type of coffee each likes.

Here in Pineland, his destination once again is the deeds office. He places a brown folder upon the wooden shelf in front of the file desk. The assistant clerk who preceded him in high school comes to the window. Natalie sidles up to the counter next to him.

"Hi, I'm Oakley Hitchcock," he starts. "I was here five or six weeks ago, researching a property. Aren't you Wanda Parker? I think you were a couple of years ahead of me at Pineland High."

"Yes. I remember you," she says, "both from high school and a few weeks back. What can I help you with?"

"This is Natalie Anderson. We're researching a reverse mortgage. We'd like to know if there are more of these mortgages out there. But we're not sure how to go about finding them."

"We don't file reverse mortgages separately from other mortgages," Wanda says.

"So when we're looking through the paperwork, how do we distinguish a Security Deed for a purchase-money loan from a HELOC, or from a reverse mortgage?"

"Well, on the purchase side, you could cross-reference the mortgage with the property tax records, which should match the new loan with a new owner if it's a sale. To distinguish a HELOC from a reverse mortgage, I'm not sure, unless the Security Deed has a due on death clause in it."

"That's it," he says. The answer has been right in front of him. Reverse mortgages are due only when the borrower dies. No other type of mortgage should have a due on death clause.

"Are you looking for something in particular?" Wanda asks.

"Just trying to get the lay of the land," he says. "Thank you, Wanda. I'm sure we'll be back with more questions."

Natalie takes the Sharon Johnson folder and settles herself at the same public computer where Hitch researched the Davidson file. In quick order she finds the executed Security Deed, which was filed the day after Sharon Johnson took out the mortgage. The promissory note the client executed is not on file in the courthouse records.

"Not much to go on," Natalie says.

"Identical to the Davidson case," Hitch responds. "Same paperwork. I bet if you look up the mortgage holder you'll find it's an LLC that's owned by a corporation in Nevada."

On her phone, Natalie navigates to the Georgia Secretary of State's website and confirms Hitch's suspicion. "No people here," she says. "Just faceless companies."

"Remember, corporations are people too. According to the US Supreme Court," Hitch says.

Natalie rolls her eyes. "You know what I mean. No person to talk to."

"Agreed. But if two transactions can make a pattern, we have one."

Natalie taps her index finger against her chin. "I bet you have some farmwork to do, or something. No reason for you to hang here while I do research."

"You trying to get rid of me?"

"I've got this, Hitch."

Hitch stands on the courthouse steps for less than a minute before he decides to attend an AA meeting at a place the locals call the clubhouse. He pulls into the parking lot, where members mill outside, some of them smoking. Maybe the two beers and two screwdrivers he had last night have brought him here. Maybe it's the fact he had a bottle of vodka hidden beneath his socks in the top dresser drawer. His old sponsor would say it doesn't matter why he's come, just that he's here.

The building is a wood-sided structure donated by a man who remained sober by going to meetings of Alcoholics Anonymous. Meetings are held three times a week at noon, and three times a week at 5 p.m., which coincides with the beginning of happy hour for the hardcore. Hitch's relationship with AA is complicated. Perhaps that is true for a lot of its members. He doesn't know if he is in fact an alcoholic. There is no consistent definition. Some say an alcoholic is anyone who has had their life adversely affected by alcohol. Well, the lawyer in him thinks in precise strokes, taking words literally, and in truth alcohol has adversely affected his life on many occasions. The morning after a bout, his mind is not sharp, and that dulled thinking has an adverse impact on his ability to reason and analyze cases and represent his clients to the best of his ability. There. Under that definition, a person who has one drink to help him sleep but lies awake all night with his mind spinning and then goes to work exhausted the next morning is an alcoholic.

Others define an alcoholic as someone with a compulsion to drink. A *compulsion*. Vague enough. Try to understand the parameters of compulsion—an irresistible urge. If a person can resist booze on occasion, is it irresistible? Is it a compulsion? Medical practitioners have tried to draw a bright line: four or more drinks a day, or fourteen drinks a week. He has breached that daily limit a few times, but he can't recall ever imbibing fourteen drinks in a week, even while on vacation in the Caribbean with Sonia, where a waiter appeared with fruit-garnished cocktails as if the tray and glasses were soldered to the palm of his hand.

AA itself doesn't define alcoholism. A stroke of wisdom perhaps, avoiding the labeling of fragile human beings, abhorring imposition of judgment. A hard swallow for someone like him, who judges people's actions daily, their motives, the impact of disastrous decisions on the lives of others. How those actions comply with or violate the law. He is judgmental to the core.

Even so, he thrusts his hands in the front pockets of his jeans and climbs the wooden steps to the second-floor meeting. He pours a cup of coffee from the urn and drops a dollar in an open shoe box. Finding a seat among the metal chairs, one row back from the center of the semi-circle, he tries to settle in. He tells himself he has come because the malaise he feels could lead him to self-medicate. If so, he needs community. He needs to hear others relate stories of battered lives and foolish deeds, some of which might dissuade him from drinking.

Though he makes his living communicating, Hitch remains silent, listening attentively to others' tales of woe. As he has at each of the dozen or so meetings he has attended in the past year. Perhaps he stays mum because he can't convince himself to say, "I'm Hitch and I'm an alcoholic." Nobody else at the meeting seems hesitant to label themselves in that way. He admires their certitude, if it is honest.

He hears stories about a five-day bender that ends with a car crash into a house, lost jobs, divorces, bankruptcy from alcohol and gambling addiction, and an older woman who fears she is falling down the same hole as her brother, who died of alcoholism at the age of 43. Barely older than Hitch.

He recognizes some of the faces who tell these stories, and some bear a familiarity, perhaps children of people he went to school with or whom he met in town long ago. The tone of these stories is varied. Some speak with rheumy eyes and the cracked voice of a person teetering on the precipice; some talk of decades of sobriety in voices *almost* assured, recognizing that most of their buried brethren were at some point sober too, before succumbing again. At the end, he doesn't pick up a white chip, signifying one day of sobriety. He silently vows to stop drinking for a week or two, he isn't sure which.

He leaves the meeting, threading his way through the smokers at the bottom of the stairs, who blow blue haze into a gentle breeze as if that will purge them of something. Maybe it works. He doesn't have the answer, but as he gets into his SUV and pulls from the lot, he isn't sure he even wants to ask the question.

He finds Natalie still in front of the computer in the deeds office at the courthouse. Her laptop is open on the desktop.

"On this list," she explains, pointing to an owner's name on a spreadsheet, "each secured party is a lender, which I've verified is registered either with the Georgia Department of Bank and Financing, or the US

Office of the Comptroller of the Currency. These lenders aren't trying to hide from anything, or dodge regulatory oversight. They're legit."

Hitch leans over her left shoulder. "I'm with you."

She clicks on another page on the spreadsheet. "These, on the other hand, are the secured parties that are not registered with any of the bank regulators. Melba Davidson's and Sharon Johnson's mortgages are on this list. I've labeled these as non-traditional lenders." She runs her index finger down the list. "In each case the secured party is a recently organized LLC, most of the names corresponding to the address of the property that's been mortgaged."

"How many so far?"

"Fifty-two in the past two years. And there's one more thing." She points to a name half-way down the list.

At first, he thinks his eyes must be deceiving him. The letters swim on the screen. "Show me the security deed," he says.

Natalie moves the mouse around and lands on the key document. The document is a mortgage in favor of a Georgia company whose name is 1447 Pond Road, LLC—the address of his parents' farm.

He grabs the mouse and navigates to the last page. His father's scribbled signature is there. There is no signature line for his mother. No mention of her at all in the document. The mortgage is notarized by Garland T. Rogers. Hitch checks the date. He grimaces. His father took out the reverse mortgage on the farm in April of this year, seven days before he was suspended from practicing law.

15

Hitch has to ask them about it. He is their son, after all. And a lawyer. Well, a suspended lawyer. He is concerned about them in both of these capacities. As he and Natalie drive back to the farm in silence, he wrestles with how to broach this sensitive subject.

During dinner at the round table in the kitchen, Hitch pushes the food around his plate, stabbing a green bean now and then, forking a small bite of mashed potatoes into his mouth. He glances at Natalie, who offers him a consoling look. He tips a glass of sweet tea to his lips an inordinate number of times, studying his parents over the rim of the glass. He practices questions in his head, but the tone is off. Everything sounds like a searing interrogation of a hostile witness. Has he forgotten how to have a simple conversation with his parents, without lapsing into lawyer mode?

He chooses something innocuous as a starting point. "We were at the courthouse this afternoon, researching a case."

"Oh?" Bridget says.

"A case?" Hale asks. "I thought you weren't supposed to do that. You know, because of the suspension."

Is this the tactic of a witness trying to throw him off? "We were researching reverse mortgages."

Hale dips his eyes. The sign of the guilty.

"Something you want to tell me, dad?"

Hale drags a fork through his mashed potatoes.

"Dad?"

"You obviously found it," he says without looking up.

"Actually, Natalie found it. Why didn't you tell me things had gotten so bad you had to take out a reverse mortgage on the farm? I know how much you hate banks."

"What are you talking about?" Bridget asks.

She doesn't know. His mother doesn't know.

Hale reaches across the table, lays his hand on top of his wife's, trying to convey an apology. She doesn't pull back, but her eyes are full of questions.

Her lips are quivering.

"I didn't have a choice, Bridget. We need the money for farm expenses this year. And to buy food and gas. Pay medical bills."

"Why didn't you tell me?" Bridget says.

"I didn't want to burden you with it, honey. It will be fine. Cattle prices will come back up and we'll build up our savings again, pay off the loan."

Hale's words of assurance do not dissipate the angst on Bridget's face. Her eyes are round and filled with worry.

"I'm sorry," Hitch says. "I didn't know things had gotten that bad."

Bridget gazes across the kitchen at a rooster clock hanging above the stove. "A lot of people have lost their farms over the past few years," she says.

"Everything has gotten ridiculously expensive," Hale adds. "It's not just beef prices that are down. Peanuts too. And blueberries, onions. You wouldn't know it at the grocery store. Everything we buy has gone way up. Middlemen. Inflation. Consumers pay more for food, but the farmer gets less."

Hitch has heard the joke more times than he can count: *How does a man eke out a living from farming? Answer: The wife has a good job in town.* For all that farm life offers, he has never been able to accept the constant worry about the weather, the impact of international trade negotiations and tariffs on product prices, the incessant criticism about the environmental effects of fertilizer and methane gas. Their financial decline has been slow, but inexorable, casting a pall over his parents, seeping into them like an insidious virus. They are barely surviving.

This is the reason he left Pineland. Not that Hitch claims any expertise for analyzing agricultural trends or predicting the next trade dispute. He has witnessed the impact on farmers in the increasing age of their rusty pickups, in the frowns of mothers at the grocery store who have to put back the package of steaks and get turkey instead, and in the slump of a farmer's shoulders who can fill his gas tank only half-way at the station this time around.

Hitch's plate is half-empty, but there is a pit in his stomach. For the past three months he has added to his parents' financial burden, ignorant of his own impact. Another mouth to feed. His dad is a good farmer, an efficient farmer, analyzing spreadsheets so he can minimize waste and maximize yield, rotating his cattle to healthier pastures at the correct time to increase their weight. He studies the price charts, hauling his cows to auction only when prices are peaking. He buys hay in the summer, when hay is abundant. He gives the herd the required shots himself, rather than calling in the vet. And still, it isn't enough. He is forced to borrow money just to live. And Hitch knows his father considers borrowing money a form of begging.

"What can I do?" Hitch asks.

His father simply shakes his head. A gesture of defeat and shame.

His mother's eyes are vacant.

Natalie sits beside him with downcast eyes, as if she's witnessed a terrible car wreck and there's a body in the median.

After dinner, Hitch takes a beer from the back of the refrigerator and sits on the front porch. Natalie joins him, a glass of wine in hand.

"Think I was too harsh?" he asks.

"Dunno. Not my place, you know."

"I'm just in shock. My dad hasn't taken out a loan in …I don't know when. Not since I've been an adult. He hates banks and hates bankers even more. He wouldn't have borrowed money unless he was desperate. He could have come to me."

"Maybe he didn't feel he could."

"Of course he could. He knows that." Hitch takes a long swig of beer.

The woods are dark ink, the nearby pasture a gray shadow before moonrise. The highway a quarter mile in the distance is a silent afterthought this time of night, with only the occasional truck sliding past. As he rocks, he gazes through the screen clouded with cottonwood seeds, drawing in his mind the boundaries of the farm, across a dirt track and a meandering creek and a high-voltage transmission line. He wonders how much of the 320 acres his father has pledged to secure the loan. Surely, not all of it. In his shock at seeing his father's name on the mortgage, he forgot to examine the property description. Even a dire financial situation would not necessitate that Hale pledge it all to a bank. He could ask, but he doesn't want to put his father through that again. Not tonight. He knows where the important papers are kept—in neat folders with typed labels in a golden oak file cabinet in his father's office. He can look there if curiosity insists.

He finishes his beer in long gulps, feeling the burn of carbonation. And maybe something else. He returns to the fridge for another, sipping this one, disregarding the commitment he made only this afternoon to give himself a week or two away from alcohol.

"We need to look at all the documents," he says. "I bet my dad has a copy of the note he signed."

Long after his parents go to bed in the parlor now converted into the downstairs master bedroom, he and Natalie creep to his father's office. The door creaks when Hitch opens it. He tries to gauge if the sound is loud enough to wake them. He concludes not. Century-old floorboards groan as they step through the doorway. After Natalie sidles into the office behind him, Hitch eases the door shut, only a light click, not even enough to alert Jasper, asleep on his pallet in the kitchen around the corner. Hitch taps the flashlight icon on his phone and pulls open the top drawer of the oak file cabinet.

"Is this what you're looking for?" It is his father's voice.

Startled, Hitch shines the light toward the voice. His father is sitting behind a gun-metal desk in his green robe, his hair disheveled, his face pasty from lack of sleep. Hale lays a manila folder on the desktop and turns on the desk lamp. It is the brass-shaded lawyer lamp Hitch gave him for Christmas a few years back. "Your mother wants you to look at the particulars. Use my desk."

Hitch steps behind the desk, chagrined, and flops into his father's tattered office chair. Natalie settles across from him in an old burgundy chair his mother purchased at Goodwill.

"You're not very good at this detective stuff, son. You make too much noise. Good thing you became a lawyer."

"Ditto," Natalie says.

Hitch opens the file and maneuvers the desk lamp's circle of light. He reads silently. First the promissory note, which reveals the loan is for $150,000, with a high interest rate.

"Who filled in the blanks on the promissory note?" Hitch asks.

"I did," his father answers, "while the guy was still here. I noticed the copies he gave me were blank."

"That was smart." In his head, Hitch calculates the interest accrual, using the Rule of 72. "You do realize that in seven years you'll owe more than $300,000 on this note?"

His father nods.

"So why did you agree to a loan with such a high interest rate?"

"No financial paperwork. We couldn't qualify for a loan based on our income, certainly not one that requires monthly payments. We don't have to make any payments on this loan."

According to the note, the lender is Pond Road Financial, LLC, a different entity from the one that holds the mortgage on the farm, though similarly named.

He peers at Natalie. "The lender and mortgagee are different, as we suspected. I'll bet it's the same MO as the Davidson and Johnson reverse mortgages."

He reads his father's copy of the mortgage. He reviews the property description, attached as Schedule A. It describes the parcels by metes and bounds, a mind-numbing array of directions and compass degrees and distances from point to point. Without a survey in front of him, these numbers mean almost nothing to Hitch. He thinks of Archie Williams, the third judge on his ethics panel, and marvels at how Archie could last so long as a real estate lawyer parsing such details. Hitch would be bored to death. He looks at his father.

"Did you mortgage …"

Hale preempts the question. "Yes, all 320 acres. They wouldn't do it any other way. I tried to negotiate a smaller parcel. They wouldn't have it."

Hitch's heart sinks. The farm is worth a lot more than $150,000. Maybe four or five times that amount. He tries to cover his despondency by nodding his head, the way he does when he gets a surprise answer from a witness in court. It's a gesture intended to convey to the Judge and jury he has expected this answer all along. "How long will the money last? I know next to nothing about farm finances."

Hale, slumped on the old couch, steeples his fingers over his stomach and blue-striped pajamas. "We've been running a deficit of about $30,000 a year for the last four years. That has depleted our savings. The funds would ordinarily last us four years, maybe five. But …"

"But what?"

"I had to use about $70,000 of the loan to pay off debt."

"You don't have debt. What kind of debt?"

His father hesitates, gnawing his lower lip. He knows his dad is deciding whether to lie to him.

"Tell me the truth, dad."

"Mostly farm debt. But I ran up some gambling debt, too. On-line," his father says, spitting it out.

"You gamble on-line?" Hitch stares with wonder at his father. He's the last person Hitch would expect to gamble. "What type of gambling?"

"On-line poker. I had a system, and well …"

"Everybody thinks they have a system."

In the dim light, his father's lips go tight.

Hitch leans back in the padded chair, slips his hands behind his head. "And mom doesn't know about the gambling."

His father shakes his head. "And I'd appreciate it if you didn't tell her."

"I'm not going to lie to her if she asks me."

"What about attorney-client privilege?"

Hitch sputters a half laugh. "There are so many things wrong with that statement. I strongly suggest you tell her, dad. She deserves to know. She's your wife. She owns half this farm."

Hale's eyes flick to the floor. He's thinking about it.

"How much do you have left in the bank?"

"About 80K. We'll be in good shape through the end of this year, and probably next year, too. Why do you care so much?"

Hitch speaks without thinking. "You wouldn't have done this if Rip were alive. You wouldn't have risked the farm if he were still here." Hitch is surprised at the acidity of his tone. The son who survived revealing jealousy of the one who died. "Sorry, I shouldn't have said that."

And yet he wonders if this is true. Rip was undoubtedly his father's favorite in many ways, probably because Rip liked working the farm, was good with the cows, never complained about the monotony or the long hours. Hitch attempts to step back, tries to view his father's actions as if he were a client. Assess the facts objectively. No payments until he dies. But his father hates banks. So, why would he borrow at such a high interest rate? Hitch answers his own question.

"You don't intend to pay it back," he says aloud. "Once you're gone, there's no one to take over and run the farm, so you're going to deplete the equity now. When you die, the farm goes to the lender."

"No. When I pass, your mother can stay here until she passes," Hale says. "That's what the mortgage broker said. Garland T. Rogers."

Hitch doesn't respond immediately. In the Davidson case, Alicia Vanderwelt foreclosed with one spouse still alive. As a result, Cordell Davidson is living out his final days in a small, subsidized apartment.

"Dad, let me help. I've got some money socked away. Maybe I can pay off the loan."

"Absolutely not. I'm not going to pay off the loan, and Bridget gets to stay here until she dies. It's not like you want to inherit the place."

Hitch sighs. "It's not about that, dad. It's about this lender, whoever it is, getting a valuable piece of land for pennies on the dollar."

Hitch opens his laptop and pulls up the website for HUD.gov. The US Department of Housing and Urban Development offers model legal forms for reverse mortgages. He scans the available forms, finds the fixed-rate promissory note. His mind buzzes with activity as he scrolls through the document. He places the hard copy of his father's promissory note next to the laptop and begins comparing terms. The note his father signed looks nothing like the HUD document.

When he reaches Section 6A, he sees the word "Death" in stark letters. He slows. The HUD document lays it out in detail. The loan is due when the borrower dies, unless an exception applies. One of the exceptions is if the borrower is survived by an eligible non-borrowing spouse who lives in the house. In this case, that would be his mother.

But the two-page note in front of him, the one his father signed, has no exceptions to the due-on-death clause. The note comes due when his father dies. Period.

Next he finds the HUD model mortgage form. He places the security deed his father signed next to the laptop. The HUD mortgage has specific provisions delaying the loan repayment trigger for a non-borrowing spouse. The mortgage his father signed has no such protection.

At first Hitch thinks this must be a mistake. The lender has in shoddy fashion forgotten to include a provision to protect non-borrowing spouses, protection that is required by regulations promulgated by the federal government. Or, the lender is simply ignoring the federal regulations.

His left hand smooths the hair on the back of his head. What is he missing? He navigates to a different part of the website and discovers there are loans called proprietary reverse mortgages—loans the federal government doesn't guarantee. Loans that HUD doesn't regulate. This is what Alicia Vanderwelt refused to tell him when he confronted her during the Davidson foreclosure sale. He hears it now, blaring at him like a bullhorn.

He clicks a link to the Federal Housing Administration so he can review the list of approved lenders whose loans are guaranteed. He knows before he scrolls the list that Pond Road Financial, the entity designated as the lender on his father's note, will not be there. He scrolls the list. Pond Road Financial is not an FHA-approved lender.

Hitch tries to slow his brain. "Dad," he begins in a voice he hopes sounds comforting, "we have a problem."

"Other than the fact you don't approve of my mortgaging the farm, what are you talking about?"

"Mom's not protected."

"What do you mean?"

"When you die, she doesn't get to stay in the house."

"Of course she does. The mortgage broker told me that because she's older than 62, she stays in the house until she dies."

"That's not anywhere in the documents."

"I know that, son. I'm not an idiot. But he showed me the federal regulations. In black and white. They are crystal clear. She gets to stay."

"If it's a federally guaranteed loan, dad. Your loan isn't."

"What?"

"This is a proprietary reverse mortgage. I didn't even know such a thing existed until tonight. Your loan has nothing to do with HUD, or any other governmental entity. The federal regulations he showed you don't apply. The guy tricked you."

"You're wrong."

"Dad, I wish I were." Hitch cannot hide his frustration, but continuing down this road will not alter the reality of what his father has done.

"How did you get this loan, anyway?" He asks this as much to re-direct his own anger as to learn the answer.

"A flyer in the mailbox," Hale says.

"Really?"

Hale purses his lips and nods.

Natalie sits quietly across the desk, perusing the documents Hale Hitchcock signed. She's back-stopping Hitch, moving slowly through each line, trying to find a loophole he may have missed in his haste. She finally looks at Hitch, shakes her head. "It's not guaranteed. There are no exceptions," she says.

"Okay then," Hitch says.

"I don't like being interrogated by my own son. You done with the third degree?"

"Yep. But you need to tell mom."

Hale stews for a minute. He closes his eyes in thought, perhaps attempting to vanquish this nightmare. Then he steps over to the file cabinet and pulls out the bottom right drawer. The metal screeches loudly enough to awaken some of the inhabitants of the family cemetery. Hale extracts a bottle of amber liquid from the drawer.

Jasper, roused by the noise, paws at the outside of the office door. Hitch lets him in, and the worried bloodhound curls on a swath of carpet in the corner.

Hale sets the bottle of bourbon on the desktop, along with three clear plastic cups. The bourbon is a limited edition from a small batch at a St. Augustine distillery, a bottle Hitch gave him for Father's Day two years ago. The paper seal is intact. Still standing, Hale slits the paper with his knife and uncorks the bottle.

"If I'm going to tell your mother ..." Hale starts.

"Tell me what?" Bridget is standing in the doorway, her pink robe draped on bony shoulders, backlit by the hallway light. She walks over and places both palms on her husband's shoulders. "Tell me what, Hale?"

16

The Hitchcock family equilibrium becomes precarious, as if they are being forced to cross a rotting log above a roaring river. The land on which the Hitchcocks have lived for 150 years is a family member, as significant to their survival as any one of its inhabitants. The farm sustains them, even as it demands all their energy, and money they do not have. The homestead is a patchwork amalgam—the collective heartbeat of cattle, a donkey, incursive coyotes, skittish deer, a rooster and hens, grand live oaks, swaying pines, quail, dove, ducks, pasture grass and invading weeds, the creaky farmhouse, straight lines of fencing, a sputtering tractor, Bridget, Hale and Hitch, and fourteen departed souls in sandy graves. A farm can thrive; a farm can die. The Hitchcock farm is moribund.

For Hitch's parents, the farm is the only home they've known since marrying. In their unguarded moments, Hitch sees the distress of their uncertain future. Hale has told Bridget the details of the mess he's created. As the import settled in, Bridget hurled a single curse at him, then slumped onto his office sofa. She has been in mourning since, as if the undertaker waits in the tree line to the west. She wanders the kitchen, opening cabinets and closing them without withdrawing anything, her eyes wide with perpetual surprise. She takes clothes from the dryer, folds them, then puts them in the dirty-clothes hamper without realizing it. She feeds the chickens in the morning, again in the afternoon, not remembering she's already fed them. She cannot contemplate living anywhere else.

When his father fills in the weekly crossword, his lips are tight and flat, not from concentration, but from despair. Word clues are insufficient distraction to this dilemma. He mopes about in the barn, picking up and putting down tools as though he doesn't understand their purpose. Hale is unable to fully accept the impact of his actions. He has imperiled his wife's future. If anything happens to him, Bridget is unprotected.

And though two decades ago he left this place without looking back, in the past weeks the farm has become Hitch's anchor. He can no longer deny it. The farm serves as safe harbor from the lashing storm his life has become—Sonia's death, his suspension, the slow erosion of his legal skills, the sinking of his ego. He has discovered some bitter comfort in the tedium, in the curious looks from the cattle, in watching them birth calves. Now, he must face the fact that his childhood home, this underpinning of support, could be gone with his father.

Natalie does not fit comfortably in this picture. She eats with the family and listens to the broken silence, offering comments about outside events to distract, but mostly she observes. She is both interloper and guest. She does not know what to say to console any of them. She does not know what to do. She does not know where to be. So she escapes the doldrums of the house and the farm and dons her running shoes and heads out onto the blacktop.

"I should go back to Savannah," she says to Hitch one afternoon as he's filling the tractor with diesel.

"To what?"

It's a pithy question. "To give you guys space."

"Space is not what we need right now. We need to solve this problem. And I'm so angry with my dad that I can't think straight."

Natalie places her right heel atop the front tractor tire and stretches her hamstring. "Is there a way he can get the money to pay it off?"

"You heard what my dad said. He's got 80 grand left from the loan but needs the money to live on. Even if the loan gets paid off, he's going to have to borrow more money unless beef prices improve and supply costs go down."

"I don't know if I'm off-base here, Hitch, but do you have the resources to pay the mortgage off for them?"

He shakes his head. "Not all of it. In case you haven't noticed, I haven't taken a paycheck in the past five months."

"Ouch," Natalie says. She walks into the sunshine at the edge of the barn, then returns. "Maybe we should temporarily shut the office down. Stacie and I can find work for the next seven months. That will save you some expenses."

"I didn't mean it like that, Nat," he says, hoisting another five-gallon container of diesel. "Sorry. I'm just frustrated. You guys have hung by me through all of this. I don't want to lose either of you. You take other jobs, you might not come back."

"Okay," she says. "I'll try to think of something else."

After a morning rain washes the sky, Hitch entices Natalie to make a trip to the swamp. The Okefenokee Swamp is the largest fresh-water swamp in North America. It covers 680 square miles, most of it in southern Georgia, though it seeps across the line into Florida. Its tea-colored water and pine-covered islands are home to a variety of fish, snakes, turtles, deer, black bear, panthers and alligators. Lots of alligators.

Hitch paddles up the Suwannee Canal in a rented canoe. Natalie sits in the bow, dipping her paddle into the water with trepidation. They slide past hummocks with the grass laid flat, evidence an alligator laid there just minutes before. They are so close, Hitch could reach out and touch the hummocks with the end of his fishing rod.

Alligator heads hover in the dark water. Thirty yards ahead. Twenty yards behind. He fixes on a pair of yellow-green eyes and a knotty brow a short cast to his left. *Ten feet,* he estimates. *Maybe four hundred pounds. Medium-sized.* He knows alligators in the Swamp get much bigger.

He has brought Natalie here and rented this canoe because … he's not exactly sure why. The dark water and humid air feel welcoming to him. This is where he grew up. He spent untallied hours here when younger, hunting deer and hogs in the pine flats. He's fished this canal at least a hundred times. In the quietude, he absorbs all of this as nourishment.

For the first time since George Colbert opened fire in his law office, his anxiety is subdued. To people who have never been victims of violence, it is difficult to explain this resonating shudder that will not go away. It is there when he sleeps. When he rises in the pre-dawn darkness. When he hears a sound that doesn't belong. There are long stretches, hours in duration, when the thrum of his encounter with death pulses within him as if it is a second heart. Yet as they slip past alligators too numerous to count, he is no longer afraid.

Natalie points as a gator thrusts itself onto a grassy bank, using its swinging head as shovel, scooping bait fish out of the water. Its tail thrashes with unquantifiable power. Splashing sounds like an explosion out here. The gator grabs a mosquito fish and, with a toss of its head, swallows the fish whole. Hitch estimates the distance from nose to eyes at eleven inches, maybe twelve, which means the gator is that long in feet.

"There's a mosquito on your neck," he warns, flipping swamp water towards Natalie's back with the paddle.

She slaps her neck with her palm, then turns toward him.

He tosses her a can of bug juice from the pack at his feet.

They are both garbed in jeans, long-sleeved fishing shirts, thick socks and hats, but the mosquitos and yellow flies still get through.

Cypress knees and water lilies dot the black water. Below, six or seven feet down, is decaying peat that gives the water its color and acidity. The cackling cry of the anhinga pierces the silence. Hitch spots it, drying its wings on an old cypress log. Its wings are raised like a black cape, its snake-like neck twisting and undulating. In Brazilian, "anhinga" means snake bird, or devil bird.

"Want to fish?" he asks.

"Not right now. I'll just watch," Natalie answers.

Hitch lifts one of his spinning rods, which is rigged with a double-bladed teal spinner. He flips a cast in the middle, hoping to entice bowfin. He's caught some here at close to ten pounds, their brownish-black bodies like a cross between catfish and eel. He's never eaten them, though some do.

He tugs the line to start the swirling action of the lure, then reels in slowly. He takes a deep inhale of air. He can almost taste the peat. Bubbles rising to the surface contain odorless methane and pungent sulfur-dioxide. The faint smell of brimstone isn't fully dissipated by the breeze. He remembers from his Sunday School days the references in Revelation to brimstone and the lake of fire. He smiles with the irony. The Okefenokee Swamp has been on fire multiple times in recent years, with methane and sulfur-dioxide prolonging each conflagration until the dried peat burns away.

On his tenth or twelfth cast, he hooks a bowfin. Medium-sized, four-to-five pounds. The bowfin fights for its life, surfacing and plunging. When he lands it, he extracts one treble hook from its mouth with curved pliers and releases the fish. He catches two more in quick succession. He hooks a fourth he judges twice as large as the others. His rod bends in a deep arc. The fish is still 40 feet away when it darts for the cover of the water lilies and the long stalks that reach to the bottom. If the fish gets there, it will likely throw the hook or tangle his line in the weeds.

An alligator reacts to the splashing fight, undulating its way toward the bowfin, hoping to make Hitch's fish its meal. The gator's spiny back, as dark as the water, is fully visible now. It's all of thirteen feet. The same length as the canoe he and Natalie are sitting in. This gator probably weighs 500 pounds.

"Too close," Natalie says, leaning against the opposite side of the canoe.

"He's not interested in us," Hitch replies. "It wants my fish."

With the gator closing the gap to the canoe, Hitch severs the line with his pocketknife. The fish stops thrashing and disappears.

The gator stops too, its hind half descending beneath the surface. Its snout is pointed directly at the broadside of the boat. Its snaggled teeth hover just above the water, slitted eyes watching them. It's no more than fifteen feet away.

Hitch puts the rod down silently. He's been closer to penned alligators before, but he doesn't recall being this close to a gator this big in the wild. Maybe this is a standoff. The alligator remains perfectly still, but Hitch knows it could be on them in seconds. This creature derives from ancestors nearly 60 million years old. The species has changed little during that span. It has been an apex predator longer than humans have inhabited the earth. At the moment, this alligator's only enemy is the man in the boat.

"It's just curious," he says to calm Natalie. He believes this, yet his right hand creeps to the leather holster at his hip and Rip's silver .357 Smith & Wesson Magnum. He releases the keep. "It's not going to attack," he whispers.

The gator disappears beneath the surface.

Hitch watches for a bubble trail, trying to track the big gator's movement. He knows alligators can stay under water for more than an hour. Therefore, he has no idea where the alligator is at this moment. The actions of the alligator, and the snakes patrolling the edges, and the bears and panthers that roam at night, are entirely predictable. They attack to eat, or to protect themselves. They do not attack things larger than they are. They feast on weakness. As Hitch slowly paddles up the canal, he comprehends that this order, this predictability, is why he feels so comfortable in the wild. He does not fear the big alligators who watch them glide by. No, what Hitch truly fears is the predator on two legs. The kind who kills without reason or warning.

17

Hitch settles his elbows on the conference table in Tobias' office. He glances at Natalie next to him before beginning.

"I have an idea about how to get to the bottom of these reverse mortgage cases," he says. "Natalie and I have vetted this."

"Okay," Tobias says. "What's your idea?"

"Background first. We've found 52 reverse mortgages made by non-traditional lenders in this county in the past two years. We've only searched the Dare County records, so that doesn't include any of the surrounding counties."

"Define non-traditional lenders," Tobias says.

"Unregulated. Not registered with state or federal banking regulators."

"How is that possible?"

"One-offs," Natalie interjects. "If you make only one loan, you don't have to register as a bank. Falls under the category of private lending."

"Okay," Hitch continues. "Sharon Johnson took out a reverse mortgage from a non-traditional lender. Melba Davidson did the same. So did my dad."

"Your dad took out a reverse mortgage?" Tobias asks.

Hitch nods. "I'm as surprised as anyone. Like every other farmer around here, he got underwater, and he needed a quick cash infusion that you don't have to pay back until you die. But there's a problem. In my dad's case, at least, the mortgage broker or insurance agent—this Garland T. Rogers—told him my mom could stay in the house if he dies first because she's a non-borrowing spouse. Even showed him a federal regulation that says so. Only thing is, the federal regulation doesn't apply."

"You're sure?"

"Yep. It's what Alicia Vanderwelt knew in the Davidson case that we didn't know. Most reverse mortgages are guaranteed by FHA, and the federal regs apply to those loans. But if the lender isn't a HUD-approved lender, as in my dad's case, the government won't guarantee the loan, and the regs don't apply. They're called proprietary reverse mortgages. Totally unregulated."

"Reverse mortgages are non-recourse, right?" Tobias says.

"Right. The lender can't collect the money back from the borrower."

"So why would any lender make a non-guaranteed loan that the borrower doesn't ever have to pay back?"

"Because they want the land," Hitch and Natalie say at the same time.

"The way I figure it," Hitch explains, "legitimate lenders want to get repaid, so they get on the approved list and have the federal government guarantee the reverse mortgage if it doesn't get repaid, either when the borrower dies or from the sale of the land. But that federally guaranteed protection becomes a loophole for a lender who doesn't want the guarantee of repayment."

"And the only reason they would forego that guarantee is because they never wanted repayment in the first place," Tobias concludes.

"Exactly," Hitch says. "That's why Alicia Vanderwelt bid $50,000 more than she needed to to win the Davidson foreclosure auction. Her client always wanted the land, not the money."

Tobias mulls this, fingering his chin. "So what's your idea?"

"A class action," Hitch answers. "My parents can be the named plaintiffs, but the suit will cover all of the other reverse mortgages where only one spouse signed as borrower."

"If the federal regs don't apply, what's the claim?"

"My dad was misled that my mother could stay in the house. If Garland Rogers used that trick on my father, he probably used it on the others as well. It's common-law fraud and deceptive trade practices."

"State law claims," Tobias nods. "So no federal court, like where we would have filed in the Davidson case to stop the foreclosure?"

"Nope. State court. Let me read you something from the FBI website:

> Reverse mortgage scams are engineered by unscrupulous professionals in a multitude of real estate, financial services, and related companies to steal the equity from the property of unsuspecting senior citizens or to use these seniors to unwittingly aid the fraudsters in stealing equity from a flipped property.
>
> In many of the reported scams, victim seniors are offered free homes, investment opportunities, and foreclosure or

> refinance assistance. They are also used as straw buyers in property flipping scams. Seniors are frequently targeted through local churches and investment seminars, as well as television, radio, billboard, and mailer advertisements.

"Is that what you think happened with your dad?" Tobias asks.

"I think this is a general warning from the FBI about reverse-mortgage scams. The particulars in my parents' case are a bit different. But my dad got a mailer, he was lied to, and he bought the pitch."

"A class action? Sounds like it could get complicated."

"Natalie and I will do all the work, Tobias. I've handled three or four class actions as local counsel. They're not simple, but it's a good way to litigate lots of similar claims in one lawsuit. The only thing I can't do now is argue in court, but by the time trial comes around, I'll be off suspension."

Tobias studies Hitch. "You want a piece of Vanderwelt, don't you?"

Hitch scratches his chin. "I won't deny it. But what I want most is my mother to be able to live in our farmhouse if my dad goes first. And maybe the suit can help anybody else who's been duped."

"Too late for Cordell Davidson, I guess," Tobias says.

"With Mrs. Davidson dead, we don't have a witness to her conversation with Garland Rogers."

"Maybe Rogers will admit what he did," Tobias offers.

"We can interview him and find out." Hitch waits a bit, allowing this to sink in, hoping Tobias is convinced this is a worthy cause. Then, "you in?"

"Probably. But before I commit 100 percent, I want to see the complaint first."

"That's fair. We'll get cracking. It will take us about two weeks to complete the interviews and draft the lawsuit."

Saving the family farm has become Hitch's self-proclaimed mandate. Just the thought of working on a complicated lawsuit, especially one that hits so close and has such implications, rejuvenates him. A class action might be the best vehicle for helping other farmers as well. His brain is coursing with ideas about discovery. Interrogatories he will draft and serve on Alicia Vanderwelt. Documents they will request from the myriad of lenders trying to hide their identities. Subpoenas they will serve.

"This is starting to feel fun," he says as he and Natalie drive up the tree-lined driveway to the farm.

"Yeah, kind of like old times," Natalie says. "Some real litigation."

"It feels great to be working again."

He wanted Tobias' commitment to serve as counsel before approaching his parents. Without that, he doesn't have a lawyer to lead the charge. Now, he has to sell his parents on the idea of filing a lawsuit.

Bridget is an easy convert. When Hitch tells her of his plan to ask a judge to determine her rights under the reverse mortgage, she nods vigorously with tears welling in her eyes. Though the turmoil has enveloped them all, Bridget has been most affected. She will be the one displaced if the loan documents are upheld and her husband dies. She signs the consent to be a plaintiff in the class action without hesitation, laying her hand upon her son's immediately after setting down the pen.

Hale exhibits an unwelcome recalcitrance. Perhaps he does not fully believe his son's conclusion that the loan dispossesses Bridget of her spousal rights in the farm, or maybe he doesn't want to admit to a judge in a public courtroom that he was duped. In truth, Hale's consent to the lawsuit is unnecessary, but Hitch wants his father's buy-in because adding him as a plaintiff to the complaint will carry some weight. Plus, Hale will be a critical witness.

Hitch charges Natalie with explaining the strategy to his father.

"Mr. Hitchcock, it's going to go like this," Natalie starts. "Bridget has consented to be the plaintiff in a class-action lawsuit to determine what rights non-borrower spouses have under these reverse mortgages. The lawsuit not only will determine Bridget's rights, but the rights of any other spouses who didn't sign the loan documents. Because you obviously have a vested interest in all of this, we want you to be a plaintiff, too. Based on what Garland Rogers told you, you didn't intend to dispossess your wife of her rights in the farm, in the land, and you agree with Bridget's legal position."

"Will I need to hire a separate lawyer?" Hale asks with a tinge of trepidation.

"No, sir. The lawyer for the class will represent you and Bridget and all the other class members.'

"How can my son represent anybody if he's suspended?"

Hitch intercedes. "Dad, Tobias Thomas—you know him—has agreed to represent the class."

"Preliminarily agreed," Natalie clarifies. "Since he's the one who will be signing the pleadings, he wants to see the complaint first. But if this case takes the normal course, Hitch will be practicing again long before anything major happens in court."

"How much longer are you suspended? Hale asks.

"Six months and eleven days. It will take us a couple of weeks to get the complaint ready."

"And you think this is a good idea?"

"Dad, I see it as the only way to get this issue in front of a judge now, before you die, when we would have to litigate it with a foreclosure looming and without you as a live witness. One of our clients already lost the chance to litigate the issue because she died before we realized there was a case. We don't want to make that mistake again."

Natalie puts on her most compassionate look. "This is for Bridget, Mr. Hitchcock. She really needs you to do this for her."

18

In a span of twelve days, Hitch and Natalie manage to interview 77 witnesses. Where possible, they conduct the interview together. When schedules collide, they split up. Using Tobias' conference room, the interviews domino upon one another until they have spoken to at least one of the interested parties in 49 of the 52 reverse mortgages they have discovered.

They decide not to bother Cordell Davidson, for they know intimately his circumstances and that he would have little factual information to provide. Hitch tucks Mr. Davidson in a corner of his mind, vowing not to forget him or his deceased spouse, but unable as yet to find him a spot at the table with the other class members.

Hitch prepares affidavits for his parents to sign. Hale Hitchcock repeated to Tobias' assistant his previous recitation of the meeting with Garland Rogers, emphasizing the way Rogers pointed to the provision in the federal regulation, a printed copy of which he had laid upon the hood of his own black pickup truck out by the Hitchcock tractor barn, confirming all spouses could remain in the home until they passed away. Hale even remembers that Rogers' index finger had a crescent of blood seeping from a broken fingernail, as if he'd peeled it back to the quick. The signed and sworn statement of Hale Hitchcock sits in its own pristine folder.

Bridget's affidavit is short, containing mostly the things she did not know: her husband's signing the documents; the meeting between Hale and Rogers at the farm; the $150,000 in loan proceeds; and her complete ignorance that her rights were being stolen from her. Hitch uses this strong declaration because his mother insists upon it. In the past few days she has gathered strength he didn't know she possessed, vowing to see the case through to the end, for herself and all similarly situated others.

The borrower on the last mortgage of the 52 has not responded to phone calls, and Hitch contemplates simply driving out to their property at the northern end of the county, but at present he has other priorities. As they review and assemble the statements, Hitch confirms the pattern he knew had to be there—in each case where there is a spouse living on the property (all but four), the borrowing spouse was promised orally by Garland Rogers that their spouse could remain even after the borrower died. In most cases, Rogers boldly supported his promise by showing them the applicable federal law in writing.

"It's time to interview Garland Rogers," Hitch says to Tobias and Natalie.

"I should do it," Natalie volunteers.

"Why shouldn't I go with you to see Rogers?"

"How would you introduce yourself? Hi, I'm Oakley Hitchcock, the lawyer son of the man you hoodwinked?"

"I see your point."

"She's going to get more information than you are," Tobias confirms.

On the drive back to the farm, Hitch and Natalie settle on a strategy for the Rogers' interview. Something sneaky but not illegal, to build her credibility before she starts asking questions. Though they have gathered a lot of information from the borrowers, whom Hitch has started to think of as "the victims," some juicy admissions from Rogers would go a long way towards building their case.

Before they turn into the driveway to the farmhouse, Natalie's phone buzzes. She glances at the screen.

She turns to Hitch. "It's Mark. I should take this." She says it almost as a question, uncertainty in her voice.

He nods. "Do you need privacy?"

"No, I want you to hear this, at least on my end." Natalie takes a deep breath and picks up on the fourth buzz.

"Hi Mark."

"You didn't go to your parents' house, Natalie. What the hell is going on?"

"Hello to you too, Mark. No, I didn't go to my parents' house. I decided to make a detour."

"Where are you?"

"Why do you need to know where I am?"

"Well, to make sure you're safe."

"I'm safe. I can assure you of that."

"Where the hell are you, Natalie?"

"Mark, your tone isn't getting us anywhere. Why did you call?"

"Because I want you to come home."

"We weren't exactly getting along, you know. Things had been rocky for a few weeks before I left. I thought it best to get some space."

"Look, I'm sorry. I know I wasn't handling things the way I should have. I just …I want you to come home, to our apartment."

"What is it you weren't handling the way you should have?"

"Our relationship. But, there was a reason. A cause. I don't want to talk about this on the phone. I want to talk to you about it face-to-face, alone. Please come home."

Hitch has pulled down the sandy driveway of the farmhouse. The car is idling between the rows of straight-trunk pines.

"I'm working on a case, Mark. I'm not sure where our relationship is at this moment, but I can't come home right now. Maybe in a week or two. I'm not sure."

"I can find you if I want to, Natalie."

"Meaning what?"

Mark is silent.

"Mark, I'm hanging up now."

"Natalie, you'd better not be …"

She hangs up before Mark can finish.

They sit in silence for a time. Hitch watches a line of cows make their way along a well-worn path to a water trough. Doves flutter in and out of pine trees.

Natalie stares at her phone, wondering whether she should block Mark's number.

19

Natalie Anderson takes the chair in front of the broad wooden desk of Garland T. Rogers. His insurance agency is a four-room office in Valdosta, about 50 miles west of Pineland. Rogers is heavy-set, red suspenders framing the mound of his belly, an extra layer of fat under his chin that wriggles when he talks. He has silver hair and a pleasant manner, a way of looking at you that makes you trust him. This is a good attribute for a man who sells reverse mortgages and insurance that triggers upon death.

"First, thank you for seeing me without an appointment," she starts. "My daddy is interested in a reverse mortgage on his property. I told him I'd look into it for him."

"Where is your father's property located?" Rogers asks.

Natalie strives to be cagey, giving less information than she gets. But if she fabricates a location, Rogers will be able to check it on his computer on the spot and know she's lying. "Columbia County, near Lake City," she says. Her father in fact owns some acreage there.

"That's in Florida."

"Yes. He has a little over 75 acres. Mostly timber."

"I'm not assisting with any home equity conversion mortgages down that way," Rogers says.

"Is that the same as a reverse mortgage?" Natalie asks.

Rogers nods. "That's not my territory." He uses a tone conveying he is only the messenger, the decision out of his hands. This restrictive policy is made in some higher place.

Natalie uncrosses then re-crosses her long, tanned legs. She stretches her arms toward the carpeted floor, which has the effect of parting the unbuttoned top of her cherry-colored blouse another centimeter. "Oh. Well, I feel like my daddy and you would get along fine. I researched you on-line, your awards and everything. Your customer reviews are amazing, Mr. Rogers. You must run a really professional, top-notch shop here."

The flattery does not sway him. Rogers shrugs his shoulders. He's better at this than she'd hoped. While he appears friendly on the outside, there's a protective shield just underneath, deflecting her.

She peers past him to the wall behind his desk, painted pale blue, dotted with certificates and salesmanship awards in cheap black frames. She doesn't see anything resembling a mortgage broker's license.

"Well, anyway, I wonder if you could tell me a little about these mortgages. You know, so I can advise my daddy about whether this is something he really should look into. It sounds like a highly regulated area, a lot of paperwork that might go along with it."

"There's very little paperwork. Just a few documents," he says.

"Do you deal with a lot of different lenders, making these reverse mortgages? Maybe you could recommend a lender who makes reverse mortgages in north Florida. My daddy could deal directly with them."

Rogers taps the balls of his fingers on a coffee-colored desk blotter, cleared of paperwork except for a note or two slipped beneath the brown leather border. His eyes fix on her—her hair, her eyes, her generous lips, the smoothness of her neck, her cleavage. It appears as if he might tap the computer keyboard and retrieve some information for her. Instead he says, "you'd get the same information if you researched it on the internet."

"You don't have a lender you can recommend? Surely you work with lenders who make loans in both Georgia and Florida. I'd hate to start from scratch. My daddy is wary of banks."

"I'm sorry Miss Anderson. This can be a complicated process. You should find someone local in Florida to assist your father."

Natalie looks down, studying her pedicure, ready to play the next card. "Well, you see, he's looking to borrow two or three hundred thousand dollars. He's burned some bridges in Florida with the banks." She dangles this as bait to a man she presumes works on commission. Her father's financial situation shouldn't dissuade Rogers because, if she and Hitch are right, the lenders he represents want the land and not re-payment.

Rogers flicks his eyes toward the ceiling. He could be making a quick calculation of the commission he might receive on a loan of that size. Natalie guesses he gets one percent. It's a number she knows some loan originators receive from traditional lenders.

The silence makes her uncomfortable. "A couple of weeks ago he went to a tent revival in Folkston, and he was talking to a couple of farmers about needing to borrow some money to get him through the next couple of years until his timber matures, and they mentioned your name as someone who could help." She puts on her best smile.

In reciprocation, Rogers adopts the funeral director's countenance. All sympathy and respect. But his refusal to cooperate remains steadfast. "I'm sorry, but I can't help you with this particular mortgage."

"Are there different types of reverse mortgages?" She's desperate to keep him talking. She needs to get something from this meeting. "From what I can tell, you don't have to pay back the mortgage until the borrower dies. Is that right?"

"That's the gist of it."

"For all types."

He shrugs. "We only make one kind."

He's proving deft at dodging her inquiries. She has little ammunition left. She decides to use her last bullet. "You notarized a reverse mortgage for Hale Hitchcock in Pineland, April 11 of this year. Did you do that here at your office, or at his farm?" She already knows the answer. She wants to see if Rogers will lie to her.

A scowl emerges on Rogers' face. Rather than answer her, he stands up from his desk. "Miss Anderson, I have another meeting."

"You don't have a mortgage broker's license."

"Please leave. Now." His tone is commanding.

"And you didn't include Mrs. Hitchcock on the loan, even though you promised her husband she could stay in the house until she dies. You showed him a federal law that doesn't even apply. You lied to him." Her voice has risen beyond accusatory, her cadence matching Hitch's when he has a witness cornered.

Rogers picks up his desk phone. "I'm calling the police."

"At least give me a phone number so we can call the lender and get a payoff."

Rogers dials 911.

"You may not want to talk to me, but you're going to have to testify in the lawsuit that's coming." Natalie leaps from the chair and hustles out of his office and through the reception area, down three wooden steps of the office to her Mustang. She slides inside and, with a shaking hand, manages to slip the key in the ignition. She pulls from the parking lot, her tires spitting gravel.

"I blew it, Hitch. I really screwed up."

They are sitting in cane rockers on the screened porch, watching the sun go down. The orange glow appears to set the horizon on fire. Natalie coddles a glass of wine in both hands.

"I'm sure it wasn't that bad. Tell me what happened." Hitch is nursing a half-full bottle of lager.

"Trust me, it was that bad. I went in with the cover story about helping my father get a reverse mortgage. Rogers totally stonewalled me. He saw me coming."

"What did he say?"

"Said Florida isn't his territory."

"Maybe it isn't."

"Hitch, why is there a territory for an unlicensed mortgage broker? He gets paid on commission. Why reject out-of-hand a prospect that might net you thousands of dollars in commissions?"

"I don't know. Why broker mortgages at all if you don't have a license?"

"I was off my game. I couldn't pry anything out of him. I tried to get him talking, to tell me something generic about reverse mortgages even."

"And he didn't bite?"

"Not a nibble. And I just kind of lost it."

"Lost it?"

"I got desperate. I told him we know he lied to your dad to get him to sign the mortgage."

Hitch takes a swallow of lukewarm beer. "That's not like you, Nat."

"I was distracted," she says.

"Mark?"

"Yes, Mark. I can't fight two battles at once." One side of her face is aglow in the waning light, the other in shadow, the epitome of conflict.

"I heard your conversation with Mark, Nat. It's an awful lot to handle. If you want to bow out of this lawsuit and focus on Mark, I wouldn't blame you."

She glares at him with eyes like burning coals. "Bow out? Just when we're getting started? Don't you need me on this litigation?"

"I do. I just don't want you to get overwhelmed."

She pauses, looking through the porch screen at something in the distance. "I'll deal with Mark tonight. Then I can focus everything on the lawsuit." She takes a long swallow of wine. "Anyway, on the reverse mortgage, I didn't get a thing. I point-blank accused him of lying to your father about your mother being able to stay in the house. That's when he threw me out of his office. I'm sorry. Back to square one."

"You gave it a shot. After we file suit, we'll put him under oath and depose him. He won't be able to dodge us then." He takes a swig of beer, draining the bottle. He wants another beer, but this is the last of the 12-pack. "You want more wine?"

"Yes, please. Bring the bottle."

He brings the half-empty bottle and another full one. He matches Natalie glass for glass. The stuff is too sweet for him, and he reminds himself to get another 12-pack of lager tomorrow. They rock for a few minutes as the sun descends to the tree line.

"So, I'm wondering how many of these reverse mortgages Mr. Garland T. Rogers has sold outside of Dare County," Hitch says. "Hard to believe he's not doing the same thing in other counties."

"Only way to know is to finish our research," Natalie says. "I'm presuming the mortgage records for the other counties aren't on-line?"

Hitch shakes his head. "Nope."

"And even if they were, there's always a short lag between execution of the document and indexing, so we could be missing the most recent mortgage filings. How many counties are we talking about?"

"Hard to say. The only way to know is to start looking. Ten or twelve, I would guess."

"Ugh," Natalie says. "That's a dozen courthouses, then."

Hitch nods. "I can't think of another way."

Natalie looks past the porch screen into the dying rays of the sun. "All right. While you're drafting the complaint tomorrow, I'll get started on the research in the other counties."

20

The scream seems to come from a dream. Hitch awakens in a murk, unsure where he is. When he hears it again, piercing the air like a bobcat caught in a trap, he runs down the stairs, flings open the screen door. Barefoot and panting, he steps down into the yard, swiveling his head, searching for clues.

Natalie is collapsed against the trunk of an oak, her hand flat against her throat. He looks to her for explanation, but all she can do is point at her Mustang. He wanders over, bends down, and peers through the side window. On the passenger seat, almost merged into the black leather, is a coiled water moccasin. The snake's jaws are agape, flashing the mouth of white cotton, two long fangs poised to strike.

"Are you hurt?" he asks.

Natalie has straightened. She shakes her head, barely able to make her voice work. "No. I was half-way in the car, setting my briefcase on the passenger seat, when I saw the snake. It struck at me."

Hitch picks up the leather case lying in the dirt beside the rear wheel of the car and examines it. On one side are two puncture marks, smeared with a clear liquid he assumes is venom. The briefcase saved Natalie from a vicious bite.

He looks back at the snake, its mouth now closed, but eyeing him through the window glass. "This is a water moccasin. It didn't just wander into your car. Somebody put it there." He searches the car's nylon top for tears or cuts, but finds none. "Was your car locked last night?"

Natalie leaves the safety of the tree trunk and steps warily toward the spot of her encounter. "I don't remember. I may not have locked it last night, but I think I did."

"You have a car alarm, right?"

"Yes."

"Is there a spare key?"

She unfolds her arms and points toward the rear bumper. "Under there, in a magnetic box."

There is not even a breath of wind, everything still. Hitch drops to his belly and scans the ground beneath the car, then the undercarriage, to make sure there are no other vipers lurking there. He finds the key box, detaches it, slides the lid open. It is empty. He then realizes that if the perpetrator was not wearing gloves, he's just compromised fingerprint evidence.

Wriggling out from beneath the car with the empty box, he announces the key is gone. "Who knew about the hidden key?"

"Anybody who's ever hidden a key on their car," she says, her tone bolder now. She's trying to ignore the fact that someone just tried to attack her with a venomous snake.

"What are you doing up at dawn?"

"I was going to drive over to the next county to start that research we talked about."

Hale Hitchcock strides up, the shotgun from his pickup dangling from his right hand. "I heard screaming. Everybody all right?"

"Someone put a water moc in Natalie's car," Hitch says.

His father peers into the car window with raised eyebrows. "We should call the sheriff."

In another hour, a deputy comes out in a patrol car, settling a brown campaign hat on his head. He is young, with bushy eyebrows and a firm jaw. He talks to Natalie first, making notes on a tablet computer. He takes a few pictures of her car from different angles, including the license plate. When he has finished her statement he peers through the windows of the Mustang. The snake is not visible. "How big was it?"

Natalie's arms are folded across her torso. She shrugs. "Big."

Hitch, who has changed clothes while waiting for the deputy, peers into the car. "Hard to say with it coiled, but I'd guess maybe three feet long, as big around as my forearm. It's still in there, somewhere," he says, scanning the seats and the floorboards.

The deputy opens the driver's door, keeping the door between himself and its dangerous occupant. He does the same with the passenger door.

They retreat to the shade of the live oak fifteen feet away. Bridget brings sweating glasses of lemonade on a bamboo tray.

"That cottonmouth didn't just wander into her car," Hitch says.

The deputy takes a long pull of lemonade. "Sometimes they do. Snakes can come in through air vents, or through small holes in the floor."

The deputy bears the tone of the non-believer, offering an explanation that does not involve additional police work or investigation on his part.

Hitch slips into attorney mode. "Then why is the spare key missing?"

The deputy wrinkles his mouth, as if it is not his job to consider all the evidence. "Maybe the key's been gone for a long time, misplaced. Or maybe the car wasn't locked. She said she couldn't remember if she locked it last night. Most people around here don't."

If he's considering the prospect that the car was unlocked, he's also considering the possibility that someone put the snake in her car.

But Hitch doesn't point that out to him. The snake slithers out from under the front seat, its diamond-shaped head dipping below the bottom of the chassis, forked tongue darting and flicking. They all watch as it drops to the ground and begin its serpentine journey across the sand and onto the grass.

"That snake's not evidence, is it?" Hale asks the deputy.

The deputy snaps several pictures of the snake on his tablet. "No, sir."

Hale follows the snake to the edge of the woods, until they can barely see his denim-clad back in the shadows. They hear two shots and see puffs of smoke from the barrel of the shotgun.

Hale comes back with the barrel pointed down and stops in front of Natalie.

"Those mocs are mean. They will sometimes chase you, or chase animals. We can't run the risk it will get in the chicken coop or come after Jasper or a calf. I don't mean to offend you." He waits a beat for a question or comment. Receiving neither, Hale walks back toward the barn.

Natalie watches him with her mouth open. "Offend me?"

"Because you're a vegetarian," Hitch says. "I guess he thinks you're opposed to the killing of animals across the board."

Her lips form a frown, dimple her chin. "My aversion to killing animals for meat does not extend to snakes. And I'm a pescatarian, not a vegetarian."

Hitch smiles, then turns to the deputy. "Are you going to dust the car for prints?"

The deputy looks down at his black boots and their dull shine, rearranges some soil with a toe. "No need for that. I'm not seeing a crime here."

"Communicating a threat," Hitch responds.

The deputy wrinkles his mouth again, unconvinced. He looks up at the house, at the security lights at the eave corners. "Y'all don't happen to have any security cameras, do you?"

Hitch shakes his head. "Didn't think we needed them."

The deputy adjusts his hat and starts back to his cruiser. "I'll talk to the Sheriff about this, and let you know if anything develops. Y'all be careful now." His tires throw sand on his way out.

After confirming Natalie has mostly recovered, Hitch asks the question he didn't want to ask in front of the deputy. "Do you think Mark did this?"

She nods. Tears well in her eyes. "I broke it off with him last night. It wasn't pretty. He said he was coming down here."

"How would he even know you were here?"

"He figured it out. If I didn't go to my parents' house, where else would I go? He's a PI. He knows how to find people."

Hitch offers to drive her to the courthouse one county over, where she was headed before the snake interrupted her journey. "I can understand if you don't want to get back in your car, right now."

"Would you mind checking it out, to make sure there's not another one in there, or it didn't have babies in my car or something?"

He hasn't thought of either of those possibilities. From the farm truck's toolbox he retrieves a long flashlight and an old broom handle with a spike in the end of it. He searches beneath the bucket seats, pulls the floor mats, scans the wires and crevices beneath the dash. As he does so, he is mindful that moccasins sometimes drop from overhead. It has happened to him more than once while fishing in the Swamp. He opens the glove box, stepping back as he lets the lid drop, waiting for a hiss or a hint of coiled movement. His skin has begun to crawl, envisioning a snake suddenly writhing out from some hidden place. He rubs his arms and searches the car again, every cubby hole inside. He checks the trunk and the well where the spare tire is stored. He even lifts the hood and inspects the engine compartment. Nothing.

"Good to go," he says. He feels less confident than his tone indicates. "I can still give you a lift if you want."

Natalie scans the length of her car. "Yeah, that would be great."

21

The next morning, Hitch rises before the rooster crows, clear-headed, looking forward to the day. With he and Natalie working long hours on the lawsuit, his dad has minimized farm-work demands. He finds Natalie in the kitchen, having coffee with his father. The first rays of sun filter through the morning fog, casting a rose-colored light. Hitch pours from the percolator on the stove while they eye him over steaming cups.

"What's up?" Hitch says after taking the first sip.

"We were just going over the draft complaint," Natalie says.

"I was going to proof it this morning, punch it up a little bit," Hitch says.

"That's what we've been doing," Natalie says.

Hitch looks at the pages stacked in front of Natalie. He notices a few red-lines on the first page.

"What did you find?" he asks.

"It's stale," Hale says first.

Natalie nods. "It's a little stale. We're punching it up. Giving it more life. Adding some description of the farm, how much it means to your parents. It's not just their land; it's their home."

"I was going to add that."

"We know you were," Natalie says. "You're out of practice, that's all. It's been six months since you drafted anything legal."

Hitch nods. "Yeah. I see all the evidence lined up, the elements of the claims. I'm just …"

"You might be too close to it," Natalie says.

"Maybe so."

"Don't worry about it. You're just getting cranked back up. We're in the transition phase. I was thinking, maybe, a little lifestyle adjustment might be good, too."

"Lifestyle adjustment?"

"I'm not trying to be critical."

"That's like saying 'no offense' before you say something offensive."

"You've put on some weight," Hale announces. "Your mother's good cooking has something to do with it, I'm sure. But once you return to office work, those pounds won't come off easily."

"It certainly could be that good southern food your mom cooks," Natalie adds. "So, I thought we could go for a run this morning."

"A run? I don't have any running shoes," he says.

"You do, actually," Natalie says. "Your mom found an old pair in the attic. Be ready in ten minutes?"

He gives her an annoyed look and, when she leaves the kitchen, utters a dramatic sigh. Though he doesn't appreciate her criticism, she's stayed on the polite side. And she's right. His skills have suffered in his six-month absence from the practice. He probably has put on some pounds since he came to Pineland.

He locks eyes with his dad for a moment. "You think I've put on weight since I got down here?"

"Don't blame me for being observant."

They meet under the spreading arms of the live oak in the side yard, dew dripping from its leaves. The fog is beginning to lift. Hitch can almost see to the end of the drive, where it crosses the abandoned railroad track. He pulls his right foot up and behind him in a semblance of a quad stretch, something he might have last performed a decade ago. His muscles are as tight as guitar strings. He repeats the effort with the other leg, holding the stretch just long enough to feel his knee pop. He slowly rotates his neck clockwise, then counter-clockwise, remembering this from football drills, though he can't fathom how it might help him this morning. He is built like a fullback, but has taken up jogging a few times in his life to keep the weight off, back when that seemed to matter. When he places his hands above his hip bones in preparation for a side stretch, he realizes they are right. He has put on a few pounds.

In contrast, Natalie has no fat on her. Not that he can see, anyway. She is wearing red spandex shorts, which fit snug and cling to her thighs. She stretches all five feet eight inches of herself, from shoulder to ankle, bending forward and putting her palms flat on the ground.

"You probably shouldn't wear those shorts. Not out here," he says.

She straightens up and looks behind her to see if something is showing, then eyes him. "You'll get over it." She measures him in his cotton shorts that hang almost to his knees, with a grey shirt that looks like it might have once been white, socks that come to mid-calf. "You might find *actual* running shorts more comfortable in the future. Let's start with three miles.

You game?"

"If I make it to the end of the driveway I'll be surprised," he says.

"What's that, a quarter mile?" An astonished look covers her face.

"About that."

"Come on, we'll go slow."

She pushes a button on her running watch and starts down the driveway, her long legs loping. She is probably 60 percent legs and covers ground with a glide he will never possess. Next to her, he plods along, each footfall awakening something unpleasant in his muscles, tendons and ligaments. His bones and muscles seem to realign themselves with each step. When he makes it to the end of the driveway, his breath is raspy. His heart pounds in his chest. He tries to remember when he last ran even a quarter mile and guesses it was on a treadmill at the gym in Savannah. His old gym, where he let his membership lapse at least five years back. They turn east onto the blacktop known as Pond Road. Natalie runs on the white line, her footfalls soft and straight. He tries to keep up, just off her right shoulder, two feet into the traffic lane.

"This is … too slow … for you," he says, each pause necessary to take a breath. He read somewhere that the appropriate pace for long, slow distance is a speed where you can comfortably carry on a conversation. It appears two words is the limit of his conversation before he needs more air.

She glances at her watch. "We're doing about nine-minutes per mile. Okay for a warmup."

"How fast …do you … usually … run?"

"Between seven and eight minutes per mile for long runs."

"How about … races?" He asks this so he can distract himself from the stitch developing in his right side.

"You're struggling. Let's walk," she says. She checks her watch. "We jogged almost a half-mile. Now we'll walk a quarter. Run/walk is where you should be right now, anyway."

He has his fists on his hips, feeling the ache of every muscle in his legs. His chest heaves. There is a tightness and throb in his left lung. Jesus, how did he let himself get so out of shape? He bends over.

"Don't bend over," she says. "Standing tall helps you breathe."

He straightens and nods, and in a dozen steps or so he feels better. "This isn't really a workout for you, is it?"

"It's fine. I can run tomorrow. This is just your first day in the program."

He gives her a sideways glance.

"What?" she says.

"The program is what they call AA."

'Oh, well, I didn't mean anything by it. Exercise program. That better?"

A pickup rattles down the road in their direction, and they sidle onto the grass shoulder to let it pass. The farmer veers to the middle of the road, waving his fingers without taking his hand from the wheel.

"How good were you?" he asks. "At running?"

"A-plus level in the 1,500. A-minus in the 800."

"You almost made the Olympics, didn't you?"

She lets out a snort, kicks at a yellow dandelion poking through the macadam. "I qualified for the US Olympic trials in the 1,500 two years after college, but couldn't compete because of a calf injury."

"Would you have made it, you think?"

She looks off in the distance, maybe envisioning a finish-line where she will break the tape, the same way he used to picture a goal line as he sprinted for the end zone.

"You know it." She laughs it off, a disappointment not that easy to shed. "Come on. Enough talk of the past. The future is right in front of us."

She pushes a watch button and starts to jog. He trudges along beside her. She leans in with her right shoulder and gives him a playful nudge. "Tactics," she says. "Got to handle the jostle." She pulls ahead, then turns and jogs backward, facing him now. "Good for the calves," she says with a twiddle of her fingers.

This is pure joy for her. He can see it in her turquoise eyes, emitting sparkles of light like laughter. He feels better, or perhaps he is simply ignoring the discomfort, absorbing by osmosis some of her ebullience.

"I'm going to do a quarter-mile pickup," she says. "You just keep jogging, or walk if you need to. I'll see you down the road."

She slips in ear buds, taps an icon on the phone holstered to her right bicep. Then she takes off, extending her bronzed legs, as natural as a gazelle bounding across savannah. Seeing her run stirs something in him. In the moment, Hitch appreciates her happiness, its contagious effect on him. He doesn't try to keep up with her. He understands his limitations, stays at a jog, his eyes on her back as her image blurs into the heat waves rising from the pavement.

Natalie stops, maybe two hundred yards out, and begins to run back to him in the same fluid motion. Behind her, a logging truck appears as if from a magician's flash powder. The cab is fire engine red, pine logs loaded to the top of the stakes. Forty tons barreling down the highway, chewing up the distance. With her music playing, Natalie doesn't hear the truck.

He begins to run faster, waving his arms, trying to direct her to the shoulder the way an airport flagger waves a jet to the gate. But she isn't looking at him. Her eyes are fixed on the road a few strides in front of her.

He stops, cups his hands and yells at her as the logging truck churns toward them, hugging the white sideline. At twenty yards out she sees him waving his arms, pointing. She turns, sees the truck barreling down on her, and dives for the ditch. He does the same. The truck wooshes by. The backdraft tousles the bushes and the low boughs of the border pines.

Hitch helps her up from the weeds and roadside detritus. She is shaking, bits of grass stuck to her clothes. In her hair. He plucks broken twigs from her clothes, and before he is done she wraps her arms around him and lays her head against his shoulder. They stand in embrace on the side of the road for half a minute, maybe more, the road barren and silent, looking for comfort in the wake of a close call. She steps back and uses the heels of her hands to rub at her eyes, then looks at him in a strange, shock-incited amalgam of fear, sadness and anger, all rolled into one face.

"Hitch, that guy tried to kill me."

"Probably on his cell phone."

"Not buying it. The snake was attempt number one. That was number two."

He thinks about it, his mind landing on the conclusion these two back-to-back incidents are not mere coincidence. "I couldn't make out the license plate," he says.

"Me either, but it looked like a Florida plate, green lettering with a big orange in the middle. Red cab."

"Standard logging truck," he says.

"It's got to be Mark. He was so angry when I broke it off. More than angry. Livid."

"You think Mark would try to kill you?"

"I don't know, Hitch. I just don't know."

Hitch wonders. The snake could have been Mark's threat. But loaded logging trucks routinely hug the white line.

They survey the road in both directions, then cross the pebbly blacktop so they are facing the oncoming traffic, which is picking up as it nears the school hour. They jog and walk along the two-lane, their blood surging with adrenaline, then sprint down the driveway to the farmhouse.

He hops up the stairs and grabs his keys and cell phone, and a pair of binoculars from a shelf in Rip's room. From the bottom drawer of his nightstand, he removes Rip's .357. In Hitch's SUV, they retrace their steps on the highway, narrowing their eyes when they reach the place where they'd been forced into the ditch. There are no skid marks, no signs the truck tried to avoid them. There are no dimples in the grass, no indicia that this is the spot where they'd flung themselves from the path of the truck bearing down on them. Hitch keeps driving.

"Look for a logging site," he says. "An active one."

In about two miles they come to a rutted path pocked with puddles, leading into a blackened field dotted with debris piles. He keeps driving until he finds a safe place to turn around. They pass the site from the opposite direction, seeing billows of smoke from the harvester and skidder working back in the trees. He finds a sandy track that allows him to pull the SUV a few yards off the highway. He parks at the edge of the pine forest. They are not dressed for reconnaissance. Certainly not Natalie, with a blaze of red short across her hips. There isn't time to change clothes. Not now. Hitch slips the gun from the holster.

Natalie eyes the gun but doesn't comment, acknowledging things have gotten serious. She doesn't disagree that the only way to counter these attacks is with firepower.

They begin traipsing through the rows of pines, the trunks evenly spaced six feet apart, shooting true to the sky.

"Watch your step," he says. She has been strangely silent, perhaps still in emotional shock. He looks behind him. She is high-stepping over the sandy terrain and blackened undergrowth. Her arms are folded over her torso, her eyes glued to the ground. He has a pair of snake boots back at the farm, but feels an urgency to reach the field and see if there are logging trucks being loaded before the evidence evaporates. He stops for a second, touches her elbow.

"Are you all right?"

Her lips are in pout, her jaw clenched. "I'm fine. Just wondering how I got myself so deep into a relationship with a sonofabitch who is so threatened by rejection that he's trying to kill me. That's the man who says he loves me?"

Hitch has learned through countless encounters with parties in the throes of legal struggles, some of them his own clients, that seemingly rational people will do things that have no basis in reason, some other force taking them over, temporarily or for the long term. In those circumstances, it's beyond frustrating trying to determine motive. It is an impossible task. People who do things that seem to spring from the loins of pure evil are not wired like the rest of us. Just read the newspaper or watch the news. Almost daily reports of senseless sprees of violence, spurred by a rabid notion or substance abuse, that leave you agape at the pure asininity of the act. Case in point: George Colbert.

He wonders if Mark Sanchez is of the same ilk?

Hitch places his left palm on Natalie's elbow and ushers her forward through the rows of pines, stepping with care across the black remnants of fires set to burn off undergrowth. The binoculars swing from his neck. When the growl of timber machinery reaches a certain level and he can see the movement of equipment through the gaps in the trees, he stops and drops to one knee, pulling the binoculars to his eyes. He sees a green grapple-skidder with an articulating arm grabbing and cutting live pines, stripping the limbs, and laying them on the ground. A loader picks them up and carries them to a logging truck, stacking them in neat rows between the stakes. This truck has a red cab, too. From this distance, he can't make out a license plate or the company name scribed on the door in faded and scratched letters.

They re-trace their steps back to his car. His eyes remain on the charred ground. He's not worried about blackening his shoes. He's worried about rattlers, whose patterns make them almost impossible to see among the litter of branches and pine straw. A surprised snake is a dangerous one. He begins to stomp the ground with each step to warn any snake of their presence.

He ponders the best way to solve this, to identify the trucking company and trace it back. He is not a trained investigator and usually hires a retired FBI agent to investigate this type of situation. But there is no time. He possesses a large measure of curiosity, which often serves him well when he is interrogating a witness under oath, but that is in a controlled environment, every word recorded by a stenographer, every grimace and eye twitch of the witness captured on video. This is a different situation. Curiosity killed the cat. He looked it up once, this saying, and that is the part people recite. The full proverb is: Curiosity killed the cat; satisfaction brought it back. He is determined to find satisfactory answers for Natalie.

They climb back into his SUV. As Natalie pulls the seatbelt across she is still unsettled, a brooding look emanating from her eyes, the sparkles of light no longer there. They return to the farm and park on the driveway, about twenty yards back from and facing the highway, straddling the abandoned railroad track. From this vantage point they have an unobstructed view for about 300 yards in both directions. He stashes the handgun under the front seat.

Hitch calls his parents' land-line. His mother answers. He explains to her where they are, providing scant details about their mission. Within minutes she arrives in her dilapidated van, one wheel grinding from shredded bearings. He notes the windshield has a star-shaped crack on the passenger side. With some difficulty she climbs out, favoring her sore hip, and appears at the driver's window of the SUV with a soft-sided cooler. Hitch gets out and opens the door for her, and his mother slides into the backseat of his SUV.

She presents them each with a sandwich in a lidded plastic container. "Tomato and cucumber sandwiches. You didn't have breakfast," she explains. She hands them each a napkin, offers them each a sports drink.

Hitch settles the plastic bottles in the cup holders in the console.

"What are y'all doing out here?"

It is a fair question; his answer isn't. He doesn't want to rattle his mother. "Waiting for somebody," he says. His tone borders on rude, and he tries to correct it. "We're just keeping an eye out for someone. I'll tell you and dad all the details when we find out more information."

Bridget meets her son's eyes in the rearview mirror, holds his gaze, then she pulls the handle on the rear passenger door. "Be careful," she says as she pushes the door closed.

In the side mirror, he watches her go back to her van, swinging her leg like it is filled with concrete, leaning hard to the left to maintain her balance. He steps out of his car as she pulls open the door of her van. "Mom. Thanks for this," he says, holding up the sandwich. "I'll fill you and dad in later today. Promise." He means it, but he also needs time to formulate an explanation, if it's even his situation to address. He realizes he has taken the lead, and is not just assisting Natalie. He wonders if he's overstepped.

Back in the car, he munches his sandwich, leaving a smear of mayonnaise on his bottom lip. "Nat, I didn't ask, but I'm assuming you want my help with this. You know, to help figure out what the hell Mark is doing."

"Of course." She stares through the windshield, lost in thought.

It is an hour before they see the logging truck emerging from shimmering waves of heat. Red cab, loaded to the gills with pine logs. It has dual chrome air horns on top of the cab. Maybe the same truck that ran them off the road. Hard to tell. The front license plate is spattered with mud. Even through the binoculars, he can see only two letters and one number.

"VJ something, and a 7," he calls out as it barrels past. "Florida plate. I think it had Shoe Lumber Company painted on the door."

Natalie types the information into her phone.

"Could you see the driver at all?" he asks.

"Too much glare from the sun as he approached.," Natalie says. "But I saw his profile through the side window when he passed. White guy, close-cut beard, average nose, sunglasses, ball cap. Not Mark."

"Describes about every truck driver I've ever seen."

"Maybe he paid somebody to do it?"

"To run you over?

"Maybe. Mark thinks I left him for you."

"Nat, I . . ."

"Get over yourself, suspended lawyer. It's not true."

He peers through the windshield at a forest of loblolly pines, the boughs furry with green needles. Something niggles him. He lays his forehead against the warm steering wheel. Then it hits him with the force of a dragonfly bouncing off the windshield at 60 miles per hour. "How would Mark know we were jogging down this road?"

"I've been thinking about that. At first I thought maybe he put a tracker on my car, but that wouldn't have told him I was jogging on the highway. He has to be tracking my cell phone."

"How?"

She holds her phone in her palms, flips it over as if this will reveal something. She scrolls through her apps but doesn't see anything amiss. "There's nothing here," she says.

"What about your running watch?"

She stares at the digital watch on her left wrist, black face with a black band, then places her hand on the dash so the watch is fully illuminated in the sunlight. "He gave me this for Christmas. Last year. Could he hack into the GPS on my watch? Is that even possible?"

Hitch can't completely dismiss the notion, but it sounds too advanced for a guy who dropped a snake in her car and tried to run her down with a logging truck. He is thinking old school—camouflage hunting clothes, camo paint on the face, binoculars, a deer rifle, walkie-talkie, a hiding place in the woods. There are dozens of places on the farm where someone could hide and watch their movements without being detected. But would Mark have had enough time to run ahead, crank up a logging truck, and come after them? Or call someone else to do it?

He puts the car in gear and heads up Pond Road toward the logging operation, scanning the horizon for something he might have forgotten since he was a kid traversing this stretch at least twice a day on his way to and from school. The land is flat, with small rises out of creek bottoms, the road bordered by endless pines and the occasional house or trailer set back off the road. He stops at US 1, which will either take them into town or to the Swamp. He scans 180 degrees of horizon with the naked eye, and there, in a haze of humidity, is a fire tower. He points to it through the windshield.

"Maybe that's the surveillance point," he says.

"A fire tower? How far are we from your house?"

"Three or four miles. I can clock it on the way back."

"And you think someone could see us running down the highway from there?"

"Not sure, but they can definitely see our farm from there. It's a big, open space."

She bobs her head, maybe coming around to the point. "He wouldn't climb a fire tower," she says. Then she looks down at her watch, remembering how Mark would remind her to put it on before she left for work in the mornings. She unbuckles the band from her wrist. She lowers the passenger window and flings her watch into the watery ditch.

22

Natalie is trying to come out of it, doing everything she can to fend off the fear. She's acting brave, but she can't hide the alarm wedged onto her face. She might be in shock. Something evil has oozed up from the sand, crawled out of the dark waters of the swamp, and infected her like a malicious virus.

"You good?" Hitch asks.

She shifts on the SUV's seat. Her hands tremble in her lap.

"Maybe we need to confront Mark face-to-face," he says He pats the holster on his right hip, the .357 Smith & Wesson snug in the clasp.

"No," she screams, as though the mention of his name brings him physically closer. "I don't want to be anywhere near him."

"Okay. But we need to figure this out. If Mark is behind this, we need to know."

When they return to the farmhouse, Hitch gathers with his parents and Natalie in the kitchen. His parents sit with anxious faces.

"Where to begin," Hitch says. His hands are clasped in front of him on the table. "You know about the snake in Natalie's car," he starts. "I'm convinced it wasn't an accident. Someone put it there. This morning, while Natalie and I were out jogging on the highway, a logging truck tried to run her down."

His mother's hand goes to her mouth.

His father shifts his haunches in the chair.

"It might have been my ex," Natalie interjects.

"That's a long story," Hitch explains. He's used to telling long stories, stories that bring life to tragedies that have befallen his clients. Narratives that highlight cause and effect and liability in sweeping arcs, seizing the attention of juries with images and sounds and sensations he ignites. But he has no patience for it now, so he gives them a truncated version.

"Her ex might be retaliating against her for breaking up with him. And maybe he's turned against me because he thinks I'm responsible."

"And you think he put the snake in Natalie's car and tried to run you both over?" Bridget asks.

"That doesn't make any sense," Hale says.

"None of it makes much sense," Hitch agrees.

"If it's Natalie's ex—what's his name?" Hale asks.

"Mark Sanchez," Natalie answers.

"If it's this Mark, what's he trying to accomplish?" Hale asks.

"Maybe the same thing as George Colbert," Hitch answers.

"Okay. I'll give you that. Maybe the guy has lost it and wants revenge against Natalie. But what do you have to do with it? You're not together, are you?"

Hitch and Natalie exchange a look. "No," Hitch says. "I mean, we work together, and Mark knows that," Hitch says. "But we're not in a relationship."

"No," Natalie says. "But maybe Mark thinks we are."

Hitch's eyes settle on the table. He can see how Mark might arrive at that conclusion. When Natalie fled their apartment, she lied about where she was going and wound up at the farmhouse, where her boss is living while he serves out his suspension. And he has no idea what else Mark could have misinterpreted.

"What if these attacks are related to the lawsuit you're going to file?" Hale asks. "Natalie interviews the mortgage broker, this Rogers guy, and the next day she finds a water moccasin in her front seat. This morning a logging truck tries to run you down. Maybe it's retaliation."

"Nobody knows about the lawsuit, dad, except for us and Tobias."

"I might have let that slip to Rogers," Natalie says. "Told him we were going to depose him. When he was ordering me out of his office. I panicked. I'm sorry."

"Well, that puts a new spin on things," Hitch says. He stares at Natalie for a few seconds. "Look, I know you're stressed about splitting with Mark. Is there anything else you forgot to tell me about your meeting with Rogers?"

Her arms crossed, she scrapes her shoe across the linoleum in the kitchen. "No, that's it. Maybe it isn't Mark. I'd like to think he's not that evil."

"It's not Natalie's fault," Hale says. The whole town knows you're going to file a lawsuit. You can't interview dozens of people and think it's not going to get out."

Hitch ponders this. His dad is probably right. The coming lawsuit is not a secret. His thoughts are spinning too fast to seize any of them. The thrum of his nerves, that unmistakable dread, has returned.

"Well, whoever the hell it is, I'm putting up security cameras."

Hitch installs motion-activated security cameras at the four corners of the farmhouse and in the live oak beside the parking area. He adds magnetic alarms on the three doors but doesn't install alarms on the windows, or motion detectors inside, because his dad won't allow it.

"This is my house," Hale declares, "and I won't have it turned into a prison. If he gets inside, he's going to get a chest full of lead. Lead shot is better than any camera."

For the briefest flicker, Hitch returns to the conference room in his law office. George Colbert stands in the doorway with a pistol dangling from his hand, a wisp of smoke escaping the barrel. Sonia lies on the floor with two red blooms on her chest. Kneeling next to her, he's almost incapacitated by an internal ache that cannot be explained solely by the bullet in his shoulder.

"That's good, dad. Keep a loaded shotgun in the house and one in your pickup. I'm packing Rip's gun," he says, patting the gun on his hip.

To test the cameras, Natalie runs at top speed across various sections of the yard, both during daylight and as darkness falls. The cameras capture her as they might a bounding deer, some images clear and others a blur. This is their early-warning system.

Hale sets up a shooting range on the edge of the woods behind the barn. A couple of silhouette targets flanked by trees. He calibrates his trap thrower to hurl orange-centered clay targets at various speeds at a height approximating a man's chest. The targets come at him from all angles in a steady flight, miniature disks that do not feint or dodge. Hale knocks down two-thirds of the targets, but even when he misses the shot scatters broadly enough to hit something as large as a man.

Hitch takes a few turns at the clays with his shotgun. He is nowhere near the shot his father is, usually shooting behind or over the target as it hurtles through the air. He is better at hitting the metal silhouettes with the pistol at fifteen yards, but he has never had to shoot a man.

Hitch has thought about this often—whether he would have put a bullet in George Colbert if he'd been armed that morning in his conference room. It is one thing to shoot holes in a paper silhouette, and another to aim at a human being who stares at you with live eyes, or who shoots back. In hindsight, he is pretty sure he could have shot Colbert. But he doesn't know if he could have done it without hesitation. Without the deliberation that accompanies his every decision, the weighing of risks and benefits, the assessment of repercussions and consequences. Before he fired, would he have analyzed the Castle doctrine, and the Stand-Your-Ground Statute, all ingrained in him by those three years of law school? He realizes it might have taken him a second, maybe two, to convince himself he had the legal right to kill George Colbert. But bullets travel faster than that.

When the first coolness of fall descends upon the farm, Hale opens the windows and doors, allowing the breezes to enter, to soothe, because it is a man's right. He will not be cowed by an unseen predator. And the truth is the cameras capture nothing but the normal roaming of the animals who call this farm home.

Each morning, even before Hitch has eaten breakfast, he sits with Natalie, staring at the computer screen, viewing the catalogue of motion-activated video that watches the mostly undisturbed night. They see a fox and her kits, does and their fawns. A big buck stands warily at the edge of the woods, as if he knows the cameras are there. Coyotes trek across the yard, heads hanging low, sometimes in a small pack, but usually alone. A huge owl surveys the darkness, only caught on tape when it swoops toward its quarry.

One night Hitch and Natalie sit on the back porch, the unscreened wooden stoop that juts from the house like a graying tongue. He coddles a bottle of beer; Natalie holds the stem of a glass, from which she has taken two small sips. The somnolent and sultry days of summer are behind them. The mosquitos are gone, mostly. The gnats that bother the cows and hover and dart about humans have abated to a bearable nuisance. Here, below the gnat line, they are never completely gone.

Hitch, with the pistol still in the holster at his side, says, "I'm sorry."

Natalie tilts her face towards him. "Sorry for what?"

"That you have to live in fear. I should have protected you better."

She scoffs, a sign of her relaxed state more than of derision. "Not your job," she says.

"Then I'm sorry about what happened between you and Mark."

Natalie shrugs. "You have to let go, Hitch."

"Let go of what?"

"The guilt that you couldn't save Sonia. These attacks have probably reignited everything. It was barely over a year ago, you know."

He sighs and looks down at the peeling step upon which his boots rest, at the pale ground, murky in the twilight.

"You need to talk to somebody," Natalie offers.

"I'm all right," he says in response. He didn't realize the gloom was so obvious, didn't realize that it must stoop his shoulders or turn down the corners of his mouth, in a way that Natalie can see. Maybe his parents see it, too.

He doesn't want to talk about it. Because he can't. He can barely think about her, much less put words to what he felt on that awful morning, what he feels now when a stray word, or a waft of fragrance, causes him to turn. It will never go away. Sonia's death will haunt him forever.

23

Joe Park, whose real name is David Chan, has been summoned to a ranch in the rolling hills of southeast Texas. It is the hideout to which a handful of Chinese diplomats fled when the US President ordered the Chinese Consulate in Houston closed. The retreat is a sprawling horse ranch with a metal-roofed main house, multiple barns and outbuildings. The seven horses are for show. The subterranean shelter was built by an oil tycoon as a place to ride out tornados.

David Chan presses his forehead to the retina scanner. Invisible infrared beams map his right eye. He has been told this is the latest in secure technology. He has been assured entry cannot be faked. He descends concrete steps, noting the block walls and ceiling are lined with sheets of steel to deflect electronic monitoring. Copper mesh covers the air gaps in the steel door. An electronic signal blocker on a wooden table provides extra precaution against eavesdroppers. All electrical service in the shelter, including the naked light bulbs strung across the ceiling, are powered by a gas generator housed in a horse barn fifty yards away.

Chan's contact does not have a name, or at least not one Chan has ever been privy to. The slightly built man with black-rimmed glasses and a cherubic face introduces himself as Tonghzi, meaning comrade. They speak in Mandarin, the comrade's accent revealing his roots in Beijing. Chan's Mandarin, after a decades-long absence from China, is rusty at best.

They have been meeting here every few months for the past two years. Before that it was a safehouse in Maryland, which replaced an ancient hotel in West Virginia.

"Status report?" Tonghzi starts.

The meeting begins this way, without the customary pleasantries or hot tea. Chan senses the urgency in his comrade's voice.

"We now control 715,000 acres of farmland and timber," Chan responds. "Approximately 1,100 square miles." Chan has been buying American agricultural land since the 1990s. Through lawyers and holding companies, he has purchased a large cattle ranch in Texas, an Iowa farm growing corn, and 300 acres of arid farmland near an Air Force Base in North Dakota. Last year, he bought 4,800 acres of timber in Northern Maine.

Tongzhi nods.

In the beginning, the scheme to acquire vast swaths of American agricultural land was driven by China's need to feed its people and to import huge quantities of timber. A 1978 United States law requires that foreign ownership of American agricultural land must be registered with the USDA within 90 days of purchase. Until recently, all of Chan's properties were acquired in transparent transactions easily traced back to Chinese corporations. For decades, the Chinese corporations complied with the mandated reporting.

With the rise of American nationalism and pending legislation in multiple states to ban ownership of property by Chinese citizens and companies, that strategy changed. China still purchases some US land through Chinese corporations and registers those transactions. Yet this is only a feint to conceal the vast acreage being secretly acquired through legally chartered limited liability companies. Like the web of companies created by attorney Tinsley Stratton for his client, Joe Park.

"You have done a commendable job," Tongzhi says. "Your work has been recognized at the highest levels."

Tongzhi issues the compliment as though it is a gesture of goodwill. Chan knows otherwise. If his exploits are not successful, his parents will suffer. They live in an apartment tower in Beijing, controlled by the Chinese Communist Party. They are under constant surveillance, sometimes by camera, at other times by armed guards. His mother has multiple sclerosis and needs expensive medicine to survive. Her medication, and thus her lifeline, will be confiscated by the CCP if Chan fails in his mission. His father has advanced dementia and round-the-clock nurses, who can be withdrawn upon a whim. During his last phone call to his parents, undoubtedly monitored by the CCP, the desperation in his mother's voice was palpable. His father was unable to come to the phone. Though David Chan believes in what he is doing, his parents' well-being is extra motivation.

"I serve at the pleasure of the President," Chan replies, because it is the only acceptable response.

Tongzhi nods. "We must accelerate the acquisitions of land here." On a laminated map whose corners are tacked to a wooden table, Tongzhi's finger traverses a swath of land stretching southwest from South Carolina into Georgia and the northern counties of Florida.

"Yes, Tongzhi. As you know, I have been securing lands in those regions for the past three years," Chan says. "It is necessary to accelerate the acquisitions?"

"Yes."

"May I ask, what is my timetable?"

"As soon as possible."

"And may I ask, Tongzhi, what necessitates this urgency?"

It is a valid question, but Tongzhi glares at him as if Chan has just hurled a personal insult.

"I ask," Chan tries to explain, "because the legal process we must undertake takes time. We only have liens on these properties. Liens do not have to be registered with the United States government. But to actually take ownership of these lands, we must do so through American lawyers."

"And when we do take ownership, you assure us this will not be traceable back to the Middle Kingdom?"

Chan nods. "Of course. The companies that hold the liens are all American companies. My name appears nowhere. But we control the lands only as a creditor. Our rights are converted to ownership when the owners of the land die. Many of these owners may live for twenty or more years," Chan says.

Tongzhi studies the map. "Everyone dies, comrade. Sometimes prematurely. Heart attacks, automobile crashes. Anything can happen. To you, to me, to your parents. To perfect strangers."

Tongzhi issues orders in this cryptic way, his words chosen carefully, so that if secretly recorded he will have plausible deniability. Whatever Chan may do, Tongzhi has ordered him to do nothing concrete. Certainly nothing illegal. Certainly no actions that will bring scrutiny upon the CCP.

Chan understands exactly what Tongzhi is demanding. He knows that his parents' lives depend on his success.

"May I ask, Tongzhi—what is it that makes these particular lands so important?"

Tongzhi considers whether to answer his subordinate. Perhaps Chan has been in the United States too long, and the Americans' propensity for questioning their government has rubbed off on Chan. In China, Chan could be jailed for challenging his superior. But Tongzhi also recognizes that of the hundreds of CCP agents operating in America, Chan is one of the Party's most-valued assets. Chan's loyalty may be deepened if he divulges a critical piece of information.

"For your ears only," Tongzhi says, locking eyes with Chan. "These areas," he points, "are rich in rare earth elements."

It is only after Chan leaves the steel-encased bunker and stops at a motel two hundred miles to the east that he begins his research. Using a VPN to search, he discovers that rare earth elements, or REEs, are a collection of 17 elements with highly valued magnetic and conducting properties. He learns that veins of REE's can be found in the placer deposits in the southeastern United States, along a line approximating where the Atlantic Ocean reached into South Carolina, Georgia and Florida 100 million years ago.

He discovers REEs are critical components of electric car batteries, computers, cell phones, wind turbines, jet engines, flat-screen TVs, lasers, and superconductors. China already controls approximately 75% of the world's production of REEs. China has been mining its own deposits and mineral veins in Vietnam, Brazil and India for the past decade. It is plain to him now. With added stores of REEs from the United States, China can control the future of technology development across the globe. In an interconnected world, the controlling nation could engineer a computer chip shortage. Limit manufacture of cell phones. Curtail the supply of batteries for electric cars. Dominating the world's supply of REEs will give China substantial leverage in the battle for world economic supremacy.

Chan stubs out his cigarette in the almost-full ashtray and reminds himself to destroy the remnants so they can't be used to extract his DNA. In the motel bathroom, he transforms himself into a beachcomber, dressing in multi-pocketed shorts and a colorful shirt with a blue tuna on the front, a white cap with a skirt that covers the back of his neck and a long bill that, along with wrap-around black sunglasses, conceals most of his face. He rubs generous amounts of zinc oxide on his cheeks, nose and jaw, which makes him look something like a ghost. He dons canvas deck shoes and walks three blocks to the beach.

He steps onto the cool sand and unties his deck shoes. He places the lace aglets inside, then arranges the shoes with the toes facing the water and perfectly perpendicular to the water's edge. He takes a few steps into the saltwater, feeling the sand compress beneath his feet. He eases in until his feet are covered to the ankles. The water immediately chills him. He recalls Tonghzi's words and the unsubtle threat in his tone. He thinks then of his parents and their frailty, their complete reliance on the CCP for every scrap of food, every pill to treat their ailments. It is there, gazing at an oil platform on the distant horizon, that Chan finalizes the plan to meet his country's demands.

24

Just before noon on a Monday, the cadre of three marches up the courthouse steps. Hitch is in the middle, Natalie to his left, Tobias on his right. This is what Hitch has been missing on the farm. This surge he has felt over the past several weeks while he prepared the lawsuit. It's not the product of adrenaline; it's something else. The feeling that comes with probing a difficult dilemma for what feels like an eternity and finally seeing the glimmer of a solution. Passion, maybe. Certainly a thrusting determination. Pounding on the doors of the house of justice until somebody answers.

He still can't practice law, not for another four months, but he will be able to do everything else. He will plot strategy. He will write motions and draft briefs. He will propound discovery. Oh yes, he will demand documents and he will demand answers. He will interrogate through written questions. He will sit next to Tobias when they put whoever is in charge of these companies in the deposition spotlight and video his every twitch and grimace and dodge.

In this new role, Hitch will be able to resume living.

Now, as they stand in the office of the Clerk of Superior Court of Dare County, preparing to file the complaint naming his parents as representatives of the putative class, Hitch is more convinced this is the only solution. He wants to slay this dragon that lied to his father and nefariously snatched away his mother's ownership rights, and yet because the dragon has no name and no face, he has mentally pasted Alicia Vanderwelt's image onto the beast. She will be the one who represents the mortgage companies and lenders who are hiding behind the opaque mask of her law firm. To incite himself, he has chosen the mental picture of her glaring down at him from the hearing bench, judging him with disdain, preparing to take his law license forever.

They could have filed the case electronically, but Hitch prefers to do so in person, to hear the clunk of the time clock as it stamps the filing date and time on the first page of each document. This imprimatur makes it real, like the whack of the gavel announcing the battle has begun.

Tobias slides the original complaint and four copies beneath the clerk's window. Only his signature appears on the lawsuit.

Once the summons and complaint are served on the defendants, they will have thirty days to respond to the claims. Sixty days if the clerk grants an extension, which is common. But Hitch cannot allow unreasonable delays. There is too much at stake. He will hit Vanderwelt with written discovery next week. He plans to follow that salvo with a request for a scheduling conference and notices of deposition soon after. As they retreat down the steps of the courthouse with three copies of the class-action complaint in hand, Hitch rejoices. The battle has begun.

25

Alicia Vanderwelt reads the lawsuit for the second time, then tosses the folded pages of the class-action complaint onto her desk. She has already begun thinking of strategies. She arranges them in her mind as she jots notes on a yellow legal pad. She outlines interrogatories and requests for production, a list of deponents. Hale and Bridget Hitchcock are the nominal plaintiffs. But she knows who is really behind this lawsuit. She'll depose their son first, the suspended lawyer, and bury them all in paper because she can.

Though the legal issues presented by the complaint are relatively simple, she can drag out a class action for three years, at least. She prefers the tactic of delay—because it usually works. As months pass and the plaintiff's attorney spends time and expense on a case that is only inching toward settlement or trial, they usually begin to lose enthusiasm and zeal. The value of the case diminishes in their minds. Delay is often a sound strategy, whether the goal is a cheap settlement or a trial.

She doesn't know Tobias Thomas—the plaintiff's lawyer—so she looks him up. He has a website that gives her scant information. He doesn't have a profile on any of the usual services. His name doesn't appear in any recent newspaper articles or internet posts. She finds a small blurb about Thomas in the University of Georgia alumni database, but nothing significant.

Of course, she has an entire file on Hitchcock. She pulls up the file on her computer. It contains details of the ethics complaints against him and his responses, a transcript of the disciplinary hearing, her notes and observations from the one piece of litigation she's had with him, all of the pleadings and motions from his divorce case, and a fifteen-page summary from a private investigator who dug into Hitchcock's background and personal life, beginning when the lead smelter litigation was filed, and updated one week before the disciplinary hearing. Mark Sanchez wrote a detailed report. She's impressed with his thoroughness. She makes a note to call him so he can update his research.

She checks the date on Hitchcock's suspension order. His suspension will end in just less than four months. She ponders whether Tobias Thomas is even competent to handle a class action. She finds nothing on his website that indicates he handles complex litigation. If he's in over his head, he could be in violation of his own ethical responsibilities. And if that's the case—that Thomas is so inexperienced he's ethically precluded from pursuing this legal matter—she will drop a ton of iron on him.

She has never litigated in the county where the suit has been filed. In fact, the only time she's ever been there was to handle the foreclosure on Cordell Davidson's farm. She checks a website for the latest census data. Dare County has fewer than 25,000 residents. The county is rural, its economy dependent on timber, tourism, farming and small manufacturing. Undoubtedly wary of outsiders. There is one Superior Court Judge presiding there, and he rides the circuit to three other counties. When she reads the profile for Alston Bass Fisher, she chuckles at the name. He's been on the bench for twelve years, elected the last two terms without opposition. She doesn't know him, but she will after she has an associate research every ruling he's ever issued in any case involving banks or mortgages or mass actions.

She glances at the scrawl on the note stuck to the front page of the complaint. It was hand-delivered to her office thirty minutes ago in a red inter-office envelope by one of the firm's couriers.

Review and call me ASAFP - TS

She buzzes up to Tinsley Stratton's office. Even as a partner in the law firm, Vanderwelt has to check with one of Stratton's secretaries before taking the elevator to the top floor. While she waits, she folds the yellow note in half and tears it into tiny pieces, drops it into the gray shred can beside her desk. Stratton's secretary says she should come right up.

The law firm has sixteen floors in Atlanta's third tallest skyscraper. Stratton's office is at the top, along with the firm's seven other most powerful partners. Vanderwelt presses her key card to the elevator scanner, goes up four floors, and exits the elevator onto the rug that anchors the small reception area. The rug was hand-made in Jaipur, India, with an abstract design of geometric shapes in jewel tones, woven from Ajgar wool and bamboo silk at a cost of almost $100 per square foot. It is a tone setter, a statement, and because neither clients nor members of the public can access the top floor, it is a message to the firm's other lawyers and staff that the top floor is a place to be revered. The reception area itself is spartan and without a chair because it is not a place where people are invited to wait. You are either granted access to the inner sanctum, or escorted back to the elevator.

The receptionist stands behind a brushed nickel lectern. She is a graduate of the Business Etiquette Institute and looks like a fashion model, wearing a sleek navy two-piece suit, with buttons on the side, purchased with the monthly clothing allowance the firm provides her.

Vanderwelt approaches the lectern as she might the hostess at a high-end restaurant. "Alicia Vanderwelt to see Tinsley Stratton," she says. Her voice is swallowed by sound-dampening panels designed to look like woven slats of wood.

"Do you have a cell phone or other electronic device?" the receptionist inquires in an accent that might be Swedish.

Vanderwelt shakes her head. "No."

The receptionist appraises her, glances at the yellow legal pad and pen in her right hand, perhaps ready with a hand-held metal detector. Instead, she says, "I will scan your face now." She holds up a computer tablet, which flashes beams of infrared light across Vanderwelt's face, mapping every contour and comparing it to the stored image. Satisfied, the receptionist taps a code into the tablet, and a steel-core door skinned in mahogany veneer swings open.

Vanderwelt nods. "Thank you."

Vanderwelt walks down a curved corridor, looking for the video cameras that are certainly watching her, but she can't spot them. She has heard the senior partners designed their suites to replicate a federal judge's chambers, closed off to all but the specially invited, with an added air of plush opulence. This floor is more grand than any judge's chambers she's ever visited. The floor is designed to lure judicial retirees to the firm with an upgraded suite of offices. There are already two ex-Judges on this floor and a dozen others in offices spread throughout the country.

She stops at a brass sign on a wall of wood panels, engraved with *Tinsley Stratton, Esq.* She pushes a button on the intercom and announces herself, then hears the door lock click open in response.

Inside the suite, she hears the first sounds since the receptionist's voice—the quiet clack of computer keyboards. Each of the five staff has a separate but small office, no bullpen. Wooden doors on either side of the short hallway, those for Stratton's two secretaries, are open. She knocks on the door frame to her right.

"Alicia Vanderwelt."

"Go on in. He's expecting you."

She passes the offices of Stratton's two paralegals, whom she may have met at a firm function, but whose names she doesn't recall. No nameplates next to their doors, just a brass plate that reads "Paralegal." At Stratton's office she depresses the brass handle of his door, but it won't budge. She glances at the small camera mounted in the wall. After a few seconds she hears the lock release, then pushes the door open.

This floor is designed with the senior partner offices in the corners, so each office has a long span of floor-to-ceiling windows overlooking at least one cardinal direction of the city. Stratton's view is north and east, a tree-filled panorama dotted with gleaming buildings and the occasional shimmering lake. The normal blight of a brown ring of pollution above the horizon is gone on this crisp day. His office seems to float on the air. Even though her office is only four floors below, Vanderwelt's view is constricted, the windows extending from waist-high to just above eye level. As she stands looking out the windows in Stratton's office, she wonders if he ever experiences vertigo.

He is on the phone, leaning back in an Italian calfskin chair the color of a polar bear. He reaches for a remote device on his desk, pushes a button, and all the windows become opaque.

She looks around the room and spots the electronic signal blocker on a tiger-wood credenza, its green light on. The devices are standard office accessories now, though she rarely uses hers. While she waits, she takes in the Remington bronze sculpture on a wooden stand in front of the bank of oak lawyer bookcases, the imported Italian sofa and armchair in red leather surrounding a low marble and chrome table. What looks like an original de Kooning sketch hangs on the wall opposite Stratton's desk. She estimates the furnishings, minus the sketch, approach her annual salary.

Tinsley Stratton ends his call and pulls his feet off the desk. He stands, all 6 feet 5 of him, smooths his silk tie, and shakes Vanderwelt's hand as if they are old friends. "Alicia, thanks for coming up." He is a decade older than Vanderwelt, with a generous amount of gray at the temples and above his ears. He motions to the seating area across from his desk.

She settles into the soft leather couch, hearing it sigh, and poises her legal pad on her knee.

"No notes on this one," Stratton says, reclining into the armchair.

"Okay." She places the pad and pen on the low marble table.

"You've read the complaint, I presume. How quickly can you get rid of this one?"

"Well, with a little paper discovery and an intimidating round of depositions, maybe a year. If we fast-track it."

"No discovery," Stratton says.

"No discovery? What are you suggesting? Maybe we can simplify the process, just go after the essentials, but I can't prepare a case without discovery. We need a ton of information for the class-certification motion itself. And I certainly can't control what discovery the plaintiff may want to do."

"No discovery," Stratton repeats.

She meets his eyes. He has a way of staring through you without blinking, punctuating his point with as few words as possible. When juxtaposed with their last meeting with his client, today he is bold, almost brash.

"What's going on?" she says. "The opaque windows, the white-noise machine. I feel like I'm in a secret meeting."

"You are. You're going to file a motion to dismiss."

"I can file it, but it won't work. You know the standard. Dismissal is appropriate only if the movant establishes the claimant could not possibly introduce evidence within the framework of the complaint sufficient to warrant a grant of the relief sought. According to the complaint, an agent of the lender lied to Hale Hitchcock when he took out the mortgage. Same for all of the class members. The allegation is fraud, and if it sticks, the loan is void. As is the lien on the property."

"Are you familiar with Estate of Jones v. Live Well Financial?"

"No." She should have researched cases on reverse mortgages, but her partner's insistent demand that she come see him ASAFP didn't allow her the time.

Stratton crosses his long legs at the ankle. He had been a small forward at Harvard, with enough talent to play Division I basketball but not enough to ascend to the next level. He attended law school at Emory instead and now plots plays in the legal arena. "Eleventh Circuit case from 2018. The case was brought by the estate of Caldwell Jones, former NBA player. He took out a reverse mortgage. His wife didn't sign any of the loan documents. The appellate court held that a mortgage company can foreclose on a reverse mortgage even if only one of the spouses signed the mortgage."

Vanderwelt nods, taking all of this in. "Did the borrower claim fraud by the lender?"

"Doesn't matter. The claim in the Hitchcock case is that the wife was dispossessed of her interest without her consent. The 11th Circuit says the husband doesn't need her consent. The wife isn't claiming she was defrauded. The broker didn't even communicate with her."

"So you want me to base the motion to dismiss on Jones v. Live Well?"

"Yes. It's all you will need."

"The plaintiffs will argue the intention of the amended federal regulations is to protect the non-borrower spouse—in this case Bridget Hitchcock. They'll argue that if Hale Hitchcock was defrauded, that voids the transaction."

Stratton sighs, pulls his hand across his mouth. "Alicia, we've been over this. The federal regulations don't apply. It doesn't matter who the regulations are intended to protect if they don't apply."

"State court judges don't always follow the law as we present it to them," she responds. "We'd stand a better chance on the motion to dismiss if we removed the case to federal court."

"In most cases, I would agree we want to be in federal court. Especially with 11th Circuit precedent. But not in this case."

"Because?"

"Because federal trial courts publish their decisions, and even when they don't, the case files are available to the public through the internet."

"You don't want any publicity on this."

He shakes his head. "The client doesn't want any publicity. Of any kind. Park is furious there's a lawsuit at all. Claims I told him my strategy was so flawless that no one would ever try to dismantle it."

"I recall you saying only a fool would try."

"Park is adamant. He wants the litigation to be as low-key and confidential as we can make it. He wants it to be over as quickly as humanly possible. Actually, faster than humanly possible. You've met him. You know how insistent he can be."

"He's intense," Vanderwelt says.

"To say the least."

"I'll do my best, but Oakley Hitchcock has a different agenda," she says.

"What do you know about him?"

"I know him, his tactics, his MO, his vulnerabilities. He's the suspended lawyer. His parents are the named plaintiffs. I'm the one who got him suspended."

"So, this is personal," Stratton says.

"My professional judgment will remain uncompromised, as always."

"Hitchcock is the lawyer who beat you in the lead smelter case, correct?"

"Yes. But that case was unwinnable."

"Revenge isn't a bad motivator, Alicia. When does his suspension end?"

"Four months."

"And Tobias Thomas? What do you know about him?"

"Local lawyer without any real credentials. Handles mostly small-time stuff. Played backup quarterback at UGA two decades ago."

"Never underestimate an opponent," Stratton says.

"I won't."

"You did once, with Hitchcock."

She glares at him. The lead smelter case *was* unwinnable. The only question had been how much the jury was going to punish her client. As it turns out, a lot. She calms herself. "It won't happen again. I'm better prepared now. But if you want to increase the chances this motion to dismiss will be granted, we need to remove the case to federal court."

"Not going to happen. File your motion to dismiss in state court."

She can tell from his expression this isn't a mere suggestion. She leans forward. "Look, I know we've only worked together on a couple of cases before, and this is a particularly demanding client, but I know litigation inside and out, and there are limits to what I can do. They've claimed fraud. That's not something we can get around with a motion to dismiss."

Stratton stands up and goes to the wall behind the couch, stands in front of the de Kooning sketch, as if its charcoal lines and squiggles are a teleprompter. His back is to Vanderwelt. "There's a strategy in place, Alicia, a strategy that I designed. The motion to dismiss is part of it. You don't need details. But that strategy involves layers of companies organized in different states, impenetrable layers, all designed to maintain the anonymity of our client and our client's operations. We cannot jeopardize that strategy. We will not jeopardize it."

She twists her body toward him. "To defend this case properly, I need to have access to this information. I need to know what entities are out there, where they're located. Who the client actually is. Skeletons in the closet. Everything."

"No."

"No? You're telling the lead lawyer on this case she can't have access to important information about her client?"

He turns toward her, his hands behind his back. His chin is tilted up. "Don't make the mistake of thinking you're the lead lawyer on this case, Alicia. File the motion to dismiss ASAP. And you'd better not lose it."

26

The courtroom is gloomy, the dusty overhead lights not bright enough to dispel the shadows in the corners. A winter storm whips a cascade of rain against the courtroom windows. Though the blinds are open, the daylight provides little illumination. The uniformed bailiff, his sidearm visible at his right hip, steps to the row of light switches, turns each one off then on again. Three sets of bulbs in the fluorescent array refuse to light.

"That's the best we can do this morning," he announces to the room, then goes back to his post and gets on the walkie to maintenance.

Tobias and Hitch sit at one table, with Natalie in a chair behind them. Her briefcase is open. Two white binders filled with case law are stacked on the chair beside her, at the ready.

Alicia Vanderwelt sits at the defense table, sliding her silver-rimmed glasses up and down her nose as she tries to read her argument outline in the dim light. A nameless associate sits next to her, literally twiddling his thumbs. Earlier, Vanderwelt introduced herself to Tobias Thomas with a smile that said they were colleagues. She shook Hitch's hand without comment. She ignored Natalie altogether.

The bailiff announces the entry of Judge Fisher, who ascends the bench with heavy steps on the wooden treads. He is robed, and the knot of a yellow tie with red and blue fish on it peeks out above the robe's zipper. He settles his bulk into a groaning high-backed chair and switches on the desk lamp. "Good morning counsel," he says. He opens the case file and readies the defendant's motion to dismiss and the plaintiff's response.

"I see we have a motion to dismiss. I've read your briefs. Very thorough. Ms. Vanderwelt, I'll hear from you."

Alicia Vanderwelt rises from her chair, clears her throat, then levels the hem of her black jacket. "Your Honor, may it please the Court." She says this in a stentorian voice that carries to the corners of the courtroom. "We have filed a motion to dismiss in this most unusual case because the plaintiffs have failed to plead facts sufficient to invoke a claim or controversy as to the validity of my client's security interest."

"We're a notice pleading state, Ms. Vanderwelt," the Judge says in retort. "Plaintiffs don't have to plead all of the salient facts. I'm sure you're aware of that. And before you talk about the plausibility standard, remember this isn't federal court, so the Supreme Court's ruling in *Twombly* doesn't apply."

Vanderwelt is caught short by the hot bench. Her associate's research into Judge Fisher has not prepared her for this stymie. She had planned to make her argument without interruption. "Of course, Your Honor. I simply want to point out that the plaintiffs have pleaded only that Mrs. Hitchcock did not sign any of the paperwork regarding the loan, a fact which we readily admit. But the loan agreement doesn't list Mrs. Hitchcock as a borrower, and it does contain a power of sale provision allowing the lender to foreclose when the sole borrower, Mr. Hale Hitchcock, dies. In the case of Estate of Caldwell Jones v. Live Well Financial, an 11th Circuit case decided in 2018, the Court held that the mortgage contract controls and the lender is entitled to foreclose against a non-borrower spouse."

"The borrower is still alive, is that correct?" the Judge asks.

"Yes sir," Vanderwelt replies. "Of course, we're not asking for foreclosure. We're simply here to defend these allegations, to discuss the interpretation of the mortgage contract. The mortgage contract governs the parties' rights. The lender is entitled to foreclose when the sole borrower dies."

The Judge pauses, rubs his fingers across his beard. "What about that, Mr. Thomas? I've read the Caldwell Jones case. Tell me why it doesn't apply."

Tobias stands. "As we know, the Hitchcock farm was acquired during their marriage. Under Georgia law, each spouse has an equitable interest in property acquired during marriage. That issue was not addressed in the Caldwell Jones case. Essentially the lender is arguing that Bridget Hitchcock, the spouse, does not have an equitable interest in the property. Her husband, Hale Hitchcock, admits in the complaint he didn't intend to dispossess his wife of that interest, and that he had no legal right to do so. And most importantly, we've alleged that the mortgage broker committed fraud when he told Hale Hitchcock his wife could stay in the house after he dies. The broker even showed Hale Hitchcock a copy of the HUD regulations protecting a non-borrower spouse. Unless Ms. Vanderwelt is willing to stipulate to the fraud, there are fact issues that have to be decided in a trial and can't be determined through a motion to dismiss."

"Ms. Vanderwelt, aren't we dealing with disputed issues of material fact here?" the Judge asks. "I assume you're not prepared to stipulate that an agent of the lender committed fraud in this transaction. So, doesn't a jury need to decide whether the mortgage broker misled Mr. Hitchcock regarding the terms of the loan agreement?"

"No, Your Honor," Vanderwelt says. Her tone is strident, even though she feels the motion slipping away. She has to keep arguing, because sometimes a Judge will rule for the party who speaks last. "The 11th Circuit has made clear that under Georgia law a spouse can sign away another spouse's rights through a mortgage. So whether Hale Hitchcock believed he had the right to do so is irrelevant. And as to the fraud, the loan agreement specifically waives any claims based on oral or written statements made prior to execution of the loan documents. It's a standard release clause."

"I've seen a thousand of them," Judge Fisher responds. "But what I find significant is that the defendants, the lender and the mortgage company, have not denied the allegations of the complaint as to what Mr. Rogers, the lender's agent, said to Mr. Hitchcock. They have not denied, at least at this point, that their agent showed Mr. Hitchcock a federal regulation that says his wife can stay in the house even after he dies. A federal regulation which you argue in your brief, Ms. Vanderwelt, doesn't apply because this isn't a mortgage insured or regulated by HUD."

"May I respond," Vanderwelt says.

"Go ahead."

"The defendants have no obligation to file an answer at this point because the motion to dismiss is pending." She sees the Judge frown. "But more importantly, what the plaintiff is alleging is not a misrepresentation of fact, it's a misrepresentation of the law. And the …"

Judge Fisher holds up his hand. "Ms. Vanderwelt, are you saying that even though the only facts before me at the moment are Mr. Hale Hitchcock's allegation that he was induced to sign the mortgage documents based on Mr. Rogers' statement about his wife's rights, and being shown a copy of the HUD regulation, that your clients are not responsible because what, Mr. Rogers' statement was a representation about the legal effect of the documents and he's not a lawyer?"

"Well, Your Honor, that's not exactly our position. Our position is that Mr. Hitchcock didn't have a right to rely on any oral statements by Mr. Rogers about the legal effect of the documents, especially given the language in the mortgage contract negating the oral statements." She knows this sounds weak, but she has to get it on the record, perhaps for an appeal, perhaps so that when Tinsley Stratton reads the transcript he will see she gave it her best.

"I'm going to deny the motion to dismiss," the Judge says curtly. "Mr. Thomas, you asked for a jury trial?"

"Yes, sir."

"All right. We'll need a scheduling order. When do you plan to address the class allegations?"

"We will be filing a motion for class certification once we get the discovery we need regarding the claims of the class members," Tobias responds.

"That's putting the cart before the horse," Vanderwelt protests. "If there isn't a class here, discovery regarding the class members claims will be unduly burdensome to the defendants."

The Judge holds up his hand. "I know I brought it up, but we're obviously not ready to address class certification. Let's schedule the motion for hearing on March 31. That gives all parties ten weeks to complete the discovery necessary to address the class-certification motion."

"Your Honor," Vanderwelt protests. "We can't be ready to address class certification in ten weeks. Discovery on the class issues alone will take six months. At least." She flicks back to her conversation with Stratton, who made it clear there would be no discovery by the defendants.

"Mr. Thomas?" The Judge asks.

"If the defense will cooperate regarding discovery, we will be ready by then, Your Honor. We already have statements from most of the class members. Their transactions were the same as the Hitchcocks', right down to being shown the same HUD regulation by Mr. Rogers. I would note for the Court's benefit that although the defendants claim they need extensive discovery, they haven't served any discovery requests or attempted to take any depositions."

"Ms. Vanderwelt, what about that? If you need all this discovery, why haven't you started?"

"We were waiting for a ruling on the motion to dismiss," she says defensively. "No reason to expend the time, energy and money if the case was going to be dismissed."

"And now you have my ruling. All right. You two work out a scheduling order on the discovery, working off the March 31 class-certification hearing. Anything else?"

Vanderwelt traces a finger down her bullet points, but finds nothing of merit, nothing that can save her now. She remains silent.

The Judge breaks the silence. "See you both at the end of March."

Vanderwelt slips her notes into a soft leather briefcase and hurries from the courtroom. She doesn't much care whether her associate follows her. She feels ambushed. She can barely contain her anger.

The winning team adjourns to Tobias' office to de-brief.

"Is Judge Fisher always like that?" Hitch asks.

Tobias sips from a huge mug of coffee. "He might have been a bit exuberant today, but he likes to point out shenanigans when he sees them. Locally, very few lawyers file motions to dismiss because he denies them the vast majority of the time. I'm surprised he didn't tell the story about how he once granted a motion to dismiss, maybe seven or eight years ago, and the court of appeals reversed him, so he hasn't done it since."

"It was fun to see Vanderwelt running away with her tail between her legs," Natalie says.

"She'll be back," Hitch says. "I'm surprised she came to court without local counsel."

Tobias nods. "Me too. Having local counsel is the smart thing to do if you don't know the Judge."

"So why didn't she?" Hitch asks.

"Ego?" Tobias says.

"I've litigated against her and she's got a big ego for sure, but she's smart enough to set that aside and develop a strategy that avoids getting home-towned," Hitch says.

"It's something else," Natalie says. "Probably more likely she doesn't want to divulge her client's secrets to someone local and then pray those secrets don't get leaked."

"I'll bet that's it," Hitch says.

They spend the next several hours developing a task list and internal timetables for class discovery. The strength of the case depends on winning the motion for class certification. If they win the motion, they'll have substantial leverage to unwind the reverse mortgages. If they lose, Bridget and Hale Hitchcock's claims may survive, but the other farmers and landowners will be out of luck. They debate whether to retain an expert and decide Hitch will have an exploratory meeting with a law professor who has written a law review article on reverse mortgages.

"I hate to bring this up," Tobias says, "but experts and depositions won't be cheap. I'm not in a position to fund a case like this."

"Of course not," Hitch says. "You've already done more than enough, Tobias. And I thank you for everything. And my parents thank you, too. I'll take care of all the expenses. And I want to pay you for your time. I hope you've kept up with your hours."

"Wouldn't think of it," Tobias says. "I'm actually having a little fun with this. What do you think their next move will be?"

"Well, Alicia's not going to just sit back and wait until the class is certified, that's for sure. She'll ramp up, send us a bunch of paper discovery to keep us busy, hire an expert or two, start scheduling depositions," Hitch says. "What do you think, Nat?"

Natalie cups her chin in her palm, elbow on the wooden table. "I don't think she'll follow the traditional process. She hasn't so far. Alicia Vanderwelt's got something up her sleeve."

27

Mark Sanchez is sitting alone in the empty apartment he once shared with Natalie Anderson when the call comes in.

"Mr. Sanchez, this is Alicia Vanderwelt. You compiled a profile on attorney Oakley Walker Hitchcock for me. I need you to update it. He's involved in a case down in Dare County. Not as attorney of record, but probably as a consultant. Plus, his parents are plaintiffs in the case. Hale Hitchcock and Bridget Hitchcock. And there's an attorney down in Dare County—Tobias Thomas—I want a full dossier on him. His family, his cases, anything noteworthy. If he's vulnerable, I want to know about it. You know the type of information I need. And a paralegal at Hitchcock's law firm, Natalie Anderson. She was at a hearing yesterday. I want a full dossier on her, too. Maybe she and Hitchcock are involved in a personal relationship."

At the mention of Natalie's name, Mark stiffens. He suspected Natalie had gone to be with Hitchcock in Pineland, but now it's been verified. "Can you give me some details on the case?"

Vanderwelt pauses. "Why do you need to know that?"

"Just interested. I can get basics from the court file when I go down there."

"Reverse mortgages. Class action. It's big. We'll need summary reports on all of the putative class members as well. There are 77 at present. No, that's 79, but I expect that number to grow. I'll get you the list by end of day. Is your schedule clear?"

He has worked with Alicia Vanderwelt long enough to know her question is actually a mandate to clear his schedule. In truth, he doesn't have much investigative work on his plate. Since his last case with Vanderwelt contributed to Hitchcock's suspension nine months ago, and almost cost Natalie her job, he's been thinking about other options. He doesn't have a clear picture of his future, but what he does see is that his secretive work blew his relationship with Natalie apart.

"Mark, can you make this a priority?"

This brings him back. "Of course. This case is now at the top of my list."

Mark drives to a mini-warehouse and enters a conditioned space that is half the size of his apartment. This is his office, to the extent he needs one. There is a lone desk, an LED lamp, and an uncomfortable chair on wheels. The desk is surrounded by file boxes, stacked to the ceiling in places. He prefers the old-school method of keeping paper files, but caution dictates he back up everything in the cloud. Paper can get wet, or stolen, or burned. But paper can't be hacked.

In his former life, Mark was a financial-crimes investigator for the Department of Justice in D.C. Because of a felony marijuana charge, he wasn't eligible for the FBI. He spent three years at the DOJ before he was fired for sleeping with his boss' wife. He fled to Savannah and took up work as a private investigator, leaning on his DOJ experience to land clients. Most of his clients are lawyers.

He pulls over two boxes containing his investigation into the love affair between Hitchcock and Sonia Summers. It's not how he thought of it at first, but after he finished his investigation, it was the only apt description. From the first box, he extracts a sheaf of scribbled notes. Notes from conversations with Natalie. Tidbits Natalie didn't know she was revealing to a man investigating her boss. Stray comments she made while they were lounging out by the apartment pool, or dining at a restaurant and, ultimately, when they were in bed. Natalie still doesn't know Mark gathered the evidence that ultimately led to Hitchcock's suspension. Mark has to keep it that way if he wants her back. And he does want her back.

When Vanderwelt hired him to find out all he could about the shooting in Hitchcock's law office, he had taken an apartment in the same complex where Natalie lived. He had approached her while she ran on a treadmill in the exercise room. It wasn't long before she became something other than a valuable witness. He had fallen for her, violating his own ethics and professional creed, but he couldn't help himself. She was beautiful, smart, athletic, and a lot of fun to be around. And Mark figured that cases came and went, but a woman like Natalie was rare.

Now, he shifts in the uncomfortable chair. He has kept the chair with the peeling leather to remind himself that although valuable information can be gleaned from computers, the best information is usually obtained by talking to people. If the chair were comfortable, he might not get out of it. In his countless conversations with Natalie about the shooting—often under the guise of helping Natalie through her own trauma—he had learned that Hitchcock and Sonia Summers were truly in love. The revelation came from Natalie. Simply saying the words out loud had softened her, opened her up to the possibility that she and Mark could have something similar. That's what he saw, anyway.

When he reported to Alicia Vanderwelt that Hitchcock and Summers had been romantically involved, she had been pleased. She had commented that perhaps Hitchcock had violated his ethical duties. She had promised Mark a $25,000 bonus if he could confirm the affair.

It took Mark only a week to find the pathway. He interviewed George Colbert in prison, where he was awaiting trial for murder. Colbert had been uncharacteristically open about his hatred for Hitchcock, blaming Hitchcock for the dissolution of his marriage and a host of financial problems that had plagued Colbert long before Hitchcock came into his life. Anger didn't begin to describe Colbert's state of mind. Seething rage was closer, but still not there. Mark had never seen a person so ready to explode, and the only similar thing he could come up with was a starving, cornered pit bull.

And Colbert had pictures. Pictures of Hitchcock and Sonia at restaurants, walking hand-in-hand along the beach at Tybee Island, and kissing at the front door of her apartment. Pictures Colbert was willing to share with Mark for a modest deposit into his prison commissary account.

When Mark shared the photographs with Alicia Vanderwelt, she was thrilled. And then she asked the question that Mark can see now as the turning point in his relationship with Natalie. The outside influence that ultimately ruined it all.

"Can you get Colbert to file a bar complaint against Hitchcock?" Vanderwelt had asked.

Mark didn't see it at the time, that he was tipping one domino that would ultimately topple others, cutting a rift between him and Natalie. He didn't exactly ruin Hitchcock's life, but he certainly greased the wheels of the rig Vanderwelt was using to get Hitchcock suspended.

When the suspension was announced, Natalie was different. "He's been through so much," she'd said, "losing Sonia like that. Getting shot. And now he's suspended for a year. How much can one man take?"

Her eyes remained hooded for days, her face taking the look of someone who was more than worried about a friend. Sympathy morphed into something else, and as she brooded around the apartment, Mark silently acknowledged what he'd done. In watching Colbert eagerly sign the bar complaint Vanderwelt had carefully crafted, Mark had hurt not just Hitchcock, but Natalie too. And the guilt had begun to pile into him. She had changed; he was changing. He couldn't look at her and lie anymore.

Now, he is not so much jealous that Natalie wound up with Hitchcock as he is ashamed that he caused it all. His relationship with Natalie had been great in most ways, certainly good enough to last. He had shopped in two jewelry stores looking at engagement rings before it all began to unravel. And though he feels the loss as deeply as he's ever felt anything, he does not want revenge. He wants to atone. He wants Natalie back, if that is even possible.

28

Bordering the Okefenokee Swamp is a large parcel of private land, more than 2,300 acres, owned by a septuagenarian named Mordecai Davis Claxton. His ancestors acquired the original 110 acres in the Georgia land lottery of 1820. The Claxton clan purchased more acreage when timbering companies abandoned their logging operations after clear-cutting the land.

The Claxton plantation is covered with pines in staggered maturities, from saplings to fully grown trees ready for harvest. A three-acre homestead at the end of a sandy road sits in the middle of the plot, surrounded by furry pines and ragged swaths of emerald grass. From the sky, the property resembles an unrolled bolt of evergreen cloth with a bleached stain in the middle, relatively the size of a shirt button. Reddish-brown needles litter the ground beneath the pines, marked by the occasional cone, most of the strobiles the color of squirrel's fur, but some still tight and green.

Mordecai Davis Claxton stands on his front porch, arms akimbo, surveying the land on which he's lived his entire life. He was born in this house. He honeymooned in this house. He and his wife raised three boys in this house. His wife died in the back bedroom.

As the sun dips below the tree line he feels a current of cool air. He can tell simply by looking at the color of the pine needles on the ground that it is time to rake the pine straw. Tomorrow he will mount the mechanical raker and drive it through perfectly straight rows of pines on section four, where 12-year-old trees will provide dappled shade and a bountiful harvest of straw. Later, he will rake the six-foot space between each tree by hand. Then he'll navigate the baler between the rows in the 40-acre stand, accumulating enough straw bales to sell to the landscapers and at his roadside stand on the highway. Money he needs to tide him over through winter.

Raking straw is tough work, but he's been doing it for the better part of six decades. He's considered hiring someone to help him this year, but on the one or two occasions when he did so in the past he was disappointed in his helpers. They lacked thoroughness, took too many water breaks, and one of them carelessly dangled a cigarette from his fingers as he lolled against a tree amid all those piles of dry straw. No, he will do it himself again this year. Claxton's heart is strong and his hands are calloused. He does not consider straw raking so much work as it is his responsibility, his obligation as the caretaker of this pine plantation.

He lost his wife seventeen months ago, and now he is alone. His three sons all moved away to cities to find work that did not involve manual labor, did not require buckets of sweat, did not gash their skin and drip their blood into the soil. Mordecai rubs his gray-whiskered chin with his right hand, the pinky finger and the one next to it each only one knuckle long, the result of a chain-saw accident so long ago he cannot remember the year.

He swings open the screen door and enters his dim living room. The door hinges groan with humidity. He reminds himself, as he heats a pan of soup on the propane stove, that he needs to apply some oil to those hinges.

David Chan traverses the edge of the Okefenokee Swamp, along a narrow, sandy track that separates the Swamp from the pine plantation owned by a man named Mordecai Claxton. The moon is a sliver, ducking in and out of cirrus clouds. Chan's night goggles give his surroundings an eerie, green glow. As he navigates the border road in the dark, he sees a white-tail buck with wide antlers bolt into the trees. He hears the howl of coyotes in the distance. From the underbrush on the Swamp side, he hears the rustle and grunts of wild pigs rooting.

As he steps onto the Claxton land, he hears a noise that chills him to the bone. It isn't a growl, not exactly. But it is unmistakably a threat. He has heard this ominous sound only once before.

As a child growing up in the Yangzte River Valley in China, he had frequently fished the cloudy river from a wooden sampan. The copper fish and carp he caught he took home to his mother. Many days, the fish he netted were the only source of protein his family had to eat. For weeks, when the river was high and muddy from the rains, he brought home nothing. His family went without.

He remembers the day as if etched in his memory by a silversmith's engraving tool. It was early, the humidity a mist hovering above the river. Visibility on the water was five feet, if that. Sound was hemmed in by the fog. The clack of his pole on the side of the boat echoed like the thunk of an axe in wood. His little tan pug, whom he had rescued as a stray from the muddy streets of his village, huddled in the bottom of the sampan. Chan and the dog had become inseparable. "Ping" he called it.

"Ping, stop moving about," he'd said in Mandarin. "Ping, stop clawing the boat. Ping be quiet. Ping sit."

When he'd heard the harrowing growl that day, he knew what it was: the bellow of a Chinese alligator. The primordial sound came from its chest as a warning to everything nearby. It sent ripples through the water. Ripples that rocked his sampan. The gator was close.

Chan poled away from where he thought the gator was swimming, the boat sitting low in the soup. But in the cloak of mist the alligator's location was just a guess. As he scanned the murky water and pushed toward where he surmised shore should be, he did not notice that Ping had climbed onto the gunwale.

The alligator's head appeared and landed on the bow, flipping the small boat. Chan and his beloved dog toppled into the murky water. For a moment, he could hear Ping's yip behind him, and then it suddenly stopped. Chan was able to right the sampan and climb back in. He called out to his dog and jabbed the water with his pole, hoping against reality he might strike the gator. That he might save Ping. He heard nothing. He struck nothing.

He searched the water for ten minutes, then an hour. In his grief, he could not discern the shore from the middle of the broad river, could not find the Chinese willow that marked his launching spot. He poled in endless circles, listening for a splash. Listening for Ping's yip. He was greeted instead by the haunting bellow of alligators.

Now, as his head swivels, scanning the tall grass on either side of the road, Chan pulls the QSZ-92 pistol from the holster beneath his right arm. He grips the gun with both hands and backs away from the sound. He tries to convince himself his fear isn't logical—that alligators rarely attack people. He feels the thump of his heart in the artery of his neck. He struggles to breathe, as if someone has covered his nose and mouth with a gloved hand. He retreats from the swampy ditches with the pistol ready, trying to put some distance between himself and the predator he cannot see. He hopes this alligator will not follow him into the neat rows of pines.

He hopes it will not hunt him. As the sound of the bellowing gator recedes, Chan's heart begins to slow.

The fires are easy to set. No accelerant is necessary. Pine straw burns quickly. And hot. Old pine boughs ignite with a flick. Chan sets a dozen fires in less than thirty minutes. The glow of trees ablaze builds an orange plume in the rural darkness above Mordecai Claxton's farm. The popping pine sap sounds like distant gunfire. Chan hustles back to his van and pulls away as sirens peal through the night.

29

Garland T. Rogers drives up the old farmer's driveway in a dove-gray pickup. The acrid smell of char is thick, even with the windows closed and the air conditioning set to re-circulate. The land on both sides looks eerie, the landscape painted in stark shades of gray and black. Blackened tree trunks stand in naked rows, their green plumes turned to gray ash. Debris lines the road. White-gray ash floats in the air like snowflakes that won't drop. Rogers imagines, though he has no frame of reference, this is what nuclear winter looks like.

Rogers is on the front porch and ready to knock before he realizes Mordecai Claxton is standing only two feet away, his image obscured behind the screen door, which is clogged with ash. When Claxton admits him to the dim interior of the farmhouse, the farmer seems but a shadow, a withered and beaten old man singed by the flames that have taken his timber. Timber he has spent decades planting and cultivating.

The old farmer sits on a bare wooden stool next to the kitchen counter, his face gray and almost bloodless.

"At least they were able to save the house," Rogers begins.

"And one of the barns," Claxton replies in a tone that hurts. "Most of my equipment, too. But there's not much use to it now. The trees are gone."

"I talked to the fire chief," Rogers says.

"Which one? They were here from Waycross and Jacksonville, the Forest Service, too. Took them four days to put it out. They're still working hotspots over on the northeast corner." Claxton points toward the far reaches of what was once his 2300 acres of trees.

"Waycross," Rogers replies. "I guess … well, he seems to be in charge of the investigation."

"Investigation," Claxton repeats, as if the word isn't familiar.

"Well sure, they have to investigate, you know. Your fire didn't start from lightning."

Claxton seems to know this, but he's still in shock, his mind not working right.

"The insurance company will probably send out investigators, too. To … you know."

"To what?"

"To talk to you. To look around."

Claxton works his stubbled jaw. "They think this was arson?"

Rogers shrugs. Insurance agents don't use that word, not unless they have to. Arson is a legal term. The insurance company will determine whether the fire was intentionally set. That's the policy provision they'll focus on. And if there's no evidence the fire started through "An act of God," the insurance company will probably conclude the fire was intentionally set.

"I didn't set my farm on fire," Claxton declares. Are they crazy?"

"The trees were insured, but they have to look into it."

"And how long will that take?"

"Months, probably."

"And what am I supposed to do in the meantime?" Claxton asks. "I'm flat broke. That straw was going to get me through the winter." His voice is high and pleading, his arms spread wide, as if through this gesture his dire plight is laid bare.

"I can help," Rogers says.

"You can help?" It is a question filled with challenge. Claxton is, like most of his fellow farmers, skeptical of outsiders. To him, help is often an illusory term. But the fire has broken him. After living on the land for 74 years in the house he was born in, he does not have the strength to re-build. Not by himself. Even before the fire, he was barely subsisting, eating mostly soup, rice and beans. Scraping together the money to buy diesel fuel for his tractor and other equipment. Until the trees matured. All his hope burned up with the trees.

"I can help you clean up and re-plant," Rogers continues.

"Re-plant? How?" Claxton eyes the man sitting across from him on a matching wooden stool.

"It takes two people, right? One to drive the tractor, and the other to load the planter with seedlings."

"You know how to run a planter?"

Rogers places both hands on his substantial belly, as if to say his girth would be hard to squeeze into the planter's small metal shell. "No, but I can drive a tractor."

Claxton adjusts his feet on the bottom rung of the stool. His hooded eyes drop to the floor. "Seedlings cost money. Money I don't have," he says, barely above a whisper.

"Oh," Rogers says, as if this has never occurred to him. One hand caresses his ample chin, contemplating something. "Well, maybe I can help with that, too. I'm not sure, but I can look into it, if that's something you want me to do."

The farmer nods, a sullen motion that seems to take most of his energy. "See what you can do."

Five days later, Mordecai Davis Claxton appears in the insurance office of Garland T. Rogers. He settles into one of the chairs in front of Rogers' desk, a chair with a curved back and arms covered in faux brown leather.

"Did the insurance company approve my claim?" Claxton asks.

"Not that I've heard," Rogers answers. "As I mentioned, these things usually take months. There might even have to be a lawsuit to determine the cause."

"A lawsuit?" Claxton says.

"That's what the lawyer says. I talked to him about it, to see if he could speed things along."

Rogers has spoken to Tinsley Stratton, his brother-in-law and the one who hired him to solicit and close the reverse mortgages. Stratton doesn't represent the casualty carrier that issued the insurance policy on the Claxton farm, but Rogers knows from experience that determining the cause and origin of the fire will take months.

"Well, if that's the sum of it," Claxton says, "you could have told me that over the phone and saved me a trip." Claxton rises from the chair in which he has been sitting for less than two minutes.

"Hold on, now," Rogers raises his hand to halt the farmer. "I've worked out a solution."

"What solution?"

"I'll tell you, if you'll just sit back down. Hear me out on this."

With a clenched jaw, Claxton settles back into the chair.

"I'm authorized to loan you $100,000 on your farm. It's what's called a home equity conversion mortgage. You don't have to pay it back."

"Don't have to pay it back? What kind of loan is that?"

"That's what a home equity conversion mortgage is. Nothing is due, not even interest, until you pass. And when that happens, what do you care?"

Claxton does care, or at least he used to. Since he inherited the farm, he has kept it debt-free. Over the years, he's taken out loans to buy equipment, but those loans aren't backed by the property. He wants to pass the farm down to his three sons, but on their last visit this wish revealed itself to be the musings of a foolish old man.

"Dad, maybe you should sell the farm." His eldest son, Zachary, had said it with his brothers behind him, both literally and figuratively, as if the committee had met and decided his fate.

"This is my home. Your mother died on this piece of land. And your grandfather and your grandmother, too. Don't you want it to stay in the family?"

"Every couple of years you have to deal with some disaster," Zachary rebutted. "Two years ago, a tornado destroyed the equipment barn. Then mom died. Before that you fell off the barn roof and broke your foot. Remember the infestation of borer beetles? What did it cost to get rid of those? How many trees did you have to destroy? Aren't you tired of it all?" Zachary didn't wait for a reply. "Dad, sell the land and buy yourself a condo on the beach or something. You deserve it." Zachary had looked to his two brothers for approval, and both nodded in agreement.

And there was a moment or two, as his sons stood before him on the front porch, as he surveyed the violence his farm had been subjected to—the destruction around him like what he'd seen in documentaries from World War II—that he was inclined to concede. He was tired. Bone tired. And he couldn't sleep with the sharp, acrid smell of burned wood invading the house, invading his bedroom, invading his nostrils so that he had to take a shower to get any reprieve at all.

Now, he locks eyes with Garland Rogers. "You say I don't have to pay this loan back?"

Rogers shakes his head. "Nope. Your heirs may have to deal with it, but so what?"

Heirs. Was that what his sons had become? Maybe so. They didn't want to help him on the farm, rarely came to visit. They didn't want this farm life, though on that score he couldn't really blame them. When he did pass, they would probably just sell the farm anyway. Especially if it happened soon. Who would want the blackened, sour mess his land had become?

"You said $100,000?"

"Yes."

"I don't need that much to re-plant. Maybe only half of that."

"And what are you going to live on while those trees mature, Mordecai?

Seeds? I'm just trying to help you out here friend."

Rogers has been his insurance agent for eight years, and the man has never steered him wrong before. He'd gotten the insurance claim on the barn paid in just a couple of weeks.

"Tell me more about this home equity thing? What's it called?"

"Home equity conversion mortgage," Rogers replied. "Some people call it a reverse mortgage, for short. But what's to tell? These mortgages are becoming really popular with people who, like you, have a lot of equity in their property. And you don't have to pay it back. I've gotten them for a lot of farmers around here. You're a perfect candidate. It's perfect for your situation."

Mordecai Claxton leaves the insurance office with a certified check for $100,000 and a folder containing the two transaction documents he didn't bother to read. He trusts Garland T. Rogers because … well, he has to trust someone. And Rogers promised to come to the farm and help him plant, as soon as the pine seedlings are delivered. The sum is enough to re-plant about 1,500 acres of the charred plantation, with enough left over for Claxton to live on for the next two years.

Claxton descends the wooden steps of the insurance office and swings open the door to his soot-streaked pickup. The old farmer is moving a bit quicker, has a little color in his pasty cheeks. As he drives toward home, he lays out the checklist to re-build: order the seedlings; repair the planter; order a delivery of diesel fuel; check the long-term weather forecast; re-stock the pantry and the freezer. Wash the truck. He's going to do that first, at the first self-service car wash he finds, to see if he can erase the sharp stench of burnt and watered wood that has infiltrated everything.

30

David Chan leans against the front fender of the old pickup truck, waiting. He has come here from the highway, shuffling half a mile through the charred debris from the fire. Acrid soot mars his boots and his pants legs to the knee. He purchased the entire outfit from Goodwill for less than $30. He wears a white mask, left over from the Covid days. The mask is smudged with a gray stain where he inhales air. For what he is about to do, he does not need a disguise.

Mordecai Claxton emerges from the farmhouse. It is still dark, the house just a shadow in the pre-dawn.

"Can I help you?" Claxton calls from the steps.

"Garland Rogers sent me. To help you plant. Or whatever needs to be done."

Claxton studies the short man leaning against his truck. He's dressed for work, with heavy canvas pants and a denim shirt. His face is partially obscured by the mask, his forehead covered by the bill of a tattered cap with a familiar implement company logo on the front.

"Couldn't make it himself?"

"Apparently not."

"Where's your car?"

"A friend dropped me off," the man answers.

"What's your name?"

"Bob," Chan answers.

"Can you drive a tractor, Bob?"

Chan shakes his head. "No. I wouldn't trust myself."

"Awright. You can ride on the sidestep, or walk behind."

Claxton mounts the tractor. It's full of diesel, and he's cleaned the engine-protecting mesh of old seeds and ash. On the front, he's replaced the regular bucket with a stump bucket, which will help him push some of the debris into piles. Behind, he's pulling a plastic water tank, which Bob can man while the debris piles burn. Fire upon fire.

Claxton places one hand on the steering wheel and cranks the engine.

The engine roars to life. Then they move off at a slow pace.

They have traveled no more than two hundred yards into a littered field, Chan walking behind the tractor, when Claxton slumps over in the tractor seat. Chan, whose every footfall raises a cloud of black dust, pulls on a pair of chemical-resistant gloves and approaches the tractor. Claxton struggles to breathe. Claxton's left hand clutches at his throat.

The carfentanil Chan dusted on the steering wheel of the tractor this morning has taken effect, entering Claxton's system through his bare hands. Without an antidote, it kills fast.

Chan mans the hose on the pressurized water tank. While he waits, his eyes scan the blackened fields, admiring the devastation he caused with a few flicks of a long-nosed lighter. He checks his watch again. When seven full minutes have elapsed, he pulls the water hose to the driver's step of the tractor and thoroughly douses the tractor's steering wheel, dashboard, and the well where the foot pedals are located. When he is satisfied the drug residue is gone, he coils the hose neatly on the water tank.

Chan mounts the tractor and pushes Claxton's limp body to the side. He shifts the tractor into gear and begins the slow ride to the border of the farm that edges up to the swamp. Once there, he drags Claxton off the tractor. The farmer lands with a heavy thump on the side slope of the sandy road. His eyes are wide, dark as black olives.

Chan positions the tractor along the edge of the raised road until the sand bank gives way. When the tractor begins to roll over to the left, Chan leaps from the right side. The tractor makes a dull thud when it lands, with a few metal parts clanging loose. Chan stoops and peers beneath the tractor.

Mordecai Davis Claxton lies crushed beneath it.

31

"Aren't you planning to take Natalie out to dinner tonight?" Bridget Hitchcock asks.

Hitch, standing in the kitchen, gives her a puzzled look.

"Valentine's Day, son. Your father is taking me to the new steakhouse in town."

"Oh," Hitch says. "Um, no plans. We're not …"

Bridget puts her hands on her hips and stares at him. "Oakley Walker Hitchcock, don't be a fool. Everybody but you can see it. You're perfect together." She hugs him for a few seconds. "There are two lobster tails in the freezer, a fresh salad in a container in the fridge, and cheese biscuit mix in the cabinet. At least make her some dinner. I'm going to get dressed."

When he is alone in the kitchen, Hitch silently defends himself. What he and Natalie have been doing for the past few months is merely work. She is here to help with the reverse mortgage lawsuit. She has stayed here because it is the safest place she can find away from Mark, her jealous former boyfriend. But Hitch knows that's not the full story.

His father returns from the fields, shedding his coat and hanging it on one of the worn wooden pegs beside the door.

"They just found Mordecai Claxton dead on his property," Hale announces. "Tractor rolled over on him. He was cleaning up debris from the fire."

"Damn," Hitch says. "First his trees burn up, then he dies on his tractor."

Hale looks absently around the kitchen, a numbness in his gaze. Perhaps he is remembering one of the many conversations he had with his neighbor over the years. Discussions that sometimes heated into arguments, often with a cold can of beer in hand at the end of a long day. There was little variety in their talk. They usually started with the weather or the price of things before getting down to it.

"You should grow timber," Mordecai would say in a strident voice. "You can build houses and barns and furniture with timber."

"But you cannot eat wood," Hale would counter. "People need to eat. They need protein. Raising cattle is the only way to go."

"Can't heat your house with a cow," Mordecai would respond. "Unless you somehow process all that methane from cow farts."

"If you want to curtail methane, start with the swamps and the rice farmers," Hale said.

And on it went, both of them with a boot on the rear bumper of a pickup, forearms resting on the tailgate, a slug of beer punctuating each point and counter. More recently, they had addressed the dilemma they both faced as old farmers with aging bodies.

"Either of your kids want to take over the tree farm when you're gone?" Hale had asked on a breathless night when not a needle on Mordecai's flush pines was stirring.

"Naw, not mine. They've gotten citified. How about your boy?"

Hale had thought about it, whether the bullet that had almost taken his son's life would alter his perspective enough to drive him home. But at the time Hitch was still practicing law in Savannah, a distance of only about 140 miles, but a world away in most respects.

"Not likely. Rip might have taken to it if he'd made it home," Hale said.

Hitch brings his father back from his reverie. "You and mom going out for a Valentine's dinner?" Hitch asks.

"Yep. Dinner." Hale shuffles from the kitchen, as though his destination is uncertain.

Hitch wants to say something to his father, but he can't get it out of his mouth. Something to ease the shock of discovering a fellow farmer is dead from a tragic accident. There really are no words when your father is visualizing the image of his own body lying beneath his tractor on the far side of the farm.

Hitch busies himself with preparing dinner, locating a boiling pot and a baking pan, seasoning the boil and smearing the pan with butter. As the stove and the oven heat up, he opens a bottle of pinot grigio, sets it on the counter on the other side of the kitchen to let it breathe. He read somewhere that's what you are supposed to do with wine.

His mother sticks her head around the door frame and announces they are leaving for dinner.

Hitch bends over, checks the progress of the biscuits through the oven glass because he doesn't trust the timer. "Okay, mom. Have a good time."

His mother comes fully into the kitchen. "Son, I want you and Natalie to have a good time tonight. We'll be home around 9:30."

He can feel his face flush at his mother's unsubtle suggestion. He conjures a retort, but she is gone before he can fully form it. He hears the rattle of the stained glass in the front door as she pulls the door to.

He returns to his ministrations, pulling the lobster tails when they turn the peculiar color of glowing embers. He removes the biscuits as the tops become gold. He melts the remnants of a stick of butter in a dish in the microwave and arranges everything at the dining table, using his mother's good china. He is lighting the candles in a silver candelabra when Natalie comes down the stairs. She is wearing a red dress that clings to her body, and black high heels.

His mouth drops.

"Court clothes," she says with a sly smile.

"You never went to court with me looking like that."

She saunters around the table.

"Sure I have. Just with a black blazer and low heels." She inspects the place settings, adjusts one of the lit candles. "Is this all for me?" she says, swinging her arm toward the table. "What a surprise."

"Mom told you."

"She might have said something. Let's eat. I'm starving."

They sit across from each other and savor the lobster, the green salad with radishes, tomatoes and carrots. Natalie eats three cheese biscuits and remarks she'll have to get the recipe from his mother. Hitch doesn't reveal the mix comes from a box. He spends long spans staring at her turquoise eyes, which look almost violet in the candlelight, at the pink hue of her skin, the way her blonde hair frames her face, the curve of her shoulders and the swell of her breasts in the plunging neckline. He wonders why he's waited so long to see her this way. Most of the bottle of wine is gone, the candles dripping wax, when he says, "Natalie, I'm sorry that I …"

She cuts him off. "Why do lawyers always think that talking is the right thing to do, no matter the circumstances?"

There is only a moment's hesitation, after he pulls her chair back, before he grasps her hand gently and leads her toward the stairs. In the master bedroom they embrace and kiss, then she turns so he can unzip her dress. She pulls it over her head, revealing a red push-up bra and panties that conceal almost nothing. He almost falls over while slipping off his pants while she unbuttons his shirt. They tumble gently onto the bed. His parents' bed, no matter.

"Finally," she says.

Once again he begins to speak, but she pulls him on top of her and kisses his lips to keep him from talking.

He feels an urgency he hasn't felt in—well, maybe never—and he raises up on his left arm while he unclasps her lacy bra with his right hand, lays it gently on the other pillow. He begins kissing her ears, then her neck, and is working his way down when he hears a faint sound from the front of the house. He gives it a momentary thought, then resumes what he was doing before. Natalie's naked body brings him back, his brain dismissing stray thoughts trying to push through.

Coupling. The joining of two things together to form one. This is what Hitch needs.

Natalie gasps when he slides inside, closes her eyes. She wraps her long legs around him and they thrust in unison. It lasts barely a minute, certainly less than two. They both shudder, then slow, and he relaxes his grip.

Natalie manages a wry smile, words unnecessary. Hitch holds her, his fingers resting just below her clavicle. He pulls her close, wanting to feel that connection. He lays his cheek on her shoulder and kisses her neck again. He feels the quiver as her skin reacts, then moves to an earlobe. His hands wander down her torso.

The second time is languid, a tangle of arms and legs and changing positions on the soft cotton sheets. Each of them is attuned to the other in discovery. As minutes tick away, their passion builds, the slow flush of blood culminating in the rush of dopamine, gasps that stick in their throats.

When it is over, she rolls onto her back and pulls the sheet up.

"That was amazing," he says. His heart is still racing, his breathing not yet settled.

She turns on her side, traces the puckered wound on his chest with her index finger. "Fair," she says with a sly smile.

"Fair? I … Oh, too much talking." He gazes at her shimmering eyes, at the glowing skin covering her cheeks. He slowly runs a finger over her pouty lower lip. For almost an hour he has been able to forget the rest of the world by turning to someone who has been right in front of him for the past three years. The word ironic slips through his brain.

They are both starting to doze when they are interrupted by a loud crash.

32

Hitch and Natalie sprint down the driveway toward the explosion. When they near the highway, the devastation becomes apparent. A locomotive sits on the railroad track, a line of bulkhead flat cars behind it, filled with logs. The locomotive's lights struggle to penetrate a plume of black smoke. In the underbrush to the side of the track, a vehicle is on fire.

His father's pickup truck.

Hitch approaches the wreck. He inches toward the flames, holding his hand up against the intense heat, but he can't get close enough. He runs back to the locomotive, climbs up the metal stairs of the engine and throws open the cab door. There is no one inside. Where the hell is the engineer? He pulls a fire extinguisher from its bracket and runs back to the flaming truck. He aims the hose and discharges the powder in the extinguisher until it is spent. The fire rages unabated.

He hopes against hope his parents were thrown clear. While Natalie punches 911 into her phone, Hitch jogs up and down both sides of the track, looking for a lump that might be a human being, listening for signs of life, shouting for them against the roar and crackle of the fire. He steps over broken glass and a damaged side-view mirror and a rusty wheel torn from the truck's rear axle. The rear bumper hangs in the limbs of a scrub oak, ten feet up. He hurries back and forth along both sides of the track.

Seat belts. His father always insisted everyone buckle up. Ever the engineer, he often explained to Hitch the forces created by tons of metal colliding. His parents must have been wearing their seat belts. They would not have been tossed from the truck when it rolled. He reaches the horrifying conclusion they are still inside the burning wreck.

He strips the t-shirt he is wearing and wraps his hands with it. He crouches next to the hulk of the overturned truck and pries at the passenger door. It is bashed in from the impact. It won't budge. Through smoke and fire he peers inside the cab. When he sees the two figures, he knows.

He races down the length of the train because he can't stop. He's too stunned to cry. He trips over protruding railroad ties and falls on the sharp gravel of the rail bed. He pulls himself up. He keeps going to the end, eighteen or twenty flat cars filled with logs. There is no caboose. No rear conductor.

The wail of sirens soon reach him, then the red lights that flash the pavement and the trees and the hulk of the locomotive in a disorienting pattern. Hitch stares at the burning truck, flipped on its roof, heat waves contorting the air. Natalie wraps her arm around his shoulders and tugs him away. They settle on a downed tree on the other side of the train, their view of the crash site obscured.

From here it is a blur of fire trucks and ambulances and cars from the Sheriff's office. Hoses and water and the stench of a doused fire. Char. Two gurneys, yellow plastic concealing remains. Remains. What an odd word.

The passage of time is marked only by the movement of the crescent moon. Klieg lights are erected. A flatbed wrecker angles past the locomotive and backs down the maintenance path. The Sheriff's Deputy who investigated the snake in Natalie's car appears out of the thick smog and begins to summarize.

"Truck . . . crossing . . . engineer is missing . . . no survivors." Hitch doesn't hear much else.

They start back toward the house. Hitch is unsteady and weaving, the overburdened man. Before he's taken a dozen steps he turns back to the deputy. "The rear bumper is up in that tree," he points. "Retrieve it, preserve it, bring in an expert, a metallurgist. My father didn't accidentally drive into the path of a locomotive."

33

The morgue. The funeral home. The Hitchcocks' church. The Sheriff's Department. Hitch visits them in quick succession, with Natalie by his side, his temporary eyes and ears. He turns to her for decisions: the make and model of the coffins; the music his parents would have wanted; the Bible passages that can't explain any of this. He feels underwater. Sound is murky, his vision blurred. He seems constantly gasping for air.

On Thursday afternoon they land in Tobias' office because it is a place where his parents haven't lived, or died, or lay waiting to be buried. They have been there for ten minutes before anyone says anything other than condolences.

"When is the funeral?" Tobias asks.

"Saturday morning."

"Do you need help planning anything?"

"Natalie is taking care of it," Hitch says in a monotone.

"Do you need help with anything else?"

"Like what?"

"I don't know, man. I've never lost a parent. I don't know what to say. I don't know what you need."

"I need explanations," Hitch says. "Why was a train hauling logs on an abandoned train track at that time of night? That spur hasn't been used since we were in high school. Why did my dad drive across the track with a train bearing down on him? Did the truck stall? Did they try to get out?" He stares off into space.

Tobias shakes his head, turns to Natalie. "Has the Sheriff been able to tell you anything useful?"

"Not really. Says it's out of his jurisdiction. The Federal Railroad Administration is taking over."

"Have you talked to the railroad?"

"We've left messages. No one has called us back. My guess is they will remain silent because they expect litigation. The crossing doesn't have any lights. Only a couple of dilapidated signs."

"I'll poke around and see what I can find out," Tobias says. "In the meantime, get him home, make sure he gets some rest, if possible. He needs to sleep."

"His Savannah doctor phoned in a prescription for sleeping pills. The pharmacy is our next stop."

Natalie leads Hitch from the office, settles him into the passenger seat of his SUV, buckles him in. She drives to the drug store and retrieves the prescription at the drive-thru. As she nears the edge of town, she stops at the highway that leads to the farm and flicks on the right blinker.

Hitch suddenly grabs her arm. "Not the farm. Not yet. It's too quiet. Make a left. Please."

She studies him with a mixture of sympathy and puzzlement. His eyes are bloodshot, his face slack and pallid. She has seen him like this only once before, in the turbulent wake of Sonia's murder.

She switches the turn signal to left. They pass more tracts of timber, the growl of heavy equipment felling and loading trees. Scalping the land, hauling off logs, scraping the remnants into burn piles. Smoke drifts above the tree line.

They have driven a couple of miles when Natalie asks, "where are we going?"

"To the high school."

"Okay."

She pulls into a restaurant and orders Hitch a double cheeseburger with fries, orders herself a catfish plate with hush puppies and coleslaw. Neither of them has eaten since yesterday's lunch. At the school they park near the bleachers at the football field and walk through an open gate, settling on a cold aluminum bench a few rows, up near the 50-yard line.

"Is this where you played?" Natalie asks over a mouthful of catfish.

Hitch nods. "Seems like forever ago."

"It was. Twenty-four years right?"

His eyes fix on something, trying to calculate. "Twenty-four." He lays his untouched burger in its wrapper on the bench seat and walks down the concrete steps toward the gridiron. It is a natural turf field. In late winter, the grass is the color of wheat ready for harvest, only a few blades of green trying to poke through. Hitch paces the sideline, his hands in his pockets, his eyes vacant. Memories try to penetrate the gloom that has descended in the aftermath of his parents' deaths. Friday night football, screaming crowds, cheerleaders waving bright pom-poms. The clunk of pads and helmets. But all those memories are swallowed by the darkness inside. He walks off the field with a heavy tread.

They return to the farm, Natalie at the wheel. She lowers the windows to allow for a breeze. She comes to a full stop at the intersection of driveway and rail line, looking both ways. The rails shoot straight away from the crossing. She can see for a few hundred yards in each direction. There are no obstructions. The acrid smell of burnt underbrush and tree limbs wafts through the open windows. She speeds on. The farm is eerily quiet. No tractor hauling bales to the hay rings. No hammering of fence posts. No sputtering old truck rattling over the cattle guards.

34

"My father did not drive into the path of a speeding locomotive." This doesn't sound weird, not to Hitch, even though he utters this from the pulpit of the First Baptist Church. He takes a deep breath. "You all knew him. He was the most levelheaded man you've ever met."

Heads nod in agreement, murmurs of concurrence from the mourners.

"Now, I know this is not what you're used to. You've all been to funerals before, and probably none of you have heard a eulogy like this. I'm doing my best. But we have a murderer out there. And my parents deserve justice.

"My parents had been married for 45 years. That night, my father took my mother out for Valentine's Day at the new steakhouse. He had a rib-eye; my mother had a filet. Sides of mashed potatoes and green beans. One glass of wine each. I checked with their waitress."

Hitch dabs his eyes with his father's white handkerchief, initials embroidered in black at one corner. Although he has prepared for this eulogy and the emotions it will spark, he has to stuff down the welling in his throat, at least for a few more minutes. He looks down at the lectern, its once-glossy finish worn by countless palms. He grips the wood with both hands.

"We don't know yet if they died from the impact, or if they burned to death. Either way it was a horrible way to go. Nobody deserves to spend their last moments on earth like that. Certainly not my parents."

Hitch meets Tobias' eyes, then Natalie's. Earlier this morning, he gave them a vague idea of what he was going to say, but he can see they are surprised. This isn't the eulogy he wanted to give. Even so, he has to do it his own way.

Natalie gives him a slight nod of encouragement.

"Am I angry? You're damned right I'm angry. I believe my parents were murdered. I don't know how, exactly, or why. It may have something to do with the lawsuit they filed a few weeks ago. I don't discount that. The police investigation is on-going, but I'm not going to wait until it's finished to speak out. We're looking for the engineer who drove that train. He wasn't at the scene. We don't know his name, or what he looks like. But keep your ears open. Keep your eyes open. If you hear or see anything that might be relevant, anything at all, call the Sheriff. Or you can call me directly."

The Sheriff, whose name is Guidry Ponder, is sitting in the third row. He stirs in the pew, eyeing Hitch. Hitch stares right back.

Others follow him to the lectern. Neighbors and fellow farmers, the regional director of Goodwill, and a nun from Sisters of Mercy, all giving traditional eulogies void of anger or accusation. Their platitudes about his parents fly past Hitch and land in the congregation. From his chair on the edge of the dais he studies the mourners. He peers into the back corners of the chapel, where overflow mourners stand in shadow, backlit by the sun filtering through the stained-glass windows. If the murderer has come to witness the pain he has caused, he would come in disguise. But no one looks out of place. Or guilty.

At the end, Hitch stands alone in the carpeted aisle of the church, in front of two closed caskets, mourners filing up to shake his hand, uttering condolences he finds utterly meaningless in his present state. Sheriff Ponder comes up last, his palms cradling his dove-gray felt hat. His fingers slide around the brim. He pushes his glasses up on his nose.

"I'm sorry for your loss."

"Thank you, Sheriff."

"I hope we can work together on this."

"I'll share whatever information I discover. I hope you'll do the same."

The Sheriff nods, non-committal. "I hope you didn't just enrage these good people to turn into vigilantes."

"That wasn't my intent. I just want answers. Have you talked to the federal investigator?"

"We're working through some things. Sorting out jurisdiction and such. But there's no evidence that …"

Hitch interrupts. "Whoever did this isn't going to leave a trail, Sheriff. Not one that's easy to find, anyway."

Ponder glances at the two ivory coffins behind Hitch. "Could just be Occam's razor, son. The correct explanation is the simplest one."

"My father did not drive into the path of an oncoming train. He'd been across that track thousands of times. Always looked both ways when he approached."

"But there hasn't been any trains on that track in twenty years or more," the Sheriff says. "Your dad couldn't have been expecting one that night."

"So why is that abandoned track suddenly in use?"

"The railroad investigator is looking into that."

"Did you talk to either of the experts I gave you?"

"On my list."

"And the truck bumper is safe, locked away in your evidence room?"

"It is. Saw it there myself just this morning. Covered with dents and scratches just like every other farm truck in this county. What's so important about the bumper? Are you thinking a vehicle pushed them across that track from behind?"

"It's a possibility. Don't you agree?"

The Sheriff looks down at his hat. "I'll look into it and keep you posted."

As the Sheriff walks away, Hitch glares at the man's uniformed back. He has nothing against the Sheriff, but he doesn't have any other place to direct his anger at the moment.

The interment at the farm is attended only by Hitch, Natalie, the preacher, and the funeral director. Two graves have been dug next to Rip's, the mounds of displaced sand covered by green tarps. Two casket-lowering devices are staged and ready, the caskets poised above the graves. The preacher says only a few words—Hitch has asked him to keep it short—then the caskets are lowered simultaneously. Not her first, or him first. Together. Hitch wants it that way. His parents would have wanted it that way. He picks up a handful of dirt in each hand, running his thumbs over the grains, and tosses them at the same time onto each casket. The falling dirt makes only a scratch of noise.

The gravestones have not yet been etched, but rest on top of the ground, temporarily propped up by wooden staves. They are identical in color and size to Rip's, but the words will be different. Hitch just hasn't composed the epitaphs yet.

The funeral director and the driver of the second hearse collect their equipment and stow it in the back of a van.

"Are you sure you don't want my workers to complete the burial?" the director says to Hitch.

"No, sir. I'm going to do it myself."

After the black hearses pull away, leaving a swirl of dust, Hitch hands Natalie his suit jacket and tie, then rolls up his white shirt sleeves. In the barn, the green tractor that has almost three thousand hours on it starts up immediately. The clean start is testament to his father's maintenance schedule. Hitch exchanges the hay spike for a bucket with metal teeth on the lower edge, then maneuvers the tractor into the family cemetery through the gap where he's removed a section of white board fence. He is soothed by the purr and gurgle of the tractor engine, the faint smell of diesel fuel, the breeze blowing nature smells across the fields. The work is quick, his hand deft on the loader stick, and within a few minutes the sand is replaced and smoothed. It looks like a beach dune partially trampled. He vows to keep the weeds out of the plots. The cows stand at the east fence of their nursery, watching it all.

He joins Natalie on the front porch. The sun has another hour of light. The wind is out of the north, cold. Natalie hands him a cup of hot chocolate. It has become his go-to beverage over the past week. He doesn't know why, exactly, doesn't try to explain it. He takes a sip. Sweet. Comforting. Evoking some memory from a more peaceful time, maybe.

"We should be out there looking for the engineer," Hitch says.

"Where would we even start?"

"The railroad must keep records. Or we could start talking to workers at the rail yard. Somebody must know something."

"The railroad won't return my calls," Natalie says.

He takes another sip of hot chocolate, then turns to Natalie. "Did you get the Kahlua?"

Natalie produces a yellow-labeled brown bottle wedged against her hip in the rocking chair. "Are you sure this is what you want to do?"

"One hundred percent." Hitch adds some to his cocoa, takes a gulp, then peers down the tunnel of trees, toward the railroad crossing he can barely see from here, trying to imagine exactly how it happened. After a few minutes, he has the thousand-mile stare. Tears sting his eyes.

35

They huddle around the conference table in Tobias' office, their faces grim.

"I don't know what to tell you," Tobias says, rubbing his jaw as if he's just been sucker-punched.

"My parents haven't been in the ground three days, and Alicia Vanderwelt is demanding we dismiss the lawsuit?"

"There's more," Tobias says. He hands across the table the one-page letter, never folded, on thick cream stationery, with cotton fiber in the sheet. So expensive it's rarely used any more. At the top, in embossed letters, is the name of Vanderwelt's law firm. It came in an overnight mailer.

Hitch runs his fingers across the raised letters as if reading braille, and the pit in his stomach enlarges. The missive is a Rule 11 letter, notice to Tobias that as signatory to the lawsuit's complaint he has an obligation to continually evaluate the validity of the facts relied upon for the lawsuit. In terse language, Vanderwelt has warned that in light of the deaths of Hale and Bridget Hitchcock, the legal dispute has evaporated and is now moot, and any continued pursuit of the litigation will be met with a motion for sanctions. Vanderwelt threatens that if they do not drop the lawsuit within 30 days, she will ask the Judge to impose sanctions against the as yet unopened Hitchcock Estate and Tobias individually, in at least the amount of the firm's attorney fees. She ends the letter in bold script, all caps, replacing the bullhorn she'd probably prefer to use:

I REMIND YOU OF YOUR DUTIES AND RESTRICTIONS UNDER THE OFFICIAL CODE OF GEORGIA ANNOTATED, SECTION 33-24-53, AND GEORGIA RULE OF PROFESSIONAL CONDUCT 7.3.

"I know Rule 7.3 prohibits solicitation of clients," Hitch says, "but what is this statute she's referring to?"

"I had to look it up," Tobias replies. "It's the anti-runner statute.

Prevents lawyers from using non-lawyers to solicit clients. First offense is a misdemeanor. Second is a felony punishable by up to ten years in prison, and a $100,000 fine."

"She doesn't want us to find another plaintiff," Hitch says. "And she's threatening us with prison if we do it."

Hitch lets this settle. The suit they filed is a putative class action, meaning Tobias doesn't represent any of the unnamed class members until the Judge grants the motion for class certification.

"The motion for class certification is scheduled for March 31, five weeks out. She's demanding we dismiss before that," Hitch says. "Before there is even a class to represent."

"She's not just tossing idle threats, is she?" Tobias says.

"Alicia Vanderwelt? No."

Natalie, who has been reading the letter over Hitch's shoulder, announces what they all have been thinking: "She's already spent $100,000 in attorney fees? How is that even possible? All she's done is submit a baseless motion to dismiss and appear at a twenty-minute hearing, which she lost."

Hitch shrugs. "She probably charges $800 an hour, maybe more. She's got a whole team of minions ginning hours." He turns to Tobias. "What are the odds Judge Fisher would seriously consider a motion for sanctions under these circumstances? I mean, our plaintiffs were killed."

Tobias drums his fingers on the table. "Slim, but can we take the risk? I certainly can't."

Hitch has faced such motions before, but never have they succeeded. It is not standard practice, yet aggressive defense litigators sometimes use the threat to cow their opponents, to sow doubt about the validity of their cases, to instill fear that perhaps the lawyer will be forced to pay attorney fees to the other side. "I'm not the attorney of record here," Hitch begins.

"This is your show," Tobias says. "I'm just along for the ride, until your suspension gets lifted in six weeks. But I don't think we're going to make it that far. Let's not forget the real issue—now that your parents have passed, we don't have a plaintiff. And even if somebody comes walking in my door, Vanderwelt will assume we solicited them and come after me."

Hitch eyes Tobias for a moment, rolling a pen back and forth in his palms. "What about the fraud?"

Tobias sighs, looks at Natalie for a moment. "Well, the relief we asked for was a ruling that your mother can stay in the house until she passes."

Hitch abruptly stands up, tossing Vanderwelt's letter on the table. He goes to the window, feeling the weight of defeat on his shoulders, the suck of despondency the same magnitude as when he was notified of his suspension. Vanderwelt is tenacious, relentless. She will continue to attack him. He should have seen this coming but, once again, he did not. He can't give up. He is close to unraveling the whole mortgage scheme. He can feel it. And he also senses, as his subconscious works to pull pieces together in that undefinable way, that his parents were murdered because he filed the lawsuit.

"Natalie, show him the subpoenas."

From her briefcase with the two fang punctures, Natalie pulls out a packet of stapled documents. She hands them across the table to Tobias.

Tobias sorts through a stack of 23 subpoenas, targeted at different individuals and entities with potential knowledge or documents related to the reverse mortgages and the companies behind them. "Who's Veronica Nobles?"

"She's the manager of the Nevada LLC that is the manager of the Georgia LLCs that hold the mortgages on these loans," Hitch says.

"And a lawyer?"

Hitch nods. "Works for the Las Vegas branch of Vanderwelt's law firm."

"You know Nobles will claim attorney-client privilege."

"Of course, but we might be able to beat it," Hitch says.

Tobias raises his eyebrows. "Because …"

"Don't know yet. I'm working on it."

"And do you expect any of these entities are actually going to comply with these subpoenas and divulge the identity of the company members who own them?"

"Not without a fight," Hitch says. He gazes out the window at white and pink dogwoods whose leaves are just beginning to unfurl. "Tobias, the subpoenas could be the key to everything."

Tobias sighs. "Hitch, I know this is important to you, but we can't win this. Not now. And unless we want to face the prospect of sanctions, and possible disbarment, which I don't want to do, we're going to have to dismiss the case, at which point the subpoenas become moot."

Hitch paces the room. "We have 30 days to decide whether to dismiss the case. The responses to the subpoenas will be due in fourteen. Let's get them served. We get the documents, then we have two weeks to decide. I need to think," he says, heading for the conference room door.

Natalie follows him.

They shuffle down the brick steps to the sidewalk, past the ruby flowers of two camelia trees, the sweet fragrance carried on a light breeze. Hitch stares at the sky, a mixture of watery blue, with cirrus clouds scuttling across like scared rabbits. The morning air is infused with moisture. He thrusts his hands in his pockets, kicks at a downed limb in the office yard. "Fuck her," he says.

Natalie stands with her arms folded, looking back at the door to Tobias's office. She starts to say something when a uniformed deputy approaches them from the street. It is not the same deputy who took her complaint about the snake in her car.

The deputy stops in front of Hitch. "Are you Oakley Hitchcock?"

"I am. Do you have an update about the investigation into my parents' death?" It is his first inclination, the only reason a sheriff's deputy would approach him here.

"No, sir." He pulls a thick sheaf of papers from his back pocket and holds them out. "It's a summons. Sorry to have to be the one."

Hitch takes the pages and the deputy retreats. Hitch unfolds the packet, his eyes growing big, rifling through the pages in quick succession, the wind rattling the paper and making it difficult to read the words.

"What? What is it?" Natalie asks.

He ignores her until he gets to the end, seeing once again Alicia Vanderwelt's signature, the precise loops and swirls in ballpoint pen. The pit in his stomach has become a sharp pain. His hand goes to his side, and an anguished look overtakes his face. He bends over and retches into the grass.

Natalie puts a hand on his shoulder to console and steady him. "What is it?"

He straightens, wipes his mouth with the back of his sleeve. His eyes sting. Whether from the wind, or the heave of his stomach, or the shock of the deputy's delivery, he cannot say. He spits into the grass, hands the papers to Natalie. "She's foreclosing on our farm," he says.

36

Hitch has barely a month to save the farm. The foreclosure sale is set for April 4, five days before his suspension ends. He wanders the pastures in a daze, kicking at pesky Johnson grass and dog fennel flourishing along the fence lines. He sits in the barn for hours, on a three-legged stool upon which his father often perched, sorting through metal parts whose functions elude Hitch. Sometimes he squats on the top rail of the birthing corral, watching the cows watching him. New calves suck for milk. The donkey stands by himself, within view of the cattle, his ears perked and alert for predators.

Hitch feels the donkey's isolation. His brother, and now his parents, have been ripped from him in the most violent of ways. Sonia was murdered before his eyes. He watched the blood leak out of her, saw her eyes turn glassy, heard the sputter of her last breath. He has been powerless to stop all this mayhem, unable to kick away the attackers with sharp hooves or deft legal maneuvers.

In the cemetery he sits cross-legged on his relatives' graves, staring at the tombstones and what lies beyond. He still has not scripted his parents' epitaphs. Nothing seems right. He is too devastated to think clearly. Their gravestones remain blank, supported by temporary wooden stakes that have begun to darken and rot. He plucks a few weeds that have sprouted on the tombs, flinging away the blades like pestilence, as if this simple act can somehow stop the impending disaster of losing the land. This is all he has left. He lays back on the coarse sand, his eyes lost in a gray sky, and tips a bottle of peach-flavored vodka to his mouth. Using the alcoholic's favorite trick, he has deceived himself into believing that something that tastes like liquid candy cannot be potent, cannot be harmful, cannot destroy his life.

He wonders what will happen to the family cemetery when the farm is gone. Will the graves be relocated? He couldn't bear it. Over the past few months he has traversed almost every square foot of the farm, the fences and the fields, the stands of trees that provide shade against a relentless sun, the creek that turns into a torrent after the spring rains and slows to a trickle as summer endures. He has grown comfortable with the feel of range grass beneath his boots, the musky smell of the swamp on a breeze, the tittering of birds and the conversations of cows. He will miss it. And the farm undoubtedly will be turned into something else. No longer nurturing and providing for the Hitchcocks. Maybe developed for housing. He doesn't know.

As he lies there in a woozy state, he composes a eulogy to the farm. The words are ambiguous and imprecise, a passage about nature and how it nurtures, peopled generations that change though the land doesn't. The land's permanence. He has been raised here, has witnessed the life cycle of animals that are not just sources of food and income, the circle of life and death of those whose blood he shares. Realizing what it will mean to lose this place, melancholy overtakes him.

Natalie finds him lying in the dirt as rain splatters the tombs. The liquor bottle is tipped over, the red cap next to it, empty save for a small puddle in the glass shoulder. She tries to pull him up but can't. His sodden form is too bulky for her to move him more than an inch. As the rain intensifies, the patter becomes a din, sheets of it tumbling from the heavens. She starts yelling at Hitch, screaming at him, using words that have no impact and are swept away like new topsoil in a flood. She reaches down and slaps his chin, a tepid tap. When this does not rouse him, she swings harder, the sting of her palm a sharp crack against his cheek. His eyes pop open.

He is beyond drunk, almost unable to comprehend the situation into which he has sunk. After a minute or two he is able to raise himself to his elbows. He stares at Natalie, drenched to the skin, her long blonde hair plastered against her forehead and cheeks.

"Can you get up?"

He grunts an inaudible response.

"I can't lift you."

The rain continues to pummel them. The first real rain of spring, plummeting from high clouds, icy on impact. Puddles have formed around Hitch's body and pooled around Natalie's feet. She crosses her arms, grips her biceps and begins to shiver.

He rolls over on his side, then onto his knees, plants one foot on the ground and rises like a wounded bull. He staggers to the right, almost falls, but Natalie catches him. They trudge through the muck toward the house. The mud sucks at their soles. They doff their muddy shoes on the porch.

With one arm she pulls open the screen door, whose hinges moan with rust, and with the other she ushers Hitch into the kitchen. He slumps into a wooden chair at the kitchen table, dripping puddles onto the floor.

He has regained consciousness but is still woozy. "You should have left me there."

"You might have drowned," she says, dabbing the water from her face with a dish towel.

He merely shrugs.

She ignites the gas on a front burner and settles the kettle there.

He gets up and wobbles to the kitchen sink, pukes the contents of his stomach, an expurgation of more than just alcohol. He needs all of this out of him. He needs to purge himself of everything dark and malevolent. Still addled, he is aware only of the raw burn in his throat as things come back up, filling his nose too. When he is done he turns on the faucet and rinses his mouth, spits, blows his nose into a paper towel, then staggers back to the chair and falls into it.

The next week is spent drying out. There is no discussion about it, just a mutual, silent acknowledgment that he has trudged to the edge of the abyss, perhaps thought about throwing himself over, but in the moment of his pause Natalie arrived to rescue him. It happened to him once before, in his first sojourn with Sonia. The end to that relationship was abrupt because there was little more than a lukewarm hope that he would not find a deeper bottom, and Sonia did not possess the strength to endure it. He wonders if Natalie will abandon him too. She probably should.

For three days he shivers in bed, his body convulsing as the alcohol drains from him. Natalie wants to take him to the hospital or a detox center, but he refuses, seeing this isolated and miserable recovery, the tremors and the fever and the retching, as his penance. His parents certainly endured more. His brother Rip suffered greater.

By the end of the week he is able to hold down warm tea and bland crackers. He can shower standing up. His first foray from the house in seven days begins with a crisp denim shirt and canvas pants, snake boots covering his shins and calves. He strides to the barn and starts the tractor, then mixes a batch of weed killer and begins spraying the fence lines to kill the nettle, Johnson grass and dog fennel that have taken over. It seems in some sense a feeble attempt at squashing the growing invasion, but it is a start.

The pallor that stayed with him through the winter, turning an ashen gray during the week of his recuperation, begins to recede. The blood returns to his skin and to his brain. He sits on the bucket seat of the tractor, his face tilted toward the sun. He gazes across the farm. He will have to sell the cows, though he hates to do it all at once. Maybe the prices have increased to a palatable level. And he will have to sell the tractor, too. He will go through the house and collect things he wants to take back to Savannah, then hold an estate sale of the rest. But he needs to act quickly. He has only two weeks before the farm will be sold at foreclosure on the courthouse steps.

Natalie wanders out to where the tractor idles. She has been for a run. If she still feels the threat of an assault, she no longer fears it. She took his SUV to the perimeter of the Okefenokee Swamp to run one of the paved entrance roads just after the sun rose. Her face is still flush, a sheen on her legs and arms. The laces of her running shoes are speckled with dirt and tiny seeds.

"How far did you go this morning?"

"Eight," she says, her face upturned to his.

"Any trouble?"

She scoffs. "Only a couple of tourists on motorcycles. Tried to race me."

"And you won," he says.

"Of course, but probably because they had to stop at the gatehouse and pay the entrance fee."

She puts her foot on the tractor's green metal step, slides her hand onto his hip. "How you doing out here?" she says.

"Good. Just applying some weed killer to the fence lines."

She nods. "Keeping the place up. Even though the foreclosure is just around the corner."

His hands tug at the steering wheel. "I don't know why I'm doing this. I mean, my parents were killed here. How many more times will I have to drive past that spot, re-living that wreck in my head?"

There is an ensuing silence, an uncomfortable one. Hitch does not notice the songs of birds in the trees, or the sparkling dew on grass the color of emeralds.

She reaches down and brushes some dirt from her damp shoe. She looks up at him in a squint. "It's the right thing to do, isn't it? The only thing, really."

He grips her right forearm and helps her up into the open cab, settles her on his lap.

"Thank you, Natalie."

"For what?"

"For sticking by me through all this. The suspension, the drinking. You know, everything."

"I'm very fond of you, you know."

He closes his eyes then presses his lips into hers, maybe too hard, reaches his hand behind her neck. He needs to hold onto something. She reciprocates without hesitation. After a time, he pulls back for a breath.

"This feels right, Natalie."

She nods her head. "It does."

They are leaning in again, lips just touching, when the anguished low of a cow reaches them. Hitch swivels his head in that direction.

"Something's wrong," he says.

"How can you tell?"

He shrugs. "Experience, I guess. That cow's in trouble."

He starts the tractor, and Natalie settles onto the hump of the metal wheel well beside him, one hand gripping the bar on the back of the driver's seat. He motors into the birthing corral, scattering a few cows and young calves to the fence lines. One cow stands in the center of the pocked field. They can hear her bellow over the idling engine.

Hitch creeps toward the cow, with Natalie at his shoulder. The donkey eyes them from his post near the water trough. The cow, with a yellow tag dangling from her left ear, has her rear legs slightly splayed, and two small hooves sticking out of the back of her.

"Her calf is breeched," Hitch says.

The cow bellows again. She is trying to expel her calf. Her hair is matted and damp, her eyes wide with pain and fear.

"We have to pull the calf, or both of them might die. Come with me."

They run to the barn. Hitch dons elbow-length rubber gloves and picks up a bottle of mineral oil and a long hemp rope. At his direction, Natalie grabs an open bag of range cubes, fills a jug with water, and slips a plastic syringe into the pocket of her shorts.

"Normally, I'd like to get her in the head gate, but I doubt we can maneuver her over there," he says as they trot back to the cow. "You stand in front of her so she can see you. Feed her some kibble. Remember, keep your palm flat or she'll take your fingers. If she swings her head or starts to charge, get the hell out of the way."

They take up their positions. Hitch talks to cow number 53 in a soothing voice, pats and rubs her haunch. He coats his gloves in mineral oil, stands behind her, and slips both hands past the hooves and rear legs of the calf. He works his hands inside, feeling the calf's position. It is too big to turn in the birth canal. The calf is still alive, but struggling. If he doesn't get it out of there quickly, it will suffocate. He slips a loop of rope around both of the calf's legs, then another just below the forelocks, and begins to pull on the rope, leaning back and using all his weight. He makes no progress. The cow is exhausted and of little help. Hitch ties the other end of the long rope to the tractor, mounts the tractor, puts it in gear and eases away. It is not the way his father would have done it, but he didn't see the calf puller in its usual place in the barn, and this is what he has. The calf slips out another half a foot, its knees clear now. Then the progress stops as the tractor begins to pull the cow backward too.

She bellows again and staggers. She starts swinging her big head side to side.

"Move back, Nat," Hitch yells as he jumps down from the tractor. The pulling rope is taut, the cow somewhat stable, as he sticks his hands into the birth canal again. He grabs the half-born calf's hips to rotate it. The calf is still moving, but barely. He runs around to face the cow.

"I don't know how, but do whatever you can to keep her still, or maybe even moving toward you, but stay away from her head. If she hits you with her head she could break a bone." He slowly reaches out to stroke the cow's white face. The cow turns her face away but does not retreat. "Do your best," he says to both of them.

He runs back to the tractor, leaps up into the cab and begins moving the tractor forward. The calf slips out another foot. Its rear haunches emerge, and Hitch accelerates until the calf comes fully out with a big sucking sound. When he gets back to the calf to untie the ropes, it is not moving. He slips off the ropes, strips off his gloves, and puts his palm against the calf's chest. The heartbeat is there, but weak. The calf is not breathing. He wipes mucous away from its nostrils then cups his hands and blows into the calf's nose. He repeats this several times. A few seconds later, the calf coughs and takes its first breath.

As he kneels by the calf, a shadow looms over him. The mother inches forward, then dips her head and sniffs her calf. Then she begins licking its head.

"Is it okay?" Natalie asks.

Hitch stands. There is nothing left for him to do. The mother cow has taken over. "I think so. We might not know for a couple of days."

They back away and stand there for a few minutes, watching cow and calf bond. The frenetic pace and adrenaline of the last half-hour ease out of them. One crisis has been averted. The engine of the tractor ticks as it cools. Doves coo from a distant pine tree.

"How did you know how to do that? Blow in its nose like that?" Natalie finally asks.

"I read about it in a cattle magazine," he says. "One of the things you do when you're bored on a farm at night."

"You're good at this, Hitch. This might be your calling."

He looks at Natalie with skepticism, his eyes narrow. "I do really love this place. Something about being out here in the fields, with the sounds of birds instead of ringing phones and electronic beeps announcing email.

"So are you going to fight the foreclosure?"

He takes another look around, the pastoral scene lifting his heart. "I have to, don't I? I'm certainly not going to just roll over and let Alicia Vanderwelt take a farm that's been in my family for more than a hundred years."

37

As they finish breakfast, Hitch receives an alert on his phone. The video camera in the live oak tree out front is capturing something. A few seconds later a camera at the front of the house also is active. He switches to the video feeds and watches as a car settles in the front parking area. It is barely light. The Sheriff emerges from the driver's side. An unknown man slides from the passenger seat.

Hitch opens the door before the first knock. On the porch stands Sheriff Ponder and a suited man who introduces himself as Ralph Lowell from the Federal Railroad Administration. Lowell hands him a business card.

Hitch shows them into his father's office, which has taken on a musty air from two weeks without occupancy. Natalie joins him behind the desk, wearing a peach sun dress. She remains standing. The Sheriff and investigator Lowell sit in the cracked vinyl chairs on the other side.

"The investigation is still ongoing, but I have something I think you should see," Lowell begins. He pulls a tablet from its case and sets it on a corner of the cluttered desk. He recites the series of steps he has undertaken, with lab tests on the engine and truck conducted by separate teams.

"The train was going 46 miles per hour upon impact. There is no evidence the train applied its brakes."

"But shouldn't the conductor have seen my dad's truck and slowed?" Hitch asks.

Lowell looks down. His feet tap the worn carpet. "I thought you knew. There was no conductor or engineer. This train was operated remotely."

"How is that even possible?" Hitch says.

"It's not new technology," Lowell says. "A little unusual out here, but this locomotive was operated by satellite."

"So no eyewitnesses?" Natalie adds.

"No, but we do have video from the train cab," Lowell says. "It's very graphic. I don't know if you really want to see it."

"Show it to us," Hitch says immediately.

Lowell maneuvers the cursor and pulls up the video. He taps a key and turns the tablet around for Hitch and Natalie to watch.

There is no sound. It is like watching a silent horror movie. The headlamps on the locomotive light the scene as it moves down the track. The clip shows an empty track, shadow-casting trees on either side. The sky has an eerie glow, as if they are traveling through a tunnel whose ceiling is only a few yards above. At perhaps 100 yards the crossing comes into view. The lamps reflect off of Hale Hitchcock's silver-gray pickup, casting a glare on the windshield and passenger-side windows. The truck is stationary on the driveway, clear of the train track, its headlights on, the red glow of the rear brake light clearly visible. The fog of the rear exhaust hovers near the ground. The inside of the truck's cab is obscured.

Hitch taps the pause button. "How many feet per second at 46 miles per hour?" He asks.

"Approximately sixty-seven," Lowell says.

Hitch taps the play button and watches the time-stamp in the bottom right corner of the screen. At that moment, the stamp reads 21:52:14. It seems to take forever, perhaps because he knows what is coming. When the train is about fifty yards from the crossing, his father's truck begins to move toward the track. It is straddling the rails, still in motion, when the train arrives. The video captures the truck at impact, the spray of glass. Hitch has to supply the sounds of metal crunching on metal and the shattering of glass. To his parents he supplies no sounds, hoping intently they died on impact. He watches as the truck is pushed along the track for a second or two before it begins to roll. He looks away, covers his eyes with his palms.

Lowell turns the computer around and taps the pause button. "It's hard to watch, even for me, and I've seen dozens of these crashes," he says. "I can't imagine what it's like for you."

Hitch stands up and goes to the door of his father's office, opens it, then shuts it without leaving. He is steeling himself. He knows he has to watch it again. And again. And again. Usually he sees only the reconstruction of accidents. He has never before seen a real train wreck, never actually watched the final few seconds of anyone's life. Yes, he has. Sonia. He watched her die. But it still didn't prepare him for this.

"I have an enhanced excerpt," Lowell says. "I think it's important."

Sheriff Ponder speaks for the first time. "You need to see this, Hitch."

Hitch nods. "Okay." He returns to the desk.

Lowell taps an icon, picks up the tablet, and sets it down facing Hitch. He stands over Hitch's right shoulder as the video plays. This clip is focused on the rear half of his father's truck as the train approaches. It is grainier, enlarged. The truck begins moving forward but is mostly out of view in this image when the train hits the crossing.

"What am I looking for?"

Lowell re-starts the video. "Look behind the truck as it starts to move. On the other side."

Hitch watches a blur of motion and a glint of light appear as the truck moves from left to right across the screen. The image is distorted, as if the video has been damaged. "What is that?"

"We've tried to reconstruct it in the lab, and the results are inconclusive. We can't enlarge the frames anymore without losing clarity. But our theory is that the blur is something moving away from the truck across the driveway."

Hitch replays the video, sees a quick flash once, then nothing. "And what is that flash?"

"Again, we aren't certain, but we think it's the train's headlamps reflecting off of metal. Maybe a dog collar or something. We don't know. We may never be sure. These videos are not high resolution, so even with enhancement the image is always going to be grainy. We found something else. We examined every square inch of that truck, every scratch and dent, even the bumper."

"I thought maybe another vehicle pushed them across the track. I mean, my father was one of the most cautious people you've ever met. This video almost makes it look like suicide."

"We don't think he voluntarily drove across the track. There may have been someone else involved."

"Who?"

"That, we don't know. When the train hit your father's truck, the driver's side door wasn't fully latched."

"You think he tried to get out at the last minute?"

Lowell shakes his head. "No, the seat belt was fully engaged. And," Lowell nods at the Sheriff.

Sheriff Ponder pulls folded papers from his shirt pocket, hands them to Hitch. "Just got this report last night. Read it for yourself, but when the coroner re-tested your parents' blood samples, he found a fair amount of tranquilizer in your parents' blood. Xylazine, to be exact. Used for sedating big animals. Your parents were probably unconscious."

"So they were drugged," Hitch says. "I knew he didn't drive into the path of that train." He looks up at Natalie for confirmation.

She nods, caresses his shoulder.

"So what's your theory, Mr. Lowell?"

"I have to stress that we don't know exactly what happened, and will probably never know all of the details. But analyzing all of this information together, the engineering and reconstruction reports, the toxicology report, the video, the data recorder, I'd say your father was unconscious when the truck crossed the tracks."

Hitch stares up at Lowell. "Are you going to put that in your report?"

Lowell shakes his head. "My theory is strictly unofficial. The report will say that the truck rolled across the track as the train approached and that the collision was therefore unavoidable."

"Unavoidable?" Hitch repeats. "Are you kidding?"

"My job is all about cause and effect. Why the truck crossed that train track at that moment in time is the Sheriff's jurisdiction."

Hitch turns to Sheriff Ponder, studies him across the desk, his face in murky blue shadow from the screen light of the tablet. "Sheriff?"

"I've seen the evidence. The presence of xylazine in both of your parents convinced me. At this point, Hitch, I'm treating their deaths as homicides."

38

As is often the case in a litigator's world, everything becomes about time. Hitch can hear the clock ticking in his head. The responses to the subpoenas Tobias served should be here in three days. The deadline for filing the motion for class certification is in seven days. Vanderwelt's demand to dismiss the lawsuit without sanctions expires in fourteen days. The hearing on class certification is scheduled for 26 days, and the foreclosure sale on the Hitchcock farm is set for four days later. His suspension will end five days after the foreclosure. *After* is the only part of that he can focus on. It is almost unfathomable how these dates line up. The word "deadline" has never struck him this way before. He knows the documents they will receive in response to the subpoenas are the lynchpin to their case. If they have any case. He also knows there are at least a dozen ways things can be thrown off course.

The revelations in the train-crash video and the toxicology report spawn more questions than they answer. The biggest question: Why? If his parents were murdered, of which he is now certain, there must be a motive beyond the class-action lawsuit itself. He can't fathom the idea that a corporate defendant would kill the named plaintiffs just to end the litigation. The George Colbert situation was different. Or was it? As he stands at the kitchen window scanning the eastern horizon, he asks this question over and over in his mind. He finds no immediate answer.

He sips coffee with creamer—no Kahlua this time—and tries to allow the unobtrusive processes of his subconscious to work. But he is unsettled. His eyes roam over Jasper, stretched out on a braided rug. He kneels next to his dog, fingers the tag in the shape of a dog bone. The dog's name and Hitch's cell number are inscribed on it. The tag is shiny. It will reflect light. He tries to remember if Jasper was inside or outside on the night his parents were killed. He can't recall.

Natalie comes through the kitchen door, a sheen of sweat on her skin. Her hair is tied back in a ponytail that reaches below her shoulders. She is dressed in a pink singlet and running shorts in a paisley design.

"I hate treadmills," she says.

He sips coffee. "It's temporary. Once we know the danger is passed, you can hit the roads again."

She blows out some air, walks over to him. "Do I smell like cow dung? I feel like I smell like cow flop. Or rotting hay."

"You smell like a woman who just ran for an hour and a half. How far did you go?"

"Eleven miles. Are you sure I don't smell like farm?"

"You do not smell like farm. But if you want, we can move the treadmill out of the barn and into the house. I'm just not sure where."

"No. It's fine."

"Hey, change of subject. On the night of the train wreck, do you remember if Jasper was in or out?"

"Out."

"You sure?"

"I am. You let him out just after dinner. He was whining at the door. He followed us back to the house after the wrecker removed your dad's truck."

Hitch nods in recognition. "He was whining at the door. I remember now. So the blurred image we saw on the video tape, the flash of light, that could have been a reflection from Jasper's dog tag."

"Sure. But Jasper didn't shoot your parents up with horse tranquilizer."

"We don't know it was injected."

"How else would it get in their bloodstream?"

"Could have been ingested. Maybe in their food or something."

"At their Valentine's dinner?"

"I don't know. I'm just exploring possibilities."

"Well, Jasper certainly didn't open the driver's door, or move your dad's truck across the tracks."

They meet with Tobias to fill him in about the train crash video. Tobias would like to see the video, but Hitch has not been allowed to make a copy. Before he left this morning, Agent Lowell reminded them the investigation is on-going, and until it is complete the video will remain under wraps.

"They were drugged, too," Hitch says. "The coroner found horse tranquilizer in their blood."

"Horse tranquilizer?"

"Xylazine. Used by vets for medical procedures on large animals. My parents were murdered, Tobias."

Tobias nods. "It certainly looks that way."

"There's no other reasonable explanation. The Sheriff is treating it as homicide."

"Motive?"

"Somebody wants our farm very badly, or will kill to get the lawsuit dismissed. But past that, I have no clue."

"There are tens of thousands of acres of farmland in this county," Tobias says. "Most of it can be had for a song. What's so special about your farm that someone is willing to commit murder to get it?"

"I don't know yet," Hitch responds. Hitch's mind keeps working, trying to find the answer. *Follow the money* keeps blaring at him, but he doesn't understand how that fits. The banks are lending money to the landowners—a fraction of the fair market value—but with no expectation of repayment. He has assumed the banks will foreclose and then sell the land for a huge profit. Maybe that's the motive.

"We need to go back to the courthouse," Hitch says.

Hitch and Natalie spend more hours on the courthouse computer. They have become an inseparable pair. With his world collapsing around him, he needs Natalie, and he has a fervent hope she needs him in some way as well.

They update the list of properties that have been subjected to reverse mortgages and security deeds. Since they last checked, an additional 22 farms in the county have been burdened by reverse mortgages held by nontraditional lenders, bringing the total to 74. Garland T. Rogers has been busy. He notarized each mortgage. These additional mortgages fit the pattern of every other one they've analyzed. When they add up the acreage, they realize these various companies have secured liens on more than 22,000 acres of timber tracts, crop land, and cattle farms in the county, an area equivalent to 34 square miles. They also discover five new foreclosure deeds. The pace of foreclosure is accelerating. His parents' farm will soon be gone.

When they check the grantor indices, they discover every foreclosed property has been transferred to a separate shadow company. All were created the day of each foreclosure sale, the deeds executed a day or two later. They scour the Secretary of State's website but reach the same dead end as they did trying to track down whomever is behind the lender and the mortgage companies. Faceless companies leading to Alicia

Vanderwelt's law partner in Las Vegas.

"Why would anyone go to the time and expense of creating three companies for every transaction?" Hitch asks. "One for the lender; one to hold the mortgage; one to hold the property after foreclosure. We have something like 175 companies here."

"That is a huge expense," Natalie muses. "Filing fees, annual reports. I've never even heard of anything like this."

"Let me check something." Hitch maneuvers the mouse, looking for evidence that any of the foreclosed properties were sold for a profit. The tax stamps on the deeds from the mortgage holders to the shadow companies all show $0, which means no money changed hands when the foreclosed properties were transferred to the holding companies.

"They're not selling the properties," he concludes. "At least not yet. They're holding onto them, which means they have to pay the property taxes on them every year. Another big expense."

They leave the deeds office and are traversing the hallway toward the front doors to the courthouse when Natalie stops. She almost falls back against a wall.

"What?" Hitch asks.

She points toward the intersection of the two hallways.

Hitch looks that way. "What is he doing here?"

Mark Sanchez strides toward them. "Natalie, we need to talk," he calls from thirty feet away. His black hair is mussed, as if he's repeatedly run his fingers through it, and his eyes carry a concerned look.

Hitch looks for a quick exit or a side door to escape through, but sees nothing. He steps between Natalie and Mark, holding up his palm as though stopping a line of traffic.

"Close enough, Mark."

"Natalie, I need to talk to you."

"She has nothing to talk to you about, not after what you did."

Confusion passes over Mark. "You know about that?"

"About the water moccasin and the logging truck? Yeah, we know."

"Water moccasin? Logging truck? What are you talking about?"

"The attacks on Natalie. You know damn well what I'm talking about." Hitch watches Mark's eyes, studies his face. Mark doesn't know. These attacks are revelations to him.

Mark tries to dodge around Hitch, concern on his face. "Natalie, someone attacked you?"

Natalie nods because she can't find words.

They eventually agree to go across the street to a diner, each satisfied that if they passed through the metal detectors at the courthouse entrance, nobody is armed. Hitch sits on one side of a booth, next to the window overlooking the street and the courthouse. Natalie settles next to him.

Mark slides into the other side. "Who attacked you?" Mark tries to focus on Natalie, but he keeps a wary eye on Hitchcock.

"I'm pretty sure it was you," she says.

"Me? I love you, Natalie. I was shopping for engagement rings when you left."

Natalie's mouth drops. She doesn't understand. "You became so distant, Mark. We were drifting apart. Way apart."

Mark sighs. "Yeah. That was my fault. I …I screwed up. I could barely look at you, seeing how much I hurt you. Hurt you both."

Mark tells them all of it. That after the shooting, Alicia Vanderwelt hired him to dig into Hitchcock's relationship with Sonia. That he interviewed George Colbert in prison, acquired the photographs of Hitchcock and Sonia and gave them to Alicia Vanderwelt. That he was the one who persuaded Colbert to file the bar complaint. "Though it didn't take much persuasion," he says. "Colbert would have done anything to hurt you."

"He put a bullet in my chest," Hitch says. "I guess that wasn't enough."

"Yeah. Look, I'm sorry. For all of it. The suspension and everything else."

"So you befriended Natalie so you could get close to me, Mark? Then you convinced her to move into your apartment?"

"Guilty. But it became something else." He reaches for Natalie's hand across the table, but she pulls away. "I fell in love with you, Natalie. You have to believe that."

Natalie has been watching it all unfold, assembling the pieces, not knowing what is true. "I wasn't in love with you, Mark. I don't know whether to believe anything you say right now, but we're over. Especially given the lengths you went to ruin Hitch's career."

"I know. It's unforgivable. But I am sorry. Truly sorry."

"What are you doing down here, anyway?" Hitch asks. "You didn't come down here just to apologize."

"No, I didn't," Mark says. He reaches into the messenger bag at his side and withdraws a gold-colored envelope, lays it on the table.

"I asked you a question, Mark. What are you doing down here?"

"Investigating a case. Your case," he says, locking eyes with Hitch.

"The reverse mortgage case? Are you working for Alicia Vanderwelt?

Mark nods and unclasps the bulky envelope.

Hitch's mind is racing. He senses this is all a trap. "Are you recording this conversation, Mark?"

Mark gives him an annoyed look. "Of course not. Why would you think that?"

"Because I can't trust you as far as I can throw you. And I certainly don't trust Alicia Vanderwelt."

"This is for you." Mark taps the envelope, begins to open it. "I've prepared a summary report. Not the same one I'll send to Alicia, of course, but it's got some explosive information in here. Did you know …"

"Stop, Mark. What you have there is confidential attorney work-product in ongoing litigation. I don't care how explosive it is. I don't want to see it. I don't want to go anywhere near it."

"But you're not going to believe what I've found."

Hitch pulls out his cell phone and hits the record button, laying the phone on the table. "We're in Chelsea's Diner in Pineland, Georgia." He checks his watch. "It is 4:37 p.m. on March 5, 2023. I'm Oakley Hitchcock, and my paralegal Natalie Anderson is sitting next to me. Mark Sanchez, a private investigator working for attorney Alicia Vanderwelt, is sitting across the table from us. He's just produced a gold envelope containing some information about the reverse mortgage class action we filed here in Dare County. He has not shown me the contents, and I have explicitly instructed him not to show me the contents. He has not divulged any information in that envelope. Correct, Mark?"

Mark stares across the table. He realizes his effort to fix what he's done is evaporating. He sees that he's lost Natalie forever. "That's correct," he says finally.

Hitch stops the recording. "Mark, my parents were murdered. Maybe because of the lawsuit I filed on their behalf. Do you really want to be working for somebody who's involved in something like that?"

Mark picks up the envelope and stuffs it in his messenger bag. He slides out of the booth, moves toward the restaurant door. He abruptly stops beside Natalie, leans down, and whispers something in her ear.

39

"What did Mark say to you, before he left?" Hitch asks. There is a jealous tone in his voice, as if Mark might once again have been able to connive Natalie.

"Nothing important." Natalie fiddles with a napkin. "Should we order some food?"

Hitch orders a decaf latte and a BLT. Natalie has a bottle of unsweetened grapefruit juice and a stuffed baked potato.

"Mark is no slouch as an investigator," Natalie says while they are eating. "He worked at the Department of Justice for a few years. Financial crimes."

"I knew he was a PI, but I didn't know he'd been at DOJ."

"That was one of the first things he told me when … anyway, he probably had some very valuable information in that packet."

"Doesn't matter," Hitch replies. "I'm not touching that. Maybe his intentions are pure, but there's a strong possibility Vanderwelt is trying to set me up. Don't forget she's already threatened us. Accepting confidential information from her side of the case would give her all the evidence she'd need to have me disbarred. Anyway, I didn't bite."

"Just wondering," Natalie says, "that if someone murdered your parents to get their land, if maybe they weren't the first." She swallows the last forkful of her baked potato.

Hitch swivels his head and stares at her for a few seconds, then flips open his laptop. He easily finds the website for the Journal-Herald, the local newspaper published weekly. He is able to research the paper's obituaries back to 2015. Hitch lingers on the obituaries of his parents, which he hastily wrote while the funeral director looked on. The separate obituaries are sterile recitations of his parents' births, dates of death, family members who predeceased them and the lone child who survived, with a blurb about the funeral schedule. The descriptions are uninspired and provide no insight into who his parents actually were. He stares at their photographs, both in color, taken a few years earlier when they had taken a rare vacation to the beach. In his mother's photograph he can see his own smile, his green eyes, the fine blonde hair they shared. Like himself, his father possessed the square Hitchcock jaw and the habit of facing the camera head on, a defiant look in the eyes.

Using their list of reverse mortgages, he reads other obituaries, summaries of men and women who were born in the county but moved on, some transplants from up north, some who served in the military. Most of the pictures seem to match the age of the deceased, but some have photos that preceded their deaths by decades, and Hitch wonders what possessed their survivors to use old photographs. Could they not find anything more recent? Did they want to portray the deceased as vibrant and youthful?"

"I wonder why so few of these obituaries list the circumstances of death," Hitch says.

Natalie shrugs.

He keeps scrolling down the list of obituaries, hundreds who have perished in the preceding two years. Comparing it to the list of 74 owners who have taken out reverse mortgages, he notes 26 have died, including his father.

"Just over a third of the borrowers have died since taking out a reverse mortgage. In two-and-a-half years. Doesn't that seem startling high to you?" he says.

"Not if they're being murdered, it doesn't."

"We need to know how they died."

"And that information isn't public. Only next of kin are authorized to know the cause of death."

Hitch's phone rings, interrupting their discussion. "Hello."

"Mr. Hitchcock?" It is a female voice. Pleasant.

"Yes."

"Can you please hold for Alicia Vanderwelt?"

"Okay."

A few seconds later, Alicia Vanderwelt comes on the line.

"How have you been?" she asks as if they are old friends.

Hitch bristles at the mere sound of her voice. He wonders if their meeting with Mark Sanchez not an hour ago and this phone call could be mere coincidence. He doesn't see how.

"I think you know exactly how I've been," he says. "It's been a helluva year. My suspension, my parents' death, being threatened with sanctions by a big Atlanta law firm. I'm really looking forward to returning to my law practice next month."

"Yes, well. I have some good news for you. About the foreclosure coming up. The foreclosure on your parents' farm."

"What other foreclosure could we be talking about, Alicia?" he says. His tone has turned acerbic.

"My client is prepared to offer $100,000 for the land. Throwing in the debt that's owed, that's a generous offer."

"It's a non-recourse loan, Alicia. Writing off an uncollectible debt is worth nothing to me. The lender can't collect on the balance anyway. You know that." He is focused now, back in lawyer mode, starting to argue the inanity of her position. "I can write you a check for the balance of the loan right now, and then the debt is satisfied. No debt; no foreclosure. I just need the number. A payoff statement I've been asking for."

"Check the loan documents."

"What do you mean?"

"The exclusive remedy upon death of the borrower is forfeiture of the property. The borrower's remedy of redemption has been waived."

He might have missed that when he looked at the security deed his father had signed, scanning instead of perusing the fine print in the dim light of his father's office. "What? That can't be right," he says.

"The language is clear," she says in response. "Paragraph 34."

He pulls up his father's mortgage on his laptop. There it is. Not in legalese, from which a clever lawyer might be able to argue the provision is ambiguous or unenforceable:

> **34. When the loan becomes due, the Lender is entitled to foreclose on the Property. You hereby fully and forever waive your right of redemption.**

"Well, the farm's worth a lot more than $100,000," he counters.

"My client is offering you cash plus debt forgiveness, which they don't have to do. They're going to wind up with the property anyway. How might a foreclosure look to your parents' friends and neighbors? You don't want to tarnish their reputation with a foreclosure, do you?"

"That's a cheap shot," he says, out of steam now.

"The offer is good for 72 hours," Vanderwelt says. "Oh, and one other condition. You have to dismiss the lawsuit. Shouldn't be a problem for you, since you no longer have a named plaintiff."

Alicia Vanderwelt hangs up on him.

He stares at his cell phone. "I hate that woman."

"You have good reason to," Natalie says. "So her client wants to buy the farm now?"

"Right. The right of redemption is waived. They've thought this through." He angles the laptop towards Natalie so she can read the language.

"Does that apply if the lender murders the borrower?"

Hitch shakes his head. "I don't see how. You can't benefit financially from causing someone's death. There are a bunch of life insurance cases on point. Where the beneficiary murders the insured, the beneficiary can't collect on the policy." He focuses his eyes on his half-eaten BLT. "I know we've been barking up this tree for a while, but it's becoming clear to me that we can't win the lawsuit by proving my dad was defrauded. That's no longer relevant. To win this thing, we have to prove my parents were murdered by the lender."

40

The next morning, they go first to the coroner's office. They don't don masks or rub peppermint oil beneath their noses this time. Instead, they are directed to a small office on the opposite end of the building from the morgue. Hitch can still smell the odor of death hanging in the air. He wonders if anybody who works here can ever fully wash it out of their clothes, or their hair.

"My condolences again on the death of your parents," the coroner says once they're seated around his desk.

"About that. Is there any way to trace the xylazine you found in my parents' bloodstream?"

The coroner shakes his bushy head. "Not that I'm aware of. The chemical compound wouldn't have a distinct marker. Plus, it's showing up in a lot of street drugs. Cocaine and fentanyl, primarily."

"So you're saying the tranquilizer could have gotten into my parents' systems through street drugs?"

"Not in their case, no. We didn't find any evidence of cocaine or fentanyl. We checked."

Hitch rubs his chin. "Doc, I'm well aware of the restrictions on the type of medical information you can disclose to me. I assume you're aware that the Sheriff is treating my parents' death as homicide?"

The coroner nods.

"Are you seeing any patterns in the people you autopsy?"

"Patterns?"

"Anything consistent about how they died. Where they died. The cause of death."

"Not that I've seen," the man says in a guarded tone.

"But you haven't specifically been looking for a pattern," Hitch says in a soft tone. He knows this could come off as an allegation of negligence. "I'm not saying there is a pattern, but ..." He nods to Natalie.

Natalie pulls out their list of the 26 deaths of the reverse mortgage borrowers, including dates of death. She hands the typed page to the coroner across the desk.

"If you could maybe re-examine your files on these 26," Hitch says. "See if you find any consistencies, any patterns."

"You obviously believe there is a pattern, Mr. Hitchcock. What do you know?"

"Those 26 people all died in the past two-and-a-half years. They all owned a farm or timber tracts in the county."

"Is there any other commonality?" the coroner asks. "Just scanning your list, I'd guess about half didn't get autopsied here."

"Because?"

"Because they didn't meet any of the nine criteria for autopsy. They didn't die violently. Their deaths weren't suspicious or unusual. Etcetera."

Hitch nods, taking this in. He understands now that if there is a common thread in the way the borrowers died, much of that evidence is buried in a casket somewhere. Hitch doesn't want to disclose that all the deceased on his list took out loans from an anonymous lender in the past 30 months. He doesn't want the coroner to know about the class-action lawsuit, or the potential connection among the reverse mortgage holders. He tells himself he's withholding this information to avoid biasing the coroner's medical judgment, but that's not entirely it. In truth, he doesn't fully trust the man.

"We're extremely busy," the coroner says. "I'm not sure we can devote the time to re-examining old files."

Hitch stands. "Given that my parents were murdered, if there is a common thread with these other deaths, can you really afford not to go back through the files?"

Sheriff Guidry Ponder invites them into his office. They settle in government-issued brown leatherette chairs across from his desk. The office walls are adorned with deer heads and pictures of the Sheriff shaking hands with various dignitaries, some of them signed. The black-framed photographs are arranged on the cypress paneling in a haphazard way. There is one with the Georgia governor, another with a now ex-president. As he scans these photographs, Hitch realizes what a political animal the Sheriff actually is. He's been in office for six terms, landslide victories in all but his first election.

Hitch starts because he assumes the Sheriff will be tight-lipped unless he first reveals something of value. "I believe there's a connection between the reverse mortgage my father took out about a year ago, and the murder of my parents."

"A connection?" the Sheriff says slowly, as if the word doesn't belong in this conversation.

"Yes. The loan becomes due when the borrower dies. We filed a civil suit to determine my mother's rights—because she didn't sign the loan, didn't even know about it—and my parents' deaths effectively end the lawsuit. So now the lender is going to foreclose on our property."

The Sheriff is non-committal, working a pinch of snuff behind his lower lip.

"You may not have known that my dad took out a reverse mortgage on our farm a few months back."

"Can't you pay it off?" The Sheriff spits into an empty Dr. Pepper bottle.

"I have the means, but the right to pay it off, what we call the right of redemption, has been waived in the loan agreement."

The Sheriff nods, pulls at the corner of his gray moustache. "So you think the lender might have something to do with your parents' homicide."

A homicide is simply the killing of one person by another. It can be intentional, or negligent, or even accidental. The Sheriff isn't ready to elevate these killings to murder.

"I do. Has to be a motive, right? Obtaining our land could be the motive."

"Lenders just want to be paid back."

"Sure, that's the usual purpose of any loan. But this one—and there are almost 80 just like it in Dare County in the past two-and-a-half years—has looked suspicious from the start. For instance, the lender isn't a traditional bank, and the identity of the lender isn't even disclosed in the mortgage that's filed at the courthouse. You have to look at the promissory note to get that information. Each mortgage holder has a different name. None of them is registered with the Georgia Banking Department."

"Is that illegal?"

"If it's only one loan, it's legal. Private, proprietary lending it's called."

"So unusual, but not illegal," the Sheriff says in a conclusive tone.

"Highly unusual that the lender doesn't want its money back, Sheriff. And none of these properties that have been foreclosed upon have been sold to recover the loan debt."

"This lawsuit you mentioned, is it still active?"

"It is," Hitch says. "But maybe not for much longer."

"And I take it you haven't made much progress through discovery or anything," the Sheriff says.

"No, sir. We've been blocked at every turn."

"Sounds like they've got good lawyers. Good at what they do, I mean."

"We have a list of the reverse mortgage borrowers who have died in the past thirty months."

Natalie pulls the list from her briefcase and hands it across the desk to the Sheriff.

"I'm wondering if you've noticed anything suspicious about the deaths of any of the people on this list. There are 26 of them. Thirty-five percent of the people who took out reverse mortgages of this type in the past two-and-a-half years alone are dead," Hitch says.

The Sheriff peers over the papers at Hitch. He is expert at not revealing information. He also is wary of lawyers, though he recognizes that Hitch isn't here as an attorney and is not representing anyone accused of a crime.

"I know a lot of the names on this list. I knew some of them personally. If there was anything suspicious about their passing, we would have investigated each one."

"Of course, Sheriff. But what if they were killed, and it was made to look like an accident. Like my parents? Carefully staged. Would there be any reason for you to investigate? I mean, what caused you to investigate my parents' death as anything other than an accidental train-truck collision?"

"We go where the evidence leads us."

"Look, I'm not making accusations, here. But I suspect that in my parents' case, after watching the train video, Agent Lowell insisted on a detailed toxicology screen. You expected to find alcohol. You didn't expect to find horse tranquilizer."

The Sheriff says nothing in response.

"I'm just trying to find out who killed my parents."

"So are we," the Sheriff says.

"But you're not looking for a connection between my parents' death and their loan. You're not looking for a connection between these other deaths and their loans. That's the motive." In the short span of a few minutes Hitch has convinced himself all the borrower deaths are related. He just needs the evidence to prove it.

"Mordecai Claxton is on your list," the Sheriff says. "His tractor rolled over on him. And the Davidson woman, she had a heart attack while going out to get her mail."

"Yes, sir. Maybe they weren't accidents."

"But probably they were," the Sheriff counters. "Son, 40 percent of murders are never solved. Do you know why?"

Hitch shakes his head.

"Because the perps we catch are related to the victims, or we have eyewitnesses. Or they're stupid and they leave a bloody trail. Where the killer doesn't leave evidence behind, we won't usually catch him. Same at all levels, whether you're the County Sheriff or the FBI. Forty percent remain unsolved cases. Forever. And the 60 percent we do solve include the mass shootings where you have multiple homicides by one killer."

"You're saying you won't solve this." Hitch's tone is now deflated, the cumulative effect of being fed nothing but bad news for weeks on end.

"No, all I'm saying is the odds are low. Police work isn't like what you see on television. On those shows, they pull evidence out of thin air for dramatic effect. We need witnesses, we need forensic evidence. We have no evidence your parents' deaths are even connected to this loan. We have no evidence any of these other people were the victims of a homicide. You don't have any clues about who is behind these companies."

"But if I'm right, you have a serial killer on your hands."

The Sheriff frowns. Two words he doesn't want to hear, doesn't want to think about. Not in his county. The Sheriff pulls at his moustache again.

"Tell you what. I'll look over your list, talk to the coroner."

"I've already talked to the coroner. He didn't seem to have the time to review the files, but I'm sure he'll be motivated if you ask him to look into it."

The Sheriff studies Hitch. Then he glances at Natalie, too, as if he's trying to determine how much of a nuisance these two will be if he doesn't offer up something. "I need you both to stay out of the investigation. Let us do our jobs. If we find anything, I'll personally let you know. But let me give you a piece of advice."

Hitch, leaning forward in the chair, nods.

"You're not the first child who's lost a parent in a terrible way. I know it's hard. I ain't a psychologist, but at some point you've got to acknowledge the reality. Unless we get a lucky break, we'll probably never catch whoever killed your parents."

Back at the farm, Natalie and Hitch immerse themselves in the care of the animals. The breached calf that Hitch pulled is doing fine, hanging close to its mother. The calf skitters away when they approach to check on it. At the chicken coop, Natalie fills the feeder while Hitch collects eggs, keeping the rooster and its talons in a corner with a pole. Hitch feeds bananas to the donkey. Jasper follows their every step, his nose to the ground. His wrinkled forehead is an emblem of constant worry.

"Do you think this is somehow connected to drugs?" Natalie asks in the barn. "The coroner said the tranquilizer is sometimes found in street drugs."

"I can't see it," Hitch says. "You know my parents. They weren't secretly snorting cocaine. I mean, even if some cartel wants our land to secretly grow something on, why go after all the other borrowers?"

"You're assuming the other deaths weren't from natural causes."

"Aren't you?"

"Maybe. I don't know. How would someone kill 26 people, and except in the instance of your parents, make it look like they all died of natural causes? It just seems too bizarre."

"You think I'm imagining a conspiracy?"

Natalie rubs his shoulder, sweeps a sweaty strand of hair from his forehead. "I think you're under a tremendous amount of stress. Who wouldn't be, with all that's happened?"

He plops down on the three-legged stool his father used to sit on. The lacquer on the seat is worn away. "We need hard evidence."

Natalie nods. "Let's start with the horse tranquilizer. Did it come from here?"

"I doubt it. My dad rarely used tranquilizers."

"Did you check? Where would he keep it?"

"In that old refrigerator," Hitch points.

Hitch pulls open the door to the avocado-green refrigerator that rests in the corner of the barn next to a long wooden table. Its door is mottled with rust. Hitch rummages the wire shelves, reading labels. He holds up a glass bottle, wiggles it to check the level.

"Xylazine."

"So it could have come from here? Did your father keep records?"

Hitch nods. "Of course. He kept records of everything." From a rack inside the front door he pulls a spiral notebook. He flips the pages until he finds the log for medications. "We should have a full, unopened vial, and about 60 milliliters in this one," he announces.

"Is the unopened vial there?"

He checks the shelves again. "Not here."

"So one bottle is missing. Do you think whoever murdered your parents could have stolen it?"

Hitch ponders all he does not know. The pieces of evidence he does not have. Evidence he may never find. The pieces he does possess lead only to supposition and conjecture, without lines connecting them to anyone.

They retreat to the house and re-examine the security footage for the period between camera installation and the night of the train wreck. They see no strangers on the tapes. They don't see any unidentified vehicles. They find nothing out of the ordinary.

"So if the tranquilizer came from our barn, then someone stole it before we installed the security cameras last November."

"Or," Natalie says. "They didn't use the driveway or come within range of the cameras on the house. Maybe they came through the woods or across the fields."

For dinner, they eat tuna fish sandwiches on the front porch, the gentle creak of the rockers creating a pleasant melody. A late afternoon breeze rattles the leaves of the live oak and sways the Spanish moss. The breeze carries the high humidity of the swamp. Hitch wipes his mouth with the back of his sleeve.

"Want a napkin?" Natalie offers him a white paper napkin.

He takes it. "Are you trying to civilize me, woman?"

"I doubt that's possible."

He takes another bite of the sandwich, begins talking before he's finished chewing. "Nat, when you look out at this farm, what do you see?"

"I see a peaceful, pastoral place with lots of trees and cows."

"Me too. Is that worth killing for? Would someone have murdered them just for trees and cows? It doesn't make any sense."

"Maybe for the trees. Trees have to be worth something, right?"

"We don't have that many. My father's eternal debate with Mordecai Claxton was that pastureland is more valuable than timber land. When Claxton died, he had no trees left. All burned. In any event, it would take fifteen to twenty years after planting saplings before you have anything to harvest."

"Maybe we can't see it."

"What do you mean?"

"Maybe it's in the ground. Water? Oil? I don't know." She exhibits a shy look, holding something back.

"What are you not telling me?"

"I'm not telling you because I want to protect you. Trust me. But there might be something valuable in the ground."

Hitch wonders again what Mark Sanchez whispered in her ear as he left the diner.

"There's nothing here but sand. It's not even that well-suited for row crops," Hitch says. "I mean there's an underground aquifer that we could tap on the eastern half of the property, but it's a big aquifer and you could drill a well into it from almost any place in Southeast Georgia. I can't see how this is about water."

"Well, maybe I'm wrong," she says, "but I know somebody we can ask. And she's got the time."

Hitch considers this for a moment. "Stacie," he says. He checks his watch. "I want to think about it before I call her."

"Are you even considering Vanderwelt's offer to buy the farm?"

Hitch bites his lower lip and shakes his head. "Nope. I'm not going to give her the satisfaction. I'm not cutting and running from this fight."

She reaches over and grasps his hand. "I'll support you in whatever you decide," she says. "But are you sure you aren't being a little stubborn about this?"

He turns toward her as the sun melts into the horizon. "I am aware that I'm being very stubborn. But I know my dad would not want me to give up this land without a fight."

41

"First, I did a little research and looked at some maps," Stacie Throckmorton says over the speaker on Hitch's cell phone. "Georgia mineral maps and a bunch of maps from the USGS."

"USGS?" Hitch asks.

"United States Geological Survey. The go-to source for issues like this. All public information."

"Continue."

"Next, I talked to a couple of researchers I know up at Georgia Tech. They're at the forefront of soil and geological research, but their studies take years to complete. You've got to do a lot of core sampling to update geological maps." Stacie is being methodical, preferring to lay out her process in chronological order.

"And what did you find?" Hitch asks. He has been waiting two days for Stacie's conclusions. He flashes Natalie an annoyed look across the kitchen table at the farmhouse.

"The geological formations and mineral content of the soil have not changed much in the last 100 million years. What's changed is our equipment and our methodology for identifying what's there."

"Stacie, can you spare me the history lesson? We're running out of time down here."

"He's a little stressed," Natalie explains. "Deadlines are coming up."

"Well, geologically, most of what's there is phosphate rock and sand. Good for growing pine trees and for certain building materials."

"That's it? Sand and rock. No oil? No gold?"

"No oil. Trace amounts of gold. There's monazite, and some recently discovered rare earth minerals in that area. In very small quantities. There's a pit mine near the Okefenokee Swamp where they're mining rare earths."

"You lost me."

"Rare earth minerals aren't actually rare. It's just that they are usually found in such small concentrations that they can't be mined economically."

"So why are they being mined now?" Hitch asks.

"Because most of our technology needs rare earth minerals to operate. Magnets mostly. Electric car batteries. Big-screen TVs. Cell phones. Jet engines. Medical equipment. I've read several articles about shortages. Not in the reserves, but in the processing."

"But there's just one mine down here?"

"At present. And according to the articles I've read, they're mining rare earths because they were already mining titanium. Plus, some rare earth is radioactive. There's a big mine and processing plant out in the Mojave Desert. Another one planned in Ft. Worth. But most rare earth is sent to China to be refined."

"China?"

"Yeah, China processes about 80 percent of the rare earth minerals worldwide. Together, China and Myanmar process 100% of certain heavy rare earth metals."

"Are there shortages or something?"

"As I said, rare earths aren't actually that rare. But demand is certainly high."

Hitch taps his fingers on the table. "Do your maps show any particular concentrations of these rare earth minerals in Dare County?"

"The mazonite is there, and rare earths are often embedded in the mazonite. But these are recent discoveries within the past few years. There's not a lot of specific research or news on what may be in the dirt in South Georgia."

"Based on what you've found so far, are rare earths so valuable they're worth killing for?" Hitch asks.

There is a pause while Stacie thinks this through. "There's a lot of rare earth in second- and third-world countries that don't have nearly the environmental and mining regulations we do. Richer deposits. So I would say, strictly from an economic perspective, the US would have to be one of the most expensive places to mine and process rare earth. That's why we don't have many mines or processing plants here."

"All right. Good work Stacie. Keep digging."

"Hitch, do you think your parents were murdered because of what's in the soil on your farm?"

"That's what I'm trying to find out, Stacie."

The next morning, Hitch watches the kitchen wall clock tick toward 8 a.m., the arbitrary hour at which he thinks most people should be in the office. He is still pondering the motive for his parents' murders. "Why?" is the seminal question in most murder investigations. The lynchpin of what leads to the suspect. And often the most difficult question to answer. Greed, lust and power are at the top of the motive list. Anger runs a close fourth. He remembers this from a psychology of crime class he took in undergrad. Often the motive does not fit the crime—robbing someone with a gun for a few dollars is an example. George Colbert was probably motivated by both lust and anger when he killed Sonia, but as far as Hitch knows, nobody ever asked Colbert why he did it. Because Colbert pled guilty, motive wasn't essential to the case.

When he glances at the clock again, it is 8:02. He scrolls his contacts list and taps one that has a gold star beside it.

Tobias picks up.

"Glad I caught you," Hitch says.

"I'm not usually in this early."

"Yeah, well, the rooster wakes me up before dawn every morning. Listen, have you heard any rumors about property around here being acquired for mineral rights? Rare earth elements, or anything like that?"

"Not that I've heard. There's an environmental battle over a mine near Folkston. I think those types of minerals have been involved. But if someone was gobbling up land for that purpose, we'd hear something about it. Like when one of Bill Gates' companies bought a big farm up near Vidalia."

"But nothing around here regarding minerals?"

"No. Hey, while I've got you—bad news. Alicia Vanderwelt objected to all of our subpoenas. I'm looking at her objections now. She says the case is moot and the subpoenas are evidence of vexatious litigation. We're apparently burdening her clients and the subpoena respondents with unreasonable costs."

Hitch cradles the cell phone against his ear and turns to Natalie. "I take it you heard most of that?"

"Yeah." She eyes the ceiling, working something through.

"So we're not getting any documents," Tobias says.

"Not unless we file a motion to compel responses to the subpoenas," Hitch counters.

"On what basis?"

"Damn her. Let me think about this, Tobias, see if there's a way through this mess."

Hitch disconnects and plops down in a kitchen chair. Their route to the truth has been blocked again. If they were to file a motion to force disclosure, he knows it would land with a big thud. The Judge would not like him continuing to pursue discovery in a case where the only named plaintiffs are his deceased parents. And with only a month to go before his suspension is lifted, the last thing he wants to do is pursue a motion that Vanderwelt will use as exhibit one that he's no longer fit to practice law.

He feels it ebbing away. The fight is seeping from him. He is burdened with the same despondency he felt as he sat on the floor in his conference room, a bullet in his lung, watching Sonia succumb with a sputtering breath.

"We know the lenders on these reverse mortgages want the land desperately," Natalie offers.

"Yeah. Sure," he says. But he's not in this conversation any longer. "Without named plaintiffs, we no longer have a civil lawsuit we can pursue. Without the lawsuit, we don't have subpoena power, or the ability to put anyone under oath in a deposition. She's cut our legs out from under us."

"Two nights ago, you said you weren't going to give up."

"I was expecting to see documents today, Nat. Without documents, we don't even know where to look."

"So we're looking for the proverbial needle in a haystack, as you farmers would say."

He eyes her and rubs the back of his neck, feeling the tension. "The rule of law is supposed to uncover the truth. Aren't you sick and tired of lawyers using the law to cover up the truth?"

"Unfortunately, it's what we have to deal with."

"Nat, do you think Vanderwelt knows, or suspects, my parents were murdered by her client?"

"I have no idea. What happens if you tell her your suspicion?"

"Without evidence? If I even make that accusation, she'll sue me for slander. And if she doesn't know what her client is doing, she'll confront her client, which will send them underground forever. Or, if she does know, she's going to destroy all the evidence."

"So if you lay out the evidence we do have, you'd essentially be relying on her to do the right thing. You'd have to trust her to investigate."

Hitch locks eyes with Natalie for a few seconds, but he doesn't say a word.

42

On the morning their motion for class certification is due, Hitch walks slowly up the steps of the Dare County courthouse. Natalie is beside him, toting her briefcase, which still bears the two puncture marks from the fangs of the moccasin. When they arrive at the Clerk of Court's office, Natalie hands Hitch the paperwork. Five originals, all of which Tobias signed this morning.

"I have a notice of dismissal," Hitch announces to the assistant clerk behind the plexiglass.

She eyes him for a moment. "There's no filing fee for dismissal."

He slides the paperwork across the white marble counter.

The clerk slips the first page of each notice into the time-clock, and with a heavy clunk each page is stamped. She hands four originals back to Hitch. The lawsuit to adjudge his mother's rights under the reverse mortgage is now officially over. In legal parlance, the dispute became moot upon his mother's death. "Moot" seems like an unworthy word to describe all that has happened. And the class action lawsuit has now evaporated.

"I know that was hard," Natalie says when they enter the hallway.

He sighs. "What else could I do? I don't want to subject Tobias to sanctions."

"The Sheriff's call," she says, "that sealed it for you, didn't it?"

"I remembered something Riley O'Reilly once told me. I know you never met him, but he was probably the best trial lawyer I ever worked with."

Their conversation is interrupted by a gang of prisoners, ten or twelve of them, who are being led along the corridor in their blue uniforms. Each is handcuffed, though there are no chains on their feet, and no chains tethering them to one another. These inmates are non-violent offenders. One deputy leads the procession; another keeps them in line from behind.

Hitch and Natalie back against the wall to let them pass.

"Anyway," Hitch continues, "Riley used to tell me that it is an indisputable fact you will lose cases. Sometimes you will lose cases you should win. When the Sheriff told me he found nothing amiss with the other deaths on our list and there was nothing to investigate, I knew it was time to dismiss the lawsuit."

He watches as the prisoners stop at the double doors to the District Court. One prisoner looks back at Natalie and gives her a wink.

They leave the courthouse, Hitch at the wheel. He passes the turnoff that will take them back to the farm.

"Where are we going?" Natalie asks.

"Reidsville."

"What's in Reidsville?"

"A stone-cold killer I need to talk to."

From the outside, the Georgia State Prison near Reidsville looks a bit like a private college ringed with high fences and curls of razor wire. This is where murderers and other heinous criminals serve out their sentences. Inside, it is nothing but bleak. Concrete floors, iron bars. The musky smell of desperate men crammed together. The din of a hundred voices behind steel doors.

Once they pass through security, Hitch and Natalie are shown into a cinder-block conference room painted a dull tan. They sit anxiously on one side of a broad, metal table when George Colbert is escorted into the room by two prison guards. One of the guards chains Colbert's hands to a D-ring bolted to the middle of the table.

"Can we be alone?" Hitch asks the guards.

The guards exchange a glance, then step to the door. "We'll be right outside."

Hitch stares across the table at the man who ended Sonia's life and almost took his.

"We don't have recorders. We're not taking notes," Hitch starts. "They took our cell phones at the gate." He holds up his palms to show his hands are empty. "You can speak freely."

Colbert stares back, his eyes somewhere between malevolent and amused. He's lost weight since his sentencing hearing and has the pasty complexion of someone who spends all of his time in a cell, far away from sunlight. In his pink prison uniform, he looks small and weak.

"What about her?" Colbert says, staring at Natalie. "She could have a recorder under her clothes. She needs to strip."

On the drive up, they had debated whether Natalie should stay in the car while Hitch interviewed Colbert alone. What Hitch wants from this interview might rattle her. She'd countered that maybe Colbert hadn't seen a woman in a long time and might be more forthcoming if he had an attractive woman to look at. Plus, she wanted to be there when Hitch confronted the man who'd attempted to kill him. They reached a compromise by agreeing Natalie would don his pair of farm coveralls, which would conceal everything up to her neck.

"Not going to happen," Hitch replies. The guards wanded her."

"Were you in his law office that morning, sweet thang?"

"I was a witness to your brutality," Natalie slings back.

Hitch tries to re-direct the interview. "George, why did you kill Sonia?"

"Why not?"

"Is 'why not' a good enough motive to take a life and land you in prison for the rest of your life?" Hitch asks.

"Good as any."

"If that's your only explanation, we're leaving," Hitch says. He wants to see how this lands. He hopes Colbert at least wants to talk to someone not dressed in prison garb.

"No, no. Hang on." Colbert casts a wolfish glance at Natalie. "What do you want to know?"

"I want to know what you were thinking in the days leading up to the murder." Hitch starts. "And what was going on in your mind when you stood there and pulled the trigger three times."

Colbert opens his mouth, stretching his jaw. If his hands were free, he would probably rub the stubble on his chin.

"Before that day," Colbert says. "I watched your office for three straight days, waiting for her to show. I bought two boxes of hollow-point bullets. I cleaned my gun. Several times."

"You used hollow-point bullets so they would fragment on impact, maximizing damage," Hitch says.

"Exactly." Colbert points a finger at him, the nail chewed to the quick. "She wasn't leaving your office alive."

It rattles him that Colbert says this with a gleeful look. It's all he can do to restrain himself from leaping over the table and choking the convict. But he wants information, and that's not the way to get it.

"Was I your target, too? Or just her?"

"Both of you. You took her from me, man."

"She left you because you beat her."

"So she claimed. Anyway …"

"Before you barged into my conference room, you planned it all the way through?"

"Every step. Getting in. Killing you both. Getting out. Getting away."

"But you didn't get away."

"Naw. Didn't count on you getting up off the floor, want to know the truth of it. I thought you were dead."

"Why didn't you fire a fourth time?"

Colbert examines Natalie again, even tries to look under the table to see what's she wearing below the waist, but the cuffs keep him tethered above the table. His dark eyes are undressing her. "Stand up for me, sweetheart."

Natalie glances at Hitch, who nods. Then she stands, showing the coveralls reaching to her shoe tops.

"Turn around for me, sweetheart."

"No," Natalie says. She sits back down, wrapping her arms around herself.

"Why didn't you fire a fourth shot?" Hitch repeats.

"I don't know. I was seeing red. Not just blood. I mean, everything was red."

"Red?"

"Red is the color of rage, ain't it? Most of the guys in here, they saw red when they took somebody out."

"And now you're wearing pink," Hitch says.

"Ain't got no choice about that."

"I'll grant you that. Why did you file the bar complaint against me?"

"You took her from me, man. You survived. I wanted to hurt you every way I could."

"I didn't take her from you; she left you."

"That supposed to change things?"

"Did you think of the bar complaint on your own, or did someone suggest it to you?"

"You don't think I can find my way around the law books, lawyer Hitchcock?"

"I know for a fact an investigator for Alicia Vanderwelt's law firm gave you a copy of the bar complaint to review."

Colbert nods. "The investigator brought it here. Put some money in my commissary account, too. Her, I never heard of."

Hitch pauses, leans back in his chair. He's been questioning almost in stream-of-consciousness, trying to get answers and keep Colbert talking at the same time. He wants details of Colbert's planning, his mindset. Not just so he can understand how Colbert can justify his actions, but how the criminal mind operates in committing murder.

"So, other than the fact that you incorrectly think I took Sonia from you, and 'why not,' did you have any other reason for what you did?"

Colbert cants his head and smiles, as though he's never fully pondered that question. "Why does there have to be a reason for everything?" he says.

Hitch thinks about this answer. About the other men in here, who, like George Colbert, will die while staring at concrete walls. He contemplates all of the lives lost to predators who don't really have a reason for what they did. It's all so senseless.

"Guard," Hitch shouts.

The door opens and both guards come through.

"We're done here," Hitch says.

After Colbert is escorted from the room, they wait a full minute, allowing the adrenaline to subside. Hitch is breathing heavily, as though he's been running 40-yard sprints in summer heat.

Natalie sits quietly, trying to still her hands. "He's not like us. The way he thinks. The way he perceives things."

"That's the main reason he's in here," Hitch says. He stands and pulls her up.

She leans into him. "That was the second scariest situation I've ever been in, Hitch. He leered at me like he wanted to eat me. He makes my skin crawl."

Hitch wraps his left arm around her shoulders. He feels her shivering beneath the thick coveralls. Two different reactions to the same murderer. She is terrified; Hitch has been wondering how he could improvise a weapon to end George Colbert then and there.

"I'm sorry it was frightening for you. I didn't know how it would go."

"Well, he's a fucking animal."

"Yes, he is."

43

Hitch sits in the family graveyard, alone. His parents' headstones are still without proper epitaphs. He has composed two versions. One version is terse, filled with a bitter sentiment, a final salvo fired at their anonymous killer. The other is palliative, a few words whose meaning may express what his parents meant to him. Something that may withstand the scrutiny of the future.

Eight miles away, on the steps of the county courthouse, the foreclosure sale of the farm is taking place. He has refused to attend because he is out of ammunition and arguments. He doesn't want to be there to watch Alicia Vanderwelt gloat in victory. He doesn't want to hear the Sheriff's Deputy announce the Hitchcock farm is officially sold.

He's contacted the mortuary about relocating the remains of his ancestors to a cemetery beside the First Baptist Church. The coffins of his great-great grandparents, great grandparents, grandparents, parents and brother will all be unearthed and lifted onto a truck that will take them to a large plot in a corner of a cemetery where their hands never touched the soil. Where their blood never spilled.

He has composed a eulogy to his parents, their legacy, the farm. Yesterday he read it to Natalie in a strained voice, his pain barely containable. He watched the tears stream down her cheeks for a few seconds before realizing his own face was wet, too. As he recites the words, silently now, without an audience, he catches a different perspective, realizes the words have varying impacts on the speaker and the listener. He hatches a macabre thought that his parents, his brother and the others are listening. It is not the first time he has found himself speaking to the dead. There is both reverence and apology in his words. He thanks them for their dedication to the land, their stewardship of it. He thanks them for the production of food to feed the hungry. He thanks them for raising him, for standing by him through all his travails.

To this point, his words mark the conclusion to a long story. The end of two lives. Final curtain. As he finishes this eulogy to the farm, the words spilling from him in uninterrupted flow, he feels empty. The farm and its living inhabitants stare back at him in verdant vibrancy. They are not dead. They endure. He is not satisfied he has done this right. In fact, he knows he hasn't. He cannot let it end like this. He cannot just walk away.

44

The newspaper article starts with the banner headline: "Rare Earth Elements in Dare County." Professor Gregory Miller, a Georgia Tech geologist and acquaintance of paralegal Stacie Throckmorton, is quoted extensively. He relates the existence and mapped location of a band of rare earth elements in and around the Okefenokee Swamp, extending along the coast of Georgia. When asked the value of the mineral reserves, Miller says the sum is incalculable.

Above the fold is a photograph of Annie Younger standing outside her cabin on a plot of almost 80 acres nestled against the swamp. Testing by Gregory Miller's field team confirms each of the mortgaged properties contain rare earth elements. Annie Younger's plot has the highest density discovered anywhere in the Southeastern United States. Though she too signed a reverse mortgage with a shell lender, she is negotiating to lease her property to a mining company. She plans to sign the lease early next week.

Hitch finishes reading the story, then turns back to the front page and begins again. This article is the spotlight he could not generate through litigation or legal maneuvers. He doesn't know how brightly the light will shine, or whether it will slow the land grab, but it is something.

Hitch fed the story to Delia Covington, the Savannah newspaper reporter who wrote the feature on the shooting in his office almost two years ago, followed by coverage of George Colbert's murder trial. Hitch emailed Delia the statistics he and Natalie uncovered about reverse mortgages and deaths and foreclosures, but that information is relegated to a sidebar. Per Delia, the publisher is hesitant to suggest a link between the reverse mortgages and the startling high rate of accidental deaths among the county's residents—now 35 in the past 32 months.

"They need more evidence before they'll acknowledge a link," Delia explained.

"So do I," Hitch responded.

The reporter contacted Alicia Vanderwelt for comment, which Vanderwelt refused.

Two seemingly unrelated events—the discovery of rare earth elements in South Georgia and the escalating deaths of county farm owners—are connected. Hitch knows this with the same certitude that he knows his blind love for Sonia Summers and George Colbert's bullets are inextricably linked. But this knowledge isn't evidence. The critical question is whether he can prove the reverse mortgage company is killing people to take their land and the minerals beneath.

He and Natalie remain at the farm. Even though it is no longer legally his. The lender foreclosed. He is waiting for the letter to vacate from Alicia Vanderwelt, which will give him three days to get off the farm. But he has vowed to stay until the Sheriff shows up to kick him off.

The morning has dawned with a heavy fog in the fields, the thick mist obscuring all but the nearby landscape. In the distance, a cow lows. Hitch listens to it, but it is not the agonized bleating of a mother in labor. It is not a distress signal. This is normal.

Natalie comes onto the porch and settles in the rocker next to him.

He flashes the front page at her. "Came out this morning," he says.

"Do you think it will work?"

"I sure hope so. It's our last shot."

45

David Chan approaches the cabin. Its outside walls are cypress logs hewn by hand at least a century ago. The windows are either covered with heavy curtains or painted over with a rust-colored paint. The steps leading to the screened porch on the front are damp, and green moss fills crevices in the wood. Insects chirp and hum in the swamp trees. It has been raining most of the day, and the earth beneath his feet is soggy. Chan likes rain. It silences his movements, covers his footprints. He is wearing black from head to toe, with black grease paint smeared on his forehead and beneath his eyes. The night sky is dark velvet, the moon cloaked in clouds.

In his left jacket pocket is a syringe containing a lethal potion made from the Gelsemium plant, also known as heartbreak grass. It grows only in Southeast Asia. *Gelsemium elegans* is difficult to trace because it is not part of the standard toxicology screen. The concoction worked on Melba Davidson, and a few others, depressing their respiration until they died of apparent heart attacks. Injecting the poison is an intimate method, bringing him close to his victims. He holds them as they struggle and kick and try to scream, the poison making its way through their bodies. Twenty-two minutes is the longest anyone has survived.

Chan has read the Savannah newspaper article about the discovery of rare earth elements in the county, a fact he has known for the better part of four years. With reporters now focused on the story, he feels the scrutiny. He has no doubt the coroner will now look more closely at the 35 accidental deaths he has so carefully orchestrated, and make connections. Traces of xylazine, carfentanil or heartbreak grass could be found. The Georgia Bureau of Investigation will likely take over the investigation. Maybe the FBI will get involved. He predicts that after his lawyers receive the first call from law enforcement, Tinsley Stratton and Alicia Vanderwelt will halt the foreclosures until things can be sorted out. And, of course, they will vehemently deny any knowledge of the scheme or the murders.

Chan has one last task before the scheme unravels. Annie Younger left him with no other choice. She should have kept quiet. If she had remained silent, he probably would not be here. He might have allowed her to live out her life. But he can't sit idly by while another company acquires the rights to mine the rare earth minerals beneath her land. They are too valuable. They are too important to the Motherland.

After he has dumped the woman's body in the swamp, where the acidic water and peat will decompose even her bones, he will drive away from this place forever. He will assume one of the covers he has been building for the past three decades. He will hide, and he will contemplate his next move. He thinks of his parents in their cramped apartment in Beijing. He may return to his homeland to care for them properly.

Chan eases himself up on the front porch, placing his weight on the balls of his feet to minimize noise. He hears music coming from inside. It sounds like a radio or a music channel on television. A country station. Hillbilly rock. Good. The music will mask his approach.

The front door is not locked. He is not surprised. When the door is barely a foot ajar, he squeezes through and enters the living room. In the corner the television is on—the source of the music. The living room is open to the kitchen, marked by a short peninsula of counter.

She is standing at the stove, stirring something in a black skillet. She is perhaps thirty feet away. To Chan's left is a bathroom, its door open. As he creeps toward her, he looks into the bathroom. Empty. Near the back, off the kitchen, is a closed door. He presumes from his surveillance this is the lone bedroom. He knows she lives alone. No husband. No boyfriend. No children. It is one of the reasons he targeted her land. Garland T. Rogers secured the reverse mortgage on her property two years ago.

She is wearing an ankle-length dress the color of squirrel fur. Her iron gray hair is knotted into a braid that hangs to the middle of her back, just like her picture in the newspaper. A small rusted refrigerator hums in the corner next to the stove. With some effort, she lifts the skillet onto a dormant burner, turns off the propane, and ladles scrambled eggs onto a paper plate. An early breakfast at 4 a.m. The smell of cooked eggs fills the air of the small cabin. From the refrigerator, she removes a plastic container of assorted fruit and a half-gallon of juice in a coated carton. She sets these on a small table next to a back counter covered with small appliances, canisters and jars. She shuffles to the single chair, pulls it out, and sits down. Her back is still to him. She has no idea he has come for her.

Chan plans his route. Around the counter, past the stove, and he has her.

Three seconds, four at most, and if he moves with stealth the syringe's needle will be in her neck before she can wriggle out of the chair. His eyes narrow to cold, black slits. A slight smile emerges on his lips.

He removes the syringe from his pocket, gripping it in his left hand. He takes his first steps in a crouch, then rises, rounding the counter-top peninsula. Less than three strides away.

He hears a tiny sound. Off to his left. The sigh of old wood settling? He turns towards it.

Attorney Hitchcock steps from the bedroom in shoes covered with blue booties, a revolver pointed straight at Chan's head. He is barely six feet away.

Chan takes a tentative step backward.

"Don't you dare move," Hitch says.

Chan swivels his head. The woman rises from the table. She removes the gray wig, revealing blonde hair held up with hair pins. He can see her face now. This is not Annie Younger. He locks eyes with her. Turquoise-colored eyes. Then he recognizes her from the dossier he put together about the Hitchcock law firm. Natalie Anderson, the paralegal.

Chan scurries for the front door, crouching low, but as he begins to cross the living room he is blocked by a man standing in the doorway. A huge man who has 50 pounds on him, at least. A man whose skin is almost as dark as Chan's grease paint. The man levels a shotgun at his chest. He does not recognize this man, but it doesn't matter.

Hitch approaches from the rear. "Raise your hands above your head."

Chan complies because he has no choice, unless he wants shotgun pellets in his chest, or a bullet in the back of his head. At this point, he is just an anonymous assailant who entered the cabin through an unlocked door.

Once the syringe hits the floor, Hitch encircles Chan's wrists with a plastic zip tie, cinches it tight. Hitch sets the revolver on the counter and pats the prisoner down, running his hands along every surface. He pulls a crystal-faced watch from the man's right wrist. He jerks the man's black watch cap from his head and rummages his fingers through the man's black hair, looking for anything concealed. He pushes the man into an old, misshapen chair hewn from tupelo limbs.

Tobias nestles the barrel of the shotgun into the hollow at the back of the man's head while Hitch securely ties his torso and ankles to the chair.

Hitch steps back and appraises their prisoner. He is smaller than Hitch imagined he would be. In Hitch's mind, he should be huge and strong to have killed so many. For a moment he questions whether this man could have murdered his parents and all those other people. He almost doesn't look physically capable. They have no description of the murderer to compare to this man who is tied to the chair.

"Who are you?" Hitch asks.

The man's eyes give up nothing. His chin is cocked in a show of defiance. He refuses reply.

"We know you murdered my parents. Tranquilized them while they sat in my dad's truck." Hitch reaches over, plucks the prisoner's watch off the table. "We have a video from the train, with you moving away from the truck as it moved across the tracks." He says this with some emotion in his voice. He can't control it. Not completely. His parents' deaths are too fresh. "On the video, there's a glint from the train's spotlight, reflecting off of something. It caught the face of your watch, I bet." Hitch examines the Seagull watch.

It is this part that thrills Hitch—the interrogation—although he has never interrogated a witness in quite this way. Here, he is not bound by rules of discovery. There is no one to object to his pointed questions. No video to capture his words or actions. No judge will corral him if he goes astray.

He's thought about how far he is willing to go. Could he shoot this man and dump him in the swamp? He doesn't know the answer. He is surprised to be here, looming over this man, who must be his parents' murderer because he came to Annie Younger's cabin at night, cloaked in black and smeared with grease paint, with a syringe in his pocket. What possible intention other than murder could this man have? What motive could he have other than to secure the rare earth minerals beneath Annie Younger's land?

Natalie has been watching from the other side of the peninsula. She steps toward the table, points at the syringe. "Is this the same tranquilizer you used on Mr. and Mrs. Hitchcock?"

The man ignores her.

Hitch lowers his face to the prisoner. "Who are you working for?" He feels the adrenaline flowing. It is different now that the man who murdered his parents is right in front of him. He never thought this day would come. "Who the fuck are you working for?" Hitch yells.

The man remains silent. Yet there has been a subtle shift in his posture. His countenance no longer holds pure defiance, but Hitch does not yet see fear.

"You have a choice," Hitch says. "We turn you over to the Sheriff, and you will be prosecuted for murdering my parents. Maybe for the dozens of others who have died under suspicious circumstances. We don't like outsiders here. A jury will not be kind to you. You will be convicted and given the death penalty. That's how we do it in Georgia." Hitch has donned a mask of sincerity, but he honestly has no idea if there is enough evidence to convict this man of anything.

The man's eyes dart to the worn wooden floorboards.

"We know what you're doing. We found the lab where you've been testing your samples. There are only a handful around that test for rare earth elements. You left a paper trail."

The man's eyes spontaneously go wide. An involuntary acknowledgment his scheme is being peeled, layer by layer. He has the look of a cornered animal. His eyes dart from face to face. He strains against the bindings on his hands, feet and torso. Still, he says nothing.

Hitch pulls out his cell phone.

Tobias steps back from the prisoner.

Hitch snaps two quick photographs of the man whose name they still do not know. The first captures him in profile. In the second, Hitch frames his full face, his eyes dark and brooding. If they ever need photographs to run through facial recognition software, they will have them.

"One last chance," Hitch says.

The man remains stoic and silent.

It takes only a few minutes to march their prisoner, gagged and with plastic ties binding his wrists and ankles, to the jon boat. They settle him in the front well. Tobias wraps a cargo strap around the man's chest, slipping it through a cleat on each side of the bow. He is now secure cargo. There is no chance he can escape. If the boat overturns, their prisoner will drown.

Hitch sits on a metal bench behind the man, the nose of his revolver mere inches from the man's head. "If you move a muscle," Hitch warns, "a hollow- point bullet will blow through the back of your head and tear off your face."

Tobias mans a paddle from the stern seat. The ten-horsepower motor will remain quiet unless needed.

Natalie settles in the middle and stows a small, soft-sided cooler at her feet. She picks up the other boat paddle.

They paddle across dark water beneath a new moon whose tiny sliver barely lights their way. When they arrive at a small island hummock, Hitch tells them to stop paddling. He pulls a pen light from his shirt pocket, flicks it on, and scans the water near the island's shore. Pairs of red eyes stare back at him, hovering just above the black water. There are ten, maybe twelve of them. Waiting.

"Hand me the bait," he says to Natalie.

She unzips the small cooler and hands up a whole, bloody chicken.

Hitch cocks his arm and hurls the chicken toward the red eyes. Moments after the splash, the water boils with thrashing alligators. As they fight over the chicken, the sound of gnashing jaws spreads across the swamp.

Sitting at the bow, David Chan has a ringside seat. His entire body recoils. Despite his training, his cold and calculated executions of dozens of innocent people, this pool of voracious alligators unnerves him. Then he hears the haunting bellows. The same primordial growl he heard when he stalked Mordecai Claxton's farm before setting his trees aflame. The same sound he heard before his dog Ping disappeared into the dingy waters of the Yangzte River, so long ago. It is the sound of an apex predator in its element.

Hitch disengages the cargo strap securing the man to the boat, then pulls him up by his collar. With his hands and feet still bound, the man tries to kneel in the bow. Hitch prods him to stand with the barrel of the pistol in lethal position.

"Any last words?" Hitch says.

The man turns half-way around. Fear is now etched on his face. His heart flutters in his chest. He briefly thinks of the syringe filled with poison. Death by heartbreak grass would be far preferable to being torn apart by alligators.

"Do you want to tell us your name? Who you work for?" Hitch asks in a whisper, though in the still night it sounds crisp and harsh.

"You mentioned a choice," their prisoner says. These are the first words he has spoken. His voice is quavering.

"Maybe you no longer have a choice," Hitch says. He presses his left palm into the small of the man's back.

"What is my choice?" the man says in a low growl.

"How did you tranquilize my parents? I know you used horse tranquilizer. Xylazine."

"And if I tell you …"

"We won't throw you to the alligators."

The man hesitates, deciding how much to disclose. He sees the dark outlines of alligator heads everywhere. Hitchcock already has uncovered key elements of his plan. He needs to buy time. Another minute could mean a chance at freedom. All he needs is a chance. In these dire circumstances, he has no choice but to give them something.

"Your father I injected with a syringe. Your mother with a blow gun."

"A blow gun?" Hitch says, unbelieving.

"An ancient, but effective weapon."

"How did you get them to stop in front of the tracks?"

"I stood on the tracks. Who would run over a man standing on railroad tracks?"

Hitch can picture his father stopping in the driveway—probably at the insistence of his mother—putting the truck in park, and rolling down the driver's window to help.

"And you pushed the truck across the train tracks?"

"I simply put the truck into gear."

"You left the driver's door slightly open," Hitch says. "That's how we knew it wasn't an accident. That's when we started looking for another explanation."

There is always a mistake in the imperfect crime. Chan sees that now.

"Why did you have to kill them?" Hitch avoids asking the open-ended "why" question during a trial, but this isn't a trial. With one hand on the man's back and the other pressing the barrel of Rip's pistol against the top of his spine, Hitch tries to maintain his composure. When the man refuses to answer, Hitch pleads, in a cracking voice, "because of these rare earth elements?"

The man merely nods.

Hitch thrusts the muzzle of the gun into the man's head, then cocks the trigger. "Say it. Out loud."

"Yes," the man hisses. "Rare earth minerals."

"Hand me the other chicken and paddle us twenty feet closer to the island," Hitch commands.

As the boat noses closer, Hitch tosses the second bloody chicken a few yards in front of the bow. The tangle of thrashing alligators rocks their boat. He's hoping for any last tidbit of information.

"Who are you?"

The man trembles, but says nothing.

"Who are you working for?"

Again, nothing.

This man, whoever he is, will not divulge further details. If being shackled in a boat encircled by voracious alligators will not compel him to say more, Hitch has no other ideas about how to extract the truth. He will never disclose his name, or who he is working for.

"You can stop recording now," he says to Natalie.

Natalie ends the sound recording and pockets Hitch's cell phone.

The Sheriff knows the license number of the man's van. Hitch caught it three days ago on a game camera he set up a half-mile down the road from Annie Younger's cabin. When Hitch phoned the Sheriff to report a strange, black van seen pulling away from his house—a necessary lie—the Sheriff called back in a few minutes, said the plates didn't match the vehicle. One or the other was stolen. That was the signal someone was stalking Annie Younger. She was a compliant, if terrified material witness. She is staying with her sister in Brunswick, a safe distance away.

This is the third night that Hitch, Natalie and Tobias have staged their charade in Annie Younger's cabin. The first two nights they stayed until dawn, aching from the wait. They left via a game trail that edges along the swamp for a half-mile before emerging onto a sandy road.

Now, Hitch has a decision to make. He has the vial containing whatever this man was planning to inject into Annie Younger. Perhaps fingerprints can be pulled from the vial. He has photographs of the man's face. He has the recording of a confession, though he is unsure if it will legally hold up. Does he have the evidence to prove what he needs to prove? Is this enough to achieve justice for his parents?

A gentle shove in the back, even ramming the boat into a cypress knee, will propel the man into the dark waters of the swamp. The alligators float temporarily subdued, but upon hearing the splash they will attack. This man who refuses to identify himself will be torn apart.

A minute passes, maybe more. Hitch feels a growing, aggravating sense this will end with the man in handcuffs in the back of a sheriff's curiser. He will sit in jail, mum and uncooperative. Hitch shakes his head at what he is about to do.

"Natalie, call 911. Tell the Sheriff we've caught their serial killer."

46

"He identified himself as Joe Park."

It is Alicia Vanderwelt's voice, void of the confidence she conveys when she holds sway in a courtroom. Or while sitting on an elevated bench, judging others. Today, she is in a hard, wooden chair in an interrogation room at the FBI's office in Atlanta. Despite her efforts to sit erectly, she keeps sliding down, her shoulders slumped. One of Atlanta's premier criminal defense lawyers is seated next to her.

On the other side of the table sit FBI Special Agent Maureen Whitaker, and Assistant US Attorney Colby Rutherford. Special Agent Whitaker takes the lead.

"And is David Chan, alias Joe Park, the man behind all of these companies?"

"Yes. We have no other contact."

Whitaker nods. "And when did you discover, Ms. Vanderwelt, that these companies were actually a front for the Chinese Communist Party?"

Vanderwelt bends toward her attorney, whispers something in his ear. He whispers something back.

"July 22nd of this year, when I was contacted by the US Attorney's Office in connection with a subpoena served upon me."

"And before that, you had no hint whatsoever that these companies your law firm created, this whole intricate web of companies, were in fact a front for the Chinese Communist Party?" There is an incredulous tone in Agent Whitaker's voice.

Vanderwelt lifts her chin defiantly. "No."

Hitch, standing one room over, behind the mirrored viewing window, notices a tic at the corner of Alicia Vanderwelt's left eye. She can't stop licking her lower lip. He relishes watching her squirm in the hot seat.

He wishes Natalie were here to see this, but the US Attorney's Office wouldn't allow it. He's permitted to watch Vanderwelt's interrogation only because he negotiated his presence before he turned over his evidence. He also negotiated immunity for Natalie, Tobias and himself. Technically, they kidnapped David Chan when they took him out into the swamp on the jon boat. But no one here thinks what they did was wrong.

Agent Whitaker continues the interrogation. "When did you first learn that this client of yours, Mr. Chan, whom you knew as Mr. Park, was killing people down in Dare County?"

"July 22 was the first I learned of the allegation," Vanderwelt responds. "Not to mince words with you Agent, but I don't think it's been proved that he murdered anyone. Not in a court of law, anyway."

Hitch bristles at this. He feels a surge in his bloodstream. The old wound in his lung pulses. Based on the evidence he obtained, he has no doubt David Chan murdered his parents. Chan confessed, and the FBI has a recording of that confession. Vanderwelt and her law partners covered for him, maybe even knew what he was doing to gain control of all that farmland and failed to stop it. In his mind, Alicia Vanderwelt is an accessory to murder.

Agent Whitaker does not appreciate Vanderwelt's semantics either, even though she is, like many FBI agents, also a lawyer. She leans forward, her forearms resting on the shining table.

"Your client already has been indicted for the murders of Hale and Bridget Hitchcock. We have his taped confession. He's also been indicted for the murder of Mordecai Claxton. We will prove it at trial. And any additional murders we discover after we exhume the bodies of the other people who died under suspicious circumstances."

Agent Whitaker taps the 8 x 11 photograph of Hale and Bridget Hitchcock, taken at their last anniversary. "These victims were killed by your client, Ms. Vanderwelt. Now, who at your law firm knew this was going on before July 22 of this year?"

Alicia Vanderwelt turns to her lawyer again. He whispers something in her ear.

"I just want to make sure," Vanderwelt starts, "this proffer letter we've signed, you can't use what I say today against me. That's correct, isn't it?"

Agent Whitaker lets out a huff of air. "You're a lawyer, Ms. Vanderwelt, and you have a lawyer sitting beside you. I'm not about to give you legal advice. The proffer letter says what it says."

Vanderwelt thinks this over. Her lower lip quivers. She closes her eyes for a moment before answering. "Tinsley Stratton. He's the architect of the whole thing."

"Tinsley Stratton is, or was, your law partner, correct?" Agent Whitaker asks.

"Yes. And Veronica Nobles, a partner in our Las Vegas office. She knew as well."

Hitch knew this had to be bigger than Alicia Vanderwelt. Based on what she's offered, he has little doubt others at the firm also knew what was going on in Dare County. But they looked the other way. Vanderwelt's law firm already is imploding. She and Stratton and Nobles have been terminated. The exodus of other partners and associates has diminished the once-prestigious law firm to half its former size.

"Who else, Ms. Vanderwelt? Who else at your law firm knew that one of its clients was murdering people in Dare County?"

She shakes her head. "No one that I know of."

"Now, in response to the subpoena issued by the US Attorney's Office, you produced some documents, correct?"

"Yes, you have those." Vanderwelt checks a note on the legal pad in front of her. "Bates numbers AV 1 through 9437."

"And these documents came from your personal files?"

"My personal files, and law firm files as well. I scoured the law firm's document storage and servers to get you everything I could."

"Everything you could? Meaning that some documents are missing?"

"We found evidence some paper files were destroyed."

"Destroyed? As in shredded?"

Vanderwelt shakes her head. "Burned."

"Where were the documents burned?"

"In a metal trash can outside Tinsley Stratton's office."

"What about electronic files?"

"It's my understanding some were deleted."

"By whom?"

"It's my understanding the process to determine who deleted the files is still ongoing. You probably know more about that than I do at this point. I'm out of the loop."

"Meaning, you got fired."

Vanderwelt nods.

"You have to answer out loud for the recording."

"Yes, I was fired."

"Let me direct your attention to AV 2338. The AV, those are your initials, correct?"

"Yes."

Whitaker lays a document in front of Vanderwelt. "Can you tell us what that document is?"

Vanderwelt slides her glasses up her nose, peers at the document. "Yes, it's a copy of a check drawn on one of the law firm's client trust accounts, in the amount of $150,000, made payable to Hale Hitchcock."

"And whose signature is on the check?"

"Mine. But I didn't sign this check," she quickly adds.

"So your signature appears there, but you're claiming you didn't sign it?"

"It's an electronic signature, Agent Whitaker."

"Did you authorize anyone to use your electronic signature to sign checks drawn on this particular client trust account at your law firm? Your former law firm?"

"Yes, generally speaking. But I didn't give specific authorization for this particular check."

"And what is the check for?"

"It's the proceeds of a home equity conversion loan that Hale Hitchcock secured for his farm in Pineland, Georgia."

Hitch has never seen this check. From behind the window, he can't see it clearly now. He hangs on every syllable coming out of Vanderwelt's mouth.

"And what is the date on the check, Ms. Vanderwelt?"

"April 2 of last year."

"So it would have been issued on April 2 of last year?"

"That's correct."

"Did you see the check before it went out, Ms. Vanderwelt?"

"No. I wouldn't have seen it."

"And to refresh your memory, you presided over an ethics hearing involving an attorney named Oakley Walker Hitchcock, correct?"

"I did."

"And what was the date of that hearing?"

"April 9 of last year."

"And as a result of that hearing, you voted to suspend attorney Hitchcock from the practice of law for one year, correct?"

"I did."

"And did you know, Ms. Vanderwelt, at or before that hearing, that this client of yours, the client that we now know is a front for the CCP, was targeting attorney Hitchcock's father's farm for a reverse mortgage?"

Vanderwelt looks down at her lap, then fiddles with the check in front of her. She glares at the one-way glass, as if trying to see if Hitchcock is on the other side.

"Ms. Vanderwelt, answer my question."

Vanderwelt nods. "Yes, I knew."

47

Nine months later, Hitch rises from the counsel table in the Superior Court of Dare County, Georgia. He is about to deliver his closing argument in the lawsuit he filed to return the properties acquired by murder to their rightful owners. The most important case he's ever filed. He buttons the top button of his coat. Though the jury box is empty because Judge Fisher will decide the outcome, the courtroom is full. The families of the murder victims stretch out along the pews behind him. A small cadre of news media are sequestered in a back corner.

"Your Honor," he says. "Over these past two and a half weeks, we have put on evidence, both forensic and otherwise, that of the 35 victims whose land was taken through foreclosure on these reverse mortgages, none of them died by accident. You've heard the recording in which David Chan admitted to murdering my parents. As for the other victims, the sheriff, the coroner, and their respective teams have done an outstanding job of exhuming and examining the bodies of the deceased. It has taken months to determine the true causes of death. In each case, homicide. And I, and all of the families of these loved ones, appreciate the work that has been done so that the truth can finally be uncovered. The only evidence you have received in this trial is that each and every one of these folks was murdered."

He looks over at the empty defense table. No one has stepped forward to defend David Chan, or his companies.

The evidence he amassed to expose the scheme has come primarily from a three-day deposition he took of Alicia Vanderwelt. It was a satisfying interrogation he conducted himself and that kept him high for a week afterward. Vanderwelt spilled everything. The legal structure, the companies, the individuals she could name. The involvement of her two law partners—Tinsley Stratton and Veronica Nobles.

Tinsley Stratton, whose legal strategies masked the nefarious land grab and enabled David Chan to murder 35 people, invoked his Fifth Amendment privilege against self-incrimination and refused to testify in

Hitch's case. He has been indicted by a grand jury in Atlanta for conspiracy to commit murder. Stratton has bigger problems than this civil lawsuit.

Veronica Nobles, the lawyer in Nevada who is listed as the manager of these companies, also invoked her Fifth Amendment privilege to remain silent. Hitch watched news coverage of her being hustled into a Las Vegas courtroom a few months ago for her arraignment hearing on charges of conspiracy to commit murder. Her criminal trial has not yet commenced.

"Now, Your Honor," Hitch continues, "this was a scheme of fantastic proportions. The Chinese government, through an American citizen whose name is David Chan but who used various aliases, including Joe Park, and who had more than a dozen fake passports, tried to perpetrate a sweeping land grab in the State of Georgia, and across the southeastern United States. The MO in all cases was consistent. Solicit a reverse mortgage from owners of agricultural land whose properties had deposits of rare earth elements, then kill the owners, at which point the loan became due in 30 days. A train wreck. Heart attacks. Electrocution. An overturned tractor. Alcohol poisoning. All staged to look like accidents. Yes, the nominal mortgagees on each loan are different, but they all lead back to one Chinese corporation—Tanjin—which an Assistant United States Secretary of State has testified before the Senate is a front for the Central Communist Party of China. The scheme was fantastic in scope and audacity. Incredible, really. And they almost got away with it. Almost."

Hitch pauses. Even now, after studying the evidence, he has a hard time believing what he has uncovered. He finds it difficult to accept that members of his profession would go to such lengths to appease a client, even if the annual fees paid to the firm were in the millions. He knows how lucky they were to trap David Chan.

"The most macabre aspect of these financial transactions, something I've never seen in almost two decades of practice, is the blockade on paying back the loan. A borrower, such as my own father, cannot even get a response to a certified letter asking how much is owed on the loan. The lender doesn't want the money, won't even provide an amount due. Because these aren't really loans. The reverse mortgages here are nothing more than a way to steal the land. The whole scheme was designed to avoid any government oversight. No bank regulator has jurisdiction over these kinds of mortgages. And with the property being acquired, at least on the surface, by American limited liability companies, there was no patent obligation to report a foreign acquisition of agricultural land. This scheme was designed by a team of sophisticated and experienced attorneys, solely as a way to trick people and defraud them into thinking they were taking out a loan, when in fact they were unwittingly writing their own death sentences. We all know that someone cannot profit from murder. So these limited liability companies that are the beneficiaries of these mortgages and foreclosures, the beneficiaries of these murders, cannot retain the land. It would be unconscionable and a complete miscarriage of justice to allow them to do so. The land must be returned to the heirs. Their parents and kin were murdered. They have suffered enough."

Hitch weighs whether to go on. He glances at Natalie and Tobias, who are sitting stoically at counsel table. There will be no rebuttal from the defense, but he senses he has not said enough, that his explanation falls woefully short of depicting the pain and horror the victims suffered. He plants his fists on the counsel table.

"This was an attack on our country, Your Honor. Make no mistake about it. A new kind of attack. It didn't involve guns or bombs or warships, but weapons that are hard to detect. Tranquilizers, exotic poisons from Asian plants, bare hands, satellites and a remote-operated train. Even Garland T. Rogers, who refused to say much in his testimony, admitted he was responsible for the attacks on my legal assistant. And his son admitted to putting a venomous snake in her car and trying to run us both down with a logging truck packed to the staves. All with the encouragement, if not the explicit direction, of an Atlanta attorney who refuses to show himself, but who represents Tanjin. None of this has been disputed in this trial."

"We cannot completely stop these attacks on our citizens and our neighbors, or our property, because the conniving and cunning nature of the criminal mind is beyond our comprehension to thwart in advance. But we can send a message now. You must send a message, Judge Fisher. Trickery and fraud and murder will not be tolerated in the courts of the United States of America."

He stops, his heart pounding. He looks behind him at the gallery, filled with his clients, but they remain quiet. They are too stunned at what a foreign invader has done to them to feel any sense of vindication, at least not yet.

Hitch looks up at the Judge, who is studying his notes. He sees it clearly. This room with high ceilings and worn carpet and dim lighting is the only place where this fantastic scheme could have been fully exposed. Thirty-five murders. Thousands of acres of land stolen.

"We all trust you, Your Honor. I have nothing further. Thank you."

Judge Fisher looks out at his courtroom over black-rimmed bifocals. "Thank you Mr. Hitchcock. And welcome back to the Bar." The Judge rolls a pen between his fingers. "I also have never seen anything like this. Maybe no Judge has. The Lockerbie bombing trial in the Netherlands comes close, but that was against two Libyan perpetrators and not against private companies, or a state actor. I've listened carefully to all of the testimony. I've examined every exhibit admitted. And I am convinced by a preponderance of the evidence, which is our standard in civil cases, that the defendant Tanjin Corporation is responsible for the murders of at least 35 of our citizens, 35 of our neighbors. Sometimes the law is an ass. And in this case the law has been cleverly used, by lawyers, not to protect people or reveal the truth, but to enable a vast criminal enterprise that almost …and I stress almost … resulted in the confiscation, because I don't know what else to call it, of thousands of acres of land by a foreign country. The law has been manipulated, as far as I can tell, solely out of greed."

The Judge purses his lips, makes a note on his yellow legal pad. "So I apologize to all of you in advance, because giving you all your land back is not going to be enough. I know that. Your loved ones have been taken from you by some companies you can't even see. Masterminded by a man who will be prosecuted in another courtroom at another time. Maybe there will be a big civil suit for damages for wrongful death and, if so, I'll welcome all of you back to this courtroom. But here's my ruling: All of the foreclosures and deeds in lieu of foreclosure involving each and every one of the plaintiffs in this lawsuit are hereby declared null and void. The loans were an instrument of murder, the product of fraud, and are hereby voided as well. The rightful owners shall get their land back. Immediately."

A burble rises from the spectators. There is no cheering from the gallery, no applause. The Judge does not bang his gavel to punctuate the finality of his ruling. But it is over.

Hitch stares at his legal pad, his eyes blurry. "We won, dad. We won, mom," he says in a choked voice.

Hitch, Natalie and Tobias emerge from the courthouse into a sky whose clouds have been vanquished. The southerly wind carries moisture from the swamp. They stand beneath the courthouse portico, where vast tracts of land have been wrested from their owners more easily than if by gunpoint or armed occupation. Foreclosures that took less than five minutes. All of it engineered by greedy lawyers to satisfy a nefarious, foreign client.

"Wrongful death lawsuits against a Chinese corporation and China itself," Tobias says. "The Judge almost seemed to invite us to file them."

"Another day," Hitch says. "Right now, it's time to return to normal, or at least try to." He fingers the Seagull watch in his pants pocket, the watch he removed from David Chan before he was hauled off in the back of a patrol car.

"You going back to Savannah?" Tobias asks.

Hitch glances at Natalie. "Maybe, but not just yet. I need to get the farm in order, tend to the cattle. Fix the fences. Things have slipped a lot since my dad died."

Natalie and Hitch return to the farm on the outskirts of Pineland. Still in their court clothes, they enter the family cemetery. The perimeter fence has a fresh coat of white paint, the last thing he did before starting the trial. Hitch finally had his parents' headstones engraved.

On his father's marker is the inscription: **Even In Death, I Will Not Leave This Land**

He places his hand atop his mother's headstone, which now reads: **This Farm Is My Blood, and My Blood In It**

He wells up, as the combined effect of death and despondency and jubilation overwhelm him. His throat clogs. He can't find any appropriate words.

After dinner, Hitch and Natalie settle into the cane-bottomed porch chairs that have conformed to their bodies, glasses of iced tea in their fists. The sun is a sharp orange disk above the treed horizon. Jasper is spread out in a corner, snoring.

"What do you think, Nat?"

"About?"

"Next steps."

"You normally plan everything out. You're asking me?" She leans back, crosses her legs at the ankle.

"Yeah, well. I'm thinking about changing the playbook a bit. Let the farm determine the schedule. Roll with the seasons, so to speak."

"You want to become a farmer?"

"Farmer and lawyer. I don't see why it has to be one or the other."

"Agreed."

"What would you think about splitting our time between here and

Savannah? Except for court appearances, I can practice law from almost anywhere."

"Our time?" she says.

He turns his head to look at her. "Well … is that presumptuous on my part … I mean, we've been together for more than a year and I guess I just assumed that we're a couple now and we want to be together and I know I want to be with you and I hope you feel the same way because …"

She grabs his hand, intertwines their fingers, and peers off into the tunnel of pines lining the driveway. "Yes, Hitch, we are together."

He takes this in, but then starts contemplating the future. "The battles aren't over, you know. Nefarious actors don't just stop. They'll change course. We've got to file civil suits for wrongful death. We'll probably have to testify in the criminal trials. We have a lot of work to do."

"Yes, we have a lot of work to do," Natalie agrees. "But can't you be quiet for a minute or two and just enjoy this?"

Hitch starts to say something, then thinks better of it.

THE FACTS

- According to the U.S. Department of Agriculture, Chinese holdings of U.S. agricultural land surged from 13,720 acres in 2010 to 194,179 acres in 2020, a 1400% increase in a decade.
- Foreign ownership of US agricultural land stands at 37.6 million acres, an area larger than the State of Iowa.
- Foreign persons or entities own 19.5% of all agricultural land in the State of Maine, and 17.7% of all private land in that State.
- Although the Agricultural Foreign Investment Disclosure Act of 1978 requires foreign owners of American agricultural land to disclose their acquisitions within 90 days, there are no criminal penalties for non-compliance.
- Experts doubt foreign owners disclose all of their holdings, especially where ownership can be vested in American companies controlled by foreign interests.
- As of 2020, foreign entities owned 133,198 acres of land in Clinch County, Georgia, almost all of it in timber. Clinch County includes the western edge of the Okefenokee Swamp.
- China controls more than 70% of the world's mined rare earth elements and 80% of rare earth refining.
- Rare earth elements have been discovered in Charlton County, Georgia, near the Okefenokee Swamp.
- In November 2021, a company affiliated with the Chinese Communist Party purchased 370 acres of farmland in North Dakota, approximately 12 miles from Grand Forks Air Force Base.
- Smithfield Farms, the world's largest hog producer and pork processor, was sold to a Hong Kong company in 2013. Hong Kong, once independent, has been absorbed into China.
- Although a substantial portion of reverse mortgages are regulated by the United States Department of Housing and Urban Development, proprietary reverse mortgages are not regulated by any governmental agency.
- Creating layers of limited liability companies, especially across state lines, makes it very difficult to determine the true owners of such companies. Even for lawyers.

THE AUTHOR

Michael Winstead is the author of four previous novels: *Ultimate Verdict; Ultimate Deception; Ultimate Truth;* and *Ella's Wings.*

Michael lives and writes in the mountains of North Carolina and in the Ancient City. You can contact him at michaelwinstead.com.

www.ingramcontent.com/pod-product-compliance
Lightning Source LLC
LaVergne TN
LVHW020709110826
845149LV00012B/2176

* 9 7 8 0 9 9 9 2 4 2 1 4 8 *